The
Queen's
Daemon

Doug L. Hoffman

ISBN 978-0-9884588-9-5

Published by
The Resilient Earth Press
http://resilientearthpress.com

Books By Doug L. Hoffman

The T'aafhal Legacy Series
Ghosts of Orion
The Queen's Daemon
Pleiad Found

The T'aafhal Inheritance Trilogy
Parker's Folly
Peggy Sue
M'tak Ka'fek

Non-fiction (with Allen Simmons)
The Resilient Earth
The Energy Gap

Preface

This is the second book in the T'aafhal Legacy series—the continued adventures of the officers and crew of the starship Peggy Sue. Once again we find Captain Billy Ray Vincent in command of the Honorable Orion Arm Trading Company's vessel Peggy Sue. After their adventures in the Gliese 667C system, chronicled in the *Ghosts of Orion*, almost a year has passed and the merchant explorers are more than 30 parsecs from home, well beyond the current 10 parsecs "safe" human bubble in space. On the way home they stumble onto a T'aafhal artifact, a developing interplanetary war, and a sinister plot by the Dark Lords.

As usual, all units of measurement—distance, mass, time, etc— have been rendered in familiar human terms. It is much easier to do that than have the reader trying to translate what a hundred ferniks per wizbat means. Most of the characters are still referred to by rank, at least on occasion, even though the Peggy Sue is now a civilian vessel sailing for a merchant company. As always, I have tried to make the science as realistic as possible, given our current understanding. Some speculative liberties are taken, particularly in the realm of faster than light travel. I also assumed the use of primitive spears and stone cutting tools by hominins a half million or so years earlier than has been documented, but then sticks rot away and knapped stones are hard to find and date.

As usual, the text is sprinkled with quotations, some from historical sources, others from contemporary humans. Not all are attributed in the story itself, people tend not to do that, but I will say that there are lines from all sorts of folks—from Samuel Taylor Coleridge to Friedrich Nietzsche, from Charlie Daniels to Dana Perino. I hope you enjoy finding the "hidden" ones.

I would like to thank the following early readers and editors of this novel. Most of these have been with me from the beginning of my writing career and without them these adventures would probably have never seen the light of day. Special thanks to Rik Faith, who helps keep my science honest and my phraseology understandable; Bobby Johnson, whose eagle eyes find errors I've missed time and time again; David Metheny, Clayton Ward, and Jesse Perkins. Mistakes that slipped through are all my fault, certainly not theirs.

This, of course, brings us to the obligatory disclaimers: all the characters in this book are fictional, not representations of any real person, living or dead; Any mistakes in the science, cosmology, engineering, etc. are purely my own and not the responsibility any of those thanked above. The book was written using LibreOffice and the cover art done using the GIMP. Ebook formatting was done using Calibre.

Finally, if you like this book please tell your friends, and if you really like it consider writing a review online at Amazon.com. Online reviews are the best way to spread the word about my books and to reach more possible readers. They also help motivate me to write that next novel.

Regards,
Doug L. Hoffman
Conway, Arkansas
May 28, 2015

For my mother,
Mary Hoffman

Prologue

Alpha Phoenicis

The primary and its companion were a mismatched pair, one a swollen orange giant, the other a small ruddy dwarf. From Earth only the primary was visible, shining bright in the southern sky it was called Ankaa by Medieval Arab sailors. It was known to more modern observers as *Alpha Phoenicis*, the brightest star in the constellation of the mythical Firebird—the Phoenix. The system lay at a distance of about 26 parsecs, roughly 85 light-years, from humanity's home world. With a mass of around 2.5 times that of the Sun and a radius 13 times solar, the star appeared to be in a short-term but stable helium burning stage. Eventually, it would expand into a brighter, larger red giant, and then, after a short time, expel its outer shell to become a tiny white dwarf; the fate of all such K type giants. Nonetheless, it currently supported a planet with indigenous life.

Near that world—a super-Earth on the outer edge of the K type's habitable zone—a starship hung in space. The ship looked like a spindle, turned out of a kilometer long shard of blackest obsidian. Tapered to slender points at either end, its central section exhibited a number of bulges, hinting at spaces contained within. Amidships, a thin silver ring encircled the shaft. Fifty meters wide, the ring's diameter was nearly a third of a kilometer. Held in position by an almost invisible tracery of dark filaments, the band seemed to float in space without connection to the glassy black spindle.

Inside a sizable bulge just forward of amidships there was a large room filled with liquid—a mix of ethane and methane, with some liquid nitrogen thrown in for good measure. The temperature remained constant around minus 166°C, almost 300° below zero Fahrenheit. Within this liquid environment floated a number of creatures, which bore an uncanny similarity to barrel jellyfish. Ranging in size from one to two meters across, they floated in place, their translucent bell-shaped mantles slowly pulsating. But, with metabolic pathways suited only to life on cryogenically cold worlds, these creatures were no relation of earthly Scyphozoans.

1

The largest of these medusoids was a behemoth two and a half meters across, with a purple fringe around the bottom of its mantle. Beneath its slowly pulsing dome hung five clusters of unripened eggs, each ending in a profusion of stinging tentacles. Situated between the dangling egg clusters was a central mouth opening leading to a digestion chamber. Having no durable hard parts—no head, no skeleton, and no specialized organs for respiration or excretion—it nonetheless possessed a distributed neural network that allowed the creature to think.

A number of its tentacles were evolved beyond the grasping and stinging of prey, forgoing the nematocysts found on those surrounding the creature's mouth. The specialized tentacles made contact with polyp like protuberances attached to the sides of the chamber, allowing the Commander to communicate with its ship and crew. For the giant pseudo-jellyfish was in command of the starship and all it contained.

"Our survey of this system has been completed," the Commander announced to its companions. "It is as the others informed us, there is an artifact on the planet orbiting the M type star—an artifact left behind by the accursed T'aafhal."

A wave of agitation spread through the creatures at the mention of the Dark Lords' ancient enemy. Though it had been millions of years since the last encounter with warm life's paladins, their name still struck fear in the minds of the dark ones and their minions.

"How are we to retrieve this artifact, Most Wise?" asked an underling, barely a meter across, floating nearby the Commander. "And why are we orbiting the terrestrial planet of the K type primary star?"

"Because, underling, I have devised a stratagem for said retrieval." The Commander's words were laced with contempt and rebuke for the presumptuous crewmember. "Have we not found that both planets are infested with warm life?"

"Yes, Most Wise," replied the senior crewmember, before the lesser crewmember could further antagonize the Commander. "The planet orbiting the M type is dominated by a form of invertebrate creatures, arthropods, while the planet below is dominated by a species of burrowing vertebrates."

"And what level of technology have these two misbegotten races of vermin achieved?"

"The invertebrates live in colonies and seem to posses no notable technology," the senior crewmember replied, "while the vertebrates communicate using electromagnetic radiation and have successfully placed artificial satellites in orbit using chemical rockets, Most Wise."

"Precisely." There was a hint of satisfaction in the Commander's terse reply. It paused to admire its solution to their mission before continuing. Into that silence the underling again rashly spoke.

"But the artifact is on the planet of the invertebrates, orbiting the other star. Why do we concern ourselves with the warm life scum on the world below?"

A shudder of rage rippled through the gelatinous material of the Commander's umbrella like body as its tentacles reached for the underling floating nearby. Realizing its peril, the underling frantically pulsed its body in a vain attempt to escape—but it was too late.

"We can not comfortably travel to the surfaces of either of these hell-spawned worlds, so we will need to act through agents," the Commander said for the edification of the remaining crew. As it spoke tentacles wrapped around the unfortunate crewmember and began dragging it toward the Commander's central mouth opening. "The surface gravity on either world is sufficient to make use of our standard cyborg workers untenable so we must recruit from the available local lifeforms."

"Perceptive, indeed, Wise One. Would you deign to enlighten your humble crew as to which species you have chosen?"

"Which would you choose, Senior Functionary?"

Edging carefully away from its commander, the senior crewmember carefully considered its answer. "Most Wise, the obvious answer would appear to be the invertebrates on the planet where the artifact resides, but I suspect that my perception falls woefully short of your superior intellect."

"It is well that you recognize your inadequacies," the Commander answered, satisfied with the senior crewmember's

3

unctuous reply. "The invertebrates are primitives, making it difficult to communicate with them effectively, whereas the vertebrates on the planet we now orbit already have the means to communicate electronically. The vertebrates also have the rudimentary beginnings of a space program."

"I float in awe of your superior perceptiveness," intoned the senior crewmember.

The Commander pulsed slowly, falling quiet as the hapless underling was drawn into its mouth opening. The pause briefly made the senior crewmember wonder if its last statement had been a bit too transparently obsequious. Eventually, the Commander continued.

"We will make contact with the vertebrates and present ourselves as beneficent higher beings from the stars, on a mission to help elevate other races throughout the galaxy." The Commander paused again to let the crew savor that bit of irony. "We will feed them enough technical knowledge to build effective spacecraft for a voyage across the system to the world circling the companion star. There they will conquer the invertebrates and retrieve the T'aafhal artifact."

"A sublimely subtle and ingeneous plan, Most Significant One."

"Yes, it is. I shall suborn the vertebrates, who will subjugate the invertebrates, and, once I have the prize we seek, both shall be exterminated."

As the Commander admired the plan of his own devising, the last trace of the unwisely verbose crewmember disappeared into its superior's digestive chamber.

Part One

Down To A Sunless Sea

Chapter 1

Ice Moon, Unnamed System

The icy moon orbited its gaseous parent, a banded giant three times the size of Jupiter. The gas giant itself orbited an unremarkable white dwarf. Too faint to have been named by ancient sky watchers, the star was known only by catalog numbers. An unnamed moon of an unnamed planet of an insignificant remnant of a dead star—pretty much the definition of a galactic backwater.

The moon's surface, composed of water ice, was remarkably smooth as lunar surfaces go. Not that it was featureless, being striated by cracks and crevasses, though craters were relatively rare. Due to the gas giant's immense gravitational field, orbital bondage kept the surface active, explaining the lack of cratering—no surface feature lasted long on the icy moon. The smoothness of the surface was a result of the ocean lying beneath it. Five kilometers of ice capped a sixty kilometer deep water ocean, kept liquid by heat from tidal flexing.

Thick continents of ice collided with each other, crumpling and grinding in a cryogenic version of plate tectonics. Volcanoes and fissures expelled liquid water into cold black space, where it instantly turned to snow that drifted slowly back to the moon's surface. The moon's white covering of ice and snow reflected the faint light from the system's central star, creating a ghostly wasteland of ridges, plains, and chasms.

Nestled between two large pressure ridges, almost invisible against the icy terrain, was a silver and crystal needle. It appeared a tiny thing, dwarfed by the scale of the terrain, but it was in fact 155 meters in length and massed more than 8,000 tons. It was the Earth starship Peggy Sue.

On the bridge, Captain Billy Ray Vincent gazed out through the ship's transparent bow and across the frozen panorama beyond. Peggy Sue's bow was a fanciful structure, composed of curved crystalline panels joined by thin flowing strips of silver. Its elegant beauty was lost on the Captain in his current frame of mind. The ship had been sitting on the moon's surface for more than three days and the Captain was becoming impatient.

After following a circuitous path from system to system for more than a year, ending up almost one hundred light years from Earth, Captain Vincent decided to stop and refuel his ship before the trip home. Unfortunately, deuterium, the fuel on which the Peggy Sue's thermonuclear reactors ran, was much less common than normal hydrogen. One good place to look for deuterium was in water where approximately one water molecule in twenty million was heavy water, at least in Earth's oceans.

"Engineer Baldursson," he called over the comm, "what is the status of the borehole?"

"Captain, we are down well over four kilometers and should reach the liquid layer in less than an hour." Arin Baldursson, the ship's chief engineer, was outside the hull in a hastily constructed enclosure, supervising the drilling of a shaft through the ice. The drill was a powerful laser assembly that could bore through solid rock or, as in this case, solid H_2O.

"Very good, Mr. Baldursson. Let me know when the ice is breached and you begin installation of the molecular filter and pumps."

"Aye, aye, Skipper."

The reason for drilling the well—indeed, the reason for the Peggy Sue's presence on the icy moon—was to access the liquid ocean trapped beneath the moon's solid surface. Once they tapped the liquid below, equipment would be lowered into the water to filter out molecules of heavy water. Heavy water contains deuterium, which makes it 11% denser than "normal" water. The deuterium substitution alters heavy water's hydrogen-oxygen bond energy. This changes its physical, chemical, and biological properties enough so that heavy water can be readily separated from its more pedestrian cousins.

"You seem a bit on edge, Captain," observed the First Officer, Beth Melaku. The strikingly tall officer was standing beside the Captain's command chair, hands clasped behind her back, keeping an eye on the bridge crew. "It's like you are anxious to be headed homeward."

"Yer right about that. We haven't found much of anything worthwhile since the mess at Paradise." The Peggy Sue was owned by the Honorable Orion Arm Trading Company, a joint venture by a group of billionaires back in the solar system. The object of the voyage was to find interesting things, which was to say profitable things, beyond the boundaries of humanity's current territory. "All we got to show for the trip is a couple of tons of oversized gemstones, a bunch of half busted alien electronics, and an empty world that kills anything that lands on it."

"That's not true," Beth said with a faint smile. "We did manage to establish trade relations with that group of six-limbed meerkat like creatures a few systems back."

"Yep, they were happy to trade carved sticks for some of the smaller gems that PO Jacobs polished up."

"We do seem to have a lock on the carved stick market, don't we?"

Billy Ray shook his head and squinted at the horizon. "The ship is safely at rest and the bridge is manned; I say we retire to the bar for a drink, Number One."

"Now that is the best offer I've had all day."

"Mr. Lewis, you have the deck," the Captain called out as he followed Beth aft.

"Aye, aye, Sir. I have the deck," replied Lt. Lewis from his station at the helm.

As Billy Ray caught up with Beth he slipped his arm through hers —not normal behavior for a captain and first officer. Of course, on most ships the First Officer is not the Captain's wife.

Armory, *Peggy Sue*

It was crowded in the armory, with a pair of polar bears, a human scientist, and most of the engineering staff in attendance. Also assisting were two of the senior crew: Petty Officers 1st Class Matt Jacobs and Steve Hitch. The reason for the assembly was fitting those going diving in the hidden ocean with pressure suits. Once the Captain's refueling plans were made clear, work began on suits for Umky, Ahnah, Dr. Krenshaw and Senior Engineer's Mate James Michaels. Quickly designed and fabricated by Chief Engineer

Baldursson's artificers, all that remained was to make sure the suits were comfortable enough for their intended wearers to spend several hours working in them.

"Tell me again why these things are so bulky," said Umky, a full grown male polar bear who was attached to the ship's Marines. "Why couldn't we just wear our normal armor?"

"Because your normal armor is meant to be worn in space, not underwater," replied Ahnah, a female bear who was a biologist on the science staff. She and Umky had a love-hate relationship that started the minute they both boarded the ship back at Farside Base.

"So?"

"She's right, Umky," Jim Michaels interjected. "A space suit is designed to keep pressure in, not keep pressure out. And at the bottom of the bore-shaft there is pressure aplenty."

"You don't say," rumbled the larger bear, attempting to stuff his hindquarters into the suit's stiff legs. "I thought we would be right at the surface."

"We are going to be underwater under the ice, and all that ice has weight. That adds to the pressure in the water below," Jim explained, as he struggled with a suit of his own. "The local surface gravity is about 1.3 m/sec^2, only 13 percent of Earth's, and the ice layer is around five kilometers thick."

The engineer paused for a second as he entered figures on his sleeve display. "That works out to about 6.6 x 10^6 Pascals of pressure, or roughly 65 Earth atmospheres, at the ice-liquid boundary."

"More than enough to crush most submarines back home," observed Matt Jacobs.

"Are you sure these suits are strong enough?" asked Will Krenshaw, a human microbiologist. He was accompanying the bears and Engineer Michaels to take samples of the water and ice below. There were a couple of similar moons in the solar system and a comparison of any microscopic lifeforms found here would be of great scientific interest.

"Sure thing, Professor, plenty of safety margin. Just don't try drifting down to the bottom," replied Jim, slipping into position. "Matt, Stevie, I'm in. Close me up please."

"Right on it, Jim," said Jacobs.

The two sailors moved to attach the suit's integrated helmet and back plate. Spurred on by Jim's success, Ahnah managed to wriggle her rear legs and bottom into her suit. Stretching her neck to look behind her she made a sort of woofing sound.

"Does this suit make my ass look big?" asked Steve Hitch in a false contralto voice.

Suit not withstanding, Ahnah whirled about and with a single paw swipe knocked Umky to the deck. The bigger male, stuck half in and half out of his suit, went sprawling.

"Hey! What's the idea! I didn't say anything!"

"You laughed, you mangy bruin!"

"I did not!"

"Well, you thought about laughing," the incensed she-bear retorted. "Besides, monkey-boy over there jumped out of paw range."

Stevie held a hand over his mouth, trying to suppress his own laughter. His normal partner in crime, Jacobs, slugged him in the arm and admonished, "Quit messing with the bears, troublemaker."

"Come on, Matt. You gotta admit it was funny."

"Any funnier and it could have got you killed, or at least sent to sickbay."

That was when Chief Zackly entered the armory to see what the commotion was all about.

"What the flying hell do yous scupper turds think yer doing?" the grizzled old sailor demanded. "Get yer shit together or I will turn ya upside down and spit in yer assholes! Do yous get me?"

"Aye, aye, Chief," the two sailors replied, busying themselves with helping Umky back up off the deck.

11

"And you, Missy," the Chief said, addressing Ahnah, "I don't care if you are on the science staff, do not go smacking things around in here."

"Yes, Chief," the she-bear said, meekly.

"Ya might damage some of the equipment, and that could delay the mission and piss-off the Captain." The Chief gave the ursine scientist a hard look and then grinned, indicating that he wasn't that upset by the brief tussle.

Ahnah gave the Chief a quick bearish smile, turned and slid the rest of the way into her pressure suit. A couple of engineer's mates moved to install her helmet section while Hitch and Jacobs assisted Umky.

"Sorry I got you walloped, Bear2," Hitch said in a lowered voice, calling the bear by his Marine squad nickname. Both Hitch and Jacobs were often detailed to work with the ship's Marines, primarily because they had as much combat experience as any on board.

"No problem, primate. That would hardly qualify as foreplay on an amorous evening. She is quick though—I should have remembered that."

"Are you saying that you two are getting busy in the polar bear quarters when no one else is around?" asked Hitch.

"Fat chance," Umky snorted. "Since Doc white implanted a birth control gadget in Ahnah she's a lot less frisky than before. But her mood swings are a lot less manic too, so the dubious loss of a piece of tail is worth it. By the way, Stevie, polar bears like big butts."

"So why did she hit you?"

"Because she knew that, coming from you, it was supposed to be an insult."

"Great job, Stevie," said Jacobs, "now you've managed to piss-off every female on the ship, not just the human ones."

"Hey, I found it funny," Umky chuckled. "Now stop chattering and seal me up. The others are almost ready to go outside."

Wellhead, Icy Moon

Located fifty meters from the ship, the borehole was in a temporary building with an open roof. A floor had been constructed around the hole itself so the crew and equipment did not have to stand on the froze surface of the moon. The walls provided a convenient place to mount monitoring equipment and an undeserved sense of security. The reason for the open roof was about to be demonstrated.

"I am recording some minor tremors, Chief Engineer," reported Katrin "Kate" Hamm. Kate had been a crewmember on an Antarctic exploration ship at one time, and knew something about drilling core samples. While drilling through ice with a laser was much different from drilling through ocean floor sediment with hollow steel, any experience was better than none, or so the Chief Engineer reasoned.

"Ja, we should be right at the ice-water boundary," the Icelandic Chief Engineer replied. With next to no atmosphere there was no sound transmission but vibrations were passed through the five kilometers of solid ice beneath their feet and transferred to the platform floor.

"We have penetration!" Kate shouted.

"Everyone back!" yelled the Chief Engineer Baldursson, motioning to the other crewmembers assisting with the drilling operation. The vibration could now be felt without the need for instruments. As the drilling crew backed against the platform walls the cause of the tremors became clear.

From the two and a half meter in diameter borehole emerged a column of water traveling at high speed. Through the open roof the gusher shot, kilometers into the inky black sky where it formed a massive plume of ice crystals.

"Trigger the seals, Ms. Hamm," shouted Baldursson.

In response, Kate closed several relays on the control board next to her. Buried ten meters down the shaft a thick, circular plate of hull material rotated. The cap plate was constructed with alternating cutouts and solid sectors. As the solid sectors in the rotating plate aligned with open sectors in a similar plate immediately above it, the column of water stopped rushing from the hole.

Even though it was capped quickly, everything and everyone in the platform building was coated with a layer of ice. The drilling crew moved their extremities, the synthetic muscles of their space armor shattering the coating of frozen H_2O.

"I did not expect it to be so... energetic," Kate said.

"Ja, remember that there was nothing but vacuum in the shaft and the water is under many atmospheres pressure, Ms. Hamm. That propelled it up the shaft with some urgency. Once the column of water began moving it built up considerable momentum, the result of which you see still dispersing in the sky above us."

Overhead the ice plume was clearly visible in the dim light of the white dwarf as it spread out and turned into falling snow. Meanwhile, outside of the building a procession had been making its way toward the wellhead when the eruption took place.

* * * * *

"What the hell was that!" exclaimed Hitch. He and Jacobs accompanied the pressure suited bears and humans in case they needed assistance—the bulky pressure suits were not nearly as agile as normal space armor.

"I'd say the drilling crew hit water, Stevie," replied Jacobs.

"Chief Engineer Baldursson, are you OK in there?" asked Michaels, leading the procession in his own pressure suit.

"Ja, ja," came the reply. "Just our first geyser. I told everyone it would be impressive."

"Being told isn't the same as seeing it, Sir. Are we clear to enter the enclosure?"

"Ja, come on to the platform. We need a few minutes to ensure the heaters in the cap are working and that the drill head is heating water to keep the shaft from freezing shut."

"Roger that, we are almost to the platform."

"What's with this shaft freezing shut stuff?" asked Umky, standing back up on all fours. When the well blew both bears sat down on their haunches and marveled at the sight. "Nobody said anything about the hole freezing shut."

"It won't be a problem, Umky," responded Dr. Krenshaw, the other pressure suited human. "The laser on the drill head will heat water at the bottom of the shaft, which will cause it to rise. That, along with heaters placed along the sides of the shaft, will circulate warm water and keep the well open."

"Why didn't you just cap it at the bottom?" asked Jacobs, who was a bit more technically inclined than his friend Hitch.

"Because access is by a plate of selectively permeable T'aafhal hull material, modified to keep water on one side and vacuum on the other. Trouble is the pressure is so great at the bottom it would be almost impossible to push anything through the barrier."

"OK, that makes sense," Jacobs replied. "So the barrier is up near the top."

"Yeah. The only real downside is that we will have to drift down five kilometers of shaft to reach the ocean below. I hope no one is claustrophobic."

"Bears are not nearly as neurotic as you humans," sniffed Ahnah. Walking behind the she-bear, Umky shook his head but made no snide remark, perhaps remembering the wallop in the armory. One by one the four aquanauts and their handlers ascended the walled platform.

Main Lounge, Peggy Sue

"Hey there, you two," called Belinda "Betty" White, the ship's doctor. Betty was nursing a cup of coffee, sitting at the table in front of the big eye shaped viewing port on the starboard side.

"Hey there yourself," replied Beth as she and the Captain claimed chairs across from the MD. Billy Ray glanced out of the viewing port just in time to see Arin Baldursson's geyser erupt.

"Now would you look at that! There's something you don't see every day."

"Oh my," exclaimed the Doctor.

"It would appear that Arin has struck water," observed Beth, "aren't you going to congratulate him, dear?"

"I think I'll let him get things under control before distracting him with a call from the captain."

"Probably a good idea," Beth allowed, gazing up at the plume. "Don't want to micromanage the crew—bad for the morale."

Billy Ray nodded absently, staring out the window. Jimmy Tosh, the chef and bartender, placed steaming mugs before the Captain and Beth—coffee black for him, Earl Gray tea for her. The officers' preferences were familiar enough for the Jamaican to bring their usual without waiting for an order. Looking up from the table Jimmy, too, was mesmerized by the scene outside the ship.

"Now dat be sometin'. Dey was blowholes at places on de coast of Jamaica, but nothin' like dat."

As quickly as the geyser had started the flow was cut off, leaving a few sad remnants to fall back on to the wellhead enclosure. The party of aquanauts could be seen outside the building, also staring at the plume in awe.

"You need anyting else, ladies? Captain?"

"No, thank you Jimmy," answered Beth for the others.

"Jus' call out if you need a refill." The Jamaican smiled a toothy smile and headed back for the curved mahogany bar that divided the lounge space from the dining area.

"I see you are sending Ahnah and Umky down to work on the extraction system," said Betty, noting the unmistakable forms of the two suited bears outside.

"Yep. I figured that the bears, being semi-aquatic and strong, would be perfect to help deploy the filters at the bottom of the well."

"And it might also help their self-esteem, having them do a task they are better suited to than humans," added Beth, looking sideways at her husband and raising her eyebrows.

"Yep." Billy Ray often adopted a cowboy drawl when at ease. Like many Texans, he figured if you don't have much to say, then you shouldn't say much.

"That's thoughtful of you, Billy Ray," Doc White said approvingly. Betty was one of the few people on board who referred to the Captain by his given name, a privilege conferred by the implicit doctor patient relationship. "Polar bears are generally solitary animals but they do socialize at times of the year. Plus, talking bears are temperamentally different from dumb bears, they miss social interaction with their own kind."

"I heartily agree, Betty. Both Billy Ray and I have decided we are lacking in two areas when it comes to the crew—we need more Marines and we need more bears on the next voyage."

"You got that right, sweetheart. Thank goodness we haven't gotten into a tussle on this trip."

"Speaking of this trip, we're pretty far away from home. I think some of the crew are showing definite signs of being homesick. When are we going to head back toward Earth?"

"We are as far away from the solar system as any Earth ship has ever gone, Betty, almost a hundred light years as the crow flies. I reckon that soon as we top off the deuterium tanks we'll head back toward more familiar space."

"As much as I love exploring the final frontier," his wife added, "I'm longing to see old friends and familiar places again—even if home is carved out of lunar rock."

"That's why I love you, sweetheart. Yer such a homebody." This last was delivered with a grin to show the Captain was speaking in jest.

"But first we need to send people down five kilometers to a hidden ocean to harvest heavy water," continued Beth, ignoring the homebody remark.

Billy Ray smiled and began to recite:

In Xanadu did Kubla Khan
A stately pleasure-dome decree:
Where Alph, the sacred river, ran
Through caverns measureless to man
Down to a sunless sea.

"Come again, Captain?"

"He's quoting Samuel Taylor Coleridge, Doctor, from a poem called *Kubla Khan.*"

"When the Captain starts quoting poetry maybe it's past time we headed for home." She fixed Billy Ray with a look of medical appraisal.

"Soon enough, Betty, soon enough." He replied with a faint smile. Between the gems and the alien devices, not to mention survey data on half a dozen habitable worlds, he figured the trip would pay for itself. Besides, there were a couple more systems he intended to visit on the way home, since Earth was too far to make in a single alter-space transit.

Outside the aquanauts disappeared into the shelter as ice crystals from the geyser continued to rain down on the ship. Chief Engineer Baldursson's voice called from the Captain's collar pip.

Wellhead, Icy Moon

The Chief Engineer was pleased how things had gone so far with the refueling effort, but the more hazardous stage was about to begin. He called the ship.

"Peggy Sue, Wellhead. We have completed the borehole and are ready to send personnel down to deploy the filtering gear."

"Roger that, Wellhead. Good job, Arin, let me know when the heavy water begins to flow."

"Aye, aye, Captain."

The members of the aquatic expedition were gathered around the borehole, peering down at the sealed cap ten meters below. Down the middle of the well ran a heavy cable, which carried power to the drill head at the bottom of the shaft. From their vantage point the cap looked a long way down.

"How are we supposed to descend to the cap?" asked Ahnah.

"I'll show you," said Jim, leaning over the hole and grasping the power cable. "You need to hit the cap barrier with a bit of momentum to help carry you through into the water below."

With that, he loosely grasped the cable with both hands and let himself slide down into the shaft. The others leaned over the edge of the hole and watched as he approached the cap. Even in the light gravity of the icy moon, Jim built up a respectable velocity falling the ten meters. He hit the cap and fell right through it, disappearing without a trace.

"Now that just looked freaky," said Hitch. "Glad I'm not going."

"Yeah, that T'aafhal hull material gives me the willies," agreed Jacobs. "Too much like magic."

"Michaels, Wellhead," called Baldursson over the comm circuit. "Are you OK?"

"Wellhead, Michaels. Everything's copacetic," came the reply. "Tell the others to come on in, the water's fine."

"Ja, the rest of you best be going, it is a long descent to the bottom of the shaft."

"Right," rumbled Umky, grasping hold of the cable. "What's that you primates yell when you jump out of an airplane? Geranium!"

Umky slid down the cable and disappeared, just like Michaels.

"That's 'Geronimo', fur ball," Hitch yelled after the now vanished bear. The smaller she-bear stepped up and grasped the cable.

"I don't know, I sort of like 'geranium'," she said.

Ahnah stepped off the edge and vanished down the well. Will Krenshaw, the last expedition member left on the platform, shook his head.

"All you need to start an asylum is an empty room and the right kind of people," he said, reaching for the cable. "Just make sure the damn hole doesn't freeze back shut."

The last of the aquanauts passed through the semi-permeable barrier without another word. The expedition was on their way to visit an ocean that had never seen the stars or sky, a world of crushing pressure and utter darkness.

Chapter 2

Borehole, The Icy Moon

The small party of Earthlings had been drifting down into the inky abyss for more than an hour. The two humans—Michaels in the lead and Krenshaw bringing up the rear—kept up a constant chatter amongst themselves and those at the wellhead. Sandwiched between the men were the two bears. They both muted their radios and quietly watched the darkness pass by.

"They do like to talk," commented Ahnah, above Umky but within suit-to-suit range. Unlike the common radio channel, suit-to-suit was short range only, allowing the bears to talk in private.

"Monkey's like to chatter," Umky grunted, the she-bear scientist intruding on his thoughts.

"And I thought you were friends with some of them."

"I like some of them well enough, it doesn't change what they are. Most of them aren't comfortable being alone, with only their own thoughts for company."

Polar bears in the wild spent much of the year alone, prowling the Arctic ice on an endless hunt for food. Males in particular spent significant time in solitude. Females were less solitary, often having cubs to take care of.

"I don't know, some of them seem to value time alone. I've seen the Captain sitting on the bridge pensing, lost in his thoughts."

"Exception to every rule. Some bears yammer on like primates."

Both fell silent again for several minutes. If Ahnah took the crack about yammering like a primate personally, she said nothing about it. As the water pressure around them slowly increased, their suits occasionally pinged and creaked. Without exterior lights there was no sense of motion, nothing to mark their descent to the hidden sea below.

"I wonder if this is how whales feel."

"What?" said Ahnah, his statement taking her by surprise.

21

"When they dive deep beneath the surface, down to where light never penetrates. It's very tranquil, like being the only creature alive in the universe."

"You are the strangest bear," Ahnah replied, a hint of puzzlement in her voice.

Umky snorted. Again the pair fell silent. Minutes passed before the he-bear resumed speaking.

"You can blame my sire, and to a lesser extent my dam." Humans often referred to he-bears as boars and she-bears as sows, which polar bears found insulting. Humans also called a group of bears a "sleuth," which oddly the bears found acceptable.

"Pihoqahiak and Isbjørn?"

"Yeah, my father was always an individualist, even for one of our species. He was the first bear recruited to serve on the Peggy Sue."

"How in the world did that happen? It's not like there was a north pole recruiting office."

"Evidently he was sought out by Jack Sutton, the ship's first captain. He found Dad out on the ice, hunting."

"And instead of shooting him he recruited him?"

Umky paused for a second while he parsed her question.

"No, it was my father who was hunting. Captain Jack just walked up behind him and introduced himself."

"Ballsy for a human."

"Especially considering Dad was hunting a group of Inuit using a modified .50 caliber sniper's rifle."

"Your father was hunting humans? And this Captain Jack not only talked Pihoqahiak into not killing him, but into going off in a spaceship?"

"Dad qualified as a serial killer in human terms but that didn't deter Sutton. He asked Dad why he was hunting the Inuit."

"What did he say?"

Umky chuckled.

"He said 'they hunt us, don't they?' Evidently that was good enough for Captain Jack. The rest, as they say, is history."

Ahnah paused to consider her next reply carefully. This was the most personal conversation the pair had engaged in since they boarded the Peggy Sue more than a year ago. Maybe it was being in the water, encircled by ice, that made the bears feel chatty. Not that their present surroundings were anything like the polar pack ice of home.

"I knew your mother from Farside Base. She was in the forefront of the 'bears forming families' movement. Isbjørn believed we had much to learn from humans. In fact, she was one of those who encouraged me to become a scientist."

"Yeah, Mom and Dad are both bears of a different kind—futurists, always looking beyond the ice flow they're on, always looking across open water to the next one. Now they are off somewhere in an ancient T'aafhal starship and I'm five klicks down a hole in the ice on a moon with no name."

Ahnah made a neutral sound in reply.

LEDs blinked insistently in both bears' helmets, signaling a call from the others. They opened the channel to hear the voice of Jim Michaels.

"I can see light from the drilling head below, we are almost at the bottom..."

Cargo Hold, Peggy Sue

The forward part of the ship's cargo hold was occupied by a flock of brightly colored butterflies and two pairs of humans. The members of each pair circled one another slowly. Wearing quilted armor and wire basket face masks, each held a *shinai*—a weapon used in kendo to represent a traditional Japanese sword during practice and competition. Occasional flurries of movement punctuated their slow dance, as one partner struck out at the other, the motion too fast to be seen clearly.

On closer inspection it was obvious that each pair consisted of an adult and a young person, a *uchidachi* and a *shidachi*—a teacher and a student. The taller pair consisted of a man, stocky of build, 5'9" in height, and a slender young woman roughly an inch taller. The shorter pair consisted of a woman, 5'7", and a younger girl around the same height.

All four were moving in accordance with *suri-ashi*, the shuffling, sliding way all movement is done in kendo. The students were practicing feints and counter attacks while trying to maintain the proper stance. Above the combatants butterflies fluttered, safely out of striking distance.

"Eiii!" cried the younger girl, stamping her right foot and pressing the attack. Her teacher easily deflected the attempted blow. The crack of clashing swords, the yelling and stamping continued until the *sensei*, the kendo master, had enough.

"*Yame!*" the woman shouted. "Stop!"

All four stepped back from engagement distance and bowed to their partners.

"Dorri, you are supposed to be practicing your technique while maintaining *okuri-ashi.*" *Okuri-ashi* is the most important form of *ashi-sabaki* or kendo footwork. It is also the most difficult. In the basic stance the right foot is in front and the left, heel slightly raised, is in back. Moving forward or backward in *okuri-ashi,* the back foot never passes the front foot.

The reprimand came from Dr. Mizuki Ogawa, the ship's science officer. When it came to kendo, she was the master, skilled beyond all others on board in the art of sword play. Others among the crew had killed using railguns, X-ray lasers, and antimatter warheads; she alone had killed other beings with a katana.

"I am sorry, *sensei,*" the young girl replied, "it's just that you are so fast, I will never be able to beat you."

"Learning *budo,* the way of combat, is not about mastering others, it is about mastering yourself, Dorri." Mizuki looked at the girl with an open gaze that some people found unsettling. "I think we have had enough practice for the day."

Dorri drew herself up and bowed again to the older woman, thanking her.

"*Domo arigato gozaimashita.*"

24

Mizuki bowed in return.

"Do not worry, you will become faster and more skillful overtime. No one becomes a master *kendōka* overnight."

"She keeps telling people that so she has people to practice with," said the man from the other couple, "or on, as the case may be."

"It must have worked with you, Bobby," the taller girl said with a smile, sultry gray eyes peering out from beneath dark seductive brows. "You are quite fast yourself."

"Yeah, but Mizuki has been whacking me with sticks for years, Shadi. It was either get better or stay covered with bruises." Bobby grinned back, oblivious to any sexual undertone in the girl's remark.

Mizuki's cool gaze shifted to Shadi, then to Bobby, and then back again.

"I will show you something that might encourage your desire to learn kendo," Mizuki said after a few moments' thought. "Bobby, please set up three mats."

Bobby's eyebrows went up.

"Sure."

As Bobby moved to comply with Mizuki's request the Japanese kendōka turned to the two young women. Standing next to each other with their masks off, it was obvious that the two were sisters. They were the only survivors of the New Mecca settlement on the planet Paradise. Together they accounted for half those who escaped that deadly planet, the Earth Colonization Board's disastrous first attempt to establish a colony among the stars.

Shadi, 16, and Dorri, 14, were originally from Iran, but had left Earth years ago. They lived first as refugees on the Moon, then as settlers on Paradise, and for the last year as the youngest members of the Peggy Sue's crew. They could be considered among the luckiest adolescents in the galaxy, being doted on by the ship's officers, educated by the science section's PhDs, instructed in armed and unarmed combat by the Peggy Sue's Marines, and generally having free run of the ship. On the other hand, they were the only young people on board.

Coming of age on board a starship where everyone was in their twenties or older was problematic for the girls to say the least. Shadi in particular was starting to have trouble coming to terms with the hormones her maturing body was pumping out. In recent days, her behavior with some of the ship's male officers had started to verge on overtly flirtatious.

"Where do you want these set up, sensei?" Bobby asked, returning with a large rolled mat on a vertical stand. It looked superficially like tatami, a type of mat used as floor covering in traditional Japanese homes.

"Place three of them in a staggered pattern, with enough space to pass between them, and bring me my katana when you have set the targets." Bobby set the first mat down near Mizuki and went back for another. Mizuki turned to the sisters, placing a single hand on the mat and striking a professorial pose.

"This mat is a target used in *tameshigiri*, a Japanese martial art with a long history. Originally it was a way to test the cutting ability of swords. To ensure that it was a test of the sword itself, and not the man wielding it, only the most skilful swordsmen performed these tests.

"The first targets for tameshigiri were human bodies. Specifically, the bodies of executed criminals. The bodies were carefully inspected before being cut, to check for disease. This was because swords were religious, almost mystical objects in ancient Japan, and it was believed that sickness would make a pure sword unclean. For similar reasons swords were never tested on low caste individuals or priests. It was believed that doing so could harm a blade's soul.

"During the Meiji period test cutting on criminals became illegal, causing the cadavers to be replaced by mats made from bound rice straw with a bamboo core and soaked with water. Side by side tests found the wet mats to have almost the same characteristics as the original human targets.

"You have practiced with the lightweight shinai, to learn proper stance and technique, and you have performed katas with the heavier bokken, which has a weight and balance as close to a real sword as possible. But neither of these forms of practice can be a substitute for actual combat, for actually using a katana against another swordsman, feeling your blade as it slices through a foe's body. The cutting of mats is as close as a swordsman can come to actually striking another human being with his weapon. To this day, tameshigiri remains the only accepted way, short of actual combat, of measuring the speed and power of a swordsman. "

Mizuki paused her lecture and looked at the rolled mat standing next to her. She looked back to her students, who were now paying rapt attention. Bobby approached her, a curved scabbarded sword in front of him. He stopped and bowed, offering his teacher the sheathed sword, balanced on his two open palms.

Mizuki bowed and accepted the sword, grasping the scabbard with her right hand. She thrust the scabbard through the belt-like sash around her waist in traditional samurai style. The flock of butterflies settled expectantly on the walls and ceiling showing excited shades of yellow, green, and cyan.

"I have shown you my teacher's katana before. It was Hiroyuki Saito's grandfather's sword and has been in their family for more than a hundred years. Their family were samurai, members of the warrior class of feudal Japan. Such swords are not just weapons, they are objects of art, and even have a sacred aspect in the Shinto religion.

"There is much mysticism surrounding the ancient samurai, their skills and their deeds. It is said a true samurai could note the positions of his opponents with a single glance, and once this was done he could strike them down without a second look."

Mizuki was standing side-on to the staggered row of targets, each as big around as a man's thigh and taller than the swordswoman herself. The first stood about five feet to her right. Bobby was to her left and the two sisters were standing in front of her, about ten feet away.

Mizuki glanced to her right and then back at the girls. Bobby stepped behind her and placed a folded strip of black cloth over her eyes. After tying the blindfold at the back of her head, he quickly moved well away. The cargo bay was dead silent.

Mizuki exploded into motion, gliding to the right, drawing the sword at the same time. An upward cut removed the top 1/3 of the nearest target. Before the severed piece struck the deck, she moved past the second target, slicing through it with a downward diagonal stroke. The last target, on her left, received another downward stroke and toppled. All three cut pieces of heavy matting lay upon the ground as the echo of Mizuki's *kiai* faded. Silence returned.

She returned the katana to its scabbard. Then she reached up and removed the blindfold. Turning, she saw the result of her attack for the first time, nodding to herself with satisfaction. She looked at her students, finding them wide eyed with mouths agape. Even Bobby looked suitably impressed and overhead the butterflies swirled in kaleidoscopic celebration of their goddess' skill.

"You see what is possible if you take the time to master yourself, focus your will and control your body? It takes time to learn the proper form, to clear your mind of distractions, but one day you may find you have acquired some small skill with the sword, as I have."

Mizuki bowed once again to her students and strode from their impromptu dojo, the flock of brightly colored butterflies trailing the warrior astrophysicist, leaving Bobby and the two sisters to clean up the mess.

* * * * *

In the aft end of the cargo hold there was a pile of tangled pipes and equipment that was meant to receive the heavy water being collected from beneath the ice. Currently the temporary processing plant was being attended to by some of the engineer's mates and several Marines. They had all stopped to watch the martial arts demonstration taking place in the forward part of the hold.

"Is old Russian saying," said LCpl Dmitry "Bosco" Boskovitch, "you can tell much about a woman's mood by looking at her hands."

"Really?" responded Vincent "Vinny" DeSilva, as Mizuki began her pass through the standing mats.

"Da. For example, if she is holding sword, is probably in bad mood."

"Did you see that?" asked PFC Hezekiah, incredulity in his tone.

"That can't be possible," said PFC Malachi, the first PFC's twin. "She cut through all three of those heavy mats in like under a second! And those butterflies are just freaky."

The two were the newest Marines on board the ship, having been recruited from the survivors of the Paradise expedition. In fact, aside from the two Iranian sisters, they were the only other survivors from among the colonists. They managed to escape from the settlement optimistically named Zion by their former leader.

Being both large and notably lacking in technical skills, they had been placed in the care of GySgt. Roselito Acuna, with the hope that she could turn them into competent Marines. The Gunny immediately christened them Jumbo One and Jumbo Two, rather than constantly trip over their unusual, biblical names.

"Believe it, Marine," snapped the Gunny. "I've fought beside Dr. Ogawa and she's just as effective against alien bug-nasties as she is against target mats. Those butterflies are actually an alien—or maybe aliens, never too clear about that—but they are basically her pet. Besides, you just saw her slice up those mats, so by definition it is not impossible."

"'I try to believe in as many as six impossible things before breakfast'," quipped Sgt. Herman "Kato" Kwan. "So get with the program, boys."

"What?" the Jumbos replied as one.

"Lewis Carroll, from *Through the Looking-Glass*," Rosey clarified. "When you find yourself stuck on some alien world, facing creatures from your worst nightmares, just remember impossible thing number six."

"Number six, Gunny?"

"'I can slay the Jabberwocky'. Now get back to work."

The Sunless Sea

Lights from the four Earthlings and their equipment shown upon the dimpled and contorted bottom of the kilometers thick ice cap. It also illuminated a silver gray flower, twenty meters across, sprouting from the end of the bore-shaft, a giant blossom of engineered origami that the bears were still tugging and coercing into place—the heavy water filtering membrane. Jim was fiddling with connections at the drill head while Will was busy collecting samples from the wrinkled underbelly of the icecap.

"I think that's about got it, Ahnah," Umky called out from the far side of the filter array. Ahnah performed a graceful back-flip maneuver, putting extra distance between her and the array. Both bears were enjoying the aquatic environment, even encased in pressure suits.

"Yes, I think that's as unfolded as it is going to get. Jim, we are ready to give the collector a test."

"Right," replied the human engineer, "let me contact the folks at the wellhead. Wellhead, Collector."

"Go ahead, Collector," came the reply from the surface.

"Wellhead, we are ready to switch the filter pumps on to test flow rate."

"Roger that, we are ready to monitor the test."

"OK, everyone stand well clear of the filter array, I'm turning the pumps on!"

Jim made a few adjustments to the drill head equipment and a slight shudder passed through the filter's petals. No other change was visible.

"Is it working?" asked Ahnah a few minutes later. The ursine scientist was impatient for a polar bear.

"Yes, Ahnah, it's working within its design parameters."

"Collector, Wellhead. We are getting positive flow of water at the head. Heavy water concentration is nominal. We are starting flow to the ship. Over."

"Roger, Wellhead. I'm maintaining the flow rate."

Both bears drifted to the same side of the filter array, surprisingly graceful in their heavy pressure suits. Thrusters in their suits' hind-legs made up for being unable to paddle effectively with the front ones, the normal mode of swimming for polar bears.

"OK, now what do we do?"

"You are awful fidgety for a polar bear, lady."

"I just like to be doing something useful, unlike you."

"Sometimes doing nothing is the right thing to do."

"Wow, he-bear zen."

"Hey, did you see that?"

"What?"

"I thought I saw motion out of the corner of my eye, just outside of the range of the lights."

"Wildlife of some kind?"

"One way to find out. Hey Jim, how about cutting the lights for a minute?"

"Sure, but everybody keep your suit lights on."

The illuminated hemisphere surrounding the Earthlings and their equipment faded to blackness. As their eyes adjusted to the darkness faint shapes could be made out, slowly edging closer. Large luminous eyes, crystalline bodies as long as a dolphin, each framed with rippling membranes, top and bottom, and tipped with a clutch of writhing tentacles.

"Wellhead, Collector. It appears that we are not alone down here."

Chapter 3

Collector Array, the Sunless Sea

"What do you make of those?" asked Umky, moving a bit closer to Ahnah as the transparent apparitions drifted nearer.

"They look like some form of squid," the ursine biologist replied. "There are deep water species back on Earth that are similar looking—almost wholly transparent."

"You're right, Ahnah, The family *Cranchiidae* comprises approximately 60 species of popularly named glass squid, the largest of which can grow to three meters in length," Will added, "though I doubt that these creatures are related to any Earth life."

"Yet another example of parallel evolution."

"Parallel evolution?" asked a quizzical Umky.

"Yes, we see the same morphologies in totally different species in response to similar ecological niches. It happens on Earth and it happens on other planets, in other star systems. For a smart bear you don't seem to have much knowledge of biology."

"Hey, I help fly a starship and, on occasion, I kill aliens. I don't have to understand how or why they evolved. I'm a simple bear with simple needs."

"'A simple man, a simple plan, the world's too big to understand'," Jim chimed in, borrowing a line from Jimmy Buffett.

"'Be good and you will be lonesome, be lonesome and you will be free'," Will added.

"Now that's a sentiment I can agree with," said Umky.

"You know Buffett stole that line from Mark Twain?"

"Marvelous, Will," Ahnah replied. "Could we get some video of the indigenous lifeforms before nasty Nanook here starts killing them?"

"Come on, Ahnah, I'm not going to kill them. Not unless they attack us or try to break the filter array."

The strange glass like creatures halted their advance a respectful five meters from the two bears. Will worked his way across the bottom of the ice, to a sheltered position next to Jim and the drill head.

"What do you think they are doing?" asked Jim.

"Trying to figure out if we're good to eat," replied Umky.

Sickbay, Peggy Sue

After returning her sword and butterflies to her quarters and taking a quick shower, Mizuki went to the medical section to talk with her friend, Betty. They had been together on previous voyages and had fought side-by-side on occasion. Betty had also healed her when she was grievously wounded on the trek across Ring Station. Of all those on board, the ship's doctor was Mizuki's BFF.

"Hey, girlfriend. What brings you to my lair today?"

"Hello, Betty. I need someone to talk to."

"And Bobby is busy?"

"Someone female."

"Oh, that type of talk. Step into my office."

Betty ushered her friend into her office off the main ward. Mizuki sat in the patient's chair and Betty set the observation windows to opaque, giving them some privacy.

"Now what's this all about?"

"You know that I love Shadi and Dorri..."

Mizuki paused, finding she lacked the words to express her concerns.

"And?" Betty prompted.

"I'm not sure how to explain this." Mizuki looked down at her lap where the fingers of both hands were intertwined and knotted together. She stopped fidgeting and placed her hands on the chair arms. "Shadi has been flirting with Bobby."

"That girl has been flirting with every man on board for months."

"But Bobby encourages her!" There was a hint of anguish in Mizuki's voice.

"Shadi is a very pretty girl. The only man who does not respond to flirting from a pretty girl is a dead man," Betty placed a reassuring sisterly hand on one of Mizuki's. "It doesn't mean anything, it's how men are wired."

"But why is she doing this? She knows Bobby and I are, are... together."

Betty leaned back in her chair and exhaled. After taking a couple of seconds to gather her thoughts she forged ahead.

"Mizuki, we think of Shadi as a girl but biologically she's not, she's a woman. All her reproductive systems are online and throbbing with natural, species preserving energy. She's starting to shop for a mate, even if she doesn't quite understand that yet herself."

"Well she can't have my mate!" There was anger in Mizuki's reply and the beginning of tears in her eyes.

"It isn't just Bobby. She flirts with Lt. Lewis and that handsome shuttle pilot and even smiles at the Captain when she thinks Beth isn't looking. She's having feelings and sensations she's never felt before, and it will take some time for her to get accustomed to them. You remember when you were a young woman, just after going through puberty, don't you?"

"I never made eyes at other women's husbands," Mizuki mumbled, looking down at her hands, which were back in her lap.

"Women are sexual animals just as much as men are. Unfortunately, she doesn't have any young men to experiment on or become enamored with. She is probably having erotic dreams and waking up aroused by them."

Mizuki's gaze snapped back to Betty's face.

"She's dreaming of sex with Bobby?"

"Not necessarily, and it wouldn't matter if she did—dream of Bobby I mean, not have sex with him. Come on, girlfriend. You telling me you never woke up with stiff nipples and dew on the grass?"

Mizuki blushed.

"Look, this is all normal. Shadi is just trying out her new found sexuality. I'm surprised it took this long, but then she comes from a repressive society when it comes to women."

Of course, so do you, Betty thought. She smiled kindly at her friend and in a softer voice said: "Has Bobby shown any signs of acting on Shadi's flirting, of cheating on you?"

"No."

"And I doubt he ever would. That man is crazy in love with you girl, has been for years. You need to give him some credit in the faithfulness department."

"I suppose so." Mizuki said meekly.

"If it will make you feel better I'll call Shadi in and give her a motherly talk about sex and boys and all that. I should probably talk to Dorri too, she's not far behind her big sister in the coming of age process."

"Great, soon I will have to worry about both of them."

"Not in the way you're thinking. Remember there are a lot more men on this ship than women, and every last one of them is horny as hell by this time in the voyage. I'm surprised there haven't been fights over the girls already."

"Really?" That thought had not occurred to Mizuki.

"Yeah, just wait. We need to get back to port and fairly soon. That or find some aliens to fight. This is why old time sailing ships had all male crews—of course they relied on saltpeter and still had widespread buggery."

Crew's Quarters, Peggy Sue

Shadi and Dorri emerged from the women's showers, dressed in crisp new jumpsuits, with their still damp hair wrapped in towels. Living and working among the crew of the Peggy Sue was a liberating experience for the two sisters. Things were much more open on board compared with their old life in the Iran of the Ayatollahs or in Imam Mustafa's flock of colonists.

Iran had not been strictly segregated by sex, as some Arab countries were, but the Imam had been only a half step away from fanatics like the Taliban or ISIS. Here men and women not only mingled but worked side by side. Of course there were some downsides—you couldn't hide a bad hair day with a headscarf or dress casually beneath an ankle length burqa. But in general the girls were having the time of their young lives.

The sisters conversed as they passed through the crew's lounge, headed forward to their quarters in the chiefs' area, known as the goat locker.

"Living in a mixed gender environment is nice," said Dorri, "but I'm glad we don't have co-ed showers like in that movie we watched last week."

The movie was *Starship Troopers*, a film loosely based on a book by Robert Heinlein. In it the soldiers of the future, male and female, all showered together.

"I don't think I could do that—shower naked with people I know," Shadi replied.

"Yeah, you would end up staring at the guys," her sister teased.

Shadi pulled the towel off her head and snapped it at Dorri, who nimbly skipped outside of towel range.

"I do not stare at all the men."

"Oh, you mean like you didn't make googly eyes at Commander Danner today?"

"I did not!"

"Did too! Why do you think Dr. Ogawa did that thing with her sword, chopping down those mats while blindfolded?"

"What? What do you mean?"

"Since you have started mooning after every handsome officer in trousers your powers of observation have gone to pot."

"I do not moon after every handsome officer, and everybody on board wears trousers... well, jumpsuits."

"You know what I mean." Dorri pressed her point as they arrived at the door to their quarters. The sisters shared a comfortable cabin with twin bunks, nicer than the average crewmember had. They also generally dined with the officers in the main lounge.

Shadi hustled her sister into the room and shut the door.

"What in heaven's name are you talking about? Dr. Ogawa was just showing us what we could learn if we practice."

"Bullshit! She saw you making eyes at her husband."

"I did not! And you are picking up too many expressions from the crew."

Dorri stuck out her tongue.

"You called him 'Bobby'. You think she didn't notice? She notices everything."

Shadi swallowed hard.

"That little demonstration was to show you what might happen if you keep messing around with her man." Dorri, sensing that she had won the argument, smiled a wicked smile.

"Was I really that obvious?" Shadi sat on her bunk and put her head in her hands. She looked up at her sister and said: "I have got to get a hold of myself, I'm not some cheap tramp. It's just that, lately, I can't help myself."

"I'd like some boys to flirt with myself. The crew, especially the officers, seem so old."

"Trust me, they get younger looking every day."

"At least stick with the younger officers, they are supposed to be gentlemen."

"You're right. Some of the crew are down right disgusting."

"No argument there, *Khahar-e Bozorgtar*."

* * * * *

Lurking in the Crew Lounge was one of the disgusting crewmembers Shadi was referring to. Raoul Mendez had been a crewman aboard the ESS Fortune, the Colony Board ship that was destroyed at Paradise. Formerly the ship's navigator, his surly attitude and general incompetence marginalized his position aboard the Peggy Sue.

He had been given a chance to become the junior navigator, under Dr. Ogawa, but he managed to blow that by constantly saying inappropriate things to her. Eventually he grabbed the astrophysicist when no one was watching. This earned him a cracked sternum and demotion to cleanup duty. If it had been up to Chief Zackly, Mendez would have ended up floating back to Earth without benefit of ship or spacesuit.

One by one, he had been rebuffed by every female crew member, or at least the human ones. Since then he had been brooding and spying on the two young Iranian sisters whenever he could. Resentment blossomed into hatred, eating at him every day.

One day, he thought, *one day I will catch you in an equipment locker or the hydroponics section and you'll find out. Just wait, you stuck up little bitches.*

He turned and left the lounge. If he lingered too long in one location the Chief invariably found him and gave him more work to do. He'd love to take care of that little SOB too, but the Chief himself was meaner than a snake and not someone to mess with. That's why Mendez was fixated on the girls, they were the only people on board he figured he could overpower physically.

CIC, *Peggy Sue*

When word came that the engineers were ready to test the deuterium extraction process, both the Captain and First Officer moved to the Combat Information Center. The big holographic projection tank in the middle of the room showed a 3D cutaway model of the wellhead, shaft, and the aquanauts around the filter array in the hidden sea. Then came word that indigenous life forms had been sighted.

"Collector, Peggy Sue. Can you send us a video feed of the locals?"

"Aye, aye, Captain," replied Michaels, recognizing his CO's voice, "adjusting the pickups now."

A large screen on the forward bulkhead showed a view of ghostly creatures, floating in darkness. Occasionally, a ripple of colored light would travel down the spine of one of the creatures, to be answered by others nearby.

"Did you see those light signals?" asked Beth. "I wonder if they are communicating with each other?"

"Don't know, Number One, could be."

Billy Ray had taken to calling Beth Number One when they were in front of the crew because calling her "Commander" or "Ms. Melaku" sounded too formal—after all, the crew knew they were married. Still, he figured that calling her "sweetheart" or "honey bunch," as he did in private or with close friends, was probably inappropriate. So, on the advice of the ship's sailing master, Bobby Danner, he settled on "Number One."

Bobby was a science fiction fan, and knew full well that "Number One" was the nickname given by Captain Christopher Pike to his first officer on the USS Enterprise in the original Star Trek TV show. Number One was noted for her exceptional intelligence and rationality, and Captain Pike regarded Number One as the most experienced officer on the Enterprise. In the script of "The Cage," Number One was described as "female, slim and dark in a Nile Valley way, age uncertain, one of those women who will always look the same between the ages of twenty and fifty." Beth's roots lay in Ethiopia, not Egypt, but Billy Ray figured that was close enough.

Beth accepted the sobriquet without comment. Like her fictitious namesake, this Number One exhibited little emotion or affection toward the Captain in public. This seeming lack of affection was largely a pretense, however, as the couple demonstrated frequently in the privacy of their shared cabin.

"You know, finding life in this system means there is long term hope for life in the solar system."

"How so?"

"This ice moon circles a gas giant, orbiting a white dwarf, the burned out ember of a star that had been about the size as our Sun. In four or five billion years the Sun will swell into a red giant and swallow Earth, before blowing off its outer layers and becoming a cooling ember like this system's star. This shows that life may survive in the solar system on the moons of Jupiter or Saturn, even after the death of the Sun."

"A happy though, Number One. Either way we won't be there to see it. Michaels, are you in any danger down there?"

"Negative, sir. So far they just seem curious."

In the blink of an eye, all the creatures disappeared from the screen.

"What just happened?" asked Beth.

"Aw, seal shit!" growled a deep voice over the comm.

Collector Array, the Sunless Sea

Ahnah had drifted closer to the strange transparent creatures, separating herself from Umky and the filter array. She was about half way between Umky and the visitors when the squid suddenly scattered in all directions. This was behavior recognizable by any predator—prey fleeing from a threat.

This thought occurred to both bears at the same time, but before either could act a large gray something flashed past and Ahnah was gone.

"Aw, seal shit!"

Umky was in immediate pursuit. The pressure suits had instrumentation and heads up displays based on the Marines' battle armor. From training and long habit, Umky reflexively brought up a tactical display that tracked the location of other squad members. On it, he could see the icon representing Ahnah traveling away and downward.

"Ahnah, are you OK?" He called.

There was no answer, just a muffled sound—half grunt, half growl. Telemetry showed she was still alive and not grievously injured.

"Umky!" yelled Jim. "What ever got her is trying to take her deep. If it dives deeper than a kilometer or two her suit could implode."

"Great!" The he-bear kicked his suit's thrusters to full, pulling in his forearms to maximize his speed.

* * * * *

"Collector, Peggy Sue. Interrogative, your situation?"

"It looks like a large predator of some kind—different from the transparent creatures we were observing—made a high-speed attack and grabbed Ahnah. Umky is in pursuit. Over."

"Roger that. Keep us apprised of the situation."

"Aye, aye, Sir."

Chapter 4

The Sunless Sea, Descending

The impact of the sea creature momentarily stunned Ahnah. The squid like creature's mantle was at least seven meters long and it carried twice the mass of the she-bear. In front of the beast's body proper, a forest of tentacles coiled around Ahnah's suited body, trying to pull her to the orifice buried among those suckered arms.

Each longer than the monster's body, the tentacles were arranged in a circle surrounding the animal's beak. Unlike Earth cephalopods, this monster's beak was a cone, formed by ten curved, pointed fangs. Ahnah could hear rasping against her suit as tentacles festooned with five centimeter suckers tightened their grip. The circumference of each sucker was lined with sharp, finely serrated rings of chitin. Normally, the sharpness of the chitin and the suction of the cups served to attach the squid to its prey, but they found little purchase on Ahnah's suit.

Polar bears are apex predators, meaning they don't take crap off of anything. The squid's position in the local food chain not withstanding, Ahnah fought back. For a few seconds, instinct caused her to try biting the tentacle arms that held her, but all that accomplished was to smear saliva on the inside of her transparent helmet. She soon recovered her wits and moved to a more effective counter attack.

A polar bear's natural fighting style is based on its claws and teeth. Years ago, Umky's father, the famous Lt. Bear, helped devised a system of retractable claws that could be mounted on suits of space armor. Though they never found a workable way of letting a bear in a space suit bite its opponents, the claws worked quite to Lt. Bear's satisfaction. Over time, suit claws became standard equipment for bear armor. Naturally, Peggy Sue's bears had insisted their pressure suits be fitted with claws, just like their armor.

Flexing her real claws within her gauntlets caused thirty centimeter long metal-ceramic blades to shoot out of their carriers on the backs of her wrists. There were three claws per paw, each knife edged and razor sharp. The claws of her right arm penetrated one of the squid's tentacles, driven with enough force for the tips to emerge on its far side.

"How do you like that, you overgrown piece of fish food!" Ahnah yelled, ripping the claws sideways nearly severing the tentacle.

This caused a violent reaction from the squid, which slowed its downward plunge and tried to reposition its remaining arms. Ahnah turned on the thrusters attached to her hind legs, deflecting the monster from its chosen course.

More flailing of tentacles ensued, giving Ahnah an opportunity to fully sever another of the beast's sucker covered arms. Unfortunately, this still left eight functional tentacles and Ahnah was soon immobilized.

* * * * *

Umky dove as fast as his thrusters could push his decidedly unstreamlined form. Not being able to close on the creature that had taken Ahnah, he was beginning to worry. Then the monster's downward plummet faltered.

Looks like Ahnah is fighting back, he thought with a sense of relief. He was finally gaining on the fleeing predator and its prize. As he drew nearer, a piece of tentacle drifted past.

Oh yeah, she's fighting back all right. He called out over the comm channel: "Ahnah! Keep it from going deeper, I'm closing on you!"

"It's about time blubber butt," came the somewhat ungracious reply, accompanied by labored breathing and grunting sounds. "This bastard's got me so wrapped up I can hardly move."

"Be right with you, sweet cheeks," Umky replied, finally laying eyes on the object of his pursuit. Unlike the other aliens, this squid was not transparent and had a wide spade shaped fin, attached horizontally to the tail end of its mantle. It was thrashing mightily but Ahnah's thrusters kept it twisting and turning, unable to hold its intended course.

Hold still just a second or two, and you're my meat squiddy. Bear extended both sets of claws as he dove for the struggling creature. An instant before colliding with his target, Umky thrust both sets of claws into its broad back. Just behind the monster's eyes and to either side of its dorsal line, the he-bear's claws sunk deep into the squid's flesh.

44

Umky landed hard on the squid's back, braced himself with his hind legs and pulled his arms to his chest in an embrace that ripped a gaping wound in his victim. The incision severed the giant axon leading from the squid's brain, the fused bundle of nerves that controlled its mantle and jet propulsion mechanism.

The squid convulsed, throwing Umky off its back.

Shuddering violently, the monster lost control of its movements. Spasming tentacles coiled about in all directions, writhing like snakes on Medusa's head. Ahnah quickly hacked her way free. Several more sucker covered arms drifted away from the now desperate creature—its intended prey had turned into a predator.

Diving in from the side, Umky ended the fight by ramming a clawed forearm deep into one of the creature's thirty-five centimeter in diameter eyes. It shuddered once, twice and went limp.

Umky pulled his forearm from the creature's corpse. Dark fluid, presumably blood, mixed with the surrounding water. The lifeless carcass resumed its trip into the abyss at a much more leisurely pace.

"You OK, Ahnah?"

"Yes, I'm fine. But I think I've lost my taste for seafood for a while."

Umky chuckled.

"Let's get out of here before the remains attract more unwanted guests."

"Yes, good idea." Ahnah turned on her thrusters and started back to the well. "And thanks, by the way."

"Not a problem. Tell the humans we're all right."

As they ascended, Umky watched Ahnah's armored hindquarters from below. *Oh yeah,* he thought, *baby's got back.*

He turned up the music that Hitch had downloaded to his suit at the start of the mission. He grinned as Sir Mix-a-Lot rapped "I like big butts and I can not lie, You other brothers can't deny..."

CIC, Peggy Sue

"Collector, Peggy Sue. Interrogative the status of Ahnah and Umky?"

"Peggy Sue, Collector. They seem to have successfully dealt with the predator problem and are returning to the filter array."

"Roger that, Collector." Billy Ray glanced at his First Officer, relief evident on his face.

"They have been down there for hours, and it will take hours more to get them back to the surface," said Beth, watching the forward display for sign of the returning bears. "If everything is working with the filter array it might be best if we withdraw the personnel from the collector."

"I think you're right, Number One. I don't see what else they can do down there except attract more local predators. I'll call Arin about bringing them up, it's his show."

"Of course, Captain." Beth smiled an unseen smile at her husband. The Chief Engineer would treat a suggestion from the Captain as an order, of course, but it was the polite way to do things.

"Wellhead, Peggy Sue."

"Go, Peggy Sue."

"Mr. Baldursson, how is the collection system working?"

"The collection is proceeding well, Captain. Flow rates are 12 percent above projections."

"How long until we have a full tank of deuterium?"

"We should have a full load in approximately thirty-six hours."

"Excellent! You and your people have done a great job rigging this up. I was wondering if we still need people at the bottom of the well at this point?"

"I don't think so, we can have them start back up the shaft. The ascent is going to take several hours."

"Will we need to send them back down to disassemble things when we're done?"

"Negative, Captain. We will reel in the laser drilling head and pump assembly, but the filter array can just be disconnected and left for the natives to wonder about."

"Roger that, and again, great job Arin. Peggy Sue out."

The Sunless Sea

As the Earth creatures began their long trip back to the surface inquisitive eyes watched them go. The eyes belonged to the same squid like creatures who had gathered earlier, prior to the attack by the giant predator. Within their transparent bodies ribbons of light flashed multihued messages to those nearby. The largest squid present was also the eldest. Its thoughts were conveyed by bioluminescent cells along its dorsal axon.

"Good. The odd creatures from out of the sky are leaving the world."

"But where are they going?" asked one of the smaller creatures.

"Who cares? As long as they leave."

"Are they really from beyond the dome of the sky? I thought there was nothing beyond the ice surrounding the world." said another youngster.

"There is nothing beyond the ice of the sky," snapped the elder.

"But where are they going if they don't come from beyond the sky?"

"They must live in the ice," answered the elder. "Yes, they must be ice demons, like in the tales of olden times."

"They sure fought like demons," said another juvenile. "They ripped that big kraken to bits."

"Another reason to be glad they are gone. Enough! We should not linger here, we will attract more hungry krakens."

With that the large adult contracted its mantle, forcing a jet of water out of its forward facing siphon. It shot away into the darkness like a glass torpedo.

"I don't care what the old one says, those creatures must live somewhere beyond the ice of the sky," the youngster said, "and someday I will go there and see for myself."

"Why do you always doubt the words of the elders?"

"Because if you question nothing you will never discover anything new."

Then she too jetted away into the darkness. But the seeds of curiosity had been planted, seeds that would eventually blossom into exploration of the wider universe.

Captain's Quarters, Peggy Sue

Billy Ray was settled in a comfortable chair, reading. His reading material was an actual book, not a pad or viewing screen. The Captain's cabin contained a sizable collection of books, most acquired by the ship's owner. The leather bound volumes were now all valuable antiques and the collection was worth a small fortune.

The Captain was a bit old fashioned, he favored real books: the heft of a volume held in the hand; the feel of paper between fingers when turning a page; the smell of ink, paper, and leather. Real books feed the senses as no pad or display screen can.

"What are you reading tonight, dear?" asked Beth, emerging from the bathroom. "Anything I would recognize?"

The text in question was a collection of poetry. Billy Ray had earned a Master of Arts in English literature after he got out of the Navy and before he joined the effort to build the Peggy Sue. His taste in poetry often tended to the obscure, but not tonight.

"Just a little Robert Frost, his *Fire and Ice*." He began reading from the open book:

Some say the world will end in fire,
Some say in ice.
From what I've tasted of desire
I hold with those who favor fire.
But if it had to perish twice,
I think I know enough of hate

48

To say that for destruction ice
Is also great
And would suffice.

"Well he was wrong all the way round. The world ended with falling rocks and tsunamis and then mud raining from the sky."

"He wasn't a prophet, he was an American regional poet. Frost was a transitional figure between traditional 19th-century American poetry and modernism. He believed in the lyrical and realistic, the rural and natural in poetry. Besides, Earth is making a come back."

"A very slow come back. Things might get back to normal in another 100,000 years, after another Ice Age."

"Glacial period," he corrected, "and for the past several million years ice age conditions have been the norm, honey bunch."

Beth um-hummed a noncommittal reply.

"You know," he said, closing the book and changing the subject. "I don't think we are being inventive enough in looking at trade opportunities. Take this place for instance."

"This frozen ice ball?"

"Sure. Do you know that there used to be a thriving trade in ice back on Earth during the 19th century?"

"You're joking. Ice? Really?"

"You bet, sweetheart. The ice trade, also known as the frozen water trade, was started by an American businessman named Frederic Tudor at the beginning of the 19th century. Tudor began by shipping ice from Boston to the Caribbean island of Martinique, where he sold it to wealthy members of the European elite who ran the place. The enterprise was called a 'slippery speculation' by Tudor's critics."

"I shouldn't wonder," Beth observed, but Billy Ray was on a roll. Sometimes she thought that her husband was really just a frustrated school teacher.

"Centered in the New England states, on the east coast of the U.S., the business grew to involve the large-scale harvesting, transport and sale of natural ice. During winter, ice was cut from the surface of ponds and streams, then stored in ice houses. Eventually it was sent by ship to its final destination."

"You're saying that ice merchants shipped frozen water all over the world and made a profit doing it?"

"Yep. Eventually, the ice trade spread around the globe where it revolutionized the meat, vegetable and fruit industries, and enabled significant growth of the fishing industry. This was all before refrigeration, you know. It even encouraged the introduction of new types of food and drink. During the 1830s and 1840s the trade expanded to include England, India, South America, China and Australia. Tudor—the so-called 'Ice King of the World'— made a fortune; not that his company was an instant success."

"And why was that?"

"At first no one knew what to do with the stuff. Tudor had to create a need so he could fill it."

"You're not suggesting we should hack up this ice ball and tow part of it back home, are you?" Beth peered closely at her husband as one might examine an inmate in a sanitarium.

"Of course not. Transporting any type of bulk commodity over interstellar distances is economic folly. You need something that's compact, rare, and impossible to get locally."

"So no ice?"

"No ice. Even those giant jewels Hitch and Jacobs found are really not worth the transport expense. The deuterium we are loading is worth ten times those gemstones. I'm just sayin' we need to think outside the box more, is all. The only thing that really makes sense is information—new science and technology—or antimatter."

"Thank goodness, sweetheart," Beth said, moving behind his chair and putting her arms around his neck. "I was beginning to thing you had gone barking mad."

"If I have, it's from boredom."

"Maybe we can come up with something to keep the boredom at bay." Beth nibbled at his neck. "Besides, we will be back in space in a couple of days and it will be back to standing different watches on the bridge."

"Why do you think I was reading you poetry? I was just trying to establish a romantic mood."

"With a poem about destroying the world? What kind of girl do you think I am?" Beth pulled Billy Ray from his chair and toward the bedroom. "Still, I guess it's better than that Xanadu poem from the other day."

"Actually, that poem always reminds me of you, honey bunch." Without waiting for a response he began to recite from memory:

A damsel with a dulcimer
In a vision once I saw:
It was an Abyssinian maid,
And on her dulcimer she played,
Singing of Mount Abora.
Could I revive within me
Her symphony and song,
To such a deep delight 'twould win me,
That with music loud and long,
I would build that dome in air,
That sunny dome! Those caves of ice!

Beth silenced him with a kiss. "Like I thought, totally barking mad."

"Come into my pleasure dome, my Abyssinian maid," he replied, slipping his arms around her trim waste, "and I'll show you just how mad I am."

Chapter 5

Surface, Icy Moon

White shapes moved stealthily across the frozen wastes, gliding from pressure ridge to pressure ridge. Points of green light, elongated by persistence of vision, lept from hiding places to strike ice spires standing on the surface ahead of the ghostly figures' advance. Orange fire blossomed briefly, noiselessly, as the spires disintegrated.

"Squad cease fire," ordered GySgt. Acuna. Since they had a day left before departure, the Gunny decided to take advantage of the open local terrain and get in a little live fire exercise. She stood erect, switching off her suit's adaptive camouflage. White faded to dark graphite, the normal coloration of the Marines' battle armor.

"All right, unload and show clear."

The tactical display on the Gunny's HUD showed the squad members' status as they secured their weapons. This was old hat for most of the Marines but there were a couple of newbies and she didn't want anyone hit by friendly fire.

"Sgt. Kwan, LCpl. DeSilva, converge on the target."

"Aye, aye, Gunny." Kato had half the squad on the left flank— Bosco, the two swabbies, and himself. Umky was in the center, next to the Gunny, with the Jumbo twins to her right and Vinny DeSilva on the far right flank.

"I think we got 'em," observed Vinny, emerging from behind a buckled ridge to view the shattered ice pinnacles the Marines had targeted. A combination of 15mm explosive shells and a torrent of 5mm flechettes, sent down range at high velocity by the Earthlings' railguns, had blasted the ice spires apart.

As the squad converged on their former targets, Hitch, always looking to stir things up, questioned Umky about his adventure beneath the ice.

"So, Bear2, tell us again how you took down that fearsome sea monster and saved the fair Ahnah."

Umky grunted in response.

"Don't be shy. Tell us how you dispatched your foe and whether Ahnah rewarded her rescuer in the traditional manner."

This brought snickers from some of the others.

"Come a little closer, primate, and I'll show you."

"Hey, don't be like that, Brother Bear," chided Vinny. "You're the only one of us to see any action in almost a year—we want details."

Umky grumbled but acquiesced.

"I went after them, but if Ahnah hadn't fought back and slowed the squid thing down I never would have caught up. Good thing we had the techs put claws on the pressure suits or we would have been squid chow."

"So you both went after the predator with your suit claws?"

"Hey, that's what we had. No weapons."

"Railguns probably wouldn't have worked very well," commented Kato. "Water is a lot denser than normal atmo or vacuum."

"Anyway, Ahnah managed to hack off a few tentacles and slow the beast down. When I caught up I tried to sever its spinal cord and then jammed an arm into one of its eyes."

"That killed it?"

"Pretty much."

"Good improvisation, Umky," said the Gunny. "This is why I want the rest of you mutts to study the physiology of different animal species."

"So we can kill squids?" asked one of the Jumbos.

The Gunny sighed.

"No, Private. So when you face some alien creepy-crawly you might have a clue as to where its vulnerable spots are. Umky disabled the sea monster with a smart attack, guessing that it would have some kind of spinal cord running down its back from its brain, which was probably close to its eyes."

"Oh."

"Of course, jamming three knives into someone's eye has got to slow them down a bit," quipped Hitch.

"The point is, we might face all sorts of strange beasties kicking around out here. It ain't enough to be good at killing icicles, we have to be ready to fight anything."

"Join the Marines and travel the galaxy," said Jacobs.

"Meet strange new creatures," added Bosco.

"And kill them," finished Vinny.

Umky and the rest of the squad laughed.

"All right you clowns," the Gunny said, shaking her head. It was an old joke. Caesar's legionnaires probably said something similar about meeting new barbarians.

"Back to the ship, two fireteams with bounding overwatch. Move!"

Sickbay, Peggy Sue

Doc White insisted that Ahnah report to Sickbay for a checkup after the predator attack. The 250 kilogram she-bear complied with minimal complaint and now lay on an oversized examination table, her vital signs painted in multiple colors on the display over her head.

"Where's that oversized roommate of yours? I asked him to come in for a checkup too."

"He's out having fun with his Marine playmates, something about live fire exercise outside the ship."

Betty harrumphed.

"Anything having to do with shooting weapons or blowing things up is irresistible to males—of both species."

Using a hand tablet, Betty examined the bear's skeleton and connective tissues, looking for signs of fractures or tears. Polar bears are a tough species, and under natural conditions collect such injuries as a matter of course—the cost of being a large predator who hunted sizable prey, none of which became polar bear chow willingly.

"So what do you think, Doc? Am I going to live?"

"It looks like the only damage is some bruising on your rib cage and some strains and contusions." Betty lay the tablet down. "Let me see your paw."

Ahnah's paw was the size of a dinner plate; short toes tipped with sharp black claws the size of steak knives. Smart bears had more articulation in their forearm toes than normal dumb bears. The toes could almost be called fingers, being more individually movable than those of their non-talking cousins. The inner toe on either paw could bend sideways, independent of the other toes, almost like a thumb in a human.

That wasn't the extent of the differences between talking polar bears and "normal" bears. There were subtle differences in their skeletons and musculature; they were more flexible than dumb bears and could walk upright more easily. The biggest differences could be found in the vocal cords, voice box, and the size of the cranium—with speech came larger brains.

They were related to non-talking *U. maritimus* more closely than humans were to chimpanzees, but more remotely than horses and donkeys. While crossing the latter produces offspring, mules, they are almost never fertile. Talking bears and normal bears cannot interbred at all. Talking polar bears were really their own species, *Ursus sapiens*—the wise polar bear.

"Not even any hairline fractures, I'd say you are none the worse for wear."

"I was wondering, Doc, how hard would it be to take out the birth control implant you gave me?"

"Not hard, why do you ask? You and Umky getting serious enough to have cubs?"

"I'm not sure about wanting a relationship, but I am beginning to think he wouldn't be a bad sire for a litter of little ones."

Betty stood back and put her hands on her hips, giving the white she-bear a look. Despite being of different species, there were strong similarities and bonds between the two females.

"Are you sure about this?"

"Yes, no, I mean, not today. I just want to know what my options are."

"It's a simple outpatient procedure, I can do it anytime you want. Just remember why you had me implant it in the first place."

If bears could blush Ahnah would have.

"It's just that there are so few of us, and Umky is fairly intelligent for a male. Plus, I don't know if I agree with this nuclear family stuff."

"You are a different species, so take this with a grain of salt, but two parent families are much more conducive to civilization than raising kids on your own. Recent history in the USA proved that —no fathers and boys run wild on their own."

"We she-bears have always raised our cubs on our own, but I hear what you're saying. Polar bears have a lot to figure out if we ever do get a planet of our own."

"Your own planet? Now you're thinking big."

"Maybe I shouldn't have said anything," Ahnah said, looking around the room. "Umky has been talking about us eventually getting a planet to settle on. Some place with a lot of ice that can be seeded with seals and walrus and other tasty animals."

"And no humans."

Ahnah looks a bit embarrassed.

"Yes, no humans—two apex predators in the same ecosystem never works out well, not for one of the species anyway."

"I'm not judging. I think you ought to be able to find your own destiny. I'm sure most of the humans on board would agree—the ones who know bears and have a half a brain in their heads anyway."

"So you don't think Umky is crazy?"

"Not at all, honey. Go for it."

Betty, who was surprisingly strong, helped the she-bear up from the exam table. Ahnah dropped gracefully to the deck.

"Thanks, Doc."

"No problem, I pronounce you fit for duty. And if you want that other matter taken care of just let me know."

Ahnah gave Betty a bearish smile and padded across the sickbay to the door, toenails clicking on the hard deck. The Doctor watched her go, thinking deep thoughts of her own.

I wish you bears luck, she thought. *I remember what it's like to be in an oppressed minority, and to long for equality and real freedom.*

3rd *Deck Hydroponics, Peggy Sue*

The top deck of the Peggy Sue was seldom visited by most members of the crew. Other than the airlocks for boarding the attached shuttles, storage space and launch bays for observation probes, there was nothing to bring people to the 3rd deck. Unless you worked on the ship's hydroponic gardens.

In the far reaches of the ship UV light strips glowed and hissing jets of water sprayed fine mist into the air, creating the proper conditions for growing plants. There were rows of lettuce, cabbage, cauliflower, egg plant, zucchini, squash, and tomatoes. Also mixed in were dwarf trees bearing apples, pears, oranges, lemons, limes, cherries, and bananas. Between the larger plants grew herbs: parsley, dill, rosemary, oregano, basil, and many others. Different sections were at different phases of growth, staggering production and ensuring a continuous supply of consumables for the hungry crew.

Alexis Garner was one of the technicians assigned to the care and feeding of the plants that provided the crew with fresh fruit and vegetables during their long trip away from home. She was a big boned girl from a farm in Washington state. Auburn hair, wide clear eyes, and a splash of freckles across her nose and cheeks gave her a wholesome, natural look.

Intending to join the family business, she attended Washington State University's College of Agricultural, Human, and Natural Resource Sciences. While at CAHNRS, she participated in research aimed at improving fruit quality and disease resistance of crops in the *rosaceae* family—apple, blackberry, peach, pear, strawberry, sweet cherry, and more—some of the principle crops of her home state. She never thought that she would be applying what she had learned on a starship light-years from Earth.

To some extent the plants helped to clean the air in Peggy Sue's closed environment, but CO_2 scrubbers and oxygen generators mostly took care of that. Even so, Alexis thought that the air smelled best in the hydroponic section, surrounded by growing plants.

Another member of the crew who agreed with her was Jimmy Tosh, the ship's Rastafarian cook and bartender. He visited the 3rd deck frequently to see what fresh ingredients were available for inclusion in his daily culinary creations. Rastafari like things simple and natural, though Jimmy created dishes by blending a number of cuisines with the cooking of his native Jamaica.

There was another reason he frequented the remote sections of the ship's garden spaces, one that also reflected his religious heritage. The crew received a daily booze ration—two drinks each that could not be saved or accumulated for a future bender—but Rastas don't drink. There is, however, a recreational chemical they do partake in—marijuana.

Ganja, weed, God's plants, Mary Jane, whatever it was called, marijuana was the recreational drug of choice for Rastafarians. To them, it was not just an intoxicant, it was a religious sacrament. Unsurprisingly, when Jimmy signed on for the voyage he carried with him a few packets of selected seeds, seeds that Alexis had happily helped him plant and cultivate in the far reaches of the hydroponics spaces.

"Dat is a beautiful plant!" Jimmy gushed, stroking the leaves of a four foot high cannabis plant. The plants being inspected spent two months under near constant sunlight being fed all the nutrients they could absorb. They were about to enter their flowering stage, when the desired buds would be produced. All the male plants had been already culled, so that the females would not be pollinated. This would result in *sin semilla* buds, from the Spanish for "without seeds." Buds without seeds have higher THC content, the main psychoactive chemical in marijuana.

"You need to be patient, Jimmy. You can only rush nature so much," said Alexis, watching the enamored Rastaman with amusement. "We will still need to top them and tie off the stems to get more even light exposure."

"I know, Alexis, dat one of de lessons Jah teach trough his blessed plants—patience."

The pair had been producing a continual supply of the hallucinogenic plants since the first days of the voyage. Early on their agricultural endeavor was noticed by the ship's computer, which monitored every nook and cranny of the Destroyer sized starship. This brought a summons from the First Officer, the imposing Beth Melaku.

The First Officer had stoically listened to the two plead their case, that they would only use the harvested bounty of their crop sparingly, in the same way that the daily ration of alcohol was consumed by others on the crew. To their shock, the First Officer agreed to let them continue to grow the marijuana plants, as long as there was no adverse impact on food production and the resulting drug was not abused.

It was the opinion of both the Captain and First Officer that the crew needed release from the tedium of a long space voyage and there was little practical difference between ethanol and THC. The company rules did not forbid drinking or other recreational drug use on board. There were, however, strict rules about rendering oneself unfit for duty, so restraint was called for. Eventually a half dozen other crewmembers opted for herb over brew in the recreational drug department.

"We need the plants to bud and form resin for us to harvest. Then we can turn the resin into marijuana concentrate for use in vape pens."

The main problem with using marijuana was that smoking it was hard on the lungs and it stunk up the part of the ship where the weed was being smoked. There was also no ready supply of rolling papers, and though the engineering section's 3D printers could whip up any number of fanciful pipes, the consumers of pot soon turned to vaping. The joint and the bong were consigned to history as those so inclined went smokeless.

"Dat still bothers I, for true. I miss de fragrant smoke from burning ganja. Notin' like rolling a big Bob Marley spliff and passing it around among friends."

"Jimmy, you know that was part of the deal with the First Officer—no open flame on board. Besides, burning stuff releases all sorts of toxins and other gunk you do not want in your lungs. Vaping is much healthier for you."

"So you say. Why would an occasional toke hurt anything?"

"You know that the ship's computer monitors everything. Do you want to explain to the Chief and the Captain why the fire alarm went off? Plus, the polar bears can smell a lit joint anywhere on the ship, even with the air scrubbers. I for one do not want to get on their bad side."

For reasons unexplained, the ship's polar bears disliked the smell of burning cannabis intensely.

"I glad we had no polar bears in Jamaican, mon." Jimmy surrendered—the same argument happened every time a new harvest drew near. The outcome was always the same, the new crop transformed into marijuana oil for use in e-cigarettes.

No matter, for Jimmy Tosh life was good. He was safe, got to cook every day, which was a joy, and had enough ganja to keep him happy. He prayed to Jah that it would stay that way.

Lower Deck, Peggy Sue

Ahnah descended the companionway from the 2nd deck, where she had been for her examination by Doc White. In her mind she was still mulling over the events that took place deep under the icy moon's surface; how Umky had come to her rescue without a second thought; some of the things he'd said. Thus distracted she dropped the last few rungs to the deck—though not often called on to climb ladders, polar bears were as capable as other bears in scaling obstacles. Looking forward toward the crew quarters, she sighted two familiar humans approaching.

"Hello girls, how are you today?"

"Hi, Ahnah!" came Dorri's happy greeting. "How are you?"

"Yes, hello," Shadi added. "How are you doing since your fight with the sea monster?"

Ahnah crinkled her long black nose and tilted her head to the left—the polar bear equivalent of a shrug.

"The Doctor just gave me a clean bill of health. Other than a few bumps and bruises it was the most fun I've had in a while. Where are you cubs off to?"

Ahnah's maternal instincts asserted themselves, even though the two sisters were not of her own species. Seven years old, Ahnah was a fully mature female polar bear. In the wild she would have already borne her first litter of cubs. The fact that Dorri and Shadi were 14 and 16, respectively, was immaterial—they were still cubs to the she-bear, the only ones on board. Ahnah's instincts told her to nurture them, protect them as if they were her own.

"We are headed to engineering for a class in gravitonics," Dorri exclaimed excitedly.

"Ah," said the ursine scientist. "That's pretty advanced stuff."

"Yeah," said Shadi, "we've already done electronics, photonics, spintronics, and a few other -onics I can't remember."

Dorri made a face at her sister.

"Don't listen to her, we are both having fun. By the time we get back home we will be able to fix deck gravity, repulsors, shields and maybe even the main engines," the younger girl enthused.

As they spoke the three passed by the spacesuit storage lockers and entered the lower crew airlock. It provided access to the cargo hold, even when the hold was depressurized. Currently, both doors were open, providing unhindered access. As Ahnah paused to let the girls go first she caught the scent of something out-of-place. Looking back at the suit storage locker Ahnah's eyes narrowed.

"You cubs go on ahead, I think I forgot something in sickbay," the she-bear told the sisters.

"OK. See you later, Ahnah!" the always bubbly Dorri replied. The two young women passed through the open airlock and into the cargo hold, heading aft.

With the natural stealth of a large predator, Ahnah turned and moved quietly down the hallway. She stopped beside the spacesuit locker door. As the door slowly opened a crack she pounced.

Ahnah burst through the door and pushed the man hiding in the locker roughly against the inner bulkhead. It was Raoul Mendez.

Ahnah placed one dinner plate sized paw against the man's chest and leaned on him. He made a sort of wheezing, squeaking sound. A low rumbling came from the she-bear's chest.

"What are you doing here, lurking?"

"N-n-nothing," the man stammered, eyes wide with panic.

"You were spying on those human cubs, stalking them." It was not a question.

"No, I swear! I wasn't!"

Ahnah leaned in close, her nose almost touching the human's face. Her lips curled, revealing an impressive array of predatory dentition.

"The next time I catch you around those cubs, I will cripple you, then drag you back to the polar bear quarters and I will begin eating you while you are still alive."

Mendez's eyes grew even wider, showing white all the way around his pupils. Ahnah notice a new odor and smiled to herself.

The she-bear snorted once, left the man fall to the deck, and left as silently as she had appeared. Raoul huddled on the deck and shook in his now soiled jumpsuit—he had shit himself.

Chapter 6

Science Section, 2nd Deck, Peggy Sue

Kate was busy disassembling the control and monitoring equipment used during the ice drilling operation, removing sub-assemblies and returning them to the lab's storage lockers. It would have been quicker to have the ship's fabrication units spit out the needed components from scratch and then scrap them but the Chief Engineer was an old fashioned type—waste not want not, he had said.

Still, it gave her something to do. A not quite mindless task that required little heavy thinking. Better this than running endless equipment checks on equipment wedged in hard to access parts of the ship. The Chief did his best to keep all members of the crew busy doing such tasks—maintenance and testing, emergency drills and weapons practice. He truly believed that idle hands were the devil's workshop.

Back on Earth, before the alien attack that killed most of the human race, Katrin was an undergraduate student in industrial engineering at the University of Duisburg-Essen. Located in North Rhine-Westphalia, a region with many institutions of higher learning, UDE was one of the ten largest universities in Germany. The pace and competition was strenuous so she had taken a year's sabbatical from studying to join an oceanographic expedition to the Antarctic. That decision had most likely saved her life when the asteroids began to fall.

Now, years later, she found herself working a similar job aboard a space ship. The biggest difference was not being cold all the time, though the drilling operation had brought flashbacks of taking core samples under freezing conditions—bundled up in a heavy parka instead of a spacesuit. Her memories put her in a melancholy mood. The thing she missed the most was friends and the ready companionship of the opposite sex.

In the time the Peggy Sue had been in space, Kate had pretty much run through all the acceptable partners among the crew. The enlisted ranks were mostly uninspired intellectually, from her point of view. She was into classical music, opera, and European philosophy—the crew were into less cerebral fare. And while the officers were more educated, they were pretty much spoken for.

Still, a girl had needs, so she had settled on a relationship with Frank Hoenig, one of the shuttle pilots. Frank had been a crewmember on the ESS Fortune, the Colonization Board transport that had been destroyed at Gliese 667C. Only four of the crew and four of the colonists were saved from that debacle, miraculously without loss among the Peggy Sue's compliment. Thoughts of the danger they barely escaped made her shiver.

"How are you coming, Katrin?" asked Gerard Leclerc, a chemist on the science staff, his sudden appearance startling the young engineer.

"*Gut, Herr Doktor,*" she replied, rattled enough to revert to her native German. "It will take several more hours to finish disassembling this equipment."

"No problem, we have almost two weeks in alter-space to look forward to so there is no rush. I'm knocking off for the day, *guten tag.*" The Belgian scientist smiled a friendly smile and exited the compartment.

I should probably quit for the day myself, she thought, *no sense hurrying. I could go see what Frank is doing. We could have a couple of beers in the crew lounge and then see what happens.*

Fakkaa Fleet, Alpha Phoenicis Prime

Grand Fleet Admiral Raqqee floated above the command deck, the long heavy claws of both digging paws clutching the backs of the admiral's observation chair. The people of Fakkaa—the cold, nearly barren super-Earth hanging in space off the flagship's port bow—were finally moving in force against the natives of the system's other habitable planet. That planet was a much smaller, much hotter world that orbited Alpha Phoenicis's small, ruddy companion star. There were already *agents provocateur* in place on that festering swamp of a world, but this was different. This was a real invasion force.

Four digging paws of warships, over ten years in construction, formed a constellation above the Fakkaa home world. On board were 432 specially trained soldiers, prepared to lay down their lives in service of the people. If the Wise Ones were correct, the very survival of the Fakkaa might well depend on their mission to the world circling the lesser sun.

More than ten years ago, the Wise Ones' ship appeared above the world, bringing a message of warning from the wider galaxy. They told the awestruck Fakkaa that their sun was soon to end its current stable helium burning phase and balloon into a red giant. The star's girth would expand to encompass the Fakkaa home world's orbit, ending all life on the planet. To back up their warning, the mysterious aliens had provided reams of data and astrophysical theory, information that advanced Fakkaa science by decades. In the end the native scientists were forced to agree, their world was doomed.

Once the Fakkaa had accepted their fate, the aliens, who called themselves only the Wise Ones, offered a way out, a path to survival. The Wise Ones claimed that there was an ancient device buried somewhere on the rocky planet orbiting the sun's red dwarf companion star. This device, they claimed, could protect the red sun's planet from the eventual explosion when the primary star ejected its mantle and became a white dwarf. This information had several implications.

First, because the other planet was inhabited, the fastest approach to recovering the artifact would be to invade that planet and enslave them. The natives would then be used as conscript labor to unearth the alien device. This would greatly reduce the number of Fakkaa needed in the initial phase of the greater plan.

Second, to invade their neighboring world the Fakkaa would need to build a space fleet—something they lacked the technology to do. Again the Wise Ones stepped into the gap, providing their newly acquired henchmen with just enough technical know-how to construct a space fleet. The result was the twelve ship fleet currently orbiting the home world.

Third and most critical, that fleet needed to proceed to the other planet, conquer its primitive natives, and find the device. Otherwise preparing a larger fleet to evacuate more Fakkaa would serve no purpose. This was Admiral Raqqee's mission and the enormity of it was resting heavily upon him. He called out to the captain of his flagship.

"Captain Tikkoo, do we have an expected flight time to the companion star?"

"Yes, Admiral. Given best estimated continuous acceleration using the impulse drives we should arrive in thirty-six days."

The Admiral nodded. The miraculous new engines that drove the ships of the fleet were like none ever imagined by Fakkaa scientists. A gift from the Wise Ones, the engines required no propellant and produced no exhaust. Supposedly, they converted microwave energy directly into thrust inside a sealed chamber—something deemed impossible by Fakkaa's best scientists.

Totally silent and highly efficient, they required only electricity, which was amply provided by compact fusion reactors—another technology far beyond the most advanced science and engineering available to the locals. They were magical devices, impossible devices, and yet they worked. The combination of impulse engines and fusion power meant they could reach the daemon star in little over a month; a voyage that would have taken years with Fakkaa's native technology, if it could have been done at all.

"The reactors are marvelous, but the drives are pure magic," Tikkoo commented, as though he heard the Admiral's thoughts.

Tikkoo had been Raqqee's friend since their academy days; but for luck their positions could be reversed, Tikkoo the fleet admiral and Raqqee his captain. There were times that the Admiral wished that was the path fate has chosen for them. Indeed, this was one of those times—Raqqee had to talk with the Wise Ones, to tell them all was in readiness for the armada to sail.

Nothing for it, he thought to himself, smoothing his quills with the digging claws on his powerful forearms. *We may be saving our people by these actions, but I can't help feeling we've made a deal with the Devil himself.*

Bridge, Dark Lord's Ship

The Commander pulsed slowly, rhythmically, not showing the disgust it felt having to talk with one of the warm life scum it had enlisted for this mission. The vile vertebrate positively glowed with heat, its very presence would have been a deadly menace if they were ever in physical contact. But the native Admiral was safely aboard his primitive flagship, and the Commander ensconced in the cold, liquid filled control center of its starship.

As part of the deception, the Admiral saw an image of a slender, furry creature—a vertebrate much like himself—not the potentially frightening sight of a massive, throbbing, tentacled medusoid. The computer generated image and voice were crafted to put the natives at ease, to minimize any anxiety the vermin might experience in the presence of a much more advanced and radically different alien species.

"So tell me, Admiral. How go your preparations?"

"All is in readiness for the Armada to sail, Wise One. We only lack your blessing for departure."

"Good, good! You have done well to prepare your fleet in such a short time." It had taken a decade of effort at a breakneck pace to construct the Armada and train the sailors and soldiers that filled its ships. This was a long time to the Fakkaa but only an instant to the cold life denizens of the black ship who mentored them. "Please extend my congratulations to all those who labored to make this fleet a reality."

"Thank you, Wise One, your praise will be most appreciated by the Fakkaa who constructed the fleet and those who sail in it. I shall signal my Captains to get underway for the daemon star."

"Excellent, Admiral. I will shadow you fleet at a distance, but within communication range if you encounter any problems. Otherwise, the next time we shall converse will be in orbit around the target planet. A good voyage to you."

"And to you, Wise One."

With that the connection was broken. A dozen warships began accelerating at the slow, constant rate that would take them to the world they intended to invade.

Bridge, Peggy Sue

All stations on the bridge were manned and the ship rigged for departure. Billy Ray sat in the captain's chair and surveyed the scene before him. Outside of the Peggy Sue's transparent bow the ice moon lay in all its white savagery, its kilometers thick ice constantly shifting, constantly grinding and buckling. This was a world none of the Earthlings would miss.

"Mr. Baldursson, are the engines ready?"

"Ja, Captain. The primary reactor is at full power."

"Sailing Master, is the ship ready to sail?"

"Aye, Captain. That she is," replied Bobby, the officers enjoying the opportunity to act out their traditional roles.

"Very Good. Mr. Lewis, lift the ship and get underway."

"Aye, aye, Captain," the Lieutenant answered from the helm.

There was only the slightest of tremors before the deck gravity came on, damping all sense of acceleration. Around the ship, snow that had fallen since they landed over a week ago streamed out in rivulets under the press of repulsors. The six large landing legs the ship had been resting on broke free of the icy surface and retracted flush with the bottom of the hull. The moon's surface dropped away and the Peggy Sue was once again a spaceship.

"Sir, the ship is underway and answering the helm smartly," reported Lt. Lewis.

"Very good, helmsman. Sailing Master, lay in a course for the next alter-space transit point. Ahead three quarters—let's burn some of that new deuterium we spent that past week harvesting."

"Aye, aye, Sir. ETA for transit point is three hours and forty-seven minutes."

"Navigation, what is the projected transit time to our next destination?"

"Alter-space transit time to Alpha Phoenicis is thirteen days, five hours and fourteen minutes, Captain," reported Mizuki from the navigation console.

"Very good, Dr. Ogawa. All hands will remain at their action stations until we transit."

"Roger that, Sir," acknowledged the First Officer as she passed the word to all stations. The general mood among the crew was a happy one, the Peggy Sue was finally headed back toward Earth with only a few stops to make on the way.

Chapter 7

Peggy Sue, Alter-space

Traveling through alter-space was boring. Nothing to see outside the ship, at least nothing that human eyes could make sense of. At best you could lose your mind to the "million light-year stare" that some experienced gazing into the nothingness. To prevent that, the viewing ports of the ship were all turned an impenetrable gray for the duration of the transit.

To keep the crew from boredom induced mischief the officers and Chief Zackly quickly found work for anyone idle. Simulated weapons practice and calls to General Quarters were frequent, but too much time at action stations tended to blunt crew performance, not enhance it. So equipment was checked and rechecked, space suits and armor were inspected and cleaned, and physical training in the cargo hold was encouraged for all hands. Regardless, shipboard life soon settled into tedium.

For Shadi and Dorri the monotony encompassed their normal school work. Dorri in particular, despite her love of all things scientific, actually asked the Chief for something different to break up her daily ritual. Grudgingly, the grizzled old sailor assigned the teenager to help out in the hydroponics gardens. She was passing through the second deck, climbing up the companionway to third when she was spotted by Raoul Mendez. Glancing around and seeing no one else, he quietly followed her up the ladder.

* * * * *

Stepping through the door to the aft hydroponics chamber, Dorri paused and called Alexis Garner, the tech in charge of the ship's gardens.

"Alexis, this is Dorri. The Chief sent me to help you... so where are you?"

"Hey Dorri! Glad for the help. I'm all the way aft re-potting some herbs. Grab something to dig with from the equipment bin and come on back."

"OK, see you in a minute."

Dorri opened the sliding door on the equipment locker and selected a shiny metal hand spade with a fat rubber grip. Closing the locker she headed aft, tool in hand.

Mendez, hearing the girl moving away, waited a couple of heart beats and then entered the chamber himself. Between lush green plants a grated pathway led aft. Overhead, light panels glared brightly, bathing the growing plants with light skewed toward the ultraviolet. Water sprays hissed, filling the air with moisture. Earthy smells assaulted his nose.

The hydroponics section was not all hydroponic. Many plants do not do well in a pure hydroponic setting so these were given individual pots, filled with soil. They were drip fed water laced with nutrients appropriate to their needs. In the largest pots were dwarf fruit trees—apples, oranges, lemons, limes, and others. Depending on the crop, the distance between pots was automatically increased as the plants grew. Starting out close together when newly planted and spread out when ready to harvest, they formed a continuum of growth.

The marvel of growing plants in a spaceship far from Earth was lost on Raoul. He had no more regard for the plants than he had for the young woman he stalked. Silently closing the distance to his target he lunged.

"Got you, you little cunt!" he snarled, grabbing Dorri around the waste with his right arm, savagely grasping her left breast with his other hand.

Dorri screamed.

"Scream bitch! You're going to scream until you can't scream anymore!" His head was pressed against hers as he shouted in her ear.

Dorri bent forward and then threw her head back, into her attacker's face. Cartilage and bone crunched as the back of her head flattened Mendez's nose.

"Ahhh!" he cried, loosening his grip.

Dorri realized she still held the spade in her right hand. Reversing her grip so the blade pointed downward, Dorri struck behind her, driving the tool into the man's upper leg. Mendez howled in pain, losing his grip on the struggling girl. Dorri escaped and ran down the row.

Mendez pulled the spade from his leg and blood began to soak his jumpsuit. Staring dumfounded at the makeshift weapon in his hand, rage swept over him. Raising the hand spade over his head he shrieked and moved to give chase.

The deck dropped away from his feet as a woman's voice behind him spat, "Not today, motherfucker!"

* * * * *

Raoul's paying unwanted attention to Dorri and her sister had not gone unnoticed by the ship's NCOs and officers. The First Officer, fearing trouble from the malcontent, ordered the ship's computer to keep track of Mendez. Peggy Sue was instructed to notify the nearest officer or senior crewmember if he approached one of the girls alone. As a result, Raoul's furtive pursuit of Dorri up the companionway triggered an alert, summoning the nearest officer to follow. That officer was Betty White.

The ship's doctor immediately left the Sick Bay on 2nd deck and hurried up the nearby companionway. She caught sight of Raoul just as he vanished through the hydroponics section door. Hearing Dorri's subsequent scream Betty broke into a run.

Racing between the rows of plants, Betty saw Raoul's head snap back, then she heard his bellow of pain as Dorri escape his grasp. As he pulled the hand spade from his wounded leg and moved to pursue the fleeing girl, Betty was on him. Grasping the man by the collar and the seat of his jumpsuit, Betty swore: "Not today, motherfucker!"

With strength born of instinct and anger, she jerked the man from the deck and threw him bodily into the overhead with such force several light panels shattered. Allowing her momentum to carry her beneath and beyond the man, Betty pivoted, repositioning her self to face Mendez if he resumed his attack. This was unnecessary.

Raoul's body fell to the deck. The tool he had in his hand came loose when he collided with the overhead and preceded him to the floor. The spade bounced and, through a conspiracy between

75

physics and the grated deck, stood on end just as he landed on it. The blade pierced his back between two ribs, puncturing his heart.

CIC, *Peggy Sue*

Beth was in the Command Information Center, reviewing the crew's performance during the last simulated weapons exercise, when the ship's voice sounded softly in her ear.

"First Officer, there has been an altercation on 3rd deck. There are casualties."

Now what? Beth thought. "What type of altercation and who was involved?"

"Crewman Mendez assaulted Dorri in the hydroponics compartment. Dr. White was notified as per your standing orders and interceded."

"And the casualties?"

"My sensors show Crewman Mendez is now deceased."

"Oh, bloody hell," Beth swore. She spoke into her collar pip, "Captain, First Officer Melaku."

"Go, Number One," came the immediate reply.

"Sir, there has been an incident involving Raoul Mendez and Dorri. Dr. White is on the scene and I'm headed there now."

There was a slight pause during which Beth could almost hear her husband's unspoken cursing.

"Very well, Cmdr. Melaku. Get me a sitrep soonest."

"Aye, aye, Captain."

Beth left the CIC headed aft at a run.

3rd Deck Hydroponics, *Peggy Sue*

Betty quickly evaluate the unmoving form of Raoul Mendez lying face up on the deck before her. *That shithead is dead*, she thought with a mixture of relief and unease. Before she became a medical doctor, Betty had been a Navy Medical Corpsman attached to the US Marines in Afghanistan. She had seen dead men in combat and Mendez was definitely dead. She turned to Dorri.

Dorri was standing a couple of meters away, one hand grasping the plant shelf, steadying her. Her eyes were wide, showing white all around the iris, her face pale, her features blank in shock. Betty moved to her and wrapped her in a protective embrace.

"It's OK, child. He ain't going to hurt you."

"He grabbed me!" she sputtered. "He did hurt me!"

"Well, he isn't going to hurt anyone anymore," Betty said, pulling the girl tight against her bosom. Dorri looked up, still frightened.

"How, how did you do that?" she demanded. "You threw him into the ceiling!"

Oh shit! I used a bit too much force and she saw me do it. "Don't worry about that now, are you injured?"

The girl shook her head "no" and clung to the Doctor. Alexis came running up with some kind of cultivating tool gripped in her hands as a makeshift weapon.

"My God! What happened?" she exclaimed, taking in the scene.

"It's all over, Alexis," Betty explained. "Here, you take Dorri down to Sickbay. Tell the nurse on duty to put her in a private examination room. I'll be right down."

Gently passing the shaken girl to the horticulturalist, Betty softly spoke reassurances. As Alexis started to lead Dorri away, the Doctor grabbed her arm and whispered.

"She's badly shaken and may go into shock. Do not let her alone until I get there, not for a second, understand?"

"Gotcha, Doc," the tech whispered back. Then she guided Dorri past the dead man, trying to shield her from seeing the body. As the pair exited the chamber another crewman entered. Steve Hitch.

"Holly crap, what happened here Doc?" the petty officer asked as Betty moved to more closely examine the man she had killed just minutes ago. The smell of violent death grew stronger, the smell of piss and shit and blood.

"Mendez attacked Dorri."

"Motherfucker!"

"Yeah, that's what I said." Betty looked up at Hitch. They had been shipmates for years, fighting side by side against aliens on several occasions. "Then I bounced the asshole off the overhead and he landed on a hand tool. Killed him instantly."

"Too bad. He should have died slowly and painfully."

Betty smiled.

"Could you go to the aid station next to the shuttle locks and bring back a stretcher? We need to take this garbage down to Sickbay so I can do an autopsy."

"Sure, Doc. I thought you said it was death by garden tool?"

"It was, a hand spade through the heart, but I still have to determine an official cause of death. Now go, I expect the First Officer and the Chief will be here any minute."

"Aye, aye. Be right back." He hurried from the chamber as the First Officer entered.

Beth paused to take in the sight of Mendez's dead body, the ship's doctor kneeling next to it. Betty looked at Beth and stood.

"Commander."

"Doctor. It would appear that crewman Mendez has expired."

"Yes, Ma'am."

"And how did this happen?"

"Peggy Sue alerted me that Mendez was stalking Dorri. I arrived in time to witness the attack. Dorri managed to free herself. I subdued him."

"Rather forcefully, it seems."

"Yes, I sort of bounced him off the overhead and he landed on a hand spade he was using as a weapon."

"You'll do an autopsy?"

"Hitch is fetching a stretcher."

"Fine, I need to brief the Captain. There will have to be an inquiry."

"Of course."

Beth nodded and turned to leave.

"Commander, Dorri saw me bounce Mendez off the overhead. She commented on it."

"Oh bollocks. We shall have to discuss that as well. When you are done with things in Sickbay come forward and we'll meet with the others."

Sickbay, Peggy Sue

The Chief arrived in Sickbay with Shadi in tow. Shadi ran to embrace her sister, who was seated on an examination table that had been curtained off from the rest of the open ward.

"Dorri! Have you been hurt? Did that son of a leprous pig touch you?" she said in rapid Farsi.

"I'm fine. Really, sister." Despite the assurances both girls started crying, speaking in the language of their native Iran. Hardly ever caught unprepared, the Chief was helpless in the face of sisterly compassion.

"Er, I'll go get the nurse or somethin'," he mumbled and left the two young women alone in the room. Eventually they both calmed down enough for Dorri to tell Shadi what happened. After the telling, Shadi was livid.

"That mongrel dog son of a whore bastard! I would kill him if the Doctor had not done it already!"

"Oh, she killed him, and you should have seen how she killed him! I had escaped his grasp and turned around to face him when the Doctor grabbed him from behind and threw him against the ceiling."

"She should have ripped his throat out!"

79

"No, you don't understand. She threw him against the ceiling so hard the light panels shattered. He fell to the deck and landed on the spade but I think he may have already been dead."

"What do you mean?"

"Think! The Doctor is not a small woman but she can't weigh more that 65 kilos. Mendez must have weighed 80 kilos. Under standard gravity there is no way she should have been able to do that. I don't even think one of the Jumbo twins could have done it, and they are as strong as oxen!"

"Are you sure? Maybe she just threw him over her shoulder, and in the excitement of the moment you saw things happen more... violently than they did."

"I know what I saw. Go up to 3rd deck and look at the light panels for yourself. He hit the ceiling and *bounced* off!"

Shadi, having calmed down, thought about what her sister said. Dorri was right, a normal human could not throw a full grown man against the ceiling with such force.

"So, what does it mean?"

"Remember how Dr. Ogawa cut through those carpets while blindfolded? Or how she and Cmdr Danner are so fast at sword practice? I wonder if some of the officers are... completely human."

That would explain a number of things, Shadi thought to herself. "Listen, little star, don't say anything about this. To anyone."

Captain's Sea Cabin, Peggy Sue

Betty was the last to arrive at the Captain's office just off the bridge. Already seated around the meeting table were Mizuki, Beth, and Bobby. The Captain, at the head of the table, looked up anxiously when she entered.

"Please close the door, Doctor," Billy Ray said in a neutral tone. Betty felt the stares of her fellow officers as she took her seat. She nodded to the Captain.

80

"Alright, let's get this business with Mendez out of the way," he said, officially calling the meeting to order. "Every one here has viewed the recoded video of the incident?"

Those around the table nodded yes.

"Let the log show that all present signaled affirmative. Doctor White, have you ascertained the cause of death?"

"Yes, Sir. The cause of death was a single deep puncture wound in the deceased's back that punctured his heart."

"And the impact of his other wounds?"

"He had a broken nose and a puncture wound in the right quadriceps muscles inflicted by his intended victim. He also had a fractured sternum and a cervical fracture from his collision with the overhead."

"A broken neck?"

"Yes, Captain, a broken neck, but it was not necessarily a fatal injury."

"You mean, if he hadn't landed on the hand tool he might have lived?" Beth prompted her. Though they were all friends of several years standing the atmosphere in the cabin was tense.

"Yes, Commander. He would have been paralyzed, but I estimate an 85 percent probability that he could have been healed with regeneration therapy."

"But the punctured heart was fatal?" repeated the Captain.

"Yes, Sir. Blood flow to his brain was cut off almost immediately. By the time he was transported to the Sickbay there was irreversible brain damage."

"OK. We have identified what killed him, now on to the who," Billy Ray looked around the room, letting his gaze linger briefly on each of his officers. "Dr. White, recordings from the ship's computer indicate that you attacked crewman Mendez from behind, lifting him from the deck and throwing him bodily into the overhead. Is that correct?"

"Yes."

"Why did you attack the crewman?"

"He was in the process of assaulting Dorri, one of the adolescent members of the crew."

Again he looked around the room before he spoke.

"All of you, having viewed the recorded video of the incident, accept that crewman Mendez was, in fact, assaulting Dorri?"

"Aye, Captain," the other three officers replied.

"Dr. White, why did you attack the crewman in the manner described in the record?"

"He was advancing on the young girl, with the bloody tool held in his right hand, above his head. He was yelling. I disabled the attacker as quickly as I could to prevent further injury to Dorri."

"You claim your use of force was warranted by the situation?"

"Yes, Sir."

"Does anyone here disagree?"

"No, Sir," said the others.

"Let the record show that the Captain and the ship's officers are in agreement in the matter of the death of crewman Mendez. Dr. White took action appropriate to the circumstance and Mendez died by misadventure."

The mood in the room relaxed and Betty exhaled, releasing a breath she didn't realize she had been holding. Mizuki reached across the table and placed a hand on Betty's arm, an astounding display of emotion for the normally reserved scientist.

"You did what any of us would have done, Betty," she said with a kind smile.

"Yeah, Doc, that was really just a formality for the authorities when we get back to port. Hell, you could have strangled him with his own intestines for all I care."

"My, Captain, you are in a bloodthirsty mood today."

"Number One, I've been regretting taking that sidewinder on board for a year now, I ain't shedding any tears over his well deserved demise. This is the second time in my life I've been in close proximity to a would be rapist and I just can't comprehend what makes a man into an animal like that."

While he spoke, Billy Ray's hands balled into fists on the table where they rested. Beth, to his right, lay her hand on his clenched right hand, insinuating her long dark fingers between his.

"That is because, love, you are in your heart a good man." He met Beth's gaze and offered a grim smile, as an awkward silence descended.

"Thank you all, but there is still the other matter to consider," Betty said, breaking the quiet. "Dorri saw me toss a grown man into the overhead."

"And you think she will have questions about how a woman your size could do that?" asked Bobby.

"Or anyone," Betty replied, "the girl's not stupid and she has a good idea of human physical limitations from combat training with the Marines."

"We decided before the voyage started that those of us who have been..." Beth searched for the right word, "*enhanced* by the T'aafhal Al aboard the M'tak Ka'fek would keep that information from the rest of the crew."

"Right, we didn't want to have them thinking that we were weird or alien in some way."

"But we are alien in some ways," said Bobby. "We are stronger and faster than unenhanced humans; our senses are keener too."

"I think our decision processes have been affected as well. When I came on Mendez attacking Dorri I acted to protect her without thinking."

"That might have just been maternal instinct, Betty. Or the reaction of a combat veteran."

"Maybe, Bobby, but the next thing I knew that scumbag was lying on the deck with a garden tool stuck through his heart."

"So what do we tell Dorri, who has almost certainly confided in her sister already?"

"Hysterical strength," said Bobby. "Most people have heard of displays of superhuman strength, usually occurring when people are in life and death situations. A common example is a mother lifting a vehicle to free her trapped child."

"The evidence for such occurrences are anecdotal at best, Bobby." Mizuki was always the rational counterpoint to Bobby's more far out musings.

"You know, that might work," said Billy Ray.

"Really?" said Beth, giving her husband a sideways look.

"Yeah, it doesn't have to be documented fact, just believable."

"Sure," added Bobby, "everybody has heard of it, it's a common legend, even if it's not true."

That last qualification did not totally placate Mizuki, but Betty latched on to the idea. "Well, it is thought to be theoretically possible, or at least not impossible."

"It's that or we have to come clean with everyone on board," Beth observed, not totally convinced.

"I say we go with hysterical strength as an explanation, unless someone has a better idea," said the Captain.

"Fine," agreed Beth, in a tone that said "if this doesn't work it's your fault."

"We need to tell the others, we all need to be on the same page on this."

"Aye, aye, Captain. I'll inform them."

"Very good. We are less than twenty-four hours from emergence, let's all get back to work."

Chapter 8

Peggy Sue, Alter-space

Anticipation of emergence in a new star system replaced talk about the death of Raoul Mendez. The dead man's corpse was stored in one of the reefers near the polar bear quarters for the journey home, prompting Umky to say he was glad there were snacks on board. Others, possessing senses of humor less gastronomically oriented, quipped that this was what happened when the Doc got bored from lack of patients. Regardless, all hands soon busied themselves for arrival at Alpha Phoenicis.

Lt. Nigel Lewis and Frank Hoenig were seated in the cockpit of the large crew shuttle, running through its test procedures. Frank had been assimilated into the crew with a rank of Petty Officer 2nd class, though no one but the ship's officers referred to him as PO Hoenig. Nigel, a junior officer, was the exception to that rule, the two having become friends during the long journey.

"So, Frank, how are you making out with the German bird you fancy?"

"You mean Kate? Things are OK, but I think she's just using me for sex."

"Oh you poor, abused sod! At least you are getting an occasional tumble. Looks like the reactor check sequence is about 80% complete."

"I saw you talking with the older Iranian sister the other day. What's her name, Shadi? She's quite a looker."

"Right, and she is all of seventeen. I was just being friendly but I wouldn't go near that on a bet. Not after what happened to Mendez."

"Come on, man. Mendez was a flaming asshole and he tried to molest the younger one. I would have enjoyed kicking his narrow ass if I had caught him."

A tone sounded as the reactor test completed.

"Reactor power test passed 100%. I knew he was a dodgy bastard but I though he was all piss and wind. I'm glad it was the Doc who caught him, she really did for him. "

"That takes care of the reactor checks," Frank said, acknowledging a prompt on the control console. "Never much liked him either. He should have kept his hands to himself, if you get my meaning. It's hard to understand how a human being can get that stupid in just one lifetime."

"No kidding. He should have stayed a frustrated tosser like the rest of us. Starting the deck gravity auto check sequence."

"Roger that. Another half hour and we should be done with this one."

"Emergence is still three hours away, we should do the pinnace next."

"You know, one of these days I need to get a check ride on the small shuttles."

"I thought you only wanted to fly the big ones."

"What can I tell you, Nigel? I'm getting bored to death with all this inaction."

"We'll see mate. Deck gravity 25% complete..."

Cargo Hold, Peggy Sue

With most of the crew preparing for emergence, Shadi and Dorri decided to get in a last run in the cargo hold before exploring a new star system disrupted everyone's schedules. The only large and relatively open space on board, the interior of the hold was a maze of equipment and storage crates, but around the edges was a clear path to allow access. There a synthetic mat had been applied to the decking to help cushion runners' knees and ankles while muting their footfalls—a squad of running Marines in an enclosed space did a fair imitation of a stampeding herd of cattle.

Running aft along the port side, the two sisters made a ninety degree turn just in front of the tangle of pipes that were part of the heavy water processor. Dorri was ahead of her sister and goading her on.

"Come on, slow poke! Your legs are longer than mine!"

"Keep talking, little star," Shadi panted. "I'm going to pass you on the straight!"

Just as Dorri was about to make the turn forward, onto the starboard straightaway, two large figures in dark green stepped from the cover of the deuterium refinery. Dorri collided with the nearest and bounced off with an involuntary shriek.

The young woman fell as she had been taught, rolling and slapping the deck with her arm to absorb energy. Ending her roll back on her feet, she assumed a defensive stance. Shadi managed to avoid Dorri's tumble and struck a similar pose next to her sister.

"Oh! Hey sorry," the other participant in the collision sputtered.

"Yeah, we didn't mean to run into you," said his companion, holding up his open hands in a sign of surrender.

"Who the hell are you! And why are you lurking around in the hold?" shouted Shadi, adrenalin bringing her to the edge of fight or flight. Next to her, Dorri seemed to be in favor of fight.

"Whoa, whoa there!" said the first man in green. "We weren't lurking, we were just taking a walk around the hold to make sure everything was ready for emergence."

"Yeah," said the other, "we're assigned to damage control with the engineers."

"And there is nothing to do," said the first.

"So we got bored and took a walk," the second man finished.

Shadi looked from one to the other.

"Do you always finish each other's sentences?"

The two men looked at each other sheepishly.

"Yeah, we do that a lot."

"Hey," said Dorri, relaxing her stance, "I know you, you're the Jumbo Twins."

Both men winced.

"Yeah, that's what they call us."

"That, or Frick and Frack."

"Or Tweedledee and Tweedledum."

"Or Mutt and Jeff, or..."

"OK, OK! We get the point." Shadi lowered her arms and straightened up. "I'm Shadi, and she's my sister Dorri."

Dorri chimed in, "Hi!"

"I'm Malachi."

"And I'm Hezekiah, but you can call me Zeke."

"And me Mal."

The two Marines stood shyly in front of the sisters. Not used to talking to female crew members, and certainly not used to conversing with two beautiful young women close to their own ages, they were at a loss. Not so the irrepressible Dorri.

"You are the other two survivors. The only other people to have lived on the surface of Paradise and escaped with their lives."

"Yes," Shadi added. "Dorri and I were colonists, like you."

"Yeah," said Mal, "we know who you are."

"Everybody on board knows who you two are," finished Zeke.

"Why haven't you ever said hello before?"

"We were sort of told not to bother you, Dorri," Zeke said sheepishly.

"Besides, we had a lot of stuff to learn to become Marines."

"We've been on board together for over a year, and you never once said Hi?"

Both men blushed.

"You're embarrassing them, little sister," Shadi said in Farsi.

Not to be deterred, Dorri continued. "We've seen you around on occasion. You're both very big, are you brothers?"

Eagerly seizing a verbal way out of their embarrassment Mal forged ahead.

"We're twins—dizygotic not monozygotic."

"Fraternal not identical," Zeke clarified.

"I can see that," said Dorri, placing her hands on her hips and looking the twins up and down.

Zeke grinned. "I'm the oldest. Mal is my little brother."

"Yeah, by about fifteen minutes."

"He's been late for everything since." He smiled at his brother.

"He doesn't look so little," quipped Dorri.

"So how old are you?" Shadi asked, her interest piqued.

"Nineteen," they answer in unison.

"Shadi is seventeen, and I'm almost fifteen. You are the youngest people on board, next to us."

The twins nodded in agreement.

"We are all lucky to have gotten this old, after Paradise," Mal replied. "You were in one of the other settlements. We would have remembered you if you were in Brother Abraham's flock."

"We were in Imam Mustafa's group." Dorri's eyes narrowed a bit. "So you are Christians?"

"Sort of," replied Zeke. "Brother Abraham had his own take on religion."

"You mean he was a total nutcase," Mal snorted.

"So you are Muslims?" asked Zeke, ignoring his brother.

"Technically, but our family was not overly religious."

"Shadi means our real family, our original family, not the Imam's band of fanatics."

An awkward silence ensued.

"I wonder what would have happened if things hadn't gone the way they did on Paradise?" Zeke said, breaking the silence. "With three groups of settlers with different religious beliefs."

"Probably would have made a mess of that planet, like we messed up Earth."

"Shadi is sometimes a bit of a pessimist. I think we would have eventually learned to get along. Most people don't agree with fanatics."

"Dorri is sometimes overly optimistic."

Dorri looked at the two young men with a thoughtful expression on her face. Before she could speak a tone sounded throughout the hold, followed by the First Officer's clipped, British accented voice.

"Attention, all hands. Emergence in fifteen minutes. Report to your duty stations. I repeat, emergence in fifteen minutes."

"We have to go back to engineering," said Zeke, looking at his brother.

"We have to run as well," added Shadi. "We need to shower and get to the forward lounge. Now!"

The sisters began running forward. Dorri looked over her shoulder and yelled, "Talk to you later, don't be strangers!"

As the two young women disappeared down the track the two young men watched then go.

"They are so pretty," said Mal.

"That they are, they're beautiful."

"You're drooling, Brother."

"What? I am not. Come on let's go or the Gunny will bust our balls for not being at our duty station."

"At least you were smart enough to not talk like a Marine in front of those women."

The pair headed aft at a run.

Bridge, Peggy Sue

"Emergence in 5, 4, 3, 2, 1..."

At the end of the computer's countdown the Peggy Sue's viewports changed from pearlescent gray to transparent and a new star system shimmered into existence before the crew's eyes. After

90

a dozen such transitions from alter-space to normal 3-space, the crew knew the arrival drill by heart.

"Any contacts on the gravitonic alter-space sensors, Mr. Umky?"

"Negative, Captain. Just the expected stars and planets."

"Very good. Any signals activity, Number One?"

"I'm detecting some EM traffic from the super-Earth orbiting the primary, but nothing else. A positive indication of some form of civilization."

"Interesting. Dr. Ogawa, please deploy the large optical telescope and start a survey of the system."

"*Hai*, Captain."

"We have a forty minute window before anyone knows we are here, let's make the most of it."

As the crew bent to their tasks a cone shaped wavefront of X-rays and gamma rays spread out from the emergence point. This was followed by a slightly slower spray of highly energetic particles, the result of the ship materializing in normal spacetime, disrupting the fabric of the Universe at the quantum level. Caused by interfering with the mutual annihilation of particle-antiparticle pairs, the burst of energy was the unmistakable calling card of a ship arriving from alter-space.

Chapter 9

Alpha Phoenicis

Because of the relative masses of the departure star and Alpha Phoenicis, the Peggy Sue's emergence point was over half a billion kilometers from the system's central orange star. It was also twenty degrees north of the plane of the ecliptic. The planet of the Fakkaa was half that distance from its sun, but on the far side from the new arrival. At nearly a right angle to the vector from the Peggy Sue to Alpha Phoenicis A, 3.2 billion kilometers from is partner, orbited Alpha Phoenicis B, a baleful red ember that held the system's other habitable planet in thrall.

Radiation from Peggy Sue's arrival passed by the Fakkaa world first, though no notice was taken of it by the planet's inhabitants. The next collection of sentient beings to receive the arrival signal was the Fakkaa invasion fleet, more than half way through their journey. They too lacked the equipment to detect the now faint emanations, but 10,000 kilometers beyond the Fakkaa's primitive fleet lay the ship of the Dark Lords.

Due to their course and the geometry of the star system the Dark Lords saw the burst of radiation two and a half hours after the Earthlings arrived. Unlike their innocent dupes, the manipulative cold life creatures possessed the necessary detectors and knew what the radiation pattern meant.

"Most Wise, we have detected signs indicating the arrival of a ship from the small dimensions."

"Yes, Senior Functionary, I have noted the signal myself. Have we identified its type?"

"We are still analyzing the combined electromagnetic and particle radiation, though the craft is unmistakably moving under gravitonic power. Perhaps it is a vessel from the Dark Lord Council or another servant race."

"Fool! Never wish away the danger hidden within the unknown. We were sent on this mission by the Dark Lord Council themselves— there is no reason for them to dispatch more servants and certainly no reason for one of the most high to personally travel to this benighted system."

This statement was accompanied by a reflexive twitch of the Wise One's stinging tentacles. The underling edged farther away from its overlord.

"Forgive me, Wise One! I should not have presumed to offer advice before you completed your analysis. You are of course correct, the drive signature does not match that of any known cold life species or servant race."

"As I intuited, it is more parasitic warm life scum coming to complicate our mission. Does the drive signature match any know warm life species?"

"No exact match, Most Wise. However, there are similarities to some old entries in the database... it is a 60% probable match for ancient T'aafhal drives!"

"Impossible! The T'aafhal passed into entropy several million years ago. It must be some other warm life refuse who adopted the forever accursed Paladins' technology. This shows why warm life is like an infectious disease, we stamp it out in one place only to have it rear its malignant tentacles someplace else."

"Frozen God's of the void, will we never be free of these foul life forms?" Cursing warm life seemed a safe response to the Senior Functionary.

"No matter. Their presence may be a blessing in disguise."

"Yes, Wise One?"

"Our kind are cold life, but we do not rank high among the other Dark Lords. It has long been our race's aspiration to join the high council. In part that is why we are here on the mission to retrieve the T'aafhal artifact. When we return with the artifact and report the extermination of two races of warm life parasites our prestige will be enhanced. But to add to that success the destruction of an obviously advanced ship sent by an unknown race of vermin, well that will be even better."

"Truly, your ability to chart a successful course in the face of uncertainty is exemplary, Wise One."

Shrugging off its sycophantic lackey's attempt to curry favor, the alien Commander continued its analysis.

"Have they detected us or the primitives' fleet?"

"No, Most Wise, at least there has been no indication from the ship's motion that they are aware of our presence."

"That is as it should be. The impulse drives we gave to the primitives are virtually undetectable and the fusion generators well shielded. Still, contact the Admiral with a low power signal and reemphasize the need to maintain radio silence."

"As you command."

"It is probable that these new creatures have never encountered a ship propelled by a dark matter, space warping drive before. Even underway we will hardly register on a scan for gravitonic drives. We cannot move between star systems with their speed but we are not limited to alter-space transfer lines between massive objects, we can go anywhere in 3-space. That gives me the greatest weapon a commander can posses—surprise!"

What the alien commander did not realize was that there was another entity in the star system that could detect the newly arrived ship. An entity that had at its disposal the full technology of the T'aafhal.

Bridge, Fakkaa Flagship

Admiral Raqqee sat strapped in his chair on the flag bridge, a raised section above the flagship's actual bridge from which he could observe operations. He was strapped down to prevent him from floating out of his chair under the fraction of a G thrust the impulse drives provided. From the bridge below Captain Tikkoo called to report an incoming communique.

"Admiral, we have just received a signal from the commander of our troops on the target planet. It says that the native queen is on her last legs and is expected to die at any time."

"Fagh! The timing is too soon. We should have been in orbit and ready to land our forces before the old bug queen dies."

"Perhaps she will cling to life a bit longer as a favor to us all," Tikkoo said in a deadpan voice. There were few on board who could get away with teasing the Admiral that way.

"If I knew the old queen's frequency I'd give her a call," Raqqee replied with a short laugh. "As I understand the situation on the ground, the instant the old queen dies the race is on."

"Yes, Admiral. On the old queen's death her royal offspring will immediately head for the capital. The plan is to back one of the princesses in the fight for the throne."

"Yes, yes, and once she is on the throne we will use her to search for and excavate the artifact. I know the plan as well as you do, Tikkoo. We must not delay when the old queen dies or we risk a different princess ascending the throne. That would greatly complicate our task."

"Agreed."

"Signal the commander to proceed with the plan using the troops he has. The natives are primitives, their weapons should be no match for our own. It is imperative that our princess wins the fight to succeed the old queen."

"Admiral, the aliens have told us to maintain strict radio silence."

"So, use a tight directional signal, and tell the local commander not to reply. I doubt even the wise ones can change the laws of physics and read such a signal."

"As you command, Admiral. I do not know why they care, the natives haven't the technology to receive radio transmissions, who are they afraid will hear us?"

"I don't know, Captain. Who can know the reasons behind anything these 'Wise Ones' do?"

As the Captain instructed his signals officer to send the message, the Admiral lapsed back into silence, worrying about what was to come—and what the aliens would do once they had their precocious artifact.

Bridge, Peggy Sue

"Captain, I have just detected a neutrino message burst," the voice of the ship's computer said in Billy Ray's ear.

"Like the one we got from the M'tak Ka'fek at the end of the battle off Sirius? I though that only the T'aafhal had the tech to do that?"

"Precisely, Captain. It seems to have originated from the planet orbiting the secondary M type star."

Clearing his voice the Captain spoke to the bridge crew.

"People, I have just been informed that we have received a message from the planet orbiting Alpha Phoenicis B. A directional neutrino burst."

Beth merely raised one eyebrow, a Spock like gesture she had mastered because it amused the crew and mildly annoyed her husband. Mizuki's response was even more appropriate for the fictitious Vulcan.

"Captain, that would imply that the sender of the message was aware of our existence, which is highly improbable."

"Why do you say that, Dr. Ogawa?"

"We have been in this system just under three hours. The propagation of a signal through 3-space is limited to the speed of light. Neutrinos have mass and are therefore even slower."

"And yer point, Doctor?"

"By necessity, the message must have been sent shortly after we emerged in this system, well before radiation from our arrival could have reached the planet of origin."

"Which means, whoever sent it must have detected our presence almost instantaneously," Billy Ray said.

"Hai."

"And that would imply gravitonic detectors that work in alter-space," the Captain continued.

"And the only species we know of who have such technology are the T'aafhal," finished Beth.

"This mission has just become significantly more important. Finding a functioning T'aafhal ship or outpost has repercussions for all humanity, not just the company. Bridge, alter course for the source of the message."

"All ready laid in, Captain." Bobby grinned at his friend from the helm. "All ahead full?"

"Aye, Mister Danner. Let's burn some D2."

"Aye, aye, Captain. ETA at Alpha Phoenicis B roughly 85 hours." In just over three and a half days the Peggy Sue would be in orbit around Alpha Phoenicis B's only habitable planet.

Part Two

Cast Upon A Hostile Shore

Chapter 10

Throne Room, Kingdom of Formicidae

The Lord Chamberlain walked slowly from behind the tall, cloth-of-gold screens hiding the Queen on her throne. Her gait was uneven, and she staggered despite having all four legs planted firmly on the floor. The throne room was nearly empty, only servants and close advisers to the Queen were present where usually masses of officials and supplicants thronged. The true sun had set and darkness was seeping into the far corners of the great hall, cloaking the high galleries in gloom. The emptiness gave the room a sad, hollow feeling.

This seems an appropriate time for her passing, the Chamberlain thought. *The orange ogre has begun its climb into the night sky, soon it will cast pallid shadows across the land. Not an evil sign in itself but not propitious either. What is more troubling are the reports of daemons about in the far provinces.*

"My Lord?" asked one of the pages, bobbing her head submissively. Others hung back, filled with trepidation.

"It is finished," the old Chamberlain said wearily. "Send the announcement to the royal princesses."

"Yes, my Lord." The page bowed her head and backed away.

And so begins the mad contest for the throne of Formicidae. The thought caused the Chamberlain to hang her head. *I had hoped to die myself before the old Queen passed. Well, nothing for it but to face the coming chaos.*

A sound caused the overseer of the royal household to look up. A keening sound, rising and falling in pitch, filtered in from outside the palace. Word of the Queen's death spread rapidly throughout the capital. Her many subjects would mourn her passing tonight; by tomorrow they would all be cowering in their homes afraid of the violence the struggle for succession was sure to bring. Over the next week or so the old Queen's scent would fade, making the colony ready to accept a new queen—which ever of the princesses wins the race, and can hold the palace long enough to establish her own scent as dominant.

The Chamberlain shook off the numbing lethargy she felt in her soul—there was work to be done.

"Captain of the Guard!" she called. "Turn out the House Guard and secure the palace. And summon the nursemaids to carry away the remains of the Queen."

The Queen's body servants had already begun the gruesome task of dismantling her corpse and removing it from the throne. Her flesh and organs would be hauled way to the nursery where they would be fed to the last of her children, still larvae—the Queen had laid no eggs for over a month.

It has always been thus, thought her faithful servant. *She who gave all of us life continues to serve her offspring, even in death. The old Queen was kind and wise, may the gods grant the next Queen those same traits.*

Outside the keening grew louder.

Princess Timushi's Palace

The eldest of the old queen's daughters was pacing the floor in the highest room of the redoubt. Disturbing news had arrived from her spies in her closest sister's fiefdom.

"Read back the message again, my Lord Castellan," commanded Princess Timushi.

"Yes, Highness," the manager of the royal residence replied with a deferential dip of her antennae. "Castle on fire. Attacked by flying dragons. Princess Shōshi feared dead."

The Princess cocked her head in a moment of thought.

"Alert my body guard, we are leaving."

"My Princess?"

"Out the tunnel to the hidden gate," Timushi clarified. "Majordomo, round up the chosen servants and make haste. Have them bring the supplies that were prepared for our journey to the capital."

"Yes, my Princess," the old head of the household staff replied with a bow. "But tradition says we must remain here until word of the Queen Our Mother's death."

"Tradition is a guide from the past," the Princess replied curtly. "To blindly follow it when it may endanger us all is foolish. Now move, and keep the staff quiet about it. I will not sit here awaiting the same fate that befell my royal sister."

The Majordomo bowed again more deeply, and backed away toward the chamber door. Once she had gone Timushi addressed her assembled advisers.

"How long does it take a messenger dragonfly to reach us from the capitol?"

"Ten hours, perhaps nine with a favorable tailwind, Highness," answered the eldest adviser.

"And from Shōshi's fortress?"

"Perhaps four."

"So, since Shōshi's fortress is roughly the same distance from the capital as we are and we have not received official word of our mother's death, the attack was launched before the dragonflies from the capital could arrive. The attack can only mean that my other dear sister, Reishi, knows the Queen has died—I cannot believe that even she would violate the laws of succession so blatantly. It also means that whatever foul sorcery befell my sister Shōshi might be well on its way to visit this castle."

"How do we know Reishi was behind the attack on Shōshi's fortress?" asked the Castellan.

"You have read the reports from our spies in the north as have I. They say she has been consorting with daemons, hideous creatures that stay in the shadows and posses terrible magics. No, Reishi is behind this, which is why we must hurry. We need to be well away before dawn."

"But these dragons attacked in the night, Your Highness. Surely there is no safety in the darkness."

The Princess's antennae twitch, a sign of royal impatience.

"Reishi has her spies here as we have in her city. We need to escape and be away from the city before her eyes on the palace can notice and send word. Now stop dawdling and move!"

"Yes, Your Highness."

As the others scurried from the Princess's chamber she motioned the Castellan closer to her. The warrior/adviser moved within whisper range.

"Have the watch light the mourning fires. The Queen is surely dead and it will be no dishonor to her to light them before the official message arrives. The commotion her passing will cause in the city will serve to mask our departure."

"A wise precaution, my Princess. What of the males?"

"What? Oh yes, I suppose it is expected to bring some on the journey. Round up a handful of the useless fops and bring them along. But be quick about it, my back is twitching as though my wings are emblazoned with a target."

"By your command, my Princess."

The Castellan acknowledged her Princess's orders with more of a head bob than a bow, and hurried from the chamber. Timushi followed closely, trailed by her body servants. They would descend the hidden stairs to the castle's storage cellars, where the entrance to the hidden escape tunnel lay. With any luck they would all be outside the city wall and under cover of the forest canopy inside half an hour.

HQ, Fakkaa Expeditionary Force

The force commander clicked the long digging claws of his main arms against each other in a display of irritation. Word of the death of the old Queen had arrived from his observers at the capital city almost eight hours ago, yet the Princess's entourage had not departed the jumbled trash heap she called her castle. In frustration he snapped at his aid.

"Lieutenant, what is keeping our pet Princess from departing? The old bug has been dead for hours!"

"She refuses to leave the palace until some kind of messenger arrives bringing official word of the Queen's death, Sir."

"Bah! It would be easier to just look for the artifact thing ourselves, and kill any insects who get in our way. Any news from the aviation unit?"

"Yes, Sir. The aviation commander reports that the attack on the nearest sister's palace was a success—they left the palace engulfed in flames and our observers on the ground report no signs of the local Princess fleeing the city."

"Damn this ban on radio communications, who does the high command think is going to intercept our messages?" the Commander fumed. "No matter, what about the airstrike on the remaining Princess's position?"

"The attack aircraft returned to base to refuel and rearm, and are now en route to the second target, Sir."

"ETA?"

"Roughly twenty minutes."

"Good, good. Too bad we have only three attack craft or we could have hit both targets simultaneously. But we still should be able to strike the second Princess's castle before they know what is happening."

"Yes, Sir. It will be dawn soon, so we will be able to get more accurate damage assessment reports on both targets shortly."

"Excellent." Operations seemed to be going well, which helped brighten the Commander's mood. "Once our positions are obscured by the bulk of the planet get radio reports from all units—the Fleet Admiral can't complain about us breaking communications silence if he never hears the messages."

"Yes, Commander." The aide saluted and headed back to the radio shack to await the dawn.

Outside the City Wall, Princess Timushi's Palace

The royal party exited the city via the secret portal—an ancient sally port constructed centuries ago and long forgotten by most. As

105

expected, the Princess's guard was well deployed and efficient in the discharge of their duties. The household servants and functionaries were less orderly in their egress from the palace. The least tidy component of the column were the five male dandies, who chittered and complained until the Majordomo threatened to have them bound and gagged. But then, what could you expect from a gaggle of useless males?

The winding column was passing over the nearest ridgeline, several kilometers from the city wall. The Princess and the Castellan stood to one side, observing the procession and looking back at the palace through a break in the jungle canopy.

"Sad to think that this is the last time I will see the palace," the Princess commented. "It has been my home since I was a pupa. One way or another, I shall never see it again."

"Bigger things await you, Your Highness," said the Castellan. She kept her compound eyes on the raged column of servants passing by, each bearing food and sundry items for the journey. "We are away in good order, my Princess. In less than a fortnight we should arrive at the capital."

The Princess sighed.

"I knew this day would come eventually, the day when the Queen Our Mother would die and one of us would have to take her place."

"My Princess, you are certainly the best qualified to take her place, but then, I may be a bit biased."

"I'm sure both my royal sisters feel the same about themselves. And since one of us will gain the throne, and the others will die in the attempt, our motivation is quite high."

"The possibility of impending death does tend to focus one's attention, Highness."

The Princess laughed. She really liked the blunt spoken Castellan but held few illusions. A Queen had many subjects but precious few friends. If one of her sisters ascended the throne all hands would turn against her. Driven by duty and pheromones, even her trusted friend would help hunt her down and kill her; that was a princess's lot in life—rule or die.

106

Dawn was breaking and the skies were clear save for a few fluffy clouds. A low rumbling echoed across the plane like distant thunder but, unlike any thunder Timushi had ever heard, this thunder did not fade. It grew louder.

"What is that sound?" asked one of the passing servants, looking up at the sky from beneath her burden of cooking pots and utensils.

"Nothing to be concerned about," the Castellan snapped. "Keep moving, quickly now."

The servant shifted her bundle and trudged on while murmurs spread through the column. Even the stoic warriors looked about and fidgeted nervously. Above the city a winged object appeared, flying through the air faster than any dragonfly.

"Your Highness, I think we are about to witness the fate that befell your royal sister," the Castellan commented flatly. As the head warrior spoke a second, and then a third flying object came into view, circling the city like flies around a dung heap.

One of the winged objects dipped toward the palace towers and spat out a much smaller object. Trailing smoke like a fire-arrow, the object's flight ended at the tower of the redoubt, the highest point in the castle. A few seconds later gouts of flame burst from the palace windows and bits of masonry exploded into the air.

"What evil sorcery is this?" the Castellan hissed, hand moving reflexively to the pommel of her long sword. The two other flying objects also made passes at the castle, resulting in more explosions and spreading fire. Loud reports were added to the constant roaring of the flying attackers.

"I expect that those are the dragons that destroyed Princess Shōshi's fortress, my Lord Castellan," Timushi replied evenly. "It would seem that the stories about Reishi consorting with daemons are true."

"Indeed, Highness. If you had not possessed the presence of mind to order the evacuation of the palace we would all be dead right now."

"Flattery does not become you, my Lord."

"It is not flattery if it is the truth, my Princess."

Timushi dipped her antennae in acquiescence. "As I said, tradition can kill you."

"Obviously, a castle is no defense against such foes," the warrior observed. "We all live and learn."

"Or we don't live long. I fear flying dragons will not be the only deadly peril on our journey to the capitol. We must hurry, there is no time to waste."

"Yes, Your Highness," the Castellan agreed, turning to the members of the entourage halted before them. "Enough gawking! Move along, back under cover of the forest, lest the dragons come after us!"

Solider and servant alike scurried over the rise and down the far side of the ridge, seeking the psychological safety of the forest canopy. Princess Timushi glanced back at her former home one last time before continuing down the slope herself. Behind the marching column the castle burned, sending pillars of black smoke high into the clear morning sky.

Chapter 11

Princess Reishi's Party

Official notification of the Queen's death finally arrived at Reishi's palace setting off a chain of events that culminated in the departure of the Princess's entourage for the capital. This column was not nearly as well organized as Princess Timushi's expedition. It seemed that Reishi was taking her entire palace staff with her; servants and drudges struggled along carrying all manner of useless brick-a-brac.

The Princess's personal retinue consisted of her castle guard and assorted hangers on. Her closest advisers jostled each other, competing for proximity to the royal personage, though they were careful not to collide with the dark figures closest to the Princess. Two creatures clad in hooded robes that flowed to the ground in a vain attempt to disguise the decidedly non-insect shapes within. "Daemons" the natives said to each other, never above a whisper, and never within earshot of the Princess or her sinister escorts.

"I must counsel we move with all possible haste, Your Highness," said the shuffling figure on the Princess's right. Its voice was harsh and mechanical, as if not of this world.

"We are progressing quite well, Commander, considering. Besides, I thought your flying mechanical dragons took care of my two royal sisters."

"The nearer target was most certainly destroyed before any could evacuate the strike zone. The strike against the more distant target, however, may have come too late. Observers on the ground report activity beyond the west wall of the city that may have been Princess Timushi escaping."

Reishi chittered in agitation.

"I would not put it past my elder sister to have set out for the capital early, she was always a schemer, bending the rules to suit herself. She was Mother's favorite when we were pupae."

"Nonetheless, Princess, we need to proceed with urgency if we are to reach the Capitol within a fortnight. I have soldiers scouting ahead; they will ensure we encounter no surprises on the way."

"Very good, Commander. I will instruct my people to pick up the pace. We certainly don't want dear Timushi beating us to the throne."

"No Highness," the Fakkaa officer replied, "I have scouts out looking for your sister's party. If they escaped the attack on her palace and are on the road to the capitol, I will see to it that they encounter an ambush that will delay them at the very least."

"It would be best to kill her outright. She is dangerous my royal sister. She may surprise even you Commander, your sorcerer's tricks not withstanding."

"Trust me, Highness. If she escaped the aerial attack she will not escape an ambush by my soldiers" *Any more than your primitive warriors could resist my commandos, you supercilious royal twit.*

The Fakkaa vanguard force had arrived on the planet nearly a year before, the first of their kind to cross the void between the local stars. The first of their kind to venture into space for any purpose. They were a pitifully small force with which to take a planet. Even smaller than initially planned since one of the spaceships crashed on landing, killing all on board. Half of the rotorcraft and twelve commandos perished even before reaching their objective. A total of thirty six highly trained commandos, a trio of attack aircraft and a single transport with its support personnel survived.

The Commander bit off the words he longed to say, knowing that eventually, when they no longer needed the insects, he would crush Reishi's head between his own two digging paws. That pleasant thought soothed him as the column continued to plod on towards the capital, nearly two weeks journey away.

Princess Timushi's Party

The column made good progress, given their early start. The Castellan called a halt as the day's light faded into dusk. The Majordomo bustled about, giving instructions to those setting up the royal camp, ordering only cold rations be distributed. No cooking fires or torches were permitted, just in case hostile eyes sought them out.

"How was the day's progress, my Lord Castellan?" Timushi asked, settling her abdomen onto a camp stool.

"We have done well, Highness. At this pace we will be in the capital in nine days, ten at the most. We only lost three stragglers: two wandered off the trail and fell into a honey pitcher, and one was devoured by a thousand-legs."

"You sent others to gather what they carried?"

"Yes, my Princess, though there was little left—the two who fell into the carnivorous plant took their load of kitchen utensils and supplies with them to their doom. I sent some of the guard to clean up the mess from the third. If nothing else, this should impress upon the other servants the importance of keeping up with the column."

As the Castellan paused a rustling was heard from the nearby woods. The Princess's guards, all warrior bred, formed a defensive perimeter, tilting their massive, boxy heads from side to side in an attempt to site a foe.

The underbrush parted in an explosion of green as a wolf spider nearly three meters across pounced on one of the guards. Knocking aside the hapless warrior's spear, the eight legged predator sank its venomous fangs into her head. The guard's legs buckled and she sank to her knees.

The other guards reacted instantly, rushing the monster spider, skewering it with their spears. The predator tried to back into the underbrush from which it had appeared, but was reluctant to release its prey. Its unwillingness to part with a meal was the spider's undoing, as more warriors joined the fray.

At the first sign of danger the Castellan moved between the Princess and the tree-line, her sword appearing in her right hand as if by magic. Even the common workers crowded around, protecting their Princess with their bodies. This was done not out of love but in response to pheromones Timushi's body released when threatened— fealty was drug induced among the workers. The precautions proved unnecessary as the spider sank to the ground, limbs twitching in its final death throes.

"That was closer than I would have liked, Your Highness."

"Only a tragedy for the one guard, Castellan," the Princess replied evenly. "Your warriors reacted well, quickly dispatching the wolf."

"This will not be the last test of their skills, I fear. In a way good training for what might happen when we reach the capital."

"Warriors are bred to fight, and live only for combat. They are fulfilling their destinies on this trek." *As hopefully I shall fulfill mine*, she added silently.

Orbital Approach, Peggy Sue

Alpha Phoenicis B glowered through the ship's transparent nose, its relatively small size overcome by proximity. As the Earth ship maneuvered for orbit above the companion star's only sizable satellite, the bridge crew kept watch for any sign of danger, though they had detected no indication of technological life on the rocky planet below. Neither had anymore enigmatic neutrino bursts been received from who ever or what ever had sent the original message.

"We are scanning the planet's surface with multispectral instruments, Captain," reported Mizuki from her station. "There are no signs of advanced technology—no radio transmissions, no industrial pollutants in the atmosphere, and certainly nothing indicating an active T'aafhal artifact."

"Unless the Peggy Sue was havin' a computer hallucination there's something down there, Doctor. Keep scanning and mapping the surface."

"Hai. There does appear to be some form of primitive civilization, there are several sizable cities and signs of land clearance for agriculture. Otherwise the surface is covered with vegetation mostly in the form of tropical rainforest. Surface temperature averages 26.7 degrees Celsius, high relative humidity, and the surface gravity is roughly 60 percent Earth normal. The atmosphere is mostly nitrogen with about 36 percent oxygen, one percent H_2O, with traces of argon, CO_2 and other gases."

"Sounds like the conditions present on Earth during the Carboniferous Era," said Samir Hosseini, the science section geologist. "Though given the planet's small size I wouldn't expect as much tectonic activity."

"If the evolutionary arc is similar to Earth's those rainforests are probably full of giant insects, amphibians and primitive reptiles," added Will Krenshaw. "It looks like a swampy place, but there doesn't seem to be any large oceans, just scattered lakes and small seas."

"Small planets build oceans quickly but can't sustain their water cycle. In a planet the size of Earth or larger, plate tectonics draws water into the mantle and volcanoes return it to the atmosphere. In smaller objects the planet's water eventually becomes trapped in the mantle."

"That may be, Dr. Hosseini," added Mizuki, "but distance from the local star also makes a difference. Look at Earth and Venus."

"Regardless, we are not goin' to the surface unless we can locate this hypothetical artifact."

"No desire to parley with the natives, Captain?" asked the First Officer.

"For what? More carved sticks and woven baskets? I'm beginning to think this trading thing won't work unless we find races as advanced as we are."

"Now you're being cynical, Captain," said Bobby. "You never know when we'll stumble upon a treasure. Hitch and Jacobs found an alien outhouse filled with gemstones."

"That's been about the only worthwhile stuff we've found and that was at the start of the voyage. I think I'd rather find some nice advanced ruins to rummage through, pardner."

"So instead of merchants we are going to be archaeologist?" asked Beth, a bit sarcastically.

"Xenoarchaeologists, Number One."

"You mean like Indian Jones?" asked Nigel.

"More like Tomb Raider," added Bobby.

"I'll issue trowels," said Beth

Mizuki shook her head, waiting for the banter to finish.

"The thick atmosphere and dense vegetation are masking any low level radiation that might indicate a power source," she said. "I think that, eventually, we will need to get closer to the surface to detect the T'aafhal installation—assuming it exists."

"You mean lower our orbit?" asked Bobby.

"No, I mean take a small shuttle, loaded with sensitive detectors, and fly a search pattern over the most likely areas at a couple hundred meters."

"Really, Mizuki?"

"Hai, Captain. I extended the signal vector back to the planet and localized where the neutrino beam originated to one of two areas on opposite sides of the planet."

"Two areas?" asked Beth, raising an eyebrow.

"Yes, a neutrino beam can pass right through a planet so the signal could have come from either point where the vector intersected the planet's surface—one on the facing side, one on the back."

"So how did we detect the signal if it can pass through thousands of kilometers of solid matter?"

"We do not understand how to send messages ourselves or how they are received, just that the M'tak Ka'fek sent such a message at the end of the battle off Sirius. Evidently, there are some peculiar molecular level circuits inside the ship's computer that can detect such messages."

"Ya know, I really dislike using technology we don't understand," said Billy Ray, "it makes me feel like a monkey flying a rocket ship."

At the weapon control console Umky snorted. Heads turned.

"Hey, I didn't say it," he said with a bearish grin.

Chapter 12

Small Shuttle, Peggy Sue

"Pass me the *schraubenschlüssel, bitte*," said Kate, her legs protruding from under the large device setting in the middle of the shuttle's passenger cabin.

"The what?" asked Nigel.

"The—how do you say it in English—the spanner."

"Right-o," he replied, handing her the adjustable wrench from the toolbox located on the floor next to the contraption she was working on. The two had been sent to install some equipment for Dr. Ogawa, needed for some kind of recon mission to the planet below.

"*Danke,*" the woman replied, grasping the tool without coming out from under the equipment. A steady stream of muted German profanity could be heard coming from the technician.

"Let me know if there is anything I can do to help, won't you Ms. Hamm?"

"Ya, ya," came her muttered reply as she squirmed deeper beneath the mound of boxes, wires and dials. After a few more grunting sounds she exclaimed, "*Endlich ist es soweit!*"

"Is that that good or bad?" the puzzled Lieutenant asked.

"It is good, I have finished securing the equipment to the deck. Take this." Her hand held out the wrench. Nigel retrieved the tool and put it back in the toolbox. He then watched with interest as Kate wriggled her way back out from under the equipment.

I can see what Frank is on about, he mused. *Even in those shapeless coveralls Ms. Hamm's femininity is not in question.*

Clearing the equipment she looked up at him. After a second's pause he offered her a hand up off the deck.

"So, are we squared away for the mission?"

"Yes, the detection device is fastened to the deck, all we have to do is connect power to it and run the self check and alignment sequence."

"And precisely what does this device do?"

"It is a detector to help locate the T'aafhal artifact. What it detects I have no idea, you must ask *Doktor* Ogawa."

"Well I'm familiar with electronics, spintronics, and gravitonics and I can't suss out how it works," the Englishman said.

"Perhaps it is a machine that goes 'ping!'," Katrina said gravely.

"What? Oh, I get it, Monty Python, jolly good." The young officer smiled. *Who said Germans don't have a sense of humor?*

"When do you think we will depart, Lieutenant?"

"Are you anxious to be underway?"

"It is just that things get so boring when we are in space. The last interesting break was on the ice moon."

"Well it could be any time now. Just as soon as Dr. Ogawa wears the Captain down, probably another hour or two." Nigel smiled. *Frank old boy, evidently you are not keeping your bird as entertained as you think you are.*

Captain's Sea Cabin

"It is as I suspected, Captain. The shipboard sensors cannot isolate any trace radiation from the T'aafhal transmitter or its power source."

"Yer just not gonna be satisfied until you get to go flyin' around down below are you?" Billy Ray said with feigned exasperation.

"Most of the crew would gladly skip their rum ration to get off the ship for a few hours, Dear." In the privacy of her husband's office Beth relaxed her normally formal demeanor. Particularly when only the four partners were present. Billy Ray shook his head and gave in to the inevitable.

"So how big a crew will you need for this little excursion?"

Mizuki hid a half smile of triumph by bowing.

"I will need a pilot and a technician to help with the sensor equipment. The needed equipment has already been installed on the small crew shuttle."

Beth cleared her throat.

"Might I suggest Ms. Hamm as the technician and Mr. Lewis as pilot?"

"I thought that I could pilot the shuttle," said Bobby, speaking for the first time.

"I don't really want half the ship's senior officers runnin' off on a recon mission, Bobby. Don't you trust young Nigel?"

"No, Nigel is a fine pilot," Bobby muttered, looking down at the table. Mizuki took his hand.

"We will be fine, Bobby. We are not even going to land on the surface, even if we find something."

Bobby smiled at his significant other, a smile of acceptance not of happiness.

"Besides," Mizuki continued, "who else could watch the *aoi chō* while I'm gone?" Mizuki's blue butterflies became very agitated without her and though they had never harmed one of the crew they could be deadly. Only Bobby could really control them in her absence.

Mizuki turned again to the Captain.

"Since we are not going to land on the planet I hope we can forgo the use of suit armor?"

Billy Ray's eyes narrowed. In his experience, sending people out without armor was an invitation to disaster. The only times he had lost personnel they had not been wearing armor.

"You know I don't like sending people out without at least light armored suits."

"The sensor equipment is not designed to be operated by gloved hands. Besides, we will not touch down and the shuttle provides better armor than a suit anyway."

"I'm with Billy Ray on this one, Mizuki-chan. I don't like the idea of you going out unarmed."

"Fine. I'll take my katana, just in case."

"That's not what I mean, and you know it."

117

"Bobby, we'll be fine, really. Captain?"

Billy Ray looked at his friend and then his wife. Finding no objection from Beth, he grudgingly acquiesced.

"OK, no suits." But in the back of his head a little voice said, *I got a bad feeling about this.*

Fakkaa Flagship

"As we suspected, Admiral, there are other forces attempting to interfere with our plans," said the voice of the alien leader. "We have detected another ship in orbit around the target planet, a ship of advanced design and unknown origin."

"A ship more powerful than yours, Wise One?" Raqqee asked. He was already suspicious of the aliens' motives and this latest development fed the fires of his suspicion.

"We think not, but safety is paramount. They have not yet detected our presence, or at least show no signs of such knowledge. A surprise attack will certainly shift the advantage to our side."

"We are going to attack the ship without warning? Are you sure they are hostile?"

There was a pause before the Wise One replied, indicative of thought or perhaps irritation.

"Yes, the radiation profile of its drives are in our database. It is a type of ship used only by a race called the Taafhal—evil creatures that have ravaged this part of the Galaxy for millions of years. We have often fought against them but have been unable to eradicate them completely."

"As you say, Wise One."

"I would like you to form your ships into an attack formation and adjust your course vector to the one I just sent your computer. We have reason to believe that they will be unable to detect your ships until you are almost upon them. At my signal I want you to attack with missiles."

"If this ship is that advanced will our missiles hurt it?"

"Probably not, but I will also launch an attack with more powerful weapons that should destroy the interlopers. Your attack will distract them and improve our combined chance for success. Do you understand, Admiral?"

"As you command, Wise One," Raqqee replied, thinking, *If these new aliens are not hostile now they surely will be after we attack them without warning.*

Third Deck Shuttle Dock, Peggy Sue

Bobby and Mizuki stood at the foot of the gangway leading into the small crew shuttle. As promised, Mizuki wore her katana strapped across her back, not the traditional way to carry the weapon but more practical than thrust through a sash on her waist within the confines of the ship.

"Promise me you will be safe down there, Mizuki-chan. No impulsive actions—I know how you get when chasing a problem."

"I promise, Bobby. We are just going to fly a search pattern and try to localize where the signal originated. No heroics, no unplanned landings, just find the artifact and return to the ship."

"I'll hold you to that."

"Why are you so worried? We have been apart under more dangerous conditions before."

"I don't know, sweetheart, it isn't rational but I feel uneasy about this whole situation. Maybe it's because things have been so uneventful for so long—it's like we are overdue for something bad happening."

He took her hands in his and looked into her eyes.

"I'm probably being silly, but remember that I love you."

"And I love you, Bobby. Now let me go, the sooner we leave the sooner we will return."

"OK." Bobby smiled and left go of her hands. Mizuki returned his smile, turned and ascended the airstair into the shuttle. As the airstair retracted, Bobby whispered, "Godspeed, my love."

He stepped out of the airlock, closing the door and cycling the lock. A hollow thump, almost unheard, signaled the shuttle's undocking. Taking a deep breath, Bobby headed back to the bridge, repeating to himself something Peggy Sue's first captain used to say: *never take the counsel of your fears.*

Chapter 13

Small Shuttle One

The night side of the planet passed beneath the small shuttle as it sped toward the day-night terminator. The shuttle cabin was in full transparency mode, the walls, overhead, and even parts of the deck showing the view outside the ship. The planet below was dark but not inky black, being illuminated by the orange giant companion star. The limb of the planet displayed a red diadem created by the M type it circled.

"This is quite something," commented Kate, seated in the copilot's seat next to Nigel. Mizuki had suggested she take the seat forward to witness atmospheric entry at its most spectacular.

"Just wait," answered Nigel, his hands on the seat arm controls, eyes scanning the glowing displays that seemed to float in space before them. "When we hit the atmosphere it will be like diving into a fiery furnace."

"Could we burn up like space junk falling out of orbit back on Earth?"

"No, the repulsor shields keep the plasma cocoon from making actual contact with the hull. Safe as houses, really."

In the rear of the passenger compartment Mizuki was alone with her thoughts. She kept trying to run through the search pattern in her mind but her thoughts returned to Bobby and his sense of foreboding regarding the survey mission. Though she prided herself on being a scientist—governed by logic, not superstition—she could not shake the feeling that something was out of kilter with the universe.

This is ridiculous, she chided herself. *There is no rational reason to think some horrid fate awaits us here. Bobby is often overly emotional, running on hunches and feelings. I guess what they say about opposites attracting is true, we are as different as night and day.*

"Dr. Ogawa," called Nigel from the flight deck, interrupting her moment of introspection. "We are about to enter the planet's atmosphere and will lose contact with the ship for close to thirty minutes."

"Understood, thank you Lieutenant."

On the flight deck, Nigel keyed the comm channel to the Peggy Sue.

"Peggy Sue, Lost Ark One." The call sign was an intentional joke based on the Indiana Jones stories. "Be advised we are about to enter radio blackout on entry to the planetary atmosphere."

"Roger, Lost Ark One. Contact us on the other side. Peggy Sue out."

A faint, cherry red glow began to show around the shuttle as the craft traded velocity for heat and a growing cocoon of plasma. Soon bright threads of light enveloped the plummeting shuttle.

Bridge, Fakkaa Flagship

"The interlopers have launched a smaller craft that is heading to the surface of the planet. Signal your ground commander to intercept that craft, it must not reach the surface of the planet."

"Your pardon, Wise One, but won't that let the aliens know our position?" Admiral Raqqee asked cautiously.

"Yes, of course, but it is of little matter now. Maneuver your fleet to attack the larger ship. This will distract them while I fire upon them with weapons strong enough to destroy their ship."

"Should we fire on the ship? None of our weapons will reach the enemy for the better part of an hour."

"No, just turning toward them and sending the transmission should be enough to get their attention," the alien Commander replied smugly. "My weapons will hit them within seconds, they will never sense them coming."

"By your command, Wise One." The Admiral turned and gave the appropriate orders to his subordinates, thinking: *If the Wise One is wrong this will be a cold, lonely place for us all to die.*

Bridge, Peggy Sue

"Captain, we have lost comm with the shuttle until it has finished entry."

"Thank you, Number One."

Beneath the starship's transparent nose the shuttle could be seen as a bright streak against the dark planet, a bright arc heading toward the daylight side of the globe. Being at a lower altitude than its mother ship, the shuttle was traveling faster in terms of angular velocity than the Peggy Sue. Eventually it would slow to subsonic velocity and the larger ship would overtake the survey mission.

"Captain, I have some anomalous readings on the sensor array from spaceward," rumbled Umky.

"Anomalous? How so, Mr. Umky?"

"It seems to be a cluster of ten or more objects approaching from deep space. Range one hundred thousand klicks and closing."

"Asteroids perhaps?"

"Sir, they are changing course and slowing down—in formation."

"Sound General Quarters, raise the shields," the Captain snapped. "Why didn't we detect them sooner?"

The klaxon rasped out its angry call to action stations as those already on the bridge sat bolt upright.

"Sir, they are not putting out much in the way of identifiable radiation. They certainly are not using gravitonic drives. If anything I'd say they are rather primitive spacecraft."

"How long have they been out there?"

Moving to Mizuki's empty console, Beth replied, "based on their current deceleration rate they may have been out there for weeks."

"Where did they come from?" asked Bobby from the helm. "I can't believe they are from this planet."

"Running some probable trajectories, I would say they came from the planet orbiting the primary star," Beth said. "Remember there were signs of a technological civilization on that world."

"Nothing capable of launching a fleet of ships, not this far, not without outside help," the Captain said. "I'd bet on that."

"That could mean interference from the Dark Lords."

"Or one of their client races, Number One."

"Incoming!" Umky shouted.

"From the bogies?"

"No Sir, different vector..."

The transparent panels surrounding the bridge went gray as the space surrounding the ship exploded with star white brilliance.

"We just lost the starboard side shields!" Beth reported with some urgency in her normally placid voice.

"Another shot like that and we're vapor! Bobby, all ahead flank! Get the planet between us and whatever hit us."

"Aye, aye," Bobby acknowledged as the ship jumped forward at eighty Gs acceleration. At the same time the Peggy Sue performed a corkscrew maneuver that put the port side screens toward the attackers.

"Instruments indicate another series of explosions, probably antimatter."

"Why aren't we detecting the incoming projectiles?"

"Captain, the readings are seal shit crazy—the incoming objects are barely registering and when they do the computer says they are moving at close to three time the speed of light!"

"But that's impossible—at least not in normal 3-space."

A shudder was felt through the deck, indicating that the inertial dampeners were close to being overloaded. If the deck gravity compensation failed the crew would be turned into a thin goo coating the interior spaces.

"Portside shields down to 30%," Beth reported in her precises English accent. In times of stress her accent grew more pronounced, while Billy Ray's cowboy twang disappeared.

"Fire control, lay down a cloud of railgun projectiles between us and those whatever-they-are we keep getting hit by."

"Aye, aye, Sir!"

"And toss a couple gravitonic torpedoes at that enemy formation. They might not be the ones doin' the damage but we can at least see them."

"Yes, Sir!" said Umky with a grin that was not at all friendly.

Jinking to throw off enemy targeting Bobby took the ship closer to the planet, following the curvature of the globe until out of the line of fire. Directly behind the accelerating ship another titanic explosion blossomed.

Bridge, Fakkaa Flagship

"By the gods of the seven hells! Did you see those explosions?" asked one of the bridge crew. "How could anything survive that barrage?"

"Keep your claws on your controls, Lieutenant!" snapped Captain Tikkoo. "Admiral! We have incoming from the enemy ship, projectiles accelerating at several hundred gravities. It must have gotten off a few rounds of its own before it was destroyed."

"Order the rest of the fleet to undertake evasive maneuvers. Break formation and scatter." The Admiral's digging claws sank deep into the armrests of his command chair. At all stations restraining belts contracted, holding the crew in place as plasma driven maneuvering thrusters fired for all they were worth.

In the end the thrusters proved to be worth little at all. The two largest troop transports were at the center of the Fakkaa formation. They had barely begun deviating from the fleet's attack trajectory when a new sun flared where the transports had been.

This was followed immediately by another burst of hellish light from the left side of the formation, as two of the lighter warships vaporized and a third was badly damaged. Admiral Raqqee shook his head hard enough to rattle his quills.

This is not believable! The Wise Ones struck the enemy ship less than three minutes ago and nearly half our fleet gone in a flash of light! The bulk of the commandos are gone!

Forcing himself to remain calm he spoke, "Have the Fleet reassemble. Send launches to pick up any survivors. Remember your duty to your comrades and the homeland!"

The bridge crew, stunned as they were, acknowledged the Admiral's orders and slowly returned to their tasks. Capt. Tikkoo looked up from the command bridge to the Admiral's bridge. For an instant their eyes locked as the two old warriors shared a common thought.

You are right my friend, we are truly out of our depth here. We are sand fleas caught in a battle between Gods. Heaven help us all!

Chapter 14

Bridge, Dark Lord's Ship

The ship commander pulsed arrhythmically, a sign of great agitation. Its subordinates all floated as far out of tentacle range as possible, busying themselves in their assigned tasks.

"Senior Functionary, did we destroy the warm life scum or not?"

"I cannot say with absolute certainly, Most Wise. We scored several direct hits on the enemy's screens and the last round struck just as it was about to be eclipsed by the planet."

"I need verification! That ship is obviously very powerful, capable of ruining our carefully laid plans."

"We are scanning for debris, Most Wise. Even if the ship was vaporized there will be signs emerging from behind the planet—traces of molecules not found drifting in space under normal conditions. Right now the only such signs are coming from the Fakkaa flotilla."

"Oh yes, our useless allies in this endeavor. The enemy ship managed to strike at them even while under attack. No matter, half of them survived, enough to accomplish the mission. It just means fewer to exterminate when I have recovered the artifact."

"Yes, Wise One. Still, our ship was not detected and the warp drive torpedoes managed to strike the enemy without warning."

"Yes, just as I planned. They were obviously unfamiliar with our warp technology, being dependent on gravitonic drives and travel through the alternate dimensions." The Commander's pulsing had resumed its normal rhythm, signaling a calmer state of mind.

"Forgive me, Wise One, but you should probably talk to the Fakkaa Admiral. He has been calling and sounds as though he could use some reassurance that things are still on track..."

Bridge, Peggy Sue

"Helm, engines all stop," ordered Billy Ray. There was no doubt about it, they had just gotten their butts kicked, and the Captain did not like it at all. "Bobby, I want you to plot us a change of course that will take us on a ballistic trajectory above the planet's orbital plane—just a short burst of maximum acceleration and then power off. I want the engines shut down before we clear the planet's shadow."

"On it," the Sailing Master replied, a glint of understanding in his eyes.

"Engineering, Bridge."

"Engineering here, Captain."

"Arin, I want you to take what's left of the deuterium processing plant and jettison it out the cargo hatch."

"Sir?"

"But before you do, get Mendez's body out of the reefer and stick it in the midst of the tubing. Then have the Marines attach a small antimatter charge to the junk on a two minute timer. Just enough to blow things to bits, not enough to vaporize it completely. Understood?"

"Aye, aye, Captain. Understood."

"Let me know when you are ready to jettison the equipment."

Cargo Hold, Peggy Sue

The Chief Engineer ran forward from the engineering spaces, headed to the cargo hold. Passing by the armory he shouted to the Marines stationed there.

"You men, get into your armor. I need you to throw some heavy equipment from the ship."

Not waiting for an answer he moved on to the ship's frozen storage locker. As he paused at the reefer, he realized that he would need the Gunny to come aft from the Marines' normal action station at the port side torpedo launcher.

"Port Torpedo Launcher, Cargo Hold. Come in Gunny."

"Go, Cargo Hold."

"Gunny, could you come aft and bring an antimatter grenade?"

"On my way."

That is one good thing about Marines, Arin thought. *They don't hesitate or ask for explanations when given an order. They might ask what the hell you were thinking after the fact, but they get the job done first.*

Two of the engineering mates hauled Mendez's frozen cadaver out of the walk in freezer and drug it toward the tangle of pipes, filters and other components of the half disassembled deuterium extraction refinery.

"Lower the gravity in the hold, that will make it easier to throw the equipment overboard."

"Aye, Chief," replied an engineer, scrambling to obey. The two carrying the body wedged it in among the pipes and duct work. Marines started arriving from both fore and aft.

"If you don't mind me asking, Chief," said the Gunny, trotting up carrying a grapefruit sized metal sphere, "what do you intend on doing with an antimatter grenade inside the cargo hold?"

"Not inside, Gunny. The Captain wants this pile of equipment, along with the dead rapist's body, thrown overboard and blown to hell and gone."

"Always something exciting going on around here," she quipped, tossing the grenade to the engineer. "Try not to set it off early."

"Ja, that would ruin everyone's day."

Arin secured the grenade to the tangle of equipment with some all purpose spray on goop. He set the timer but did not start it. Then he turned to the Jumbo twins, who were just clumping up in their heavy armor.

"You two, grab either side of this pile of equipment and, when I tell you, throw it out through the starboard cargo door."

"Aye, aye, Sir!" came the response over the suits' speakers. On suit-to-suit Hezekiah said, "You think we can move this pile of junk by ourselves?"

His brother replied in kind, "Sure, they got the gravity turned down and that mess can't mass more than four or five tonnes."

As the hulking armored Marines moved into position, Arin checked the antimatter grenade one last time and called the bridge.

Bridge, Peggy Sue

"Damage reports coming in, Captain," said the First Officer. "We seem to have gotten off with no casualties among the crew and minimal structural damage to the ship. The shields, however will need repair."

"Fortunately we took that last shot on the stern. Reinforcing the rear shields was one of the things I insisted on last time we were in space dock."

"We do seem to spend a great deal of time running from things."

"Funny, Number One. Tell all sections to rig for zero G. When we emerge from behind the planet I want everything shut down, including the deck gravity. And I want the shields, such as they are, in stealth mode, deflecting any EM that might come from a search radar."

"If we point the stern in the direction of the alien fleet we should be able to mask ourselves fairly effectively." Beth paused for a second before full comprehesion of the Captain's plan struck her. "You intend on playing dead, no, invisible, and drifting away from the planet so we can effect repairs."

Her husband grinned as the comm squawked.

"Bridge, Cargo Hold."

"Go, Cargo Hold."

"Captain we are ready to jettison the equipment as ordered."

"Good. Wait one." The Captain turned to Bobby, seated at the helm. "Ready to make our escape?"

"Course laid in, Captain," he replied, his hands resting lightly on the controls that would send the ship accelerating madly in a new direction.

"Mr. Baldursson, eject the debris."

"Jetsam away, Captain."

"Mr. Danner, put us on our new trajectory."

"Aye, aye, Captain." Bobby initiated the maneuver.

Cargo Hold, Peggy Sue

"And what do you suppose that was all about?" asked one of the junior engineers, staring at the empty space that used to contain the deuterium refinery. The whole exercise seemed rather anticlimactic—they threw out the explosive laden pile of junk and nothing else seemed to happen.

"I think the Captain has got a trick up his sleeve," replied the Chief Engineer.

"It's the Romulan trick from the old Star Trek series," said Jumbo Two.

"Yeah, from 'Balance of Terror' where the Romulan captain dumps his friend's body with a bunch of other junk to trick Kirk into thinking he destroyed the bird of prey," added Jumbo One.

"Wasn't that whole scenario copied from some old war movie?" asked one of the engineers.

"'The Enemy Below', with Robert Mitchum and Curt Jurgens," said another. "Even some of the dialog was repeated."

"Not exactly," said the Gunny. "The trick with the dead body was from 'Run Silent, Run Deep', another movie about submarine warfare."

"Well, wherever he got the idea I hope it works," said Arin, as the zero gravity alarm began to sound. "Because we have a lot of repair work to do on the shields before the Peggy Sue can fight again."

Bridge, Dark Lord's Ship

"Commander! We have detected debris emerging from behind the planet," exclaimed the Senior Functionary.

"What vector?" demanded the Commander.

"It is on a course consistent with the last observed movements of the warm life vessel, Wise One. Sensors show that there are metallic fragments and complex molecules embedded in an expanding cloud of cooling plasma."

"But is it from the ship?"

"The debris matches the hull composition of some T'aafhal ships and there are also organic molecules present, the type found in warm life infestations. I think the vermin have been destroyed, Most Wise."

"Excellent, now to get this plan back on schedule..."

Chapter 15

Small Shuttle One

As Nigel promised, the display outside the shuttle's hull during atmospheric entry was spectacular. Fiery ribbons of plasma twisted and turned like living creatures in a fervid display that obscured the world outside. The craft had passed into the daylit hemisphere of the planet by the time the light show abated.

"You were right, Lieutenant, the light show is spectacular."

"You don't have to call me 'lieutenant', Ms. Hamm. This isn't the Navy. Call me Nigel, at least when there are no senior officers present."

"OK, Nigel," Kate smiled at him, "and you can call me Kate, all my friends do."

"Jolly good, Kate." Nigel took his eyes off the instruments long enough to give the woman what he hoped was a winning smile. Outside the glow diminished. "I think we are about through with the exciting part of deorbiting."

As both world and sky faded into view a brilliant white light flared behind the shuttle, causing its viewscreens to overload and turn black.

"What the bloody hell was that?" asked Nigel as the cabin darkened, lit only by the glow of the cockpit instruments. Seconds later the shuttle tumbled as a shockwave struck it. Just as Nigel managed to right the craft a second blast shook the shuttle.

"Christ, that one did some real damage. I've got warning lights on both the shields and propulsion systems."

"What is that blinking red light?" asked a terrified Kate.

"Missile warning. The blasts must have been antiaircraft missiles with nuclear warheads of some type."

As Nigel struggled to right the craft Mizuki's voice came from the passenger cabin, "Is this normal, Lieutenant?"

"No Ma'am, we seem to be under attack. Something exploded in the atmosphere near us. Two somethings, both damned big."

Still traveling several times the speed of sound the damaged shuttle descended rapidly toward the surface of the planet. The viewscreens recovered in time to show a wrinkled green carpet racing past—jungle draped across sharp rocky ridges.

"Oh bollocks! Everyone strap in, we are going down!"

Pilot skill managed to slow the shuttle to subsonic speed and stay out of a flat spin before the planet rose up and hit them. The shields and deck gravity held as the shuttle grazed the top of a verdant plateau. Leaves, vines, and branches were shredded by its passage, flying past the cabin viewscreens in a green maelstrom. Then they were in clear air again, but only for a moment.

Twice more they bounced. Careening off the rugged terrain slowed the speeding shuttle but it was still moving far too fast. Barely clearing the next ridge, they descended into the following ravine. Nigel looked out the windscreen and felt the bottom drop out of his stomach. Rising up out of the jungle was a dark wall of stone.

"Sorry love, we're going in!" he shouted.

There was tremendous noise as the shuttle plowed headlong into the rock face. Deck gravity took most of the deceleration but failed in the end as the nose of the shuttle crumpled. Failure was accompanied by a crushing blow, followed by darkness and then nothing at all.

HQ, Fakkaa Expeditionary Force

"Commander, we have just received word from the interceptor flight. They say the alien was hit by two missiles and crashed into the jungle."

"Thank you, Lieutenant." The Commander had been annoyed when the approaching fleet finally broke communications silence to inform him that he needed to have his air assets intercept a hostile alien craft that was trying to land. He barely had time to get the attack craft armed with nuclear tip interceptor missiles and into the air before the craft appeared.

It was only dumb luck that they were in a position to fire on the descending craft, which was traveling much faster than his atmospheric aircraft could fly. Even so they only hit the target as it passed by.

"Any sign of survivors?" After the interceptors had been scrambled word came from the fleet that these new aliens had managed to destroy five ships, including ships containing half of the reinforcements and all their air assets.

"There was only time for a single flyby before the flight hit bingo fuel, but they reported that the alien ship struck the ground at high speed and was most certainly destroyed. The flight leader said nothing could have survived that impact."

"Excellent! Report our success to the Fleet Admiral." *Over 200 commandos dead in space! This was at least some small vengeance to soothe the souls of those departed warriors.* The ground force commander tapped his digging claws together in agitation. *I hate to question the wisdom of this operation, but it has been a total cluster fuck from the start.*

"Where is the Princess's traveling circus?"

"They are still a week's march from the capital, Sir."

"Fucking useless insects," he muttered. After marching with the column for several days the Commander had returned to HQ. It was that or he was going to kill the ant Princess before accomplishing the mission. He left a lieutenant and sergeant to herd the ants in the proper direction. "Now that radio silence has been lifted I want constant updates on their progress, Lieutenant."

"Yes, Sir."

Princess Timushi's Party

The kilometers long procession of guards and servants wound its way along the trail, passing in and out of woodlands. They had been marching uphill for days and were now crossing a stretch of highlands where the overhead cover was less dense. On the far horizon two bright flashes appeared in close succession.

"What in heaven's name was that?" demanded Princess Timushi, throwing up her arms to shield her large compound eyes.

"I don't know, my Princess," said the Castellan, who was always near her royal charge. "Perhaps more daemonic sorcery."

"Daemonic or not, at least it did not fall upon us." In truth, since leaving the palace little had befallen the column. The occasional worker was lost to a predator here and there, but that was to be expected. At least they were not assailed by dragons or other monsters.

"Indeed, Princess," the Castellan agreed, making a sign to ward off evil with her left hand. As if reading Timushi's thoughts she commented: "We will soon descend to the river basin, where the increased number of predators will keep the guards busy. We will be lucky to reach the high pastures on the other side with fewer than a dozen casualties."

"The price of command is high, Lord Castellan, and I fear that it will be higher still when we reach the Capital. If my dear sister reaches the palace first the Queen's guard will start to defect to her. We may well be outnumbered."

"I'm more worried about the allies she may bring with her to the fight. Your warriors will acquit themselves with skill and honor against all opponents, but daemons... who can know?"

"Truly these times are rife with strange signs and evil portents, my loyal friend." The Princess nervously stroked the vestigial wings attached to her shoulders. Like the similar wings adorning the males of her species the wings were an evolutionary artifact, serving no purpose except to advertise her virginal status. "If my fate is to fall victim to dark magic, I cannot avoid that. All I know is I must fight for my rightful place on the throne, regardless of whatever evil comes from the stars to interfere with the affairs of mortals."

"Making deals with daemons seems a dangerous thing to me, Highness. Besides, if the stars have sent daemons to aid Reishi they may yet send one to help us."

"Dangerous such a compact might be, but I would not refuse the help of a daemon, should the Gods see fit to send one my way."

Loud booming, like the sound of distant thunder, rolled across the hills, as though the Gods had heard the princess's words and were acknowledging her request.

Bridge, Peggy Sue

The bridge crew sat in silence, as though talking or making any sound could give them away to their enemy. The ship was adrift, the engines powered down. Even the deck gravity was turned off, in case their still unseen foe could detect those gravitonic devices in action. The officers and ratings floated in zero G, restrained by belts seldom used on a craft that could barely function without artificial gravity and inertial dampeners—the Peggy Sue was effectively dead in space.

"We are approaching a million kilometers from the planet, Captain," reported Bobby from the helm. "If they were going to detect us they should have done so by now."

"Yer probably right, Mr. Danner." The return of Billy Ray's cowboy twang indicated that he was feeling more relieved than he was willing to show the crew. "Mr. Umky, any sign of our invisible nemesis?"

"Not even the faintest scent, Captain."

"Now that we appear to have made good our escape, how do you propose we deal with the situation, Captain."

"First we have to get our ship put back together, Number One. Officers and chiefs in my sea cabin in five minutes."

* * * * *

The ship's officers, Chief Zackly, and Gunny Acuna all crowded into the Captain's cabin off the bridge. Present over a comm link from engineering was Chief Engineer Baldursson, as was the ship's omnipresent computer. Notable by her absence was the ship's science officer, Dr. Ogawa.

"Ladies and gentlemen, our first order of business is getting the Peggy Sue back into fighting condition. Arin what's the status of all critical systems?"

"The worst damage was done to the shield generators, Captain. On the starboard side most of the gravitonic circuitry was damaged when the shields overloaded. The other shield generators were also stressed and should be checked and rebuilt where necessary."

"What caused the overload?" asked Bobby.

"From the sensor recordings and the impact on the shield hardware I can only guess that it was caused by several near hits by sizable antimatter warheads."

"But how did they deliver them? And how do we fight back?" asked the Gunny. The Marines disliked being sucker punched by invisible aliens even more than the officers.

"We'll get to that next, Gunny, but first I need your estimated time to repair, Arin. How long until we can fight again?"

"I would say four or five days, a week at the outside, Captain. We are probably going to need to regrow all the shield circuitry on the starboard side and much of it elsewhere. Thankfully, the structural damage was light and can be re-knitted by the hull nanites in less than 24 hours. As far as I can tell, the reactors and drives came through with no damage."

"At least there is some good new there, thanks Arin. Dr. White, what about the crew, any casualties?"

"None during the attack, though we did have one crewmember sprain an ankle when some of the large plants shifted in the hydroponics section."

"Yeah, Tosh secured the galley and went up to 3rd deck to help with the... plants," added Chief Zackly. "They didn't quite get things squared away before we went to zero G, and somehow a dwarf fruit tree landed on our cook."

"Chef Dread will be fine," Betty concluded, "that boy does love his plants."

"OK, we can be thankful for that as well. Let's turn to our foe, do we have any analysis of who or what hit us?"

"You mean other than we were caught with our knickers around our ankles?" Beth raised a single eyebrow.

"Yeah, we almost screwed the pooch, but we didn't. We did manage to get in a few licks of our own." The Gunny was feeling a bit defensive about the torpedo crews' performance.

"Yes, Gunny, the torpedo crews reacted well," Billy Ray said, soothing ruffled feathers. "Sensor readings indicated we took out four or five ships in the alien formation."

"Yes, sorry," added Beth, "the crew's performance was exemplary once we knew we were under attack."

Both Chief Zackly and the Gunny looked mollified with the officers' response. They were not used to coming off second best in an engagement and the outcome of the ambush was weighing heavily on both of them.

"Whatever it was that hit us, it wasn't those primitive tubs. There was something else out there, using the formation of slow ships as a decoy. How can we fight something we can't see?" the Chief growled.

"Not only that, Umky said the sensor readings, slight as they were, indicated objects moving at superluminal speeds," added Beth.

"But not in alter-space, the T'aafhal sensors should have picked up objects moving in alter-space."

"No, Captain, the tracking computer clearly indicated that the objects were moving faster than light in 3-space."

"How is that even possible?"

"Captain?" the ship's computer said. "I have information that might shed some light on the situation."

"Please enlighten us, Peggy Sue."

"As usual, observing events has triggered retrieval of data I was previously unaware of. It seems that there are entries in our database regarding an alternative way of superluminal travel."

"Other than alter-space transit?" Bobby said, looking for clarification.

"Correct, Sailing Master Danner. There is a way to create a Lorentzian manifold, a region of flat space known as a warp bubble. By warping space—compressing the space in front of and stretching out the space behind the bubble—it can move through 3-space. In the context of general relativity, this allows a warp bubble to appear in previously flat spacetime and travel at effectively superluminal speed. Inhabitants of the bubble feel no inertial effects and relativistic effects, such as time dilation, do not apply."

"You're saying these unknown hostiles have a warp drive?"

"That is correct."

"Cool!" In spite of himself, Bobby was still a science fiction geek to the core and finding out that warp drives were real impressed the hell out of him.

"Why didn't we know about this before?" asked the Captain, exasperation in his voice.

"As I explained, though I have access to the T'aafhal database from the artifact found on Earth and enhanced by the M'tak Ka'fek's AI, useful information often remains dormant until events trigger recognition."

"OK, fine. What else can you tell us about this warp drive thing —like how we can track it."

"A space warping drive is not very efficient and requires a quantity of what human physicists call dark matter to create the necessary spatial gradients. Our existing sensors will not detect a ship using warp propulsion, but the warping of space does cause disturbance, gravitational ripples. Though in 3-space such gravity waves cannot exceed the speed of light either, so no warning is possible if the ship is coming at us head on—the ripples would not be detected until after the ship passed by."

"Like a jet flying faster than sound, it can fly past with the boom arriving after it has gone by."

"An apt analogy, First officer."

"So yer saying we can never see these jokers coming?"

"Not in 3-space, Captain. However, the movement of a warped bubble of 3-space does cause ripples in some of the alternate dimensions where the distance metrics are different. I have found information that describes a form of subspace interferometer that should be able to detect a working warp drive."

"That's good news Peggy Sue, pass the info to the engineers and let 'em get started."

"It will require extensive modifications to the shields and deck gravity circuitry to detect the subspace gravitonic resonances but construction should take only a week and can be combined with the current repair work."

The Captain smiled for the first time since the attack. "One last question, Peggy Sue, can we destroy something traveling in one of these warp bubbles?"

"Yes, the space in front of such a bubble is merely compressed, once targeted the ship's X-ray lasers will be able to detonate the enemy torpedoes well away from the hull."

"I'm more concerned with blowin' the bastards' ship out of existence."

"The superluminal particle cannon should prove quite sufficient for such a task. I will interface the new sensors to the main fire control system."

"OK, do it. Unless there are any other questions you're all dismissed. Bobby, could you stay a minute, please."

The others rose and quickly exited the cabin, anxious to get on with the needed repairs. The door slid shut, leaving Bobby and Billy Ray alone for the first time since before the enemy engagement began.

"How're you holding up, pardner?"

Bobby looked his friend directly in the eye.

"I'm OK, been too busy to think about it."

"We're going to get her back."

"Yeah, but first we've got to repair the ship and neutralize the alien threat. I understand, Billy Ray, I've had a ship of my own."

"Sure thing, Bobby. I just wanted to make sure you knew we're going after Mizuki and the others. We don't leave our own behind."

Bobby smiled wanly.

"Damn straight, Captain. So let's fix the ship, kill us some aliens, and then go find my girl."

Chapter 16

Shuttle Crash Site

Mizuki's first indication that she was alive was the stabbing pain in her head. Creaking and groaning sounds punctuated the silence, the sounds of cooling metal and tortured airframe members. Even with her eyelids closed the world spun crazily around her. As the spinning slowed she hazarded a peek at her surroundings. Pyrotechnic spots flashed before her eyes as she tried to focus.

As her vision adjusted to the darkness she detected dim light filtering in from above her head. Then she realized that she was laying on her back and the light was coming from the rear of the shuttle—or what was left of the shuttle.

She tried to move and was rewarded with more pain, particularly from her right leg. She was pinned beneath a rack of equipment. Trying to free her legs, Mizuki pushed up on the rack, moving it slightly. Her palms slipped off the top lip, dropping the rack and causing a rush of pain from both legs.

This isn't fair, she thought, on the edge of hysteria. *This is my second set of legs and Betty might not give me a third.*

Again, the world went black.

* * * * *

Pain, like an unwanted but reassuring old friend, signaled the return of consciousness. The stabbing head pain had diminished to a dull throbbing. Gingerly she felt along her sides, down to where a metal cross bar rested across the tops of her thighs. There was no feeling in her legs.

I'm not getting out of this unless I can raise the equipment rack, she thought, distantly pleased that her ability to reason had returned.

Feeling around in the darkness she located several empty equipment boxes and a length of angle iron laying nearby. Carefully working one of the metal boxes under the edge of the fallen equipment rack, Mizuki inserted the angle iron, forming a lever. Pulling down on the end of the makeshift lever raised the rack

143

several centimeters, enough to allow blood to rush back into her legs. She gasped as feeling returned and pain reasserted itself.

Breathing in short, panting breaths while holding on to the lever, Mizuki waited for the pain in her legs to subside. Time passed, the pain became bearable again.

Gathering up her strength, Mizuki pulled her body a few centimeters toward the rear of the cabin while struggling to hold down the handle of her improvised lever. Renewed waves of pain forced her to stop.

More panting breaths, small painful movements in preparation for another move aft, followed by another couple of centimeters progress. Another respite, another small slide aft, rest and repeat. Eventually, her knees were clear of the bar that had pinned her legs. Leaning on the lever, using the weight of her upper body to hold it down, she reached behind her and slid the second equipment box under the edge of the rack.

Gingerly she eased off on the lever, allowing the rack to lower until it rested on the equipment box. Her legs remained unpinned. Removing the angle iron, Mizuki quickly slid the box that had served as the lever's fulcrum under the other side of the heavy rack, securing its new position. The now freed scientist fell back, exhausted.

After an unmeasured number of minutes, Mizuki returned to full consciousness. Wriggling on her back, being careful not to dislodge the supporting boxes, she fully extracted her legs from their former trap. Clear of the rack, she sat up and delicately probed her lower extremities, checking for serious damage.

Ouch! The right knee is badly swollen, but I don't think anything is broken. Not too bad, both will be bruised but the left leg seems undamaged.

Gently massaging life back into her abused legs, Mizuki looked around what was left of the shuttle. The cabin forward was crushed, with no space to even crawl under. In fact, the racks of sensor equipment had probably saved her life, holding up part of the roof.

Nigel and Kate! The realization struck her like a physical blow. There was no way anyone in the front of the shuttle could have survived—she called out their names anyway, receiving no reply.

They're both dead!

Hot tears ran down her cheeks as she squeezed her eyes tightly shut. It was not that they were close to her, but there was something about shared calamity that bonded people together. Then another realization struck her: *I'm alone!*

HQ, Fakkaa Expeditionary Force

"Yes Admiral, I understand the importance of verifying the destruction of the alien lander, but by the time I can get troops to the site it will already be dark," the ground commander opined. "Might I propose we send a squad to the area in the early morning, to arrive at the crash site around sunrise?"

"I'm being pressured by our allies, Commander," came the Admiral's reply. "For some reason they are highly agitated by the presence of these aliens, who ever they are."

"I understand, Sir, but we might not be able to even find the crash site in the dark. The vegetation cover down here is unbelievable." Their home world was cold and arid, with persistent gusting winds. What vegetation there was clung closely to the ground in a forlorn bid for survival. This world's luxuriant jungle vegetation was overwhelming to the Fakkaa.

"All right we'll compromise. Send one of the attack craft to fly recon over the area tonight. If the pilot can spot the wreck fine, otherwise the troop carrier can search in the morning. Either way, I can truthfully tell the 'Wise Ones' that we are actively searching for the crash site."

"Yes, Admiral. I understand." *I understand we are not masters of our own fate in this endeavor.*

In truth, the Commander was not sure that the alien craft had been destroyed. After viewing the attack craft gunsight footage it looked like the aliens were hit by two of the three interceptor missiles launched at them. He would have expected the target to

145

have been blown to bits, or at least knocked out of the sky. Yet the recordings plainly showed that it kept on flying in a more or less controlled descent.

What type of craft can take hits from two nukes and stay in the air? The attack craft pilot's report of the intruder crashing into the jungle and being destroyed seemed a tad premature. The Commander wasn't sure he wanted to meet these aliens, particularly in the deep jungle after dark. *Whatever, ours is not to reason why.*

"Lieutenant! We have orders from on high. Call the aviation unit commander and tell him he needs to lay on a reconnaissance flight over the area we think the alien landing craft crashed in."

"Yes, Sir!"

"And inform second squad they are to go look over the remains in the morning. I want them on site by sunrise."

Captain's Quarters, *Peggy Sue*

After the stress of the ambush and close escape, both Beth and Billy Ray were overdue for some down time. As usual, Beth had grabbed the shower first and was now sitting at the vanity doing those post-bathing things that women find essential and men find mystifying. Billy Ray emerged from the shower draped in a towel, padded bare foot across the carpet and gave her a peck on the cheek.

"I don't know about you, love, but it's good to have the deck gravity back on," she said, "even if it's only a tenth of a G."

"I never did get the hang of sleepin' in zero G, honey bunch, and I definitely need some rack time."

"Too tired even for a little fooling around?" his wife asked with a smile.

"Well, maybe not quite that tired." Billy Ray grinned back. After almost four years together they still were as frisky as a couple of newlyweds. Different officers dealt with the strain of duty in different ways—for Beth and Billy Ray sex was the best treatment for job related stress ever devised.

"How is Bobby dealing with the situation?"

"He's doin' better than I though he would. I guess he has matured a bunch over the years. There was a time something like this would have sent him into an all out panic."

"I would hate to be faced with the same situation. I wouldn't rest until I found you."

"I think that's why Bobby has been working so hard on the repairs, he was wearing himself to a frazzle. I finally had to order him to get some rest."

"Hopefully he'll realize that he will need to be at his best when we confront our attackers."

"Oh I think he'll be ready to take on those bushwhackers. And even more ready to go planetside looking for what happened to the survey crew."

"You think letting him lead the ground search is wise?"

"If our positions were reversed and you were missing, do you think anyone could stop me from headin' up the search party?"

"I should hope not, love. But I worry about the fallout if they didn't make it. It's one thing to confront the possibility, another to face the fact."

"Sweetheart, I know just what type of pain such a loss can cause." A look spread over Billy Ray's face, a look filled with great sadness. "But I also know that people can live through it, and even live to love again."

"Yes, of course you do, how insensitive of me," she apologized, caressing the side of his face with her hand. Billy Ray had lost a previous lover, Peggy Sue, the woman the ship was named after. The pain in her husbands eyes faded quickly, and he wrapped his arms around her.

"No sense borrowin' trouble, honey bunch. Now I think we need to work on easing our own stress a bit, don't you?"

Bobby & Mizuki's Quarters, Peggy Sue

Bobby had worked on shield repair and sensor renovation for sixteen hours straight, until he couldn't focus anymore and the Captain ordered him to get some rack time. It wasn't that the work was so urgent, they had obviously made good their escape and the course he put them on would not arc back down to the planet for almost two weeks. He had stayed at his console to avoid coming back to their cabin, having to face the fact that Mizuki was not there, maybe would never be there again.

They had cohabited for more than a year back on Farside and when they signed on for the current voyage most people on board assumed that they were husband and wife. That was not the case—though not from lack of asking on Bobby's part. Though Bobby had no doubt that Mizuki loved him she simply refused to entertain the idea of marriage. His repeated proposals so agitated her that he eventually gave up, willing to accept her on her own terms. Once he stopped asking for her hand things settled into a state of unwedded bliss. The past year had been a good one—up until now.

Bobby sat on the bed, eyes shut, his clenched fists on his knees. *What will I do if they didn't make it? What if she's dead? No, I won't believe that until I see her body.*

At best they are down there, on the surface of a hostile planet, with no armor or weapons. Just her katana, a Medieval weapon to face God knows what. While he wrestled with his emotions the room filled with fluttering wings, the *aoi chō*—Mizuki's blue butterflies.

The butterflies had adopted Mizuki during the trek across the ring station, when the crew of the M'tak Ka'fek was desperately searching for a supply of antimatter to refuel their ship. Why they chose Mizuki out of all those on that journey remained a mystery, but since they helped the crew escape the station with the needed fuel, Captain Sutton had them brought along. Since then they were Mizuki's pets and protectors—they may look like harmless butterflies but they were, in fact, a form of communal alien intelligence that was quite capable of killing a man or other attacker. Fortunately for Bobby they accepted him as Mizuki's mate and companion.

The butterflies were not their normal sky blue color, but rather darker somber shades of purple and indigo, some almost black.

They gently fluttered down to alight on Bobby's rigid frame. It was as though they sought to comfort him over the loss of the woman they both loved. Bobby opened his eyes and unclenched his fists. Seeing the flock perched all around him, many on him, he smiled.

"Don't worry little guys, if she is alive I will find her and bring her back." Saying it out loud helped bolster his hopes.

The butterflies became more animated, almost as if they understood his words. With a single finger he gently lifted one of the delicate looking creatures, which opened and closed its wings and then took flight. Before him the flock gathered in a fluttering, swirling cloud, their wings beating a complex, syncopated pattern.

In the quiet room a whispered voice could be heard: "We know you will rescue our goddess, we will help you."

Chapter 17

Shuttle Crash Site

After salvaging what she could from the wrecked shuttle, Mizuki managed to exit the craft through the partially deployed rear airstair. Whether Nigel had opened it just prior to the crash or it sprung on impact, had it not opened Mizuki would have been trapped inside. All she managed to salvage from on board was her katana and a basic survival kit. The kit contained an emergency beacon, a knife, a first aid kit, some survival rations, a camouflaged poncho, a water purification straw, and a small computer that could also function as a simple translator.

As dusk approached, she found herself standing outside the almost unrecognizable wreckage of the shuttle with her pitiful clutch of possessions. The wreck was almost covered by fallen rock from the cliff. In a way that was a good thing—the rubble would make the crash site harder to identify from the air. Nigel had said they were under attack, so Mizuki had to assume that she was in hostile territory and that those who shot them down would be looking for any survivors.

Unfortunately, for other reasons the site would be hard to miss, at least in the daylight. The racing shuttle had cut a swath through the dense vegetation that was like a kilometers long arrow pointing straight at the impact point. There was even a notch visible on the crest of the last ridge they had bounced off.

If someone is looking for us I had best be moving, she thought. While she still ached all over, her legs seemed functional; another benefit of having a blood stream filled with T'aafhal medical nanites. She was both stronger and faster than a normal human being, and healed more quickly as well.

Securing the survival kit to her back, along with her sword, she set off into the jungle on a path roughly bisecting the angle between the rock wall and the shuttle's last heading. The red sun was setting and ahead the forest waited, dark and menacing.

151

Princess Timushi's Party

Traveling the winding pathway through the lowlands near the great river, progress was frustratingly slow. Bellowing calls by the reptiles that lurked in the murky waters had everyone's nerves on edge, though the threat of attack by wolf spiders, thousand-legs, and other forest predators was greater. The great lizards did not stray far from the river's banks and the road had been constructed far enough inland to escape their attentions.

"How much farther, Castellan?" Timushi asked for the tenth time that day.

"About as far as the last time you asked, Highness. A day to the river crossing and then another to the grazing fields of the capital. From there only four more days march."

"So half our journey remains ahead of us, how I long to be at its end."

"The true sun is setting and this day is almost behind us, Princess. The day of your arrival will come in the fullness of time. Best to remember that there may be other dangers lurking along the path."

"So you have counseled me before, my Lord. At least we have only lost a handful of servants thus far."

"Normal for such a journey, Highness, the jungle demands its toll of those who would pass through it. I am more worried about the river crossing, it is a natural place to stage an ambush."

"Ambush? How would my sister get a party of soldiers ahead of us on the road? Her retinue must be struggling along the northern road, much as we are here in the south."

"It is not her I am concern about, it is those who assist her. You heard the roar of those dragons in the distance, as they destroyed your palace. If they could strike there surly they could attack the bridge to prevent our crossing, or worse, wait until we are on the bridge and vulnerable."

"How truly wonderful! I am sure to rest easy tonight knowing what may lie in store for us tomorrow."

"Your pardon, Princess, but it is my duty to advise you, even when the advice is not comforting."

"I did not mean to criticize you, my Lord." Timushi's antennae dipped in apology. "I am cranky and out of sorts and in need of a meal. I am sure that tomorrow will see us safely to the north side of the river."

"Your warriors and I shall endeavor to make it so, Your Highness."

Mizuki In The Jungle

Light was fading rapidly, as it does near planetary equators. Mizuki was carefully picking her way through the undergrowth, trying to stay on the thick, corded roots that splayed out in all directions from the sixty meter tall trees. This was proving tricky enough without the failing light. Retrieving a headlamp from the survival kit, she adjusted it to shed only ultraviolet light.

The lens of a human eye ordinarily filters out UV rays, but the photoreceptor cells of the retina are sensitive to near ultraviolet light. People lacking a lens—a condition known as aphakia—can see near ultraviolet light as whitish blue or violet. One of the "enhancements" made by Mizuki's T'aafhal nanites was the ability to see these wavelengths with her lenses intact.

Using the lamp was a risk worth taking, since the alternative was stumbling around in near complete darkness. She reasoned that on a planet lit by a red M type star most creatures vision would not extend into the near ultraviolet frequencies. Moving from one large runner to another she caught movement out of the corner of her eye.

Mizuki pivoted to face the movement, drawing her sword over her head at the same time. Something large and black with too many legs flew directly at her. Years of training had taught Mizuki's body to react almost instinctively, without conscious thought—an ability that saved her life.

Turning the drawing motion into a downward stroke, the katana split the creature's nightmare of a face in two. Despite the power of the two handed blow, the creature still collided with the

153

swordswoman, knocking her off the root and into the detritus on the jungle floor. Drawing her legs up beneath her as she fell, Mizuki rolled onto her back and thrust upward with all of her strength.

On this low gravity world, the musculature of any normal human being would seem brutally strong. Mizuki's enhanced physique combined with years of conditioning resulted in power that was literally out of this world. Her legs thrust the hairy black body five meters through the air where it struck the trunk of a nearby tree.

It hit the tree with a meaty thud. Seeing her attacker clearly for the first time, Mizuki realized that it was a giant spider like creature. As it slid down the trunk, several smaller, multi-armed shapes attacked the now dead monster. The body was torn apart before it reached the ground.

Hearing more movement in the darkness, Mizuki rose on crossed legs, pivoting 180 degrees as she stood. In front of her was another monstrous creature, reaching for her with a pair of meter long claws. She hopped up, out of the way, as the monster's claws snapped shut on empty air.

Nimbly landing back on top of the root placed her above the attacking beast. Rearing up the creature reached out with its claws, but it was only a ruse. The creature struck out with its real weapon, a curved multisegmented tail as long as its two meter body, topped with a wicked looking stinger.

Mizuki took the stinger first, with a diagonal slash to her left. The return stroke to the right sent the creature's left claw flying, the third followup cleaved through part of the scorpion thing's face and separated the right claw at its base. The creature pulled away but was already dying. As it thrashed in the fallen leaves more scuttling arthropods emerged and began devouring the scorpion alive.

I have got to get out of here!

Mizuki looked around in alarm, her only thought to escape this ravenous menagerie. Her sword work had undoubtedly saved her life, but it was as though she had rung the dinner bell for every creepy crawly in the area. Before anything else could try claiming her for diner, Mizuki turned and fled, bounding from one large root to another.

In front of her was a junction formed where two buttress roots joined a gigantic main trunk at nearly a right angle. The result was a vertical inside corner reaching ten meters up the tree. Like a Hollywood ninja scaling a building by bouncing from wall to wall, she ran up the cleft between the massive buttresses until she was well above the feeding frenzy on the forest floor.

Clinging to the tree's wrinkled trunk single handed, Mizuki re-sheathed her weapon. Free to use both hands, she climbed higher up the tree, headed for someplace, any place, safer than the ground. Eventually she came to a spot where several branches split from the main trunk, forming a sheltered fork. Above, branches reached skyward, bifurcating again and again before ending in leafy profusion at the forest canopy. Trying to make herself as small as possible, Mizuki nestled into the fork, back against the main trunk.

My God! Is everything on this planet trying to eat everything else?

Though an astrophysicist, explorer, and traveler to the stars, Mizuki was a city girl through and through. This much nature was more than she ever wanted to see up close. Then she noticed the ichor smeared down the front of her jumpsuit—blood, guts and venom from the creatures who had tried to make a meal of her.

Eww! Gross. How do I get this yucky stuff off of me? It might attract more hungry predators.

Exploring her little bower she found some damp, moss like growth that would have to suffice. Rubbing as much of the gore from her clothes as possible, Mizuki calmed down and her breathing quickly returned to normal—the local air had a lot more oxygen in it than Earth standard. As she settled in for the night she reluctantly switched off the little UV lamp on her forehead.

It's amazing I didn't lose it during the fight, she thought. *No sense wasting the battery, and no more walking around during the night. If this is what the Carboniferous was like back on Earth I'm glad people evolved 300 million years later.*

Just as she was about to drop off into fitful sleep, a rumbling sound echoed across the hills. The sound that the natives thought was the roaring of a dragon was not nearly so mysterious to Mizuki—

she recognized it as the sound of a jet engine, something that was as out-of-place on this primitive world as she was.

HQ, Fakkaa Expeditionary Force

"Commander?" asked the aide, "Sir, the aviation commander says that the flight sent to look for the downed alien aircraft has spotted nothing in the darkness."

"What?"

The Commander was one of those individuals who could transition from a solid sleep to full awake in an instant. This was a good thing for the aide, as the Commander recalled that he left orders to be awakened when the reconnaissance report arrived.

"Fine, tell the command sergeant that second squad needs to be on station at local dawn. And make sure they take heavy weapons, not just rifles."

"Yes, Sir. The squad is awaiting the arrival of the troop transport. They are anxious to see what these aliens look like."

"Fine, let me know when they are in the air so I can report to the Fleet Admiral." The Commander rolled over on his cot and tried to get back to sleep.

I'm not sure if we want to find these new aliens or not. Hell, we have no idea what the mysterious 'Wise Ones' look like and they are supposed to be our allies. There are too damn many moving parts to this operation, and that's a sure invitation to disaster.

Chapter 18

Mizuki in the Jungle

In the thin light of the morning gloaming Mizuki awoke from a restless night's sleep. The cacophony of night sounds faded, replaced by less frequent but more urgent calls from creatures that prowled the daylit hours. As illumination increased Mizuki discovered that the tree she had taken refuge in was almost at the crest of the ridge she originally spotted from the crash site. She stood and gazed toward the impact point.

The last tendrils of morning fog clung like evanescent lace to the tree tops in the valley, preventing identification of the shuttle's wreckage. Shrugging, she turned and looked the other direction, across the valley beyond the ridge. It looked pretty much like the valley she had treked through last night, a carpet of green stretching kilometers to another ridge. A ridge much like the one she was currently on top of.

Face it, one stretch of jungle looks much like any other, Mizuki thought. *But I seem to remember a valley with a river running through it just before we started crashing into things. That's as good a destination as any, I guess.*

Having chosen a goal, it was time to descend from her hide to the forest floor fifty meters below. Moving carefully down the trunk, using the multitude of thick vines for purchase, she was startled when a brightly colored flying creature dove right for her face.

Snatching the squirrel sized creature out of the air with her left hand, Mizuki saw that it was not a rodent but a lizard of some kind. Iridescent blue green skin stretched between four splayed legs, each ending in hooked claws for hanging on to trunk or limb. It could almost have been an Earth creature, except for the mouth. The lizard's mouth was open wide displaying a tripart jaw—one lower and a split upper—lined with needle sharp teeth. The inside of the mouth was colored pink and orange with a yellow tongue, looking strangely like an orchid or other tropical flower.

The quick grab resulted in Mizuki holding the squirming creature by the neck as it futilely tried to bite and scratch her. Its intended trajectory would have landed it, mouth agape, on Mizuki's face. Realizing that the little predator's delusions of grandeur could have caused her to fall, Mizuki angrily crushed its throat and threw the body out of the tree. As the lizard fluttered to the ground something dark and fast jumped out of a clump of leaves, snagged the dead animal in midair, and disappeared back into the foliage with it.

It would appear that daylight is just as dangerous as nighttime around here. I had best get moving.

Descending the tree, keeping a careful lookout for more hungry local fauna, for the second time since entering the rain forest, Mizuki heard a sound that could not be natural. Peering through a gap in the canopy she sited a strange craft several kilometers away, a quad tiltroter with ducted props. It was obviously some kind of troop carrier and it was most likely looking for her.

Rapidly finishing her descent she paused to don the poncho from the survival kit. It was not raining and certainly not cold, but the poncho provided adaptive camouflage, much like the Marines' battle armor. Hopefully it would help hide her from those who hunted her, be they in the troop carrier or lurking in the forest.

2nd Deck, Peggy Sue

Everyone on board was pressed into service, helping to repair and upgrade the Peggy Sue's damaged shields and other systems. In a crawl-way off the port side torpedo launcher Dorri and Zeke were in the process of fixing shield circuitry that had stopped responding. Wielding a cutting torch, Zeke finished carving an access hole in the inner hull to expose the circuitry in question.

"That should do it," observed Dorri, "use the hand grapples to lift the plate clear."

"I'm on it, keep your pants on," the large Marine replied. Since the two had been assigned the repair task Dorri had assumed command, somewhat to Zeke's annoyance. After all, she was only fourteen and he was almost twenty.

"I have no intention of taking my pants off," she replied.

Using a pair of hand grapples to seize the meter by half meter chunk of ceramic metal, Zeke carefully pulled the plate free, sliding it aft and out of the way.

"All right, Commander Dorri, have at it."

Dorri stuck her tongue out at him.

"I'm not sure why Chief Engineer Baldursson trusts you to repair critical gravitonic circuitry, you're only a teenager. Shouldn't you be playing with dolls or something?"

Shooting Zeke a scorching look, Dorri unpacked some test equipment from the pouch on her belt. Over her shoulder hovered a small drone, about the size of a softball—the eyes and ears of the ship's computer.

"I am here fixing the shield circuitry because I am best qualified, whereas you are here to provide muscle."

"No need to be insulting," Zeke sniffed.

"Just because I am the youngest person on board doesn't mean that I'm not good at things. I've been outscoring Shadi and even some of the junior techs on test in gravitonics and other stuff. And you insulted me first."

"Sorry, I didn't mean to. My brother and I are often treated as though we're dummies. I guess working for a kid rubbed me the wrong way."

Dorri sighed.

"I don't think you're a dummy, Zeke. You or your brother. I guess we are both a bit over sensitive."

As she was apologizing she attached a number of probes to the exposed superconductive wiring. Looking at the readouts on the hand-held scope she frowned.

"I think this thing is fried."

"How can you tell, it looks like a jumble of spaghetti to me."

"The test probes show no signal continuity. We are going to have to remove the whole mess and regrow a new control nexus."

"I concur," the ship's computer said, speaking through the drone. "remove the old unit and grow a new one with the nanite template in your kit. Once it is done test for continuity before regrowing power connections."

"Yes, Peggy Sue, I have been briefed on the procedure."

The computer remained silent.

Dorri took out a cutting torch, smaller than the one that Zeke used to cut the access hole, and started severing the leads to the shield nexus. With the precision of a surgeon she quickly isolated the damaged circuitry from the ship's power grid.

"Stay back, I'm going to spray some removal nanites on the dead device. The should pretty much turn the damaged stuff into a layer of gunk stuck to the hull."

"Gunk?"

"Yeah, we can reuse the raw material in the decomposed circuitry to grow its replacement. But you don't want to get any of the removal nanites on you, they can also turn organic material into gunk."

"No problem." Zeke backed away from the opening and slid down the crawl-way next to the piece of covering material. "So why isn't your older sister out here doing this stuff?"

"Like I said, I'm better at this than Shadi. I mean, she's smart about a lot of things, just not tech."

"Like what, for instance?"

"Well, like history, economics, and politics. I'm more interested in making things, or raising animals, or building a new city."

"Sounds like you have big plans. Maybe Shadi would like talking with Mel. He's always been a history buff."

"What about you? What interests you, Zeke?"

"Me? I'm more interested in military things, weapons tech and such. I really like being a Marine."

"But you really haven't fought in any big battles or anything, have you?"

"Not yet, but I have a feeling that there will be plenty of fighting coming up. First to knock out that alien ship that waylaid us, and then going down to the surface of the local planet to look for Dr. Ogawa and the others."

"There is an old saying, be careful what you wish for because you just might get it."

"You say that like it's a bad thing." Zeke grinned and Dorri raised her eyebrows.

"Hey, look. The old nexus has been reduced to raw goop. Now I have to apply the new nanite template to start growing a new one..."

Princess Timushi's Party, Nightfall

The lead elements of the Princess's column had reached the bridge that spanned the river. They had been paralleling the slow moving stream for most of the day. The Castellan called a halt and set the servants to pitching camp for the night.

"Your prediction was correct, my Lord Castellan," said Timushi, observing the controlled chaos swarming around her. "We have, indeed, reached the river crossing before nightfall."

"Not all of us, Highness. There will be stragglers stumbling into camp til an hour past sunset. Those who don't end up providing the local wildlife with dinner."

"I see we are camping well away from the river, a prudent precaution."

"Yes, my Princess, no need tempting the river beasts with an easy meal. Once we have gathered the remaining host we will set out across the bridge in the morning, well fed and well rested."

"Then on to the highlands and the pastures where the queen's herds graze."

"With any luck we will camp in safer territory tomorrow evening."

Mizuki, Ridge Above The River

Pushing herself mercilessly, Mizuki crossed the next ridge and then the one following that. As daylight was waning she ascended another tree, seeking shelter for the night. As she climbed she reflected on her day's journey. In all, not as exciting as the previous evening—she was only accosted by predators twice.

The first time was by another oversized spider, striking from ambush. Mizuki spotted the trapdoor covering the spider's lair move slightly before it pounced, giving ample time to draw her katana and dispatch the meter and a half long beast with a single stroke. As before, small scavengers quickly emerged to harvest the sudden windfall of food. The second attack was more harrowing.

* * * * *

As she hurried through the forest, staying on roots and runners as much as possible, Mizuki detected occasional scuffling sounds in the underbrush. These persisted for more than a half a kilometer. There was no doubt that she was being stalked. Arriving at a break in the forest cover, she decided to confront whatever was hunting her.

Sprinting to the center of the opening she halted with a clear field of action and drew her blade. Seconds passed with agonizing slowness until finally a large black shape burst on her from the right. It was at least ten meters in length, with an elongated, segmented body. From each body segment sprouted a pair legs, giving the creature the appearance of a gigantic centipede. Rising like a serpent the beast struck out with its forcipules—venom claws —thrust toward Mizuki from either side of the creature's flattened head. But she was prepared and in a proper stance.

The katana's blade was a blur as she struck first right, then left, relieving the attacking centipede of its poisonous grapples. The next stroke took off the creature's antennae, causing it to pull back and gather itself for a second strike.

Dodging its second lunge, Mizuki skipped to the left avoiding large, fanged mandibles that snapped shut where she had been standing. The centipede's strike left its body stretched out on the ground before its intended prey—an opening for a counter attack. Mizuki hopped onto her attacker's back holding her sword in a two

162

handed grip, blade pointing downward. On the back of the monster's head was an oval membrane surrounded by a dozen unblinking eyes. She sank the katana's blade deep into the membrane with a stabbing stroke.

Writhing in agony, the centipede bucked and threw Mizuki off. Sword in hand she did a back flip and twist, landing in position next to the beast, ready to strike again. It was not necessary, the oversized carnivore was finished.

"I thought centipedes were nocturnal," Mizuki said to her fallen foe, cautiously circling around the still twitching body. "I guess when you are on the top of the food chain you can hunt whenever you like."

Still pumped up from combat, Mizuki took several deep breaths, cleaned her blade with a piece of cloth, and resheathed her sword. A last look around the open glade and she quickly resumed her trip toward the next ridge.

* * * * *

Reaching the upper branches of the tree Mizuki's spirits soared. Ahead she could see a river slowly winding through the valley below. Not only that, along the near side of the river was what looked like a road, or at least a well traveled path. As she watched in the fading light, a number of creatures moved along the road. Some carried things on their backs, other carried spears!

"Well," she said to the forest surrounding her. "I guess we have found what passes for civilization around here."

Night was falling fast, and Mizuki did not want to chance continuing to the road in the darkness. She would seek the road in the morning, and try to pick up the trail of the creatures she saw. Perhaps she could make contact with the natives, they couldn't be more dangerous than trekking through this green hell alone.

Chapter 19

Mizuki in the Jungle

Mizuki awoke feeling as though her left ankle was on fire. So intense was the pain that she cried out and almost lost purchase on the branches she had slept among. Looking down, she spotted the source of her misery, an ant as long as her index finger with mandibles two centimeters long—the mandibles pierced her boot and the flesh within.

Kicking out with her right food killed the ant, removing its body from its thumb sized head. The head, however, remained firmly attached, even in death. Releasing the miniature attacker's hold required using the survival kit knife to pry open its oversized mouth parts. Bending down to inspect her wounded foot, Mizuki glanced down the trunk of the tree.

Below her the trunk swarmed with more ants, several headed toward her position. As she watched, an ant crawled into her hideaway and she stabbed it with the knife—it emitted a strong, disagreeable odor that seemed to attract even more of the miniature predators.

Giant centipedes and spiders I can handle, but how do I kill hundreds of finger length biting ants?

Gathering up her things and strapping on the backpack she fled in the only direction she could—upward. Picking the largest fork she climbed toward where it intersected a branch from a neighboring tree. Once near enough to grasp the other branch, Mizuki reached out and swung from one tree to the next. Not daring to look down, she wrapped her legs around the limb, feeling safe for a second. Then the new branch tilted down with a loud cracking sound.

Fracturing near where it joined the main trunk, the branch pivoted back toward its parent before severing completely. Mizuki found herself falling head first toward the forest floor thirty meters below. Twice she collided with protruding limbs until she finally managed to grasp one and hold on.

Hanging upside down like a tree sloth, she edged down the branch to the main trunk. Struggling to sit upright on the branch, Mizuki finally dared to look down. She was ten meters above the ground, sitting astride the last sizable branch before her fall would have ended on the jungle floor. The next thing she noticed was that the jungle floor was moving.

More ants! They're everywhere! What do I do now?

As she watched, the carcase of a scorpion thing moved past the base of her refuge, carried along by a carpet of ants. There was no sense in climbing down the rest of the way just to be overwhelmed by an army of ravenous insects. Forcing herself to stand up, she resumed climbing, looking for a way to cross to another tree, farther away from the tide of insects flooding the surface below.

Princess Timushi's Party

The river crossing went without incident. The water in the river was fairly low, giving the river beasts no chance to dine on those crossing the bridge. Spirits among the servants was lifted as the column started up the winding road toward the more settled highlands. The warriors, however, became more skittish, knowing that the chance of an ambush or attack grew as they neared the capital city.

"Hopefully the river crossing was the last bit of excitement before reaching the capital, my Lord Castellan," the Princess commented as they walked side-by-side in the middle of the procession.

"Yes, Your Highness, but then things will become truly exciting."

"Then things will be brought to a conclusion, my Lord. I cannot say that I am not anxious to be done with this entire affair. One way or the other, this will be my last trek across the wilderness."

"To be sure, Your Highness. Once you claim your mother's throne you will be cared for and coddled for the rest of you life. You should savor this trip through the lands you will soon rule over."

"Lands that I will not see again in person. Strange, don't you think, to live every day planing and struggling to win the throne, knowing that success will mean becoming a captive in my own palace?"

"No one gets to chose her position in life, my Princess. It is a worker's lot to labor, and a warrior's lot to fight and die. A princess's lot is to seek the high throne and, if she succeeds, spend her life giving birth to the next generation of her subjects. We are all born with our futures charted by fate."

"More like by genetics and nurturing in the egg chamber and crèche. None the less, I shall endeavor to enjoy these last few days of freedom. This is, after all, the adventure of my life."

"Yes, Ma'am. And it is your subjects' great fortune to share that adventure with you."

Main Lounge, Peggy Sue

Dorri and Zeke entered the main lounge through the second deck doorway. Having finished their tasks, they were searching for their respective siblings and had been sent to the lounge by Chief Zackly. Sitting at a table in front of the large viewport were Shadi and Mal, both drinking hot beverages from heavy china mugs.

"So here you two are, goofing off I see," said Dorri in a haughty tone. She seldom left a chance to tease her sister pass by.

"Unlike you, we are good enough at our work to finish early," was Shadi's retort, the smile on her face saying it was all in jest and she was happy to see her little sister.

"Hey," said Mal in greeting, to which Zeke replied with a noncommittal grunt.

"Are you two always so talkative?" Dorri said to her escort.

"We're twins," Zeke replied, "we have a psychic bond and don't have to waste a lot of words like other people."

Mal just nodded. The two sisters looked at each other.

"See, you two do it too!"

"We're sisters," said Shadi. "It's well known that sisters are closer than brothers when it comes to sharing each other's thoughts. We can have whole conversations without saying a word."

Both brothers rolled their eyes, then all four laughed.

"So sit-down and tell us how your day went," said Mal, motioning toward the two empty chairs at the table. "Shadi and I have been slaving away carrying spare parts and tools to repair teams all over the ship."

"Yes, Mal and I are now intimately aware of every nook and cranny within the Peggy Sue."

"Well, Zeke and I were down in the bowls of the ship regrowing shield circuitry and rewiring power runs."

"Yeah, we had to cut into the inner hull and then nanoweld the holes back shut. By the time the nanites were done you couldn't even tell we had been there."

As the two newcomers took seats at the table, Jimmy Tosh came over to take their order.

"Welcome to I and I lounge," the barkeep said with a dazzling white smile. "Can I bring you someting to drink, or maybe a snack?"

"Hi, Jimmy, just a cup of tea for me," answered Dorri. She and her sister normally took their meals in the main dining room while the two Marines generally ate in the crew lounge on first deck.

"Could I get a cup of coffee?" Zeke asked shyly.

"Comin' right up, mon," Jimmy replied and hustled back to the bar.

"Why is he always so happy?" Zeke asked.

"Because he's always vaping ganja oil," replied his brother with a smirk.

"Ganja oil?" asked a puzzled Dorri.

"You know," said her sister in a hushed tone, "*qínnab hindiyy.*"

"Marijuana? I didn't know there was marijuana on board."

"Yeah," added Mal with a knowing nod. "The Captain allows those who favor reefer over grog to use e-cigarettes to inhale cannabis extracts. I think our cook and bartender is always a bit high."

"That would explain some of his more fanciful culinary creations," Dorri commented with a look of enlightenment on her face. After a few seconds of hesitation, she spoke again. "You know, since we are all here together, there is something I think we should talk about."

"Oh?" the brothers said in unison while Shadi subtly shook her head 'no'.

"Why not, Shadi? We are as alone as we ever get aboard this ship."

The sisters had been hanging out with the twins more and more frequently in recent days, to the point where Dorri suspected that Shadi and Mal were becoming closer than just friends. Dorri had shared her idea with Shadi a while back, but the opportunity to talk with the two brothers had not presented itself until now.

"OK," said Mal, "now you have to spill the beans."

"Spill the what? Oh, figure of speech. OK, I will. You know that the four of us are the only survivors of the colony on Paradise."

"Yeah, some paradise," said Mal.

"We were lucky to escape with our lives," added Zeke.

"Hear me out." Dorri gave the others a stern look before continuing. "I've talked with the scientists in Dr. Ogawa's section and they are pretty sure that, having observed the black death that attacked the colony, a way of getting rid of the contagion can be found."

"OK, so what?" asked Zeke, while Mal nodded thoughtfully.

"So, I think that we four, as the only living survivors of the colony can stake a legal claim to the planet."

The brothers were speechless as Shadi glanced nervously from one to the other. Eventually, Zeke broke the silence.

"Claim the whole planet... yeah."

"Do you have any idea what a whole, habitable planet would be worth?" asked Mal, as the idea sank in.

Just then Jimmy arrived with two steaming mugs for Zeke and Dorri.

"Here you go, if you need anyting else just give a shout."

"Thanks, Jimmy."

Dorri smiled at the Jamaican, who nodded and happily returned to his work.

"So, you two. What do you think? Would you like to share a planet with Shadi and me?"

Chapter 20

Mizuki in the Jungle

Having worked her way through the treetops until the ground below was free of ants, Mizuki descended to the forest floor and resumed her quest. As she searched for the road by the river she gave thanks that her evolutionary ancestry was shared with apes and monkeys—being able to climb nimbly from branch to branch while escaping the army of ants saved her life.

As she neared the river the plant life seemed to be changing. There were large plants growing out of the loamy soil, with slick curved openings that narrowed to vertical throats. From those openings came odd smells, perfume mixed with rotting flesh, a most unpleasant odor. Walking on a fallen log next to a particularly large pitcher plant a strange creature blocked her way.

Mizuki had never seen an animal like the one in front of her. It had the head of a toad attached to a fat lizard's body with splayed legs and a stubby tail. With an overall length close to two meters the beast probably outweighed her and the look in its eyes was definitely along the lines of "now how do I swallow this thing?" Mizuki reached over her shoulder and drew her katana.

Her sword had barely cleared its scabbard when the toad lizard's mouth opened and a long pink tongue, capped by a fat fleshy tip, shot out. Striking her in the right thigh, the tongue hit with the force of a mule's kick, knocking Mizuki back a step. The impact ruined her sword stroke and she only managed to nick side of the fleshy appendage.

The cut inflicted on the right side of the creature's tongue caused it to hop to its left—right onto the slick curved surface of the giant pitcher plant. Madly scrambling in an attempt to escape the plant, the amphibian slid into the flared opening and out of sight. Unfortunately, its adhesive tongue was still affixed to Mizuki's thigh.

The dead weight of the falling toad lizard pulled Mizuki over the plant's flared lip and into its throat. Reacting in the blink of an eye, the swordswoman reversed her grip on the katana's handle, holding it point down with the curved sharp edge facing away from her body. As she was pulled over the lip, she drove the sword into the surface of the plant with all her strength. When things reached equilibrium, Mizuki was left hanging from her sword, with the still affixed toad lizard hanging by its tongue from her coverall leg.

Unable to pull herself from the plant with her assailant still stuck to her leg, Mizuki let go of the sword's hilt with her right hand and retrieved the survival knife from her belt. Reaching down she began sawing away on the lizard's tongue. After what seemed an eternity of hacking and cutting the tongue finally parted, freeing Mizuki and sending the toad lizard to whatever well deserved fate awaited it in the depths of the pitcher plant. A faint splash sounded from the depths of the carnivorous flower.

Keeping the knife in her hand, Mizuki swung to the right and sank the stout blade into the almost frictionless material of the pitcher's flared mouth. Pulling herself higher using her grip on the knife, she managed to slowly extract her sword from the plant's flesh. Lunging forward she again sank the long blade into the curved surface.

Repeating the process she finally reached the edge of the deadly pitcher, only to find that her efforts had drawn the interest of another member of the local fauna. Staring at her with multiple pairs of eyes, was a hairy grey spider.

"*Chikushō!*" *Oh shit!*

Princess Timushi's Party

"We lost no one crossing over the bridge, excellent." In the grand scheme of things a few workers or even warriors meant little. Still, a ruler must care for her subjects, or so Timushi had been taught. Queens were revered by their subjects, it seemed only fair that she be concerned about her subjects' well being.

"Luck was with us, Your Highness," replied the Castellan. She was just making conversation. The only losses that concerned the Castellan were among the warriors—about the common workers she cared not a whit, they were the Majordomo's problem.

"Just five more days journey to go, prior to arriving at the capital."

"Yes, Ma'am."

"And does not the repeated appearance of strange flying creatures give you concern, my Lord?" This said in a lowered voice.

At least twice a day for the past several days, strange apparitions flew by, low on the horizon, almost at the limit of vision. What the flybys portended was unknown to both the Princess and her Castellan, but neither thought them harbingers of good fortune. It was as though the creatures were following the column, monitoring its progress.

"Whatever evil magic animates them, the flying creatures stay well away, for which I am grateful. Neither the warriors nor the servants seem to have noticed them." *The last thing we need is panic among the drudges,* the crusty old warrior thought.

There were many specialized castes among the Formicidians, each with different physical attributes suited to their duties. Common workers had no need for good distance vision and large eyes would have been a vulnerability in a warrior. Only members of the higher castes sported large compound eyes—architects, engineers, scientists and so forth. The Princess had the largest eyes of all; glittering, golden compound eyes shaped like canted almonds on her heart shaped head.

"Yes, but still I can see that an enemy would have the advantage of us if they were able to track our every move."

"If one of them would pass close overhead I would have the archers try to bring it down, though such a result is not a certainty."

"Indeed, it might make it angry. After seeing what my dear sister's sorcerers did to my palace from the air, perhaps it is best to count our blessings and leave well enough alone."

"Perhaps. But the question is moot as long as the creatures only appear briefly on the horizon. I will tell the warriors to be on heightened alert for an ambush as we draw nearer the capital."

"A prudent precaution, no need for them to know why our risk may be heightened."

"Precisely, Highness."

HQ, Fakkaa Expeditionary Force

The situation, in military parlance, was fluid. Reconnaissance flights showed Princess Timushi's column within five day's march of the capital with no major impediments in her way. The vanguard of her sister Reishi's party was a similar distance from its objective. Meanwhile, hurried preparations for landing reinforcements from the Fakkaa fleet were underway.

"Lieutenant, how soon will the reinforcements be ready to deploy?"

"The first shuttles will land in another day cycle, Commander. It will take a couple of hours to disembark the troops and their equipment. Then they will need to be briefed on the operation and the terrain they are expected to operate in."

"Very good. Once they have landed, I want a squad of fresh commandos to prep for an insertion in front of the enemy princess's column. Right now both claimants to the throne are in a dead heat. I want to drop in a blocking force to slow down the competition a bit."

"Yes, Sir! I will inform the appropriate officers."

The Lieutenant saluted, waving his right digging claws in the neighborhood of his forehead. He turned and waddled from the room. Fakkaa were neither swift nor graceful, being built for burrowing and covered with sharp quills. On the other hand, they were strong, low to the ground, and particularly hard to kill.

Finally, we are getting somewhere, the Commander thought. *In one more day I will be able to reinforce the native column and launch an operation against our opponents. As long as there are no unforeseen complications, victory is within our grasp.*

Mizuki in the Jungle

The gigantic spider raised two hairy legs and hissed at the Japanese astrophysicist hanging on the lip of the carnivorous pitcher plant.

"Kutabare! Enough!"

Releasing her grip on the katana, with a lung she grabbed the two closest legs on her left. Twisting her body, she flung the twenty kilo spider over her shoulder and into the pitcher plant. Another faint splash sounded below.

"Kuso kurae!" She yelled over her shoulder. Still incensed, as she pulled herself from the plant she swore in labored breaths.

"Why... is every... *saitei* thing... on this *koitsu* planet... trying to kill me!"

After spending several minutes catching her breath and recovering her composure, Mizuki staggered to her feet and resheathed her weapons. She limped off in what she hoped was the direction of the road, a piece of lizard tongue still adhering to her thigh. Another ten meters brushing aside large fern fronds, and Mizuki found herself standing on a wide, well beaten path—the road she had spotted from the ridgeline.

Walking to the middle of the road, the exhausted scientist looked both directions and then sank to her knees. Tears of relief blurred her vision, running hotly down her cheeks. Taking a deep breath, Mizuki left out a primal scream, a roar of rage and defiance. For the next few moments the jungle around her fell silent, its denizens no doubt wondering just what sort of horrible monster could make such a sound.

* * * * *

Paralleling the river for several kilometers, Mizuki came upon a clear area that had obviously been used as a campsite by a large group of somethings. A number of stone circles contained the damp ashes of campfires, all properly extinguished.

Must have been a disciplined group, she thought.

Finding a raised natural basin filled by a bubbling spring, Mizuki used the filter straw to drink her fill. The water was clear and flowing but there was no telling what microorganisms made the miniature pond their home. Laying her poncho out on the ground, the bone-weary survivor sat down and stripped off her boots—her left ankle was swollen and red inflammation showed around the two bite marks inflicted by the ant's mandibles.

175

That ant has been the only foe to get through my defenses so far. I guess I'll live, but best to put some antibacterial cream on it anyway.

Retrieving a tube of unguent from the first aid kit, Mizuki treated her wounds and then wrapped the swollen ankle with an elastic bandage. The weather was hot and muggy, no chance of catching a chill. Looking around the camp site, finding no threat and having a clear field of view, she arrived at another decision.

Standing barefooted, she stripped the blood and entrail encrusted jump suit from her body. Thankfully, the remnant of the lizard's tongue lost its grip and fell off during the hike to the campsite. Still, Mizuki's clothing was a mess. Standing next to the basin she propped her sheathed katana against the rim and proceeded to wash her jump suit. A fleeting thought passed through her mind.

Bobby would love to see me standing here in my underwear, all disheveled. Men find the strangest things erotic.

The thought of her lover almost made her breakdown, but she willed herself not to burst into tears. This was not just a matter of love, it was a mater of duty, of honor. Bobby would not rest until he found her, his honor demanded it. It was her duty to survive until he could come for her.

I know you will come for me Bobby, my love. And I swear to you that I will be alive when you do.

After hanging the jump suit on a bush to dry in the sun, Mizuki washed herself and cleaned up as best she could. Then the nearly naked woman sat on her poncho, slowly consuming a ration bar and massaging the spectacular bruise on her thigh where the toad lizard's tongue struck. The red sun was warm on her skin, drying the remaining drops of water. Under different circumstances this could have been a pleasant way to spend the afternoon. From where she was seated she could see a bridge across the river just upstream.

I guess that is my next objective. I don't know how far ahead the natives are, but they must be a large party and large parties do not move swiftly. Perhaps I can catch up to them by nightfall.

Chapter 21

CIC, Peggy Sue

Repairs and refurbishment of the ship were progressing rapidly. The crew were working round the clock to return the Peggy Sue to fighting shape and to modify the sensor suite to add new capabilities. Chief Engineer Baldursson and Chief Zackly were everywhere, urging the crew on and keeping an eye on the work. The ship's officers, including the Captain, were also wandering the ship, adding to the crew's stress levels. The Captain or the First Officer were apt to pop up anywhere at anytime. Currently, however, the senior officers were together in the CIC, where the large holographic light table displayed a detailed 3D model of the ship.

"It looks like things are progressing nicely," said the First Officer. Despite the punishing schedule she looked as neat and proper as always. Her unwilted appearance mildly annoyed her husband, who was beginning to look a bit ragged around the edges.

"Yep. At this rate Arin says we have two, maybe three more days left at the outside. As soon as we can get everything squared away we can go and kick ET's ass."

"Yes, Sir," Beth and Bobby replied in unison.

"Speaking of the varmints that bushwhacked us, have we been able to locate them using the passive instruments?"

"We've been keeping the flotilla of primitive ships under surveillance while using the large telescope to scan for the main attacker," Bobby said. In Mizuki's absence he had assumed command of the sensor section, driving himself and the techs mercilessly. "We have a sighting of an anomalous object about 300,000 kilometers from the planet."

"Is it in a planetary orbit?"

"In a sense. It's in a Lissajous orbit around the star-planet L2 point, so technically it is in orbit around the M-type star."

"Is it a tight orbit or a wide one?" asked Beth.

"Pretty tight, right at the edge of the planet's umbra, but well inside the penumbra so the planet blocks most of the star's light."

"That sounds like Dark Lords fer sure."

"Yeah, I imagine they don't much care for light even from a red dwarf. IR data show that ship is cold, like seventy Kelvin cold."

"Definitely Dark Lords then. What else?"

"It's a big bastard, Sir. Looks to be more than a kilometer long and as black as space. We've never encountered anything like it and Peggy Sue says it doesn't match anything in the T'aafhal databanks. The computer concludes that it is some form of Dark Lord vessel and that the primitives are a client race, being used because they can work on the surface of the planet we all seem to be fighting over."

"I'm not worried about the minions, it's the mother ship that we need to take out first. Do we have any analysis of the ship's armaments and capabilities?"

"Between the initial attack and the optical surveillance the computer suggests that it is powered by some form of warp drive, capable of superluminal travel through normal 3-space," Beth responded. "The supposition is that we were struck by multiple torpedoes using the same form of propulsion. Because they don't use gravitonic drives they are difficult for our sensors to detect."

"Beth's correct, the location from the optical observations is uncertain because their warp field seems to be distorting the space around the ship. But if we can get a firing solution with the new sensors we ought to be able to hit them with the particle cannons."

"So yer saying that this new warp detector had better work or we have a big problem?"

"Aye, Captain. They are pretty much maintaining station now, but the range makes a railgun attack a long shot, and torpedoes would be detected in time for them to get underway. We don't know how long it takes them to accelerate to superluminal velocity, but once they do a torpedo hit is not very likely."

"Sounds like our best mode of attack is to bring all the systems on line, get a quick fix on the Dark Lords, and hit 'em with the cannon battery."

"That would appear to be the best course of action, Captain. Realizing that once our engines power up they will probably be able to detect us."

"Yeah, and if the new sensors don't work we may need to go to plan B."

"Plan B, Bobby?"

"Head straight at 'em. Once it's clear they see us and start moving we hit them with everything we got while throwing up a cloud of junk from the close support guns."

Beth raised a skeptical eyebrow.

"That sounds just a tad desperate, Bobby."

"It is, but once they know we are here there is no way we can run to a transit point before they catch us."

"Sounds like an old fashioned gun fight, pardner—who ever clears leather first wins."

"Only if we kill them with that first shot." Bobby's eyes held a malevolence his friends had not seen before, a smoldering hatred. Billy Ray nodded.

"Well then we better not miss."

Mizuki on the Queen's Highway

Refreshed and feeling considerably more human after her stop at the campground, Mizuki made good time in her pursuit of the unknown natives. Her aches and pains subsided to the point that she broke into a trot on several occasions. Miziuki suspected that the T'aafhal nanites coursing through her veins not only helped her body heal, they suppressed pain and provided stimulants as needed.

It was dusk when she came upon the large party of strange, insect like creatures. Her quarry had already stopped for the night, and were busily setting up camp and starting cooking fires. Around the camp's perimeter armed guards patrolled in pairs.

I guess there are still dangers about if even a large group of armed natives feels the need for sentries, Mizuki thought, observing the insects from the vantage point of a large tree well off the main road. *Now that I've caught up with them how do I make contact? Simply walking into camp in the dark doesn't seem like the best way to proceed, not with armed guards patrolling the perimeter of the encampment.*

Even in the failing light, the scientist in her could not help but make observations.

They seem to come in different types and sizes. That large one next to the fire in the middle of the camp, the one with the big eyes, must be the leader. I guess introductions can wait until the morning, until after I've studied these creatures a bit.

Having decided on a course of action, Mizuki settled in for another night, in another tree top. Just being in close proximity to the natives gave her an odd sense of security, a feeling that could easily be misplaced.

* * * * *

The sound of the natives noisily breaking camp and preparing to embark on another day's journey woke Mizuki from the best sleep she had since crashing on the planet. Chittering and chirping the odd creatures moved along the roadway, many bearing bundles on their backs, others pulling two wheeled carts, and some grasping spears or bows and quivers of arrows.

The countryside became more open as the elevation increased. Instead of dense rainforest the road passed through open meadows dotted with copses of trees. With the help of the adaptive camouflage provided by her poncho, Mizuki remained unseen as she paralleled the marching body of natives. She still had no idea how to approach the creatures. Even worse, she had no way to communicate with them.

The survival kit did contain a computer translator, but unless these creatures used one of the ancient trade dialects it would take time to build up enough vocabulary to communicate effectively. Given the conditions, she could not get close enough to the natives to start working with the translator without being spotted. Running from hiding place to hiding place, Mizuki watched the natives as her frustration grew.

Princess Timushi's Party

The procession was now moving through pastureland where the royal aphid herds grazed. Rounding a wide curve, the road entered a straight stretch where the land on both sides opened up into wide green pasture. Scattered about the knee high ferns were grazing aphids, slow moving thousand kilo mounds munching their way across the meadow. Their triangular bodies looked like green sails three meters tall, afloat in a sea of waving ferns.

The large, mostly defenseless beasts were kept for their sweet milky secretions, collected daily and sent back to the capital. Occasionally, some of the beasts were roasted on special feast days. The herds were watched over by a special cast, yet another variant of the polymorphic natives. Not warriors but still versed in the use of weapons, the herd-keepers were not considered among the brightest of the Formicidians. But then, their job required patience and immunity to boredom, not excessive cogitation.

"Your future herds, Your Highness," the Castellan announced. "Surely a good sign that we are drawing nearer to the capital."

"This countryside certainly seems more amicable than the jungle we have thankfully left behind. Four days to go."

"Three at the end of this day, Ma'am, and though our surroundings seem more benign the threat of an ambush cannot be discounted."

"You always think such bloody thoughts, my lord Castellan."

"It is my job, my Princess, to see you safely to the throne." *Or die trying.*

"At least we are no longer threatened by all manner of wild beasts as we were in that accursed swamp."

As Timushi finished speaking the high-pitched bugling of aphids in distress drifted across the pasture. Both the Princess and her guardian quickly located the source of the herd's distress.

"I fear you may have spoken too soon, Your Highness..."

Chapter 22

The Royal Pastures

From a hiding place in the treeline, Mizuki saw the herd of large green insects turn as one and head toward her side of the open field. As the beasts made a panicky if slow stampede across the pasture their guardians, clutching spears, ran the other direction, evidently to head off the threat. Looking in the direction of the herders' charge Mizuki saw the cause of the panic.

Emerging from a copse of trees was a tall slender creature, its elongated body a mottled brown, ending in an upper third colored bright green. Mizuki's vision telescoped, bringing the beast into closer focus. Atop the trunk like body was a large triangular head— huge compound eyes widely spaced at the upper corners, narrowing down to a collection of obviously predatory mouth parts at its lower apex. Held in front of the long green neck were a pair of arms folded, as though in prayer. It was a giant *Mantodea*—a praying mantis ten meters tall.

As Mizuki watched in fascination the first of the herders reached the predator. The herder tossed its spear, which bounced off the mantis's wide spiked forelegs. The mantis's raptorial legs shot out, moving with impressive speed for such large appendages, neatly snaring its attacker. The smaller creature struggled as the mantis improved its grip on body and thorax. Bringing the herder up to its mouth the mantis ended the herder's resistance by biting a large chunk out of the herder's head.

The casual savagery of the mantis's attack shocked Mizuki. *That's horrible! The herders don't stand a chance against that monster.*

Without further thought Mizuki bolted from cover and ran across the field, avoiding the running aphids who were now in total panic— to them she was another predator and as much a threat as the mantis. In the lower than Earth gravity, long strides quickly brought the angry woman close enough to the tall predator to attract its attention. It swiveled its head for a better view of the alien creature charging toward it.

What the mantis thought of the Earth woman was unknowable, but it hesitated for a few crucial seconds. Mizuki drew her katana and, with a twisting leap, launch an attack. With both hands she brought her sword down in a vertical blow that struck the beast's left arm at the junction of its upper arm and spike-fringed femur. The arm severed, letting the dead herder's abdomen dangle.

Not giving the mantis time to react, Mizuki completed her airborne pirouette, landing on one foot like an ice skater finishing a twirling jump. The mantis lost track of her as she charged beneath its body. Two steps brought the swordswoman to the first walking leg on the right side. She severed it *en passant,* then stopped to look back at her opponent. The mantis staggered.

A step and a leap took her to the creature's inclined back. Running up the trunk like body, she was almost startled when the mantis's head swiveled 180 degrees to look back at her. A horizontal strike from left to right sent the monster's head toppling to the ground.

With its head missing and standing on only three legs, the dying mantis tottered and began to collapse. Mizuki nimbly lept from her defeated opponent's back, rolling on impact and coming up in a defensive stance. The headless mantis toppled to the ground, the courageous but unfortunate herder still locked in the spiked grip of the predator's remaining grasping leg.

Standing up, Mizuki gave her katana the traditional swing and flick to clean body fluids from its blade. Hearing shuffling sounds behind her she turned, sword held one handed, her left arm out to balance the weapon in her right. Five meters from her three more herders formed a ragged half circle, their spears held before them.

"Well now," she said aloud, "the next move is up to you."

* * * * *

As the mantis launched its attack the Princess's party halted on the road, near the middle of the meadow. Her guards moved to form a protective wall between Timushi and the violent drama being played out farther across the field.

"Mantis," said the Castellan, succinctly.

"Yes," replied Timushi. "but what in the name of the gods, old and new, is that?"

As she spoke an odd four limbed creature ran swiftly across the meadow, heading straight for the towering predator. As it ran it seemed to shimmer, wraith like, the shifting color pattern of its body blending in with the background.

"I have never seen anything like that, Your Highness," the Castellan admitted, right hand on her sword's pommel. "But those herd-keepers stand no chance against the mantis, it will eat of them until sated and then move on."

As the Castellan spoke the ghostly bipedal figure reached the mantis and did not stop. Instead, it drew a blade and attacked the predator that was already consuming the first herd-keeper. The strange creature lept into the air and severed one of the mantis's raptorial legs.

"Did you see that, my Lord Castellan?"

"It must be a daemon!" the old warrior hissed.

The daemon emerged on the other side of the mantis and lopped off another appendage. Then it jumped upon the predator's back, ran to its prothorax and decapitated the monster.

"The gods preserve us!" one of the Princess's advisers exclaimed.

"Spear bearers form a shield wall," the Castellan bellowed, drawing her sword. "Archers behind the spear bearers."

"Hold, Castellan, do not attack the creature."

"I was thinking more along the lines of a rear guard to cover your escape, Your Highness."

"No, I want to see what the creature does next."

"Fine, Ma'am, but if it attacks the other herd-keepers you must flee."

* * * * *

Standing in front of the three highly agitated herders, Mizuki made a show of producing a cloth and cleaning the blade of her weapon. Trying to act as nonchalant as possible she removed the

185

scabbard from her back and positioned it properly in her belt, curved side up. Then, with a theatrical flourish she sheathed her sword.

The herders chittered excitedly to each other, looking back and forth among themselves and Mizuki. Eventually they came to some form of consensus—the three backed away, opening a pathway between them, and grounded their spears. It was then that Mizuki noticed the much larger martial formation across the field, shielding the party on the road.

Well, I couldn't figure out a way to introduce myself to the locals. It looks like the mantis solved that problem for me. The herders seem to be taking a pass and referring the matter to the party on the road.

Straightening her poncho and adjusting her sword, Mizuki made a slight bow to the herders.

"*Yoi ichinichi o,* have a good day, I am going to have a word or two with your friends on the highway."

Dismissing them from her mind, she marched toward the group of armed natives clustered near the road. They seemed to be guarding the big eyed individual, perhaps the large native was someone in authority.

Captain's Sea Cabin, Peggy Sue

"Naturally, I want you at the helm when we engage the Dark Lords' ship, Bobby." Billy Ray had called Beth and Bobby to his private cabin off the bridge to go over the action plan for after repairs were completed. "Umky will be on the new fire control sensors and will direct the superluminal particle cannon."

Bobby nodded in assent. "Once we blow them out of space are we going to remove the slow ships?"

"I'm thinking no."

"Not good form to leave an enemy, even a primitive one, in your rear. They might try something when the Marines shuttle down to the surface," Beth observed.

"I don't think they can do us any harm with the weapons they have, at least none that we wouldn't detect in plenty of time to avoid. Besides, I've had Shadi and Dorri working with the computer to decode their language."

"Speaking of which, we've been collecting SIGINT for the last several days, have they made any headway?"

"Actually yes. We have a pretty good idea of what they are up to. Seems there was a small force already on the surface, infiltrating the local native power structure. Only a platoon's worth of soldiers but some air support assets as well. We managed to destroy about half the reinforcements in space, but they are in the process of landing a couple hundred fresh troops."

"Shouldn't be anything the Marines can't handle, Captain."

"Why give the task to the girls?" asked Bobby.

"The translation? Well, they are both smart as a whip and they speak a half dozen languages between them. I figured it was a good way to keep them occupied now that most of the heavy repair work is done."

"You realize that they have been spending quit a bit of time with the two young Marines?" Beth was not really asking a question, she knew full well that, since the incident, her husband was keeping close tabs on their youngest crew members. She posed the question to inform Bobby of the situation without being too obvious. With Mizuki among the missing, his recent attention to shipboard matters was cursory at best.

"Yup. I didn't want them distracting part of the landing party before the balloon goes up."

"Smart move, Captain," Bobby said, comprehension of the situation dawning on him. "If I were a younger man those two would certainly be a distraction."

"A much younger man," Beth said archly. She was happy that Bobby was not wallowing in deep depression, but was instead taking an active and productive part in the coming rescue mission. "How do you propose implementing the search for the missing shuttle?"

"We have a good idea where it went down. From sensor and atmospheric readings it looks like they were hit by multiple air-to-air missiles tipped with low yield nukes. They must have damaged the shuttle but it kept on flying for several hundred klicks before going in."

"And we have a fix on their final position?" asked Billy Ray.

"Yeah, the emergency transponder was stationary for several hours before it went dead." Bobby's face was grim when he uttered the word 'dead', though he continued his description of what they knew about the crash. "I figure we will go to the impact point and assess the damage. If it looks like there were survivors we will try to figure out which way they headed."

"You don't think they would have stayed with the craft?"

Bobby shook his head.

"No, they had to know they were under attack. If they lived, and were able to move, they would have gotten away from the crash site, in case the hostiles came looking for survivors."

"Well, pardner, it sounds like you got things under control. I figure we will give the crew a double watch of down time once the techs have done all the testing they can without powering up the drives. I want the crew well rested before we begin operations."

Beth nodded. "The crew is anxious for round two, Captain. The sooner we can neutralize the Dark Lord threat the sooner Bobby and the Marines can go after our people."

"One more thing, Captain."

"Yes, Bobby?"

"I want to take the butterflies with us. Sometimes the damn things seem almost telepathic, maybe they can help find Mizuki down there."

"What ever helps, pardner. Let's get back to work."

The three officers departed, headed back to their duties. All three felt the strain of Mizuki's absence. Both Beth and Billy Ray prayed fervently that Mizuki would be found alive, for Bobby's sake and for their own. She and Bobby were a couple but the four of them had been close friends for years, through the early voyages of the Peggy Sue and the battle to save Earth. Like every human alive, they had lost more loved ones than could be counted. They were not just friends, they were the only family they had left.

Cargo Hold, Peggy Sue

"Alright, listen up people!" the Gunny shouted. "Some of you cream puffs have never been in real combat before, so pay attention."

The joking and playful banter quickly faded away, leaving the end of the hold where the deuterium plant had sat filled with expectant faces.

"We do not know for sure what we are walking into downstairs, but we are going to start at the crash site where the shuttle went down. Our primary mission is search and rescue. We are looking for survivors, not a firefight with the locals. Understood?"

"Aye, aye, Gunny." the group of green clad men and one large polar bear replied.

"Commander Danner is in charge of the mission; once we get dirtside he will assess the situation and decide how we proceed from there. From what intel we've been able to gather, there are at least two different groups of alien critters running around down there. The most numerous are the natives of the planet, arthropods that seem to be at a Medieval technology level."

"What does that mean, Gunny?" asked Vinny. The other Marines snickered.

"Knock it off, you chuckle-heads! Playing smart while staying dumb is a good way to get dead." She gave them the hard stare. "If you got a question now's the time to ask it."

"Yes, Gunny." the squad replied, more or less in unison.

"We are talking bows and arrows, spears, and swords—nothing that can directly threaten a Marine in armor. The other creepy critters are the ones in the antique spacecraft hanging out in orbit. The word is that there are several hundred of these douche-nozzles on the planet trying to pull off some kind of stealth invasion or something."

"Are these the ones who shot down our shuttle?" asked Kato.

"By process of elimination, yeah. We think that they have the equivalent of late 20th Century weaponry, including tactical nukes."

That got the Marines' full attention.

"They have limited air support, probably some kind of fighter bombers. No armored vehicles that we've been able to spot from orbit. We can expect projectile weapons, maybe RPGs and light artillery. They've been consorting with the Dark Lords, so its possible they may have been given some energy weapons as well."

Umky gave a low rumbling growl. "What's the weapons load, Gunny?"

"We are going in heavy: flechette and 15mm railguns, AM grenades, and full armor. We'll be in the armored shuttle so it can supply air defense, and we can use the battle bots if needed. I repeat, our mission is not to engage these alien slime-balls, our mission is to find our people and get them back. Is that understood?"

"Aye, aye, Gunny!"

"Good. Now everyone go to the armory and go over your kit, twice. Then grab some rack time, because the balloon is going up in about 24 hours. After that we're all gonna be busier than a one legged man at a butt kicking contest."

As the Marines left for the armory, talking in low voices among themselves, the Gunny thought: *Damned if this ain't another well organized stampede.*

Chapter 23

The Royal Pastures

Striding across the field came the strange bipedal creature, its body coloration shifting as it moved through the knee high ferns. Its pace seemed purposeful but unhurried.

"It's coming right toward us, Your Highness," simpered one of the servants.

"Quiet! Let her Highness think," the Majordomo chastised the servant, secretly glad that she had pointed out the obvious danger. Ignoring the household help, Timushi turned to the Castellan.

"I believe that it wants to have words with us, my Lord Castellan."

"You think that wise, Ma'am?"

"I think we would be hard pressed to out run it if we flee and it decides to give chase. Besides, it did not harm the other herd-keepers. I don't think that bloody murder is what it has in mind."

"Yes, Your Highness," the Castellan acquiesced. "Archers, stand at ease! Spear bearers ground your weapons! Do not provoke the, er, stranger."

"Strange indeed," the Princess mused. "I've never seen anything that walked upright like that, balanced on only two legs. You'd think it would topple over."

"It seems to get about just fine, Ma'am, considering it crossed the meadow faster than any warrior could, and then sliced up the mantis without missing a step."

"In doing so it did us a good turn, my Lord. I wonder what it wants?"

* * * * *

Mizuki forced herself to remain calm and maintain a steady pace on her march across the pasture. She had hung the translator computer around her neck, not that she expected it to be of immediate help. She was still draped in the camouflaged poncho, with its hood up covering her head. She felt like a cowled monk as she approached the line of spear men, or rather, spear bugs. As she drew closer they all grounded their weapons, much like the herders had.

I hope that is a good sign, she thought. *At least they aren't going to skewer me out of hand.*

Mizuki halted three meters from the line of soldiers and put her hands on her hips. The spear bearers remained as unmoving as statuary.

These are obviously different from the herders. They have much larger heads and bigger mandibles. They must be warriors. I wonder if all these creatures are specialized for the kind of work they do?

Lacking any flash of inspiration Mizuki simply spread her arms, displaying her empty hands. Behind the line of warriors there was shuffling as the archers and other types of insect parted. Through the open path strode the big individual she had spotted from the trees. Beside it was another, smaller individual who also sported large compound eyes, but was wearing body armor and a sword—a warrior commander perhaps?

At a word from the smaller of the pair, the spear bearers stepped sideways, clearing the way. The leader took another step forward but did not fully leave the cover of its warriors. The leader stood as tall as Mizuki, though it did so on four legs, not two. From a heart shaped head with two antennae, large almond shaped, compound eyes stared levelly at her.

It cocked its head to one side, as if in contemplation, then straightened up. It nodded its head and lowered its antennae in what could only be a gesture of greeting.

Mizuki bowed in response.

Straightening up she thought, *Well, here goes nothing.*

Slowly she reached up and drew back the hood of the poncho, revealing her head and face.

* * * * *

"Ye gods, its hideous!" said the Castellan in a low voice.

"I must admit, it is not like anything I've ever seen," said the Princess in a conversational tone. "It looks soft and fleshy, like a grub."

192

"Look at that mouth! How does it eat with that mouth?" Even the crusty old Castellan was having trouble maintaining a calm demeanor. The warriors remained stoic as ever but a wave of chatter swept through the servants and other retainers.

"At least it had the good manners to bow, so it must be civilized for all its horrible strangeness." Timushi paused for a second. "Consider, my Lord, that we must appear as hideous to it as it does to us."

"You are wise as always, Your Highness. Still I find the thought little recompense for having to gaze upon its terrible visage."

At that point the daemon pointed to its chest and said, "Mizuki."

The princess nodded and gesturing to her own chest and said, "Timushi."

The daemon's face distorted and the ends of its freakishly mobile mouth turned upwards. This gesture, so ghastly and unnatural, almost made the Princess turn and run, but she persevered. Spreading her arms in an all encompassing gesture, she said, "We are Formicidae."

Touching its chest with both hands, the daemon replied, "Human."

HQ, Fakkaa Expeditionary Force

"I am sorry, Commander, but the landing of the reinforcements has been delayed by at least a half a day due to damage to the landing craft." The voice was that of Fleet Admiral Raqqee himself.

"Yes, Admiral, I understand," replied the Ground Commander, carefully controlling his voice in an attempt to keep his frustration from boiling over. *We are approaching the end game and now this happens! Damn it, I need those fresh troops!*

The Ground Commander's temperament was well known throughout the fleet and the Admiral was a crafty old dog. He knew that if anyone of lesser rank had delivered news of the delay the Commander would throw a fit. As it was, he was barely keeping his temper in check.

"I apologize for the delay, but several of the landing craft did not pass their pre-flight inspections. I'm sure you will agree that we have already lost enough troops without having more perish while deorbiting."

The Admiral's words brought back bitter memories of losing half his pathfinder force a year ago, when they first came to this god's be damned planet. As much as it galled him, the Commander had to admit that old Raqqee was right—losing more assets at this point could put the entire mission at risk.

"Yes, Sir. We will make do until you can safely land the reinforcements. Please keep us advised of your progress."

"I will, Commander. Raqqee out."

The channel went dead.

After a few moments thought the Commander bellowed, "Lieutenant! Get the aviation commander on the radio. We don't have troops of our own to spare so I am going to call on our native levies to provide a delaying force."

"Sir?"

"Contact the First Sergeant with the native column. Tell him he is to requisition half a dozen of the insect warriors for an ambush of Princess Timushi's party."

"We are going to use natives for the ambush, Sir? Will they be able to pull it off?"

"Who cares? I'm hoping that attacking the opposition column will unsettle them enough to slow their progress a bit. Besides, we cannot weaken our force accompanying our Princess's column without endangering the mission. Should the opposition win the race to the capital I sincerely doubt that Reishi's warriors could take the place by storm without all the help we can muster.

"What if Princess Reishi refuses?"

"Tell her to come up with the ambushers or forfeit her throne. We'll see how much the high and mighty insect Princess really wants her dead mother's empire. Have the troop carrier meet the column and pickup the warriors."

"In front of all the insects, Sir?"

"Hang 'em all. Let them see what type of power we have, maybe it will help motivate them."

"Yes, Commander."

Lower Deck, Peggy Sue

Mal and Zeke were headed from the cargo hold, forward to the crew lounge when they encountered Shadi in the passageway. She was standing just outside the shower room, looking nervous and alone.

"Hey you," said Mal, smiling at the young woman.

"Hey yourself," she replied.

"Where's Dorri?" asked Zeke, looking past her down the passageway.

"She's in the crew lounge, being entertained by some of the sailors. I wanted to talk with Mal alone."

"Oh," Zeke answered, somewhat disappointed.

A glance and raised eyebrows from his brother sent him down the passageway toward the lounge. Glancing over her shoulder at the departing Zeke, Shadi turned back to Mal and looked down shyly. It was unusual to find Shadi at a loss for words, and Mal regarded her expectantly.

"I just wanted to speak with you before the attack," she began.

"Hey, I don't think anything bad is going to happen. If the Captain didn't think we could take these Dark Lord clowns we would try something sneakier."

"It's not the attack on the alien ship that I'm worried about. It's what happens after, you know, going down to get the missing people back."

"There's gonna be nine of us, ten counting Commander Danner, and we'll all be in battle armor. Umky's a walking tank and we'll have cover from the armored shuttle and its battle bots on the ground if needed. We'll be fine. It's the others that I worry about, the ones who went down in the first shuttle."

"Just promise me you won't do anything... overly heroic."

"You mean stupid," he said with a grin.

"I guess so. It's just that Dorri and I have lost so many people—family and friends, and even the other settlers—I don't want to lose you."

"I promise, I'm coming back."

"You'd better," she said, forestalling any reply by quickly kissing him on the lips. She turned with a swirl of dark hair and ran down the passageway, leaving behind the lingering fragrance of jasmine and a dumfounded young Marine.

It was Mal's turn to be at a loss for words, standing mute as Shadi disappeared forward. All he could think was: *Holly shit! I didn't see that coming.*

Princess Timushi's Party

The group of natives continued their trek toward the capital city, marching until twilight forced them to camp for the evening. Along the way the daemon Mizuki and Princess Timushi conversed as best they could. The magic amulet around the daemon's neck started to translate the daemon's language into that spoken by the natives, rapidly improving as they walked along.

"Well Your Highness, you asked the gods for a daemon of your own and it looks like they granted your request," said the Castellan in a hushed tone.

"So it seems," Timushi replied. "The only problem is that the gods usually extract a heavy price for the gifts they bestow on mortals."

"We will see, Ma'am. Just a couple more days and we will settle things with your royal sister and her daemons." *I hope this daemon is up to it.*

* * * * *

Mizuki walked along with the leader's party, an easy pace despite the natives using twice as many legs for locomotion. They were unlike anything found on Earth. Obviously arthropods and

196

anatomically similar to insects, they possessed six limbs, two of which acted as arms and the rest legs for walking. Their bodies were also segmented into insect like parts: a head with compound eyes, two antennae, and a mouth; a large abdomen in the rear; and a thorax where the arms and legs attached, connecting the other two parts.

They reminded Mizuki of ants from back home, but the thorax was different from Earthly ants, consisting of two distinct parts. The rear half was parallel to the ground and from it sprouted the four walking legs. The front half bent upward almost 90 degrees, the two arms attached to its sides with a short neck supporting the head on top. There were vent openings along the sides of the chest section and below that the thorax expanded and contracted rhythmically—an indication of some form of lung within the chest cavity.

On Earth, insects breathed through a network of tiny tubes called tracheae. Air entered the tubes through holes along an insect's abdomen allowing oxygen to be absorbed. But these creatures were much too large to breath without some form of forced respiration, even with the higher atmospheric concentration of oxygen. Back home, the only arthropods to develop lungs were arachnids and scorpions, and those were just primitive book lungs.

During Mizuki's travels it had become obvious that evolution charted a similar course on most Earth-like worlds, but the details were different. This world never experienced the asteroid collisions and massive volcanic eruptions Earth had, events that triggered mass extinctions that repeatedly reset Earth's evolutionary clock. As a result, this world never progressed to the age of dinosaurs or the later age of mammals. Here insects had many millions of additional years to evolve.

In spite of the substantial differences, Mizuki could not help thinking of the natives as giant ants. That is the name she gave to the translator and that is how she saw them in her mind. The translator itself was progressing nicely, the neuromorphic circuits within it building a bidirectional translation network between English and ant speak. On the road Mizuki and Timushi had time to learn a bit about each other.

Mizuki discovered that Timushi was a Princess and that she was in some kind of race for the throne of her recently deceased mother. She also learned that all the ants were female, except for a few males kept for breeding purposes. More unsettling was the news that "daemons" were actively helping Timushi's rival, Princess Reishi. This was the topic of discussion as they settled into camp for the evening.

"You say your sister Reishi has enlisted daemons and dragons to help her gain the throne, Princess?" Mizuki asked through the translator around her neck.

"Yes, Lord Mizuki," the Princess replied. "Three flying dragons destroyed my sister Shōshi's palace and her with it. They also spat fire and burned my palace, though I had already departed for the capital."

"And these flying dragons make constant roaring sounds?"

"Yes, they do, do you know of them?"

"I have knowledge of similar 'dragons'. If they appear overhead your party should scatter and seek cover."

"My Lord Castellan offered similar advice."

"Your advisers are wise, Your Highness. There is little defense against dragons save other dragons."

"Do you have dragons of your own, Lord Mizuki?" asked the Castellan.

"My companions do, but they are not here at the moment. I am afraid that avoidance is the only counter I can recommend in our current situation."

"You say that you are from beyond the sky, is that correct?" Timushi changed subjects to cover the Castellan's dissatisfaction regarding Mizuki's paucity of dragons.

"Yes, my group of... fellow daemons, travel from world to world among the stars. We look for other... people to exchange ideas and goods with."

"Your fellows are not the same type of daemon as the ones helping my royal sister?" From the descriptions forwarded by her spies this would seem to be so, but she wished to hear it from Mizuki herself.

"No, Ma'am, we are not the same as those helping your sister. In fact, they attacked us without warning when we arrived."

"Were your companions killed?" the Castellan asked, leaning forward with interest. The balance of power could depend on whether this was the only daemon allied to their cause or if others existed who might come to the aid.

"My two companions who accompanied me to your world were killed," Mizuki said, haltingly. "But most of my people escaped." *I've got to believe that, otherwise I'm stuck on this world alone until I die.*

"When will they be back?" The Castellan pressed his interrogation.

"I do not know, Lord Castellan, but I am sure that it will not be long." *Do you hear me, Bobby?*

"Enough questions for our guest, my Lord Castellan. Lord Mizuki came to our aid today and dispatched the mantis in a most convincing style. Surely our bid for the throne has been strengthened by her joining our host."

The Princess tilted her head and looked directly at Mizuki. Obviously this was a ploy to see if Mizuki intended to accompany her to the capital, and by inference fight for her if necessary. Recognizing that Timushi's not so subtle question required an answer, Mizuki quickly reviewed her options.

Decision time! I must either flee the company of this Princess and her war party or pledge my allegiance to her cause. I doubt I will get better terms from her sister, or her sister's daemons. What is that saying of Beth's? In for a penny, in for a pound.

"Princess Timushi, I would be honored to accompany you and your warriors to the capital as you claim your mother's throne."

Both the Princess and the Castellan had been tensely awaiting her response, heads slightly lowered, antennae slanting forward. Hearing Mizuki's answer they both relaxed visibly.

199

"I accept your gracious offer to accompany me to the capital, Lord Mizuki," the Princess replied with a nod of her head, dipping her antennae, a gesture Mizuki took as the equivalent of a polite bow. Mizuki bowed in return from her seated position near the fire.

"Majordomo!" Timushi cried out. "Bring food and drink for our guest and new companion."

Oh crap! Mizuki thought. *Now I have to eat some of their food! If I refuse they may take it as an insult and that won't do. I hope there is nothing poisonous in whatever is on the evening's menu...*

Chapter 24

Princess Timushi's Party

Mizuki stirred from a tempestuous sleep. Last evening's meal lay heavy in her stomach, a heaping pile of finger-sized white grubs that had the texture of tofu and tasted faintly of garlic and lemon grass. At least they had been cooked. But it was not indigestion that woke her, it was the whistling and clicking sounds coming from the servant the Majordomo had assigned to her. It was cowering beside her waiving arms and antennae at something behind her.

Instantly awake, Mizuki did a kip-up, drawing her sword while springing to her feet like a ninja. Whirling around she was confronted by a warrior in the act of driving its spear into the ground where a fraction of a second before she had slumbered. Converting her rotation into a right to left sword stroke she cut the warrior across the junction between upper and lower thorax, bisecting both ant and spear.

Standing back and raising her katana for another stroke she discovered that it wasn't needed—the upper part of the warrior toppled sideways, separating from the rest of its body. The torso-less body sank unsteadily to the ground, its four legs buckling. On the ground next to it lay the severed thorax and head, the deceased ant's mandibles opening and closing, not quite resigned to death. Satisfied that her foe no longer posed a threat, Mizuki spun around and confronted the Castellan, who had come up behind her.

"Why are you trying to kill me!" she shouted, raising her katana above her head in preparation to strike.

"Not us, Lord Mizuki, them!" The Castellan pointed beyond the severed upper body of the warrior Mizuki had dispatched, toward the woods beyond. Mizuki glanced over her shoulder in time to see another warrior loose an arrow at the Castellan.

With her left hand Mizuki snatched the arrow from the air in mid-flight. This confounded the archer sufficiently that it stood unmoving, frozen in place for the few seconds it took Mizuki to close the distance between them. On arrival she delivered a right to left diagonal cut from shoulder to hip, a cut called *kisa giri* in

Japanese—the monk's robe cut. The archer fell, its upper body split in two.

All around the sound of battle rose and as quickly abated. Warriors ran past, into the woods seeking out more attackers. The Castellan directed the counterattack with gestures and shouted commands, moving into the woods with her warriors. It took several minutes for the chaos to subside but eventually Timushi appeared, surrounded by more jittery guards.

The Princess surveyed the remains of the attackers who had drawn Mizuki's attention and nodded as if this was added confirmation of the daemon's prowess in combat.

"I see you put down two of the attackers, Lord Mizuki."

Mizuki wiped down her blade and returned it to its scabbard.

"Yes, Your Highness. Would you care to enlighten me as to the nature of our attackers?"

"They must have been sent by my sister, Reishi, though how they came this far this fast eludes me. If she has already arrived at the capital and claimed the throne all she need do is wait for my arrival."

"You would surrender to her?"

"Oh no, surrendering would just hasten my death. My warriors and I would attack and die. Her forces combined with the palace guard would far outnumber us but we would still try."

There is no second place in this contest, Mizuki realized. *This is a fight to the death.*

As Timushi and Mizuki conversed several of the large eyed servants—types that Mizuki had tagged as scholars and sages—busily examined the head of the first warrior Mizuki struck down, removing it from the already severed upper thorax. The sages chittered at each other as the Castellan came hurrying up, intent on reporting to the Princess.

"Your Highness, we have killed all those who participated in the attack. They ambushed and overpowered four of the perimeter guards and snuck into the camp. From the tracks, there were only six, including the two Lord Mizuki dispatched."

"How did they get here, my Lord, did you question any of them?"

"No, Ma'am. They all fought to the death."

"A shame. I could have interrogated any that lived." The Princess sounded disappointed none of the attackers survived.

"Your pardon, Your Highness," intoned one of the scholars. "But I doubt you could have extracted any information from these assassins."

"Why, Senior Sage? They would have been soon overcome by my pheromones, changing allegiances in spite of themselves."

"Again, begging your pardon, Ma'am, but the antennae of the attackers have been coated with resin, rendering their olfactory sense useless. They could not have smelled your royal emanations, Your Highness."

As proof two other sages held up the assassin's head, displaying the doctored antennae. The Princess was outraged.

"That is barbaric! Warriors without their sense of smell are almost helpless at night. My royal sister has stooped lower than I would have ever suspected."

"We also found this on one of the assassin's, Ma'am," added the Castellan, holding out a cellphone sized metallic object.

"Might I examine that?" Mizuki asked, extending her arm. The Princess nodded and the head warrior passed the device to the Earth scientist. Mizuki turned the object over in her hands, peering closely at it from all angles. Looking up, she addressed Timushi.

"Your Highness, this is an alien device, a device made by other daemons. It may let your enemies pinpoint your location, possibly to help guide aircraft, dragons, to attack you. We need to get it away from you and your servants. Now."

"Give it to me, Lord Mizuki," the Castellan responded. "I will have a servant carry it out into the field."

Handing over the device, Mizuki continued. "Good, that is a start. Your Highness, we need to move and quickly. We must be away from this place as soon as possible."

Timushi nodded her assent and called for the Majordomo. In less than five minutes the Princess's party had vacated the campsite and was once again on the road to the capital. If anything, the ambush had hastened their departure and lent greater urgency to their steps.

HQ, Fakkaa Expeditionary Force

"Have we received an update from the ambush force?" demanded the Commander. The six native warriors had been inserted in front of Princess Timushi's party last night, with instructions to move along the road until they made contact. The plan was to attack just before dawn, when the camp guards' attention would be at its lowest.

"Negative, Sir. The last report was over an hour ago when the bug leader said they were launching their attack."

"Then we must assume that they were all killed in the attempt. Blast it! We have no idea of how much damage they caused, or if the rival princess still lives."

"It is highly unlikely that the Princess was killed, given that she is surrounded by a hundred of her own warriors and servants. We can schedule the troop carrier to surveil the area, homing in on the beacon in the communicator we gave to the insects."

"No, Lieutenant, there is no time. The reinforcements are finally arriving from the orbiting fleet and we will need all the troop carriers to ferry us to Princess Reishi's column."

"We only have the one, Sir. Moving our entire force to the head of the column will take quite some time."

"Yes, fortunately there are two additional quad-rotors in the landing shuttles. Also, get the attack craft prepared for the assault tomorrow. We may not need them but I want everything in readiness. Sometime tomorrow we shall cross the line of departure and the battle for this stinking ball of mud will begin."

"Yes, Commander. I will notify the aviation commander."

Bridge, Peggy Sue

Billy Ray looked around the bridge of his ship, finding all stations manned and ready. This was it, time to throw down on the Dark Lords that ambushed them more than a week ago. On reflection, he decided he liked their odds. The aliens seemed to be limited in offensive power, relying on their FTL torpedoes and surprise to take out their opponents.

On the other hand, the Peggy Sue had weaponry that even Navy ships did not, specifically the new superluminal particle cannon that could penetrate all but the most advanced shields. Of course you can't hit what you can't see. Everything was riding on the new sensors being able to detect the Dark Lord's ship.

"What is our status, Number One?"

"All weapons manned and awaiting power up, Captain."

"Sailing Master?"

"A rough course is laid in, Captain, awaiting better resolution of the enemy's location."

"Mr. Umky?"

"Ready for power up, Sir."

Surveying the bridge one last time, the Captain nodded to himself.

"Mr. Baldursson, reactors to full power. Power up all shields, sensors, and weapons systems."

"Aye, aye, Captain," came the Chief Engineer's reply from the engine room.

Around the bridge panels and displays illuminated, coming fully to life for the first time since they shut down for repair and refitting. The holographic display overlaying the view forward through the bow blinked into existence, status indicators and a cross hair symbol marking the enemy's position seemingly floating in space.

"Fire control, do you have a fix on our target?"

"Aye, Captain, that we do. As clear as the scent of a seal sunning itself by an air hole on the pack ice," Umky replied, a smile spreading across his ursine features that had more to do with predatory instinct than happiness, though for a polar bear they might be one and the same.

"Helm, all ahead flank. I want to close the range to the target as much as possible before they spot us."

"Aye, Sir. Engines all ahead flank," reported Bobby from the helm.

The Peggy Sue lept ahead, accelerating at 80G. Sensor and status readings danced on displays around the cabin. Tension among the crew was palpable. Some were nervous, while others stared hard eyed, looking for payback.

"Sensors, I want the large optical scope slaved to the new warp sensors. Put our target on the forward display."

"Aye, aye, Sir!" The excited reply came from Dorri who, along with her sister, was manning Mizuki's usual station. The view forward rippled and an alien craft swam into focus—a long space-black needle banded by a ring of silver. There was nothing in the display to provide a sense of scale, but everyone on the crew had heard the Dark Lord ship was over a kilometer in length, far larger than the Peggy Sue.

A minute passed. The Peggy Sue was traveling toward her enemy at 47,000 m/sec and still accelerating. A second minute, a third. Now closing at 141,000 m/sec, and 25,000 kilometers closer to the target.

"The prey is moving, Captain," Umky called out.

"I guess they've seen us," Billy Ray said. "Do you have a firing solution, Mr. Umky?"

"Working, Captain..." The bear's response trailed off into a low rumble, his eyes shut, receiving tracking data through his sense of smell. On the forward display the target's image rippled as the fabric of space surrounding it distorted.

From the helm Bobby called out. "The target seems to be heading away from us, Sir. They're running."

"You may fire when ready, Mr. Umky."

There was no sound, no flash of light, only changing status indicators at various stations marked the event. Two concentrated bursts of subatomic particles, traveling more than ninety-nine percent the speed of light, streaked toward the alien vessel. But the beams' effective velocity was much greater than that, as the particles traced a shallow dip into alter-space. Instead of taking a slovenly two seconds to strike their target the twin bursts struck home in microseconds.

The light returning from the alien vessel had no choice but to obey Dr. Einstein's speed limit, delaying confirmation of the salvo's impact by two seconds as it traveled across the 600,000 kilometers separating the Peggy Sue from its foe. As the photons finally arrived the view forward blossomed in a star-bright explosion.

"Pull back the view, Dorri," ordered Beth, as the forward display was overloaded. Dorri immediately complied, zooming out until the miniature sun that had been the Dark Lord ship fit on the display.

"I think it would be safe to say we hit them," said Beth with typical understatement.

"Good shooting, Mr. Umky," Billy Ray responded. *Shoot at my ship will you, you froze assed bastards!*

Umky opened his eyes and bared his fangs at the sight on the forward display. Cheers broke out on the bridge and all throughout the ship.

The explosion stuttered.

"What the hell?" said Bobby.

The glaring matter-antimatter explosion was sucked back into itself, a million degree swirling backdraft of tortured particles and hard radiation. As quickly as it was sucked in the explosion expanded again, flashing briefly and fading to black.

A shudder passed through the Peggy Sue.

"That ain't normal," Billy Ray muttered.

"We have just experienced a space-time compression wave caused by the destruction of the Dark Lord ship," said the ship's computer in Billy Ray's ear. "The wave was probably caused by the dark matter kept in containment aboard the alien vessel, which was released in the explosion."

"The computer says that the shudder was caused by dark matter released from the target vessel. Nothing to worry about," the Captain relayed to the bridge crew, hoping he sounded authoritative and convincing.

"I'm glad we didn't get much closer before we blew the bastards out of space," said Bobby.

"Speaking of which, Mr. Danner, reduce our velocity and lay in a course for a high planetary orbit. It's time to go find our missing people."

"Aye, aye, Captain!"

Flagship, Fakkaa Fleet

"What in the seven hells was that!" Capt. Tikkoo swore as the main bridge display flared brilliant white. The others on the bridge of the flagship stood transfixed, all eyes on the tortured display screen. A tremor passed through the ship.

On the flag bridge above him, Fleet Admiral Raqqee tumbled into his chair and yelled. "What's happening, Captain, are we under attack?"

The radar observer on the command bridge was staring at his scope in disbelief when he realized that his captain was yelling his name.

"Y-Yes, Captain?"

"What's out there, sailor, what can you see? Are we under attack?"

"N-No, Sir. It's gone, Sir!"

"What's gone, son?" said the Admiral, not unkindly.

"The Wise Ones, S-Sir. Their ship is gone. It exploded."

"What!" said the Admiral and Captain together.

The Admiral grasped the rail of the flag bridge with his claws, staring again at the now blank display. "Is there any wreckage? Any debris?"

"No, Sir. Signal returns show no debris, the echo is consistent with a cloud of expanding plasma."

"Plasma?" said the Captain in disbelief. "Nothing left? No possibility of survivors?"

"No, Captain, nothing. Not only are they gone, Sir, there is a contact decelerating at 50 Gs on a trajectory that will bring it into planetary orbit." The radar operator looked up at his captain, his digging claws trembling slightly. "It matches the other alien ship, the one the Wise Ones destroyed over a week ago."

"Thought they had destroyed is more like it," the Captain observed, the implication of the radar operator's information sinking in.

After a moment's stunned silence the Admiral spoke. "Captain, what is our status? Are all the troops away?"

"Yes, Admiral, all the troops and their equipment are en route for the planet's surface. They should be down safely within the hour."

"And this alien ship. How soon will it arrive in orbit?"

"Five or six hours, Sir," the frightened radar operator answered.

"Feed the crews. Action stations in four hours," Raqqee snapped, thinking, *we are so screwed.*

Daylight Side, Formicidae

Orbiting the star-planet L2 point, the Dark Lords' ship had constantly faced the night side of Formicidae until the Peggy Sue blasted it into fundamental particles. Those on the daylight side of the planet did not observe the temporary blossoming of Alpha Phoenicis' third sun, but they did feel the passing of the gravitational compression wave that the explosion released.

Of the three biological races embroiled in the current struggle, the ants themselves were the most puzzled by the slight temblor.

Their world had been geologically stable for a hundred million years, making earthquakes almost unheard of. When the quake shook the capital around noontime, most just waved their antennae and went about their business, passing it off as another manifestation of the evil times afflicting their world.

The Fakkaa commandos, allied with Princess Reishi, came from a world with considerable tectonic activity. For them an earthquake was not anything noteworthy, particularly if they happened to be above ground at the time. They also shrugged and went about their business, getting into position for tomorrow's assault on the capital and the royal palace.

The lone representative from Earth present had grown up in Japan, where earthquakes were a frequent occurrence. The mild tremor that gently shook the roadway beneath Mizuki's feet hardly warranted notice. That it signaled the Peggy Sue's reemergence on the local scene would not be realized until later, after the battle for succession between Reishi and Timushi was fully joined.

There was, however, a fourth form of intelligence that marked the passing of the seismic disturbance. This intelligence was not organic in nature. Instead, its mind inhabited a network of entangled quantum dots constructed from exotic particles seldom seen in nature. The mind belonged to a T'aafhal AI, an artificial intelligence left on Formicidae over a million years ago.

In the north of the ant empire, burred deep under layers of rock, the AI patiently waited to either fulfill its mission or be recalled by its creators. The AI was awakened by the arrival of the Dark Lords' ship. As it monitored events, wondering if it would have to take action, the artificial mind was surprised again by the arrival of another ship. This ship arrived via alter-space, and bore similarities to ships built by the T'aafhal.

Perhaps surprise was too strong a term—the AI merely noted that the arrival of a T'aafhal ship after all this time, particularly only twelve years after the arrival of the warp drive vessel, was highly improbable. Its response was to send a message to the new arrival encoded in a beam of neutrinos, a narrow beam that no one else could intercept. If the ship responded to the message it would be proof enough that it was related to the T'aafhal in some way.

When the newcomer altered course for the AI's planet new possibilities had to be considered. The Dark Lords' ship and the flotilla of primitive vessels, which no doubt carried minions in thrall to the Dark Lords, were about to enter planetary orbit. The possibly T'aafhal ship managed to arrive first, only to be attacked without warning—not that Dark Lords ever gave their victims warning.

Not T'aafhal then, concluded the AI. A real T'aafhal ship would not have been surprised by a warp drive vessel. This observation spawned several other avenues of speculation regarding the nature of the newcomers, their possession of unmistakably T'aafhal technology, and the fate of the AI's creators. Observing how the ambushed ship managed to escape its attackers, the AI pondered the meaning of these new data, awaiting the next act in the drama to unfold.

A brief time later, the ambushed ship launched an ambush of its own, destroying the Dark Lords' craft in decisive fashion. As the ship maneuvered for orbit the AI noted how quickly it had recovered, and how quickly it adapted. Probability fields, quantum representations of uncertainty, collapsed as the AI reached a conclusion: *The newcomers are not T'aafhal, but they are probably allies (probability 0.78). I will await more data.*

Part Three

Cat's Paw

Chapter 25

Rescue Mission Departure, Peggy Sue

Once the ship made orbit, the Captain sent Bobby and all the Marines aft to suit up for the trip dirtside. After a brief stop at his quarters to don a skintight pressure suit and collect the *aoi chō*, Bobby headed aft to the armory. Trailing behind him the butterflies flashed excitedly through colors red, orange, and yellow. No longer the somber shades of sorrow for their missing goddess, but rather hues reflecting excitement with an underlying hint of menace.

Bobby too, was contemplating actions to come, wishing for the thousandth time that they possessed a Star Trek like transporter that could place him on the surface almost instantly. He had about come to the conclusion that such devices were not possible. After all, the insanely advanced T'aafhal—possessors of technology that could create wormholes through space and throw black holes at their enemies—did not have such a device. Mizuki would have argued why such a mechanism was impossible, citing conservation of energy and differences in velocity vectors between transmitter and arrival point. He smiled in spite of himself.

God I miss you Mizuki-chan, he said to himself, eyes blurring at the thought of her. Behind him a ripple of indigo and deep blue passed through the cloud of butterflies, reflecting his emotions. *If you are down there I will find you.*

Arriving in the armory, Bobby found the Marines already in full armor. He quickly climbed into his own suit, what was euphemistically called "light" armor. Once encased, he would weigh more than 200 kilos. Made from overlapping thin bands of highly refractive metallic-ceramic composite, the armor could turn away small arms fire up to .50 caliber armor piercing rounds. To offset its weight, electroreactive synthetic muscles augmented his own natural ones, making movement easy and amplifying his strength nearly threefold.

For armament he carried a combination railgun that had a rapid fire 5mm flechette gun mounted atop a 20mm shotgun/grenade launcher firing configurable explosive rounds. The nano-engineered explosive in the 20mm rounds could be adjusted by displacing the electrons in the material, bumping them to higher orbitals and enhancing the explosive yield. The pattern of the explosion itself could also be adjusted between an antipersonnel bursting charge and an armor piercing shaped charge. The laser rangefinder could automatically set the distance a round would travel before detonation, making it possible to fire above an entrenched position and rain down shrapnel from overhead bursts.

As imposing as Bobby's kit was, it paled next to the Marines' heavy battle armor. In heavy armor the humans stood seven feet tall and weighed in at over 400 kilograms, Umky topped 12 feet and weighed over a ton. Multi-barreled flechette and 15mm railguns attached to the forearms of the suits with ammo feeds linking them to large magazines on their backs. The armor essentially turned them into tanks with legs.

As the technicians closed up his armor, Bobby looked around the room at the Marines. They looked like hulking gray robots, faceless in their enclosed helmets. It had been a long time since he had led Marines into battle, but the feel, and the smell, of armor brought it all back. Over the squad frequency he spoke, "Gunny, move 'em out."

"Aye, aye, Sir," the Gunny responded. "You heard the man, get your worthless hides up to the shuttle bay on 3rd deck."

* * * * *

The Marines and two Petty Officers headed for the cargo lift with a minimum of grumbling and banter. They knew that they were likely to find bad news on the planet's surface—the odds that any of the crewmembers survived the small shuttle's crash were slim. The missing three were well liked by the crew and the loss of any one of them would be a blow to morale. This was particularly true of Dr. Ogawa, her being Cmdr. Danner's wife and all.

In general, all of Peggy Sue's officers were popular with the enlisted personnel. The Captain was highly respected as was the First Officer, though some might admit to being slightly intimidated by her. It was the Sailing Master, however, that the crew felt the most genuine affection for. He was always approachable and never talked down to crewmembers. Even his sometimes wacky conspiracy theories and slightly off center observations helped endear him to the rank and file.

As much as it would suck if Kate or Lt. Lewis bought the farm, the Marines headed for the shuttle silently agreed, it would be a fucking shame if Dr. Ogawa was dead. With that in mind they somewhat somberly boarded the large armored shuttle for the trip to the planet's surface.

Princess Timushi's Party

After a brief soaking by afternoon rain showers, the Princess's party crested a small hill and finally caught sight of their objective —the capital city. Standing above the city, the towers of the royal palace glowed a warm reddish-orange in the light of the setting sun.

"Are we going to push on to the city?" asked Mizuki, anxious to be done with the journey.

"No, Lord Mizuki," the Castellan answered. "We cannot make the southern gate before night fall. The gates will be locked until tomorrow's first light."

"You are correct as always, my Lord Castellan," Timushi added. "There is a good place to camp just ahead according to the scouts. We will eat and take a good night's sleep so we are ready for an early start in the morning."

"And you are sure that your sister has not already arrived, Your Highness?"

"If she had there would be signal fires burning in the palace towers, announcing her ascension to the throne. No, we have either beaten her party to the capital, or tomorrow we will both arrive to contest the royal succession. I fear if that is the case, tomorrow will be quite unpleasant."

The Castellan's antennae twitched and her hand strayed to the pommel of her sword—a tell-tale sign that the old warrior was anxious or worried. The Princess remained poised as always, causing Mizuki to contemplate the coming day in silence.

A shining city on a hill, didn't some old politician talk about that as a symbol of hope? No matter. One way or another, this journey will end tomorrow. What comes after that, I haven't a clue.

Princess Reishi's Party

On the north side of the city, Princess Reishi's procession came to a ragged halt. She had pushed her subjects unmercifully, mostly at the behest of the daemons who accompanied them. Reishi was no longer sure the arrival of the demonic creatures was a blessing, sent by the gods to aid her cause. She had begun to suspect that they were using her for some purpose known only to themselves. In any case, it was far too late to back out of the deal now.

The head daemon shuffled up to her side. "Princess, we should press on to the city."

If they were sent by the gods, how can they not understand the protocols? The succession must be done according to tradition, observing ancient rituals whose origins are lost in the mists of time. "No, my Lord Daemon. The gates to the city will be barred at sunset, and it would be a grave breach of protocol for a claimant to the throne to arrive in the night."

The daemon's frustration was almost palpable. The Princess twitched her antennae in annoyance and explained.

"Tomorrow, after the city gates are opened at dawn, my procession will enter the north gate. There are three gates, one for each of the three traditional claimants for the throne—north, east, and south. Each opens onto a broad boulevard that runs straight to the royal palace. It is important that you and your fellow daemons remain cloaked and hidden behind my warriors. If you are seen it could spark hostility on the part of the palace guard."

"They cannot stop us, Princess," the hooded daemon grumbled.

"I'm sure they can't, Commander, but an altercation would greatly upset the populace. It could take days, even weeks to settle them down after such an... event."

"And what if your sister is there?"

"The lack of signal fires in the palace towers say she has not arrived before us. We need just to march to the palace, right to the throne room and I can claim my birthright."

"And if Timushi arrives at the same time? Won't getting into a battle with her upset the city's inhabitants?"

"Not at all. They will be expecting us to fight for the throne. If she arrives late, the palace guard will already be in thrall to me, and her attack will be short and fatal for her and her warriors. The services of your daemons will only be necessary if she, by some miracle, gains the upper-hand. Hopefully any such confrontation will happen within the palace and hidden from the prying eyes of the populace."

"Does Your Highness have any objections to my commandos guarding your person as we attempt to gain access to the throne room?"

"Of course not, in fact I am counting on you to keep me safe so my warriors can devote all their energies to defeating my foes. The day will not be won until my royal sister has been dismembered and the scent of her dying can be sensed by all. Only then can I claim what is mine, only then can I be seated on my mother's throne and begin my reign as Queen of all Formicidae."

Chapter 26

Rescue Mission, Shuttle Crash Site

The armored shuttle full of Marines made a high angle of incidence approach to the crash site, decelerating rapidly while scribing a bright arc across the predawn sky. Sonic booms announcing its arrival echoed from the ridges and valleys, causing animals large and small to stir beneath the jungle canopy. Knowing that he would be accompanying the Marines after landing, Bobby, with great trepidation, let Frank Hoenig pilot the shuttle to the planet's surface.

"Set her down there, Mr. Hoenig, next to the base of the cliff."

"Aye, aye, Commander."

Next to Frank was Jay Taylor, serving as copilot, while Tamara Wilson manned the shuttle's armaments—there had been no shortage of volunteers among the crew for this mission. In the end, the First Officer selected those she thought steadiest under fire, hence the presence of the Aussie and the Canadian along with Hoenig, arguably the best shuttle pilot among the noncoms.

The furrow the small shuttle plowed on its violent encounter with the local terrain had faded significantly during the time since the crash, but was still visible from above. The surrounding jungle's tenacious flora had not yet reclaimed the open space in front of the ill fated shuttle's final resting place at the base of the ancient escarpment.

Frank edged up to the cliff face, pivoted the shuttle so the rear ramp faced the wreckage, and gently sat the armored craft down.

"We're down, Commander. You can drop the ramp when ready."

"Thanks, Mr. Hoenig. Pop a recon drone if you would." Bobby headed aft to the passenger compartment where the squad of armored Marines waited. "Secure the site, Gunny."

"Aye, aye, Sir," Rosey replied. Releasing the ramp she called out assignments. "Kato, Vinny, take the starboard side, POs on overwatch; Jumbo Twins take port, Umky and Bosco on overwatch. Move!"

The rear ramp dropped onto the hardscrabble debris brought down from the cliff face by the small shuttle's impact. The two designated teams of Marines sprinted down the mild incline and around the armored shuttle's flanks. Bosco and the bear moved at a less hurried pace, taking up position beside the ramp on the port side. They correctly interpreted the Gunny's assigning them overwatch to mean "keep an eye on the newbies."

The Gunny exited next, headed directly for the wreckage. She was followed by Bobby in his light armor, looking small and childlike next to the Marines. Overhead, a basketball sized recon drone appeared, drifting silently above the investigators.

As Bobby examined the wreckage using the drone's ground penetrating radar the butterflies explored the cliff face and surrounding debris. Umky and Bosco watched the Jumbo Twins as they approached the edge of the clearing.

* * * * *

"Zeke, don't get too close to the underbrush," said Mal on suit-to-suit.

Zeke paused and turned toward his brother. "Come on, bro, there ain't nothing here. The shuttle's repulsors blew this crap all around as we landed—it would have scared any local critters off."

As he was speaking the brush in front of him quivered ever so slightly. The large green fronds parted and a gray spider-like creature the size of a wild boar burst from cover and landed on Zeke's shoulder. Proving its intentions beyond a reasonable doubt, the spider attempted to sink its venomous fangs into the Marine's helmeted head.

"Ayyyiii," Zeke cried, waving his arms around. As flexible as the armored suits were they did restrict the wearer's arm movement. The spider had landed in the one place that Zeke could not easily reach with his armored mitts.

"Get it off! Get it off!" he shrieked, hopping around like a spastic humanoid robot.

Answering his brother's cries for help, Mal stepped up beside him and delivered a roundhouse, open handed blow that swatted the spider from Zeke's shoulder. In a jumble of legs and squirting body fluid the hairy attacker flew through the air and disappeared into the thick foliage. The blow also knocked the hopping Zeke off his feet, leaving him face down in decaying organic matter.

"What the hell did you do that for," the now spider free Zeke demanded, pushing his upper body up out of the muck.

"You said get it off of you," Mal replied, a bit indignant at his brother's lack of appreciation for his actions. "You were freaking out, man. That thing looked like it was trying to eat your head."

"You could have just pulled it off of me. You didn't have to almost knock me out!"

"That's BS and you know it, I didn't hit you that hard." Mal attempted to give his brother a hand up but the proffered hand was knocked away as Zeke struggled to his feet. As he stood upright both brothers' attention was drawn to a violent shaking of the oversized ferns and tree limbs in the area where the spider had landed. The commotion continued as other, unseen predators made a quick meal of the now deceased arachnid.

* * * * *

Back by the shuttle, Umky nudged Bosco and said, "What's with those two?"

The human Marine watched the antics of the two brothers as they hopped around trying to fend off their hairy, multilegged attacker.

"Not my circus, not my monkeys," Bosco commented. He looked up at Umky and explained. "is old Russian saying."

"Heh, that's a good one," the bear replied. "Not my monkeys. I'll have to remember that."

Their observation of the twins was interrupted when the Gunny called them over to the wreckage at the base of the cliff. Most of the wreckage was covered in fallen rock but what was left of the small shuttle's rear airstair door was still identifiable. The crumpled opening was far too small to allow any of the armored Earthlings access. The Gunny had sent her suit's recon drone—a baseball sized robot that was intended to scout ahead for enemies—into the small opening. The video it returned showed a jumbled mess, but no bodies.

"The ground penetrating radar from the big recon drone shows that the front of the shuttle was totally crushed by the impact," Bobby said grimly. "I can't really tell what happened to the crew without going inside. Let's see if we can excavate around the opening a bit—maybe I can wriggle in for a look."

The bear looked first to the Gunny, then back at Bobby. "If you don't mind, Commander, I think I have a faster way of telling what's in there than that."

"Really?"

"Yeah." Umky's helmet unfolded from around his face, retracting into his suit, leaving his head exposed.

"Oh wow," he exclaimed, waving a platter sized armored paw in front of his muzzle. "Damn this planet stinks!"

"Er, what does it smell like?" asked Bobby, somewhat at a loss to comprehend the polar bear's actions.

"It smells like insects, lizard shit, and rotting plants. And I thought it smelled bad on the ship!"

The humans looked at each other, trying to figure out what the bear hoped to accomplish by opening his suit to the native atmosphere. Umky moved forward and stuck his nose into the hole that was the only entrance into the wreck. He sniffed.

"Well, there's dead humans in there, too far gone to tell who or even how many."

He pulled back and started sniffing around the area, nose down like a bloodhound. He moved ten meters away from the wreck and then sat back on his haunches. "One of them made it out alive."

Bobby was flummoxed. "What? Can you tell who it was?"

Umky looked back at him. "Yeah, it was Dr. Ogawa."

Bobby's head swam. He was torn between anguish over the lost crewmembers and elation that Mizuki had somehow lived through the crash. "Are you sure it was Mizuki?" he asked.

Umky snorted.

"You primates are real visual critters, Commander. Is there any one of the crew you wouldn't recognize on sight?"

"Well, no."

"A polar bear's primary sense is smell and I have been locked up with you humans inside a metal tube for more than a year. There isn't a one of you I don't know by scent."

"I didn't mean to doubt your word, Umky," Bobby apologized. "I just never realized that you could do that. No offense intended."

"None taken." Umky looked back at the surrounding forest. "Dr. Ogawa exited the shuttle and headed out that way, through the jungle."

CIC, Peggy Sue

Billy Ray, Beth and Betty White were in the CIC monitoring the surface party on the big 3D display tank. Views from suit cameras appeared on the displays lining the walls, as did medical readouts for each of Marines and crew down below. Those present had refrained so far from peppering the ground personnel with questions, not wishing to distract from their investigation. Finally the comm channel squawked.

"Peggy Sue, Rescue Leader."

Billy Ray replied. "Rescue Leader, we read you five-by-five. Go ahead."

"We have ascertained that two of the shuttle crew died in the crash. One survived and left the area on foot."

"Copy that, Rescue Leader. Interrogative the names of the KIAs?"

"Katrin Hamm and Nigel Lewis."

"Does that mean Mizuki survived?" Beth asked her husband in a harsh whisper.

Billy Ray held up a hand to forestall more questions. "We copy, Shuttle One. Crewman Hamm and Lieutenant Lewis are confirmed as deceased. Please verify the survivor."

Bobby's reply was laced with emotion. "Affirmative, Peggy Sue. Dr. Mizuki Ogawa was not found in the wreckage and Mr. Umky says there is a scent trail leading from the crash site into the jungle."

Relief lit up both women's faces when Bobby confirmed that Mizuki survived the crash. Their elation faded quickly as they realized their possibly wounded friend had been stranded on a hostile planet for over a week. That her body was not among the wreckage kept hope alive, but the odds of her survival were still not good.

"It's great news that Mizuki survived the crash, Bobby. What are your next steps?"

"When we came in I noticed there was a river a couple of valleys to the north, with what looked like a road alongside it. I have a hunch that's the way Mizuki was headed and I'm thinking we should go to the road and let Umky check for signs she passed that way with his Mark 1 Mod 1 sniffer."

"Roger that, Rescue Leader."

"Peggy Sue, interrogative regarding the remains of the deceased?"

"Wait one." The Captain muted the comm.

"Aw hell," He said to the two women gathered around the display table. "Betty, what do you think? Is there any reason to try and recover the remains?"

"I don't know, Billy Ray. It doesn't sound like there's much to recover."

"And they would have to excavate the whole wreck to get at them." Beth shifted uncomfortably. "I know we don't leave our people behind, but to expend a lot of time and energy to recover some nearly unidentifiable body parts doesn't seem a reasonable thing to do."

"Neither of the deceased had any known family back home, so there'd be no reason to repatriate the remains. Which means we'd do a burial in space." This had been done for other lost crewmembers on other missions—their remains launched from the ship in sealed coffins, which were then vaporized by the X-ray laser batteries.

"From the images of the crash site, they both died instantly on impact," Betty said. "They are beyond caring what we do with the aftermath."

"Betty's right, Captain. And we need to destroy the wreckage in any case."

"Right." Billy Ray made a command decision. "Rescue Leader, Peggy Sue."

"Go, Peggy Sue," came the immediate reply.

"Unless you've got a compelling reason not to, pardner, I want you to blow the wreckage with an antimatter charge. Enough to vaporized the shuttle and the remains."

After a slight pause, Bobby replied. "Aye, aye, Peggy Sue. We'll take care of it, and then head for the river."

"Very good, Rescue Leader. Peggy Sue out."

Shuttle Crash Site

Bobby and the Gunny stood near the wreckage. The Gunny handed Bobby a grapefruit sized silver sphere. "Everyone's back on board, Sir. The charge is set to fifteen minutes delay."

"Thanks Gunny," Bobby said, accepting the AM bomb. "Get aboard, I'll be right behind you."

The Gunny turned, jogged to the shuttle and up the rear ramp. Bobby walked over to the jagged hole leading inside the fallen shuttle. Above him, the butterflies formed a swirling wreath in dark somber colors reflecting his mood. Boby was not a very religious man, but the circumstances seemed to call for some form of prayer. From memory he recalled the words from a Navy funeral he once attended.

"Grant eternal rest to them, O Lord, and let perpetual light shine upon them. May their souls and the souls of all the faithful departed, through the mercy of God, rest in peace. Amen."

He armed the bomb and tossed it underhand into the dark hole in the wreckage. Before heading back to the shuttle he spoke a final benediction, words heard at the funerals of many a mariner. "Farewell shipmates, may you have fair winds and following seas."

* * * * *

As soon as Cmdr. Danner was back on board Frank secured the rear ramp and lifted the shuttle from the clearing. They had all heard Bobby's words over the comm and, religious or not, they all mourned the loss of their shipmates.

"They died too young." Frank's voice held both sadness and anger.

"That they did, Frank-O," Jay added. "Kate was a fine sheila, a good mate, and Lieutenant Lewis might have been so British that he farted scones, but he was a top bloke."

"Right you are, Jay," said Tamara from the weapon's operator station behind the two pilots. "I just hope we run into the fuckin' asswipes who shot 'em down."

"You and me both, Tam," Frank replied, heading the big shuttle toward the river. "I think we would all like to find the bastards who did this."

Chapter 27

Princess Timushi's Party, The Capital City

Dawn broke, painting the walls of Formicidae's capital city red. Ruddy rays of light revealed Timushi's warriors standing in formation before the southern gate. Behind the soldier ants, who stood in regular ranks five abreast, were the Princess, Castellan, and a strange hooded figure. They were followed by a less orderly mass of attendants, functionaries, and servants.

The gate itself was monumental in scale, standing ten meters wide and fifteen high. Its construction was cyclopean, the uprights and lintel consisting of single gigantic stones. The gate obviously predated the surrounding walls, which were made of smaller, dressed stone blocks. An attempt at integrating the massive stones with the surrounding walls had been made by carving designs into the gate's frame. Atop the walls the heads of warrior ants could be seen through the crenelations.

"Do you need to announce your presence, Your Highness?"

"No, Lord Mizuki. The guards can sense that I am a Princess of the royal linage. There can be only one reason for my presence—to complete my journey to the castle and claim the Queen's throne."

As if on cue, the massive doors creaked and swung slowly open. The warriors moved their grounded weapons to port arms and marched forward through the gate. Timushi and her companions followed, trailed by the rest of her entourage.

Passing into the city proper, Mizuki looked about as innocuously as possible, the hood of her poncho up to hide her alien features. The wide boulevard was paved in stone, with a slightly arched cross slope to aid runoff from frequent rains. Storm gutters lined the pavement along with planters filled with large ferns.

Set back from the planters were buildings, two and three stories tall, also constructed of stone blocks. Their moderately pitched roofs were made of slate, their windows unglazed, with shutters open to the new day. Whether the buildings were shops or domiciles was not clear. Everything was very clean, very orderly, very unlike any human city at a preindustrial level.

The boulevard ran arrow straight for several kilometers ending at a second wall, above which the royal palace stood like a Medieval cathedral. The morning sun glinted off tall windows framed by flying buttresses—impressive even to Mizuki who had been raised in modern Tokyo.

I can't wait to see what the palace looks like inside, Mizuki thought, playing tourist in a strange city. *Hopefully we will just march into the palace and Timushi will claim her throne—then I can concentrate on signaling the ship to come rescue me.*

Princess Reishi's Party, The Capital City

As Timushi's column advanced on the palace from the south, Reishi and her warriors approached from the north. Her soldiers' ranks were not as orderly as her sister's, but they were more numerous. And hidden at the center of the formation were dozens of bulky shapes wearing hooded cassocks. Like sinister monks on an unholy pilgrimage, the Fakkaa Commander and a hand picked platoon of commandos shuffled along thinking bloody thoughts. It was bad enough being stuck on this open sewer of a planet, with too much heat and too much humidity, without having to walk around wrapped in heavy cloaks so as not to frighten the natives.

Unimpressed by the city and the palace's graceful spires, the Commander thought only of completing his mission. What neither party knew was that they were in a dead heat. Their long race to the capital was about to end in a tie, a tie that would transform a foot race into armed combat. If the Commander had known this his mood might have been lighter, and his anticipation keener.

"What will we find when we arrive at the palace, Princess?"

"As I explained last night, Commander, the palace is laid out with vaulted halls pointing north, south, and east. The throne itself is where the western arm would be, behind it being the royal brood chambers. We will enter the northern door and proceed to the steps leading to the throne itself."

"So you just walk in and sit down? That's it?"

"No, of course not. There are dignitaries and officials in the palace that will come forward to inspect me—to ensure I am not deformed or in someway defective in mind or body. Once that formality is taken care of I will be led to the throne itself."

"And then you are queen?"

"For all intents and purposes. The palace guard will come to view me and be bonded to my service—my pheromones will ensure all the lesser castes are faithful to me. There will be a coronation ceremony later to allow my subjects to see their new queen."

"Sounds fairly straight forward."

"It should be, Commander. You and your warriors stay with my person and let any fighting be handled by my guards. You are my insurance, my fallback—I must ascend the throne in the traditional way if at all possible."

The Commander mumbled something under his breath, and then spoke aloud. "Understood, Your Highness."

"Look! There ahead, my warriors are climbing the steps to the palace grounds. We must hurry to catch up!"

The Queen's Palace

Drawing closer to the palace revealed a more complex layout than apparent from a distance. The palace itself sat on a raised platform, higher than the surrounding city. The raised plaza itself had sloping sides encased by more ancient stonework—massive stone walls ten meters high, built from large irregular stones of varied sizes and shapes. The stones were closely fitted to their neighbors with no visible gaps or mortar, like the walls of the Incan fortress of Saqsaywaman. A wide flight of stone stairs led from the boulevard to the plaza above.

In the center of the raised area sat the palace itself, a collection of spires, flying buttresses, and panels of colored glass that could rival any Gothic cathedral. Marching with Princess Timushi's party, Mizuki found herself heading across the stone paved plaza toward the south transept of the castle. A squadron of warriors led by the Castellan preceded the Princess and her daemon through the ornately carved wooden door.

231

Mizuki lowered her hood and looked around the interior in wonder. The walls were shimmering curtains of light suspended between intricately carved stone columns. Galleries and side chambers were adorned with pointed arches, and the ceiling sixty meters overhead was a ribbed vault that would have done any Medieval cathedral proud. Light from the multihued windows danced off the polished stone floors, themselves containing delicate inlaid patterns.

If the Queen's palace took on the cruciform shape of a traditional cathedral it was certainly not for the same reasons. Still, while there were no pews for worshipers, the soaring ceilings and monumental architecture might well be considered appropriate for a place of worship. After all, those who came to these halls to petition the Queen of Formicidae revered her as a living goddess, the font of all life for her people.

Entering the main part of the hall, the intersection of the four great vaults, the queen's throne sat on a stepped platform to Mizuki's left, where the chancel and ambulatory of an Earthly cathedral would have been. The throne was an alabaster cradle meant to support the queen's abdomen—there was no high back as on a human throne.

"This is truly stunning, Your Highness," Mizuki said in wonder.

"As well it should be, for I will never leave this room again so long as I shall live."

Before Mizuki could ask the Princess why that would be, figures approached from the northern transept.

"You are right about that, sister!" came a strong voice from among the newcomers, echoed and amplified by the chamber's excellent acoustics.

Looking to identify the source of the comment, Mizuki spotted a large native that looked nearly identical to Timushi. No doubt this was Princess Reishi, Timushi's sister and rival for the throne.

Reishi's warriors spread out across the north side of the nave, filing down the side aisle, as Timushi's warriors did the same on the south side. Both sides dressed their ranks and faced each other with weapons drawn.

Chikushō! Mizuki thought, drawing her katana, *I guess this isn't going to be simple after all.*

Rescue Mission, The River

Frank took the shuttle low over the river to gain cover from the surrounding ridges. As they sped westward along the river valley a bright flash appeared off the port side—the detonation of the AM grenade left in the wreckage of the small shuttle. Seconds later the shockwave arrived, causing the shuttle to wobble, though its passengers felt nothing, all motion filtered out by the deck gravity.

"How much juice did you put in that thing, Commander?" Frank asked, correcting the shuttle's attitude and heading.

"About 90 terajoules, the equivalent of roughly 20 kilotons of TNT."

"About the same as the bomb dropped on Nagasaki," observed Tamara.

"About that," Bobby agreed. "Temperatures at the heart of the explosion should have exceeded five thousand degrees—hot enough to vaporize the shuttle and those left aboard her."

"Where to now, Sir?"

"Look over there, off to port. That looks like a sizable open space just before the bridge up ahead. Put her down in the clearing, Mr. Hoenig."

"Aye, aye, Sir."

* * * * *

Minutes later the shuttle was on the ground and the Marines fanned out across the clearing. Partially sheltered by nearby trees was a small raised pond with water running out of an overflow.

Umky was once again seeking the scent of the missing Mizuki. "She was here alright, Commander."

Bobby kneeled down next to the outflow from the pond. "Indeed, Mr. Umky. Even I can tell she was here."

The bear looked at the human with a puzzled expression on his long face. Then he noticed that Bobby was pointing at the ground. There in the moist soil was an eroded but recognizable boot print.

Umky grinned. "Yeah, that'll work too."

"So we know that she passed this way," the Gunny said, coming over to look at the boot print. "Do we know where this road goes?"

"I don't but we can ask the ship." Bobby changed frequencies. "Peggy Sue, Rescue Leader."

"Go, Rescue Leader."

"We have found evidence that Dr. Ogawa made it out of the jungle and was headed along the river road. Can you tell us where the road leads?"

"Roger that, Rescue Leader. It turns after the bridge and runs north for a couple hundred klicks. It ends up at a large city... wait one."

The rescue mission leader waited impatiently.

"Rescue Leader, be advised that there seems to be a great deal of activity around a big structure in the middle of the city. It looks like there are two columns of armed natives converging on a cathedral like building—one from the south and one from the north."

"I copy, Peggy Sue. The natives are having a dust up in the city to the north."

"Affirmative. Be advised that the northern party is accompanied by aliens of some other form, presumably the ones landed by the primitive fleet."

"What does that mean?" the Gunny asked Bobby.

"It means that something important is happening at the end of this road, something involving the aliens that shot down the shuttle. And if I know Mizuki she'll be in the thick of it. Let's saddle up, Gunny!"

While the Gunny got the squad back on board the shuttle, Bobby talked to the ship in orbit.

"Peggy Sue, I'm going to take a leap of faith and assume that Mizuki is involved in the situation to the north. We are headed there now. ETA is fifteen minutes."

"Roger that, Rescue Leader. Good hunting."

Chapter 28

Queen's Palace

Warrior ants poured from the northern transept, moving eastward along the aisle on the north side of the nave. To keep themselves from being flanked, Princess Timushi's warriors did the same on the south side. Once both sides had fully deployed they rushed to meet in the middle of the vaulted hall, spears thrusting and swords slashing. Unlike humans, the insect warriors fought in eerie silence, making no battle cries and not calling out in pain when wounded.

Mizuki, her katana drawn, positioned herself in front of the Princess, standing a few steps down from Timushi and the Castellan. From the north side came a volley of arrows. Behind her several warriors moved to protect the Princess with their shields and bodies. Mizuki's approach was more direct—she knocked three of the incoming arrows from the air before they could strike.

"Stay under cover, Your Highness," the Castellan shouted, motioning for her archers to counter volley. The return flight of arrows scattered the opposition archers temporarily, but on the front line things were not going well. The superior number of Princess Reishi's warriors was slowly but surely overwhelming Timushi's force.

I signed on for this and I doubt they will show mercy if my side loses, Mizuki thought grimly and waded into the fray.

A warrior in front of her went down with a spear through its thorax. Mizuki stepped forward and removed the attacking warrior's head. The attacker sank to the floor still grasping its spear.

Fixing the nearby attackers in her mind, Mizuki focused her *ki* as she had been taught. Much as she had with the target mats back on board the Peggy Sue, the swordswoman danced among the attacking warriors, her sword a silver flash, harvesting heads, limbs, and torsos.

A monks robe cut to the left. To the right a *kote* or wrist cut, severing a sword arm, followed up by a *do* cut across the ant's belly. Again to the left an upward *kiriage* cut laid open an opponent's body from hip to opposing shoulder. The ant warriors were no match for her speed and her skill with a sword. Mizuki cut a terrible swath through the opposing warriors until she stood alone surrounded by a dozen dead.

* * * * *

On the north side, near the foot of the stairs leading to the throne, Princess Reishi stood surrounded by dark hooded figures. Among her guardians was the Fakkaa Commander.

"What in the seven hells it that thing?"

Reishi hissed. "It seems that my dear sister has brought a daemon of her own to the party. This is your area Commander."

"Right. Sergeant, deploy a squad to the left and drive back the opposing force. That should draw off the attacking alien."

Mizuki's rampage had turned the tide of battle and Timushi's warriors now pressed their advantage. The once cathedral like audience chamber was now a charnel house, with insect corpses littering the polished stone floors.

"Yes Sir! And what should we do with the alien?"

"Kill the damned thing."

A dozen of the Fakkaa commandos threw off their outer garments, revealing their true nature. Each was about man height but much stockier. They stood on splayed feet that ended with stout curved claws. Their upper limbs were thick and strong, each with three long digging claws similar to a giant sloth or an anteater. Beaver like front teeth protruded from pug faces with deep set dark eyes, but the most prominent feature was the quills.

Each Fakkaa was wrapped in a coat of needle sharp spines, much like an Earthly echidna or porcupine. Individual quills—modified hairs coated with a thick layer of keratin—were interspersed with normal hair and a furry undercoat. The quills themselves were up to thirty centimeters in length and embedded in the skin musculature, allowing their owners to bristle when wading into battle. Against an unarmored foe they were close to invulnerable.

The daemons joined the fray, knocking aside ant warriors, inflicting grievous wounds with their massive claws. The long stiff spines warded off blows from edged weapons and their digging claws handily deflected the warriors' spears. Princess Timushi's warriors faltered and again, the tide of battle shifted.

Rescue Mission, Arriving at the Palace

"There seem to be a whole lot of arthropods with Medieval weapons converging on that big building down there, Commander," Tamara called out from the weapons console.

"Drop lower and circle the building, Mr. Hoenig. Let's be sure of what we are getting into here."

"Aye, aye, Sir."

The armored shuttle banked and circled the queen's palace at two hundred meters. To the south, ant-like warriors were entering the structure, while a throng of smaller insects crowded around.

There seemed to be no activity in front of the eastern wing of the building, but to the north an even larger body of armed ants crowded in. A hundred meters back from the structure there was another set of creatures, these decidedly not ant-like and each wearing garb akin to a monk's habit.

All the Marines were viewing the shuttle's video feed as they orbited the scene below. The Gunny asked the question they all were thinking. "I get that the ant things are the natives, but what are the things in the dark robes?"

"I'm guessing they are the other aliens, the ones from those primitive spacecraft in orbit."

"That would be the aliens who shot down the shuttle," said Frank.

"Affirmative, Mr. Hoenig. Take us around to the east side of the structure and land with the ramp facing the building."

"Aye, aye."

"Sir, IR shows a bunch of creatures moving around inside that building, and from the way they are moving I'd say they are either having a rave or there's a battle going on in there."

"I'm not sure if Dr. Ogawa is in there but anything having to do with the off planet aliens can not be good," the Gunny observed.

"I agree. Once we're down, form up the squad and we'll go around to the north side of the building and see what the interlopers are up to. Mr. Hoenig, send out a couple of recon drones —one to orbit the building and another up high to keep a watch on the surrounding airspace. Remember, these critters have some form of air support."

"Aye, Sir. We are down and the rear ramp is unlocked."

"Sit tight and keep an eye out for incoming," Bobby said to the pilot. Then he turned and headed aft. "Gunny, deploy your Marines."

The rear ramp dropped onto the flagstone pavement and massive dark shapes pounded down it. The jogging Marines swung to the right, spreading out and taking up firing positions. Bobby was the last one down the ramp, along with his halo of butterflies.

Walking clear of the shuttle, he looked up at the east face of the building. From the ground, the structure looked much larger than it did from the air. The main portion stood some eighty meters tall at its central peak, though it was surrounded by even taller spires. The facade rose in four tiers, the lower one taking the form of a pointed arch and archivolt framing ten-meter wooden doors. The tiers above that contained windows of various sizes and shapes, some glazed in stained glass and others open.

As Bobby marveled at the palace's architectural grandeur, his winged entourage was also making some observations. The butterflies formed a whirling torus above Bobby's head—flashing excitedly in vermilion, magenta, and gold—before heading *en masse* for the building. Like a Chinese dragon, the flock described a sinuous path, pulling up sharply at the doors. Rising to the second tier, the *aoi chō* entered the palace through the open windows and disappeared.

Inside the Palace

Seeing the carnage the spiny "daemons" were wreaking among the ant warriors, Mizuki charged forward, though she was not sure of how best to attack the creatures. Approaching the nearest quill covered attacker from the side, she struck its left arm where she estimated its wrist to be. The clawed hand was cleanly severed and fell to the floor.

The creature made a high-pitched bawling sound, almost like a human baby crying. Stepping behind her victim, carefully avoiding the wicked looking spines, Mizuki aimed a second strike at the back of its right knee. This brought the crippled alien to the ground.

Sensing a threat from behind her Mizuki spun about while sliding sideways. Her motion took her to the right side of a second alien who stretched upward, spread its arms and revealed its unprotected belly. But the creature's naked front held a deadly surprise—sprouting from black wrinkled flesh was a second set of arms, lower and smaller than the heavily clawed upper arms. The smaller arms ended in three fingered hands with opposable thumbs, hands that held what was obviously some form of firearm.

The alien pivoted, trying to bring its weapon to bear. Mizuki cut upward, slicing through both secondary arms, sending the short barreled weapon flying. Finishing the upward cut with her blade horizontal above her head she drove forward in a straight thrust, driving the point of her katana fifteen centimeters deep into the creature's left eye. She pulled the blade out and her foe collapsed.

Victory was short lived. The other daemons produced their own firearms and began to fire short bursts into Princess Timushi's remaining warriors.

Oh crap! I need cover. As good as she was with a sword she knew swords do not win over firearms except in martial arts movies. Mizuki turned and ran for the side aisle, seeking cover behind the stone columns that supported the gallery above. Bullets ricocheted off stone as she ducked behind an ornate column.

In the shelter of the column she raised the hood of her poncho and activated its adaptive camouflage mode. Running down the aisle toward the Princess's position on the throne platform, Mizuki was a shimmering phantom, dodging bullets, arrows and an occasional thrown spear. As she neared the cluster of warriors protecting the Princess she noticed more of the spiny aliens entering the fray.

This is not going well at all, she thought, breaking from cover and heading toward the daemon nearest the Princess. In front of her, an ant warrior was in the process of collapsing from gunshot wounds. She took two steps and jumped onto its back. Landing on both feet, she launched herself into a front flip over the head of the alien who was still pumping rounds into the dying ant. Landing in a crouch she spun to her left, moving to the shooter's side.

Striking with all her strength she cut the barbed alien below its second set of arms, where she hoped the creature's stomach was. Drawing back on the sword as it cut, her hands barely avoiding the spines, she pulled away and stood up. The daemon dropped its weapon and sank to its knees.

The alien began keening pitifully while trying to hold its intestines in, but they slid from its slit belly and spread wetly across the floor. The smell of blood and manure filled Mizuki's nostrils—evidently the porcupine like creatures were herbivores. Almost causally she cut down an attacking ant warrior as she backed toward the stairs. Looking toward the enemy Princess she saw more of the deadly aliens. Looking back down the nave to the east she saw her death.

Another of the spiny daemons stood well out of sword reach, pointing its projectile weapon directly at her. As fast as she was, she could not reach her foe in time, nor could she hope to evade an automatic weapon with no cover nearby.

"Shinjimae, kono yarou!" She shouted at the alien in defiance and then she noticed a cloud of bright fluttering color descending from the air above the battle.

A flock of butterflies danced around the gun welding alien, spoiling its aim and distracting it from shooting Mizuki. It waved an upper arm, trying to shoo way the winged distractions but instead they landed on its spines and body. Blue-white sparks lit up the creature, which shrieked, spasmed, and crumpled to the floor.

Under her breath Mizuki said a single word. "Bobby!"

Chapter 29

Rescue Mission

"Now where in the hell are they going?" Bobby said out loud as the last butterfly disappeared. Then it struck him that maybe, just maybe, Mizuki's winged pets knew something the rest of them didn't.

"Umky! Take out the doors," he cried, pointing toward the massive stone structure.

"Aye, Commander," the bear replied happily, raising his left foreleg. A six round burst of 15mm HE rounds issued from the triple barreled rail cannon on Umky's arm. The resulting string of explosions detonated so close together they formed a single rippling mass of flame. Fragments of wood and stone flew in all directions as the doors disintegrated.

Bobby blinked. He had intended for the large ursine to break through the doors bodily, not blow them to splinters. *Probably our own fault for teaching the bears they should use weapons and only fall back on physical strength as a last resort.*

As the smoke cleared, the stone lintel from above the doorway fell to the ground with a hollow thud. The Gunny and several of the other squad members were looking back at him, no doubt wondering what was going on.

"Gunny, take the squad to the north side of the building and remove any hostiles from the area."

"Aye, aye, Commander."

"You three," he said indicating the Jumbo Twins and Umky, "follow me." Breaking into a run, he headed into the building.

Inside the building was chaos. Insect bodies were everywhere, some places in mounds. A number of strange creatures—porcupines with huge claws—also lay among the dead. The wounds on their bodies and missing limbs immediately conjured thoughts of Mizuki and her katana. Looking to the far end of the hall he caught site of the object of his search. Then he noticed that not all the aliens were dead—in fact, several turned and attacked him.

Inside the Palace

In shock and disbelief, the Commander and Princess Reishi watched Mizuki's butterflies electrocute the commando who threatened her. It was the Princess's turn to question reality.

"What in the name of the old gods are those things?"

"Damned if I know Princess, but they seem to be on your sister's side."

"Timushi's daemon has summoned an evil spirit from the nether regions!"

At that point the east end of the nave exploded.

Through the smoke and debris dark shapes moved, coming on at a run. Large, larger, and larger still, they charged through the melee of warriors and commandos. Leading the charge, the smallest of the new monsters wielded some form of weapon that struck down any who got in its way.

The Commander sent more commandos into the fray. *This is going from bad to worse!*

* * * * *

Bobby cut down several of the armed ants before coming upon a live spine covered alien. It stood erect, opening its upper arms to reveal a second pair of arms holding a weapon. It opened fire.

Responding reflexively, Bobby sent a six flechette burst into the creature's chest, just above its firearm. Tumbling on impact, the flechettes blew fist sized holes exiting the creature's back, spraying blood, tissue, and quills on the ants behind it.

Not breaking stride, Bobby knocked the slumping alien out of his path. In full combat mode his helmet was opaque, his suit's cameras providing a view in all directions overlain with tactical information. Glancing at the view behind him, he saw the two human Marines charging through the hostiles.

"To the platform at the end of the hall!" he shouted. While he was watching the twins, the holographic display inside his helmet alerted him to movement overhead. One of the spiny aliens arced through the air, its trajectory reaching apex ten meters above his head. The source of the airborne alien was quickly identified—Umky had both sets of mechanical claws extended and was cutting a wide swath through the hostiles. With every swing of his claws, heads, arms, and less identifiable body parts flew into the air. The heavier spiny aliens he impaled and threw toward the front of the nave.

Now he decides to use brute force, Bobby thought in exasperation. Seeing more porcupine things heading toward Mizuki's position Bobby sped up.

* * * * *

Mizuki stood, katana held at port arms, as the dark shape pounded up to her position. The armored figure's bubble helmet changed from translucent gray to fully transparent, revealing the human within. Her heart skipped a beat as her hopes were realized. "Bobby!"

Bobby grinned and moved closer to her. She came forward to embrace him but stopped. Pointing with her sword she screamed, "look out, behind you!"

Bobby turned sideways while moving to shelter Mizuki from whatever threat she was trying to warn him about. Multiple bullets ricocheted from his armor. Off-handed, Bobby fired a single 20mm round from the lower barrel of his weapon, high explosive set to contact detonation. The projectile struck the alien standing seven meters away. It penetrated the gunner's chest ten centimeters before exploding.

The exploding shell caused what might euphemistically called "energetic disassociation" of the alien hostile. Gobs of tissue and body fluids flew in all directions, leaving behind a fine pink mist and two short stubby legs where the alien had stood. Some of its quills were propelled with such force they impaled the ant warriors standing nearby.

Bobby turned back to Mizuki, who rushed forward and draped her left arm across his armored chest, as close as she could come to hugging him in his bulky armor. "You came for me."

"Always, Mizuki-chan," he replied, carefully embracing her slight form with his left arm. After a few brief seconds of mutual relief, they disengaged. "Stay under cover while I see to the rest of the hostiles."

* * * * *

"Kill her! Kill her! Kill her!" Reishi screamed over and over, pointing in the direction of her sister. Victory that had seemed so close at hand was snatched away by the arrival of these horrific new daemons.

The Commander swore silently. *What a cluster fuck! Still, if we kill the other princess we may yet complete the mission.* "Sergeant, fire on the enemy Princess with the breaching rocket! Ignore the large alien. Kill the Princess."

"Roger, Sir!" The Fakkaa Sergeant took the rocket powered grenade launcher from one of the commandos. Holding the launcher's tube with his right upper arm, he brought it to his shoulder. Grasping the firing handle with his secondary hands, he sighted on the cluster of ants surrounding Princess Timushi and fired.

* * * * *

Bobby looked to the north side of the throne platform and spotted one of the porcupine things with what looked like a rocket launcher. "RPG!" he shouted.

Closest to the platform was Mal, already in motion. Seeing the backblast from the launcher he threw himself into the air. The explosive projectile flew true toward its target but Mal's timing was perfect. Halfway between the two princesses, grenade and Marine collided.

The grenade detonated against Mal's abdomen, knocking the airborne Marine backward. Landing on his back the stricken Marine slid toward the clutch of warriors surrounding Princess Timushi. He came to rest several meters away, with wisps of smoke rising from a hole in his armor.

"Malachi!" his brother yelled, pulling up short. He rounded on Princess Reishi's party of Fakkaa and warriors, and with an inarticulate scream opened fire with both cannon and flechette guns.

246

From his right arm came a stream of 5mm flechettes, three thousand a minute, traveling at 4,000 fps. Every fourth round was a tracer, drawing a line of green fire from weapon to target. From his right came 15mm explosive rounds, twelve hundred a minute, filled with nano-engineered high explosive set to maximum bursting charge. Reishi, the Commander, and everything else on that side of the hall disappeared in a cascade of explosive fire.

Palace Grounds

Outside the palace, the rest of the Marines spread out into a skirmish line and advanced on the milling crowd of armed aliens on the north side of the palace grounds. Weapons at the ready, the Marines moved closer to their prospective enemy until one of the aliens in a monk's robe noticed them.

Something yelled and the ants charged. Green fire lanced out from the armored Earthlings, mowing the native warriors down like wheat in a hailstorm. Behind the ants, the monks shed their habits and opened fire.

"What's with the spiny Ewoks?" asked Stevie.

"What is Ewok?" asked Bosco, assuming a kneeling position.

The Fakkaa attacked the Marines with machine guns and grenade launchers.

"Ewoks from hell maybe!" yelled Kato, switching from flechette fire to 15mm cannon.

"Take 'em out," the Gunny ordered. "Aimed and measured fire, you mutton heads. There's enough of them to go around."

* * * * *

Back in the shuttle, the flight crew was watching the Marines engage the large alien force on the north side of the building. The recon drone loitering above the structure provided a bird's eye view of the developing battle. Observing the firefight, Tamara noticed a warning sign flashing on her display. Switching to the second drone, maintaining position a thousand meters above the ground, she immediately saw the reason for the warning.

"Frank, I have three contacts inbound about six hundred klicks out."

"Crap! What type of craft are they?"

"Fast movers, fighter-bombers or attack jets, headed right for us, velocity 800 kph. They must be the interceptors that shot down the shuttle."

"Let's go kill the bastards," Jay snarled from the co-pilot's seat.

Frank nodded and called Cmdr. Danner. "Rescue Leader, Shuttle One. We have incoming aircraft. Request permission to intercept."

Inside the Palace

"Cease fire!" Bobby commanded. It took several yelled repetitions before Zeke stopped pouring rounds into the north side of the hall, but finally sanity returned and he quit firing.

Umky had finished off the last of the hostiles in the eastern part of the hall and rambled forward to join the humans. He examined the results of Zeke's fusillade.

Most of the glazing had been blown from the windows, and the stone work in the gallery and the supporting columns were badly pitted by flechette fire. In several places holes had been blasted clear through the masonry. Of the enemy Princess and her alien henchman there was nothing left except stains on the walls and floor.

"Nice job, Zeke," the bear said approvingly. A sizable chunk of a support column toppled and shattered on the floor.

"Those bastards killed my brother!"

Checking the medical telemetry from Mal's suit, Bobby could see that the wounded Marine was not dead, but he was in a bad way. "Your brother is alive, Zeke. I'm calling the Doc, you and Umky clear the north end of the hall. Now!"

Zeke looked back at Bobby and his brother's still form, torn between concern for his twin and his orders. In the end duty won. He and Umky jogged off toward the north door.

"Peggy Sue, Rescue Leader. I have a Marine down."

"Go, Rescue Leader. This is Dr. White."

"Mal got hit by an RPG. There is a hole in his suit that looks like the charge burned through his armor. Over."

"I've got his suit telemetry on the display now, Bobby. It looks pretty serious, significant internal injuries. I'm going to put him out and flood his system with antibiotics and nanites to stop the internal bleeding. You need to get him into a position where he can be carried and immobilize his suit. He needs to brought back to the ship inside of three hours, four at the outside."

Bobby leaned over Mal's recumbent form. The stricken Marine spoke to him on suit-to-suit.

"I guess I fucked up, Sir."

Bobby clasped Mal's armored shoulder. "Hell no, Marine. You saved the day. Now lay still while the Doc gets to work on you."

"Aye, aye, Sir..." Mal's voice drifted off as his suit injected him with anesthetic. The hole in his suit was already growing shut as its self-repair nanites went to work. A different voice came over the comm. *Now what?*

"Rescue Leader, Shuttle One. We have incoming aircraft. Request permission to intercept."

"Say again your last?"

"We have three incoming aircraft, tentatively identified as the alien interceptors that shot down our shuttle. Request permission to take Shuttle One and intercept them."

"What's the hostiles' ETA?"

"Around 45 minutes, probably less than that to missile range."

Shit! That's right, they have nukes. "Copy, Shuttle One. Deploy the battle bots to maintain an air defense umbrella, then go shoot them down, Mr. Hoenig."

"Aye, aye, Commander. Shuttle One out."

Bobby looked down at Mal's unmoving suit of armor. *Sorry, son, but taking out those possible nukes takes precedence. If the porcupines slip one of those in we could all be in a world of hurt.* He called the ship back.

"Peggy Sue, be advised that I have sent Shuttle One to intercept hostile aircraft headed our way."

"Roger, Bobby." It was Betty's voice. "I really need the wounded Marine in sick bay soonest."

"Understood, but the hostiles may have nukes and I can't risk them getting much closer."

There was a brief pause.

"We copy, Rescue Leader. We'll handle it from our end."

CIC, *Peggy Sue*

A grim faced Billy Ray looked at his officers. "We haven't lost anyone in combat on this mission yet and this ain't the day to start. Number One, send the Chief in the pinnace to medevac the wounded."

Beth nodded. "I'll go myself."

The Captain acknowledged with a nod of his own. "Do you need to go with them, Doctor?"

"No, Captain. There's noting I can do for him until he's in Sick Bay. In fact, I should get to the lab and start growing him some new intestines and tissue stock so I can repair the damage when he gets here."

"OK, make it happen people."

The two women departed on their separate missions.

Damn these idiot aliens, they don't even know they are fighting on the wrong side. "Peggy Sue, find Shadi and Dorri and have them come to the CIC. I want to give the alien commander a call and explain the facts of life to him."

"Certainly, Captain. They are on the way."

Chapter 30

Inside the Palace

Bobby stood up and walked over to where Mizuki was huddled with the largest of the ants. Doc White's magic nanobots were busy doing God knows what inside Mal's busted gut, and there was nothing more he could do until transport arrived. As he approached he saw that Mizuki and the big ant were bent over another ant who had sunk to the floor. On either side they were holding the fallen ant's hands.

Bobby figured that it was some kind of warrior since it wore armor and a sword. It must have been hit during the firefight—a row of holes stitched a ragged line across its breastplate. He tapped into Mizuki's translator pendant to find out what they were talking about.

"Hold on, my Lord Castellan, the healers have been summoned," the big ant said.

"Sorry, my Princess, but I have failed you..." the fallen ant wheezed. "If not for Lord Mizuki's friends we would have lost."

"Nonsense, Lord Castellan, you could not be expected to defeat enemies from another world," Mizuki protested. "If Reishi had not made a deal with those quilled devils things would have gone much differently. In any event we have won, and Timushi will be queen."

"Thanks to your friends... those gray monsters are your friends, are they not?"

"Yes, my Lord, those are my friends."

The Castellan coughed and emitted a wheezing sound. "And right proper daemons they are, too..."

"Don't try to speak, my old friend," the Princess implored, "save your strength."

"I'm sorry, but my strength is at its end... at least I will be able to say this once before I die... it has been an honor to serve you... Your Majesty." With a final rattling breath the Castellan lowered her head and died.

The Princess, now all but officially the Queen, lowered her antennae and remained silent for what seemed to Mizuki a very long time. Finally Timushi raised her head and spoke.

"She protected me from the time I hatched, and tutored me when I was a pupa. I have never known a time when I could not call on her for advice. She was my oldest friend... my only friend."

Mizuki gently left go of the Castellan's hand and looked up at the Queen. "I did not know her long, Your Majesty, but I also liked her a great deal."

"I knew the day would come, Lord Mizuki, when she would pass away—queens are the longest lived of our kind—but my world will be a much poorer place without her." Caressing the Castellan's head the new Queen addressed her deceased servant. "Rest easy my faithful sister, you served me better than all the others."

After a respectful silence Mizuki addressed the Queen. "She was also your sister, Your Majesty?"

"What? Oh, of course. You are not our kind; you do not understand. All of these Formicidae are daughters of my departed Mother the Queen. They are all my sisters." She made an all encompassing gesture with one arm. "In time, they will all pass away while I will live on. Eventually all the inhabitants of this land will be my daughters."

Mizuki was stunned. "I didn't realize, Your Majesty."

"That is why I will never leave this palace again. Once on my throne I will be fed and pampered for the rest of my life, first by my sisters and then by my daughters. I will sit on the throne and give birth to millions, and never again see the empire I rule."

Bobby shuffled a bit closer, clearing his voice over the suit's PA system. This attracted the attention of both Mizuki and Timushi.

"I'm sorry, Bobby, I didn't see you there." She looked back at the dead warrior. "Princess Timushi just lost her dearest friend, the Lord Castellan. She was also my friend."

"Who is this?" Timushi asked.

"Your Highness, I mean Your Majesty, this is my husband, Commander Bobby Danner. Bobby, this is my friend, Princess, now Queen Timushi."

Bobby took the hint and executed a graceful if limited bow in the large ant's direction. "Honored to meet you, Queen Timushi. Sorry about the mess, and the casualties."

"It is I who am honored by your presence Lord Bobby, and do not worry about the damage, it can be repaired given skilled hands and sufficient time."

While Bobby tried to frame a diplomatic reply the Gunny called on the command circuit. "Commander, we've chased the spiny aliens off of the plaza and killed most of the ants. Funny thing is the ants have stopped fighting and are just sort of milling around. What do you want us to do next?"

"Your Majesty, there are a number of opposing soldiers wandering around outside, do you have your own warriors to take them in charge?"

"Why? Ah, I understand, like Lord Mizuki you do not fully comprehend the ways of the Formicidae. When your warriors eradicated my sister the release of her body chemicals would have spread to her warriors, telling them that she was no more. They now belong to me and will become integrated into the city guards."

"We killed quite a few of them, ah, I'm sorry."

The new Queen waved a dismissive hand. "There will be more warriors if they are needed. Do not trouble yourself over the matter, Lord Bobby."

Inside his clear helmet Bobby nodded, and then called the Gunny. "Gunny, you can ignore the ants, they should give you no more trouble. What's happening with the other aliens?"

"The hostiles have pulled back from the surrounding area and are retreating to the north. They did try to drop some mortar fire on us but the battle bots took care of it—counter battery fire took out their tubes. Now they just seem to be hotfooting it outta Dodge, Sir."

"Stay in contact with them until they leave the city, just to make sure they don't try to leave some bad actors in place, but

253

don't pursue them into the forest. Keep 'em under drone surveillance while I check with Hoenig regarding the airborne threat."

Shuttle One

Frank was concentrating on the holographic display overlaying his view from the shuttle. His left hand grasped the side-stick controller and his right rested on the thruster controls. The synthetic vision display showed his intended targets closing at close to 2,000 kph.

"I'm going to split their formation. Tam, you take the two on the left, Jay the one on the right. Get locked on and let the computer decide when to fire."

"Roger that," Tamara replied from the weapons station behind the pilots. She was engrossed in the view inside her helmet, which showed the world outside of the shuttle as though she was a bird flying across the sky. Sitting next to Frank, Jay was similarly engaged.

The bogies were in a staggered delta formation at 1,500 meters and coming on fast. The shuttle was above them at 2,000—fighter pilots liked to engaged their opponents from above. The greater altitude gave them an edge in potential energy, and a dogfight was really a mater of energy management. Displays showed them closing with the alien aircraft at high speed, glowing lines on target displays converging at an accelerating rate.

"Looks like they've seen us," Frank called out, though his two gunners already noticed that their targets were trying to maneuver. "On them in three, two, one..."

The big shuttle passed through the alien formation in the blink of an eye. As it did the fire control computer triggered bursts from the shuttle's two, independently targetable rail cannon. Two of the three targets disintegrated in gouts of fire and clouds of debris.

"I missed the third bogie!" Tamara called.

Frank pulled the big delta shaped lifting body into a climb, exchanging speed for altitude—the primary flight display showed altitude increasing quickly as airspeed drop like a rock. Frank was planning a wingover, an energy-management maneuver used to change directions during a dogfight. Also called a box-canyon turn, it was popular with crop-dusters because the aircraft does not roll as it does in a split-s or an Immelmann. This keeps the cockpit facing the same direction throughout.

"Got 'em, mate, he's headed east and diving for the dirt," Jay yelled excitedly.

Frank kicked the nose over and dove, locking on to the alien craft's tail. The jet's pilot was jinking to save his life, but Frank closed with him rapidly. Though it was big and ungainly looking, the shuttle was more maneuverable and had a better power to weight ratio than the alien attack craft.

"Damn, I wish we had missiles," Tamara opined.

"Sorry, the shuttle was not designed for air-to-air combat. Get ready, who ever gets a shot take it."

The alien pilot was growing desperate and tried a rolling scissors maneuver. Frank was having none of it. Using thrust vectoring from the bottom repulsors he rolled inside of the alien pulling 20G and put his nose on the fleeing fighter.

"Guns to me," Frank commanded. Targeting information popped up in his field of view. The reticle followed his eye movements to the target and he fired a burst of 15mm shells.

The Fakkaa pilot knew his time was up when the huge attacking craft out maneuvered him in the barrel roll. He targeted his missile on the ant queen's palace and launched. The last thing he saw before his plane came apart around him was the bright dot of the missile's exhaust as it accelerated toward its target.

"Missile launch! He got a shot off!" cried Tamara. "It's climbing, velocity holding steady at thirty-five hundred kph."

"Christ, it'll hit the city in less than a minute," said Jay.

"Rescue Leader, you have incoming! Repeat, you have incoming!"

The Queen's Palace

Before Bobby had a chance to call the shuttle, they called him. Frank's frantic voice crackled in his ears. "Rescue Leader, you have incoming, repeat you have incoming!"

Calmly Bobby called up the tactical display that combined sensor data from the recon drones with the disposition of all the Marines and the two battle bots. Though he might not look it, Bobby was a pilot from the same mold as Chuck Yeager and the Right Stuff astronauts—he did not panic under pressure, instead he became almost supernaturally calm.

"Roger, Shuttle One. Break. Squad, take cover for possible incoming." As he spoke he identified the incoming missile's track and designated it the priority target for the battle bots. They mounted railguns like the Marines but they also had air-defense X-ray lasers that were effective out to more than ten kilometers.

Outside the Marines all dove for the ground, the Gunny yelling "Suck planet! Now!"

Behind them on the terrace, the two battle bots stood like statues. As the missile crossed the ten kilometer mark crackling sounds could be heard from the robotic weapons platforms. In the distance there was a puff of smoke, marking the missile's destruction.

"Shuttle One, Rescue Leader. I'm showing no more incoming. Interrogative the situation on your end?"

The crew of the shuttle started breathing again.

"Roger, Rescue Leader. Scratch all three bogies," came the voice of a very relieved Frank Hoenig. "They only got one off before we took them out."

"Copy that. Since you are out that way, see if you can identify where the aircraft came from and make sure there are no more waiting to surprise us."

"Roger that, we're on it. Shuttle One, out."

Shuttle One

On their displays the shuttle's flight crew received a visual of the missile being shot down, the puff of white smoke that marked its demise seeming almost disappointing. Sitting in momentary silence, they realized that they had just dodged a bullet.

"I though you said it was a nuke, Tam?" asked Jay.

"It was, sensors are picking up radioactive debris."

"Then why didn't it make a big explosion? An air-burst nuke only ten klicks away could have ruined everyone's day."

"It doesn't work that way, Jay. It was a small warhead, probably an implosion fission device."

"So?"

Tamara sighed. "It's easy to set off a nuclear explosion if you have a lot of fissile material—some of the early atom bombs were more or less cannons that shot two hunks of enriched uranium into each other. Making a smaller bomb takes a lot more finesse. A small bomb is usually a sphere of fissile material surrounded by precision high explosive that implodes it to achieve critical density. The timing of the detonation must be just right."

"Like I said, so?" Jay reiterated.

"So, it's really hard to make one explode except on purpose."

"Really?" asked Frank.

"Really," Tamara replied with a grin. "Trust me, I'm a weapons tech. We know these things."

"Crikey, Tam," Jay said, doing his best Crocodile Hunter accent. "That's good to know for next time some alien tries to hurl a nuke at us."

"Yeah, I thought we had screwed the pooch there for a minute," Frank added. "Well, you heard the Commander, let's go see if we can find some other targets to shoot up."

"Right you are, mate!"

Chapter 31

CIC, Peggy Sue

"Peggy Sue, can you match the alien's signal encoding so I can talk to them?" asked Billy Ray.

"Yes, Captain. Do you wish me to hail them?"

"Yes, do it." He turned to the two sisters, standing by to assist in translation if necessary. "Are you two ready?"

"Yes, Captain," Shadi replied excitedly, while Dorri nodded in agreement. This would be the first time either of the sisters saw an actual space alien, even if only on a video display. "Please try not to use big words or figures of speech if you can avoid it."

"I have a response and I am decoding their video algorithm. You have voice now and picture will follow momentarily."

"This is the captain of the Earth ship Peggy Sue, calling the commanding officer of the flotilla of ships in planetary orbit. Respond or I will be forced to take action against your ships."

Static and strange harmonic noise came from the comm channel as colored confetti painted the display screen. Slowly words emerged from the chaos.

"...calling...fleet...is Fleet Admiral Raqqee, over."

Pretty grandiose title for the leader of a collection of tin cans. "Admiral Raqqee, this is Captain Vincent. Are you reading me clearly?"

There was a slight pause, during which a picture congealed on the display, revealing a spine covered beaver with two deep set dark eyes and two large yellowed teeth. Shadi and Dorri were totally captivated.

"Is that a real image?" asked Dorri. The Captain made a motion with his hand to silence the girl.

"Yes Captain, I can hear you, and see you clearly. What do you want?"

"You have landed troops on the planet below and they have interfered in the affairs of the natives. You will signal your forces on the surface to cease all military actions and surrender their weapons."

"Why would I do that? We...are acting to save our species."

"If you do not surrender immediately my Marines will destroy your invasion force to the last soldier and I will blast your 'fleet' into plasma."

"I think that garbled word is what they call themselves, Captain," Shadi whispered as Dorri typed furiously on a keyboard. "You can call them 'Fakkaa' from here on."

Billy Ray nodded as he waited for the Fakkaa Admiral's reply. "Bridge, CIC, sound General Quarters and prepare to fire on the alien fleet."

Bridge, Fakkaa Flagship

Admiral Raqqee stared at the alien on the forward display. The creature was mostly clothed, with dark brown fur on its head. What could be seen of its face and neck was naked pink flesh—ghastly to behold.

"Should I order the fleet to battle stations, Admiral?" asked Capt. Tikkoo. The bridge crew were looking at Raqqee nervously.

"No, Captain. I doubt our weapons would make any impression on that ship." *After all, it turned the Wise One's vessel into plasma in an instant. We are as primitive to them as the ants are to us.* "What is happening on the surface? Has the plan been successful?"

"No, Sir. The ground commander has been out of communication for more than a half an hour. The second in command reports that alien warriors landed at the queen's palace and attacked our commandos inflicting heavy casualties. Our forces have been forced to retreat into the forest."

"What about an air strike?"

"One was mounted using all of our assets—the aliens shot them all down. Admiral, we've lost more than half our personnel, all our air assets, and the mission commander. We are..."

"Screwed, Captain. We are screwed. Call the ground force and tell them to stand down."

No teeth, no claws no quills, how can creatures that look so harmless be so deadly? How will I explain this failure to the ruling counsel back home—assuming they let us go back home?

Raqqee cleared his throat.

"Captain, I have ordered my ground forces to stand down. What else would you have me do?"

CIC, Peggy Sue

"A wise decision, Admiral," Billy Ray replied. *OK, they surrendered, now what do I do with them? Tell them to go home? What's to keep them from coming back after we leave? I need to make them understand that they are fighting for the wrong side.*

"Admiral, why were you fighting for the creatures in the black ship?"

"They came to us over a decade ago. Told us they were an ancient race dedicated to helping less advanced races. They said our sun was going to explode, killing all life on our world. According to the Wise Ones, this planet held a secret, ancient device that could save our people."

"But to find it you needed to suborn the natives. Force them to turnover the device if they had it or help find it if they did not."

"That is correct, Captain."

Billy Ray sighed. "I am afraid that you have been used as a cat's paw, Admiral Raqqee."

"A what?" the alien replied.

"It comes from an old Earth fable, 'the monkey and the cat'. Monkeys and cats are... two other alien species. The story goes like this: Bertrand the monkey persuades Raton the cat to pull chestnuts from the embers where they are roasting. Bertrand promises him a share but as the cat scoops them from the fire one by one, the monkey gobbles them down. Raton burns his paw in the process and ends up with nothing for his pains."

"You are saying that the Wise One's were using us?"

"Precisely. In truth these 'wise ones' belong to a group of species we call the Dark Lords. They inhabit rogue planets and the moons of brown dwarfs that lurk in the dark space between true stars."

"But we saw their ship! They had technology so advanced we could hardly imagine it. The technology they gave us to mount this expedition was almost beyond our best scientists' understanding. Why did they need us if all they were after was this mysterious device?"

"They are a form of life that lives at temperatures which would freeze your kind or mine solid. They could no more go running around the surface of the planet below than you could take a hike across the surface of your sun. Easier to enlist some unsuspecting locals to do the dirty work."

"And this device exists?"

"A device exists, though whether it can save your people is not evident."

"Will our sun explode soon, as the aliens told us?"

"Soon is a relative term. To them it probably is soon, for you not so much. Our calculations show you have another hundred thousand years or so before your primary star turns itself into a white dwarf. You should have plenty of time to develop the technology to leave for safer pastures."

"So if they were using us as tools, what was their plan for us, their endgame?"

"For reasons known only to themselves they find creatures like us—warm life—anathema. I don't know this for a fact but I suspect that both you and the Formicidae would have ended up extinct."

There was a long silence while the Fakkaa Admiral conversed with those on the bridge, his sound pickup muted. Eventually, he faced the camera and restored the sound.

"Captain, I don't know what to say—I feel like such a fool. What do you wish us to do next?"

"Does your ground force have a way to get back to your ships?"

"Yes, the landing craft can bring them back to orbit."

"Then I would suggest you get your troops back to their landing craft and off the planet, as soon as possible."

"As you command, Captain."

* * * * *

"That was great, Captain!" Shadi enthused. "Using *Le Singe et le Chat* to explain how they were being used."

"Yes," added Dorri, looking up from her keyboard. "There were only a few terms that couldn't be translated without rewording. I think we have a much better translation algorithm for Fakkaa now, you probably won't need us to help next time."

"Thank you for your assistance, ladies." Billy Ray smiled at the two beaming teenagers, then touched his comm pip. "Bridge, this is the Captain. Secure from General Quarters."

As the all clear sounded the Captain called Bobby on the planet below. "Rescue Leader, Peggy Sue."

"Go Peggy Sue."

"You can tell your Marines to stop shooting things, the aliens have surrendered. I just talked to their admiral and he agreed to cease fire and have his remaining ground forces leave the planet."

"Copy that, Peggy Sue. I don't know how many are left to surrender, the Marines killed most of those who tried to take the palace. Interrogative an ETA for the medevac?"

Checking a status readout, Billy Ray replied, "they are in atmo-entry comm blackout and should be on site in fifteen minutes. Over."

"Roger that, Peggy Sue. Rescue Leader out."

Queen's Palace

Bobby looked up to see two suited figures coming toward him from the eastern doorway, one tall and one short. Since active hostilities ended a few minutes ago, he had been kneeling over Mal's inert body praying that the young Marine wouldn't die. Mizuki was still by the Queen's side as servants and functionaries appeared from everywhere to fawn over Timushi. The body of the fallen Castellan had been taken way and the cleanup of the palace had already begun.

"Well I see that you found her," the taller of the two newcomers said. The shorter stood legs apart, hands on hips.

"That I did," said a smiling Bobby, standing up. "She even saved some of the nasty spike covered beavers for us."

"Is that big bug the queen?" the Chief asked, scanning the scene. "Nobody here seems to care if we come or go, nobody tried to stop us coming inside or nothin'."

"The Chief's right," said the First Officer, towering over the diminutive sailor. "There are insects running about everywhere; none even gave us a second look."

"Naw," Bobby replied to his shipmates, "Mizuki introduced me to the Queen. She politely said hello and has ignored me since. I think it's because she sees us as warriors."

"What's wrong with warriors? Particularly warriors who saved her chitin covered carcass from her evil sister and a pack of demonic hedgehogs?"

"In her world everyone is some kind of underling—servants, workers, warriors—you know, like an ant colony."

"Really?"

"Really. I apologized for the damage we did to her palace and all the ants we killed. All she said was the palace could be repaired and there would be more warriors if she needed them."

"Damn, glad I ain't an ant," the Chief muttered.

"She didn't care that we wiped out several hundred of her subjects?" Beth asked incredulously.

"I think it's ant arithmetic." Bobby replied with a grin.

"Ant arithmetic, Commander?"

"In ant arithmetic there are only two numbers, Chief: Zero, which means anything less than a million, and Some."

Beth grinned. "Very good, Bobby. Neal Stephenson if I recall."

264

"Right, from *The Diamond Age*. So using ant arithmetic we killed zero of her warriors."

"And there are zero of us," Beth Finished. Then, turning serious, the First Officer looked down at the immobile suit of heavy armor laying on the throne platform. "I guess we better get him to the shuttle."

"Right, Ma'am. I'll fetch a hover sled," the Chief said. He turned and headed back to the small shuttle parked outside.

"Doc says she wants Mizuki to come back to the ship as well. She's concerned with possible contamination by alien life forms. If you want, you can fly the pinnace back to the ship and I can take over here."

"No, thanks. I brought them down here I'll see it through."

That was the answer Beth had expected—an officer stayed with his men until they all went home. Still, she had to ask. "OK, you help the Chief with Mal and I'll go tear Mizuki away from her new BFF."

"Good luck with that," he said with a smirk and turned to get the fallen Marine ready for transport.

Well, that's a good sign, Beth said to herself. *Bobby is back to making obscure jokes based on science fiction books. Hopefully Mizuki is in good spirits as well.*

The First Officer's tall armored figure headed toward the cloud of brightly colored butterflies, knowing that Mizuki would be somewhere beneath their happy display.

Chapter 32

Sick Bay, Peggy Sue

Half of Sick Bay had been sealed off as a clean room and isolation ward. Mal's armor encased body was brought into the room by four crewmembers, where he was decanted by a technician and several medical personnel. The armor was resealed and taken away to have its interior sterilized.

Dr. White and her team, all clad in air tight pressure suits with clear bubble helmets, gathered around their patient who now resided on an instrumented operating table. An endotracheal breathing tube was inserted into Mal's mouth, with a mask sealing off his mouth and nose. He was connected to a heart lung machine so his respiration and heartbeat could be stilled during the surgery to come. Betty examined the wounded Marine with her hand tablet, peering beneath his skin to evaluate the tissue damage inflicted by the Fakkaa RPG.

"Looks like the ileum and part of the jejunum are ruined as well as most of the descending colon and the upper end of the sigmoid colon," Betty informed her physician's assistant and surgical nurse. "We are going to need all of the replacement intestine I've got growing in the lab and then some."

"Should I start more in the growth tank?" asked the PA, who would be assisting Betty during the reconstructive surgery.

"Yes, but let's get the wound opening and the abdominal cavity cleaned out first. We need to remove any burned or necrotic tissue. Then we can plan out the reconstruction in detail while the nanites finish the cleanup. Thank goodness neither the ileocecal valve nor the rectum were damaged, and the spleen and liver are intact."

Betty tapped the screen on her tablet, initiating the surgical procedure. From above the surgical table, slim robotic arms descended and began the process of cleaning Mal's wounded abdomen.

* * * * *

In a separate room within the isolation ward, Mizuki stripped off the skintight space suit she had donned during the trip to the Peggy

Sue. The suit was to keep her from contaminating the ship, not for her protection. Still, she was happier than she had been in weeks, safe back on the ship and among friends. Bobby had come for her as she knew he would. Even though he was cleaning up loose ends on the surface, all was right with Mizuki's world.

Though not wounded like the unfortunate Marine in the other room, she, too, had to be decontaminated inside and out. Much of the decontamination was unpleasant, but part of that process was a long hot shower that reminded her of how fantastic modern technology really was.

Shuttle One, Formicidae

While the Marines contained the few remaining Fakkaa commandos, Bobby supervised the tiltroter troop carriers that ferried them back to the Fakkaa landing site. Surveillance drones scanned the area for heat signatures, ensuring that none of the invaders remained behind. Only two score of the spiny aliens survived, but they had to load their dead as well.

The Earthlings wished to minimize contamination of the planet's environment by outside organisms, but that ship had probably already sailed. More than a hundred Fakkaa corpses littered the palace grounds, some more intact than others. Indeed, Mizuki had spent more than a week trekking across the planet during which time she had to answer nature's call. For better or for worse, Formicidae was irreversibly tainted with alien lifeforms.

"That should be the last flight of them, Commander," the Gunny called from the ground as the alien tiltroters lifted off. The Marines were all ready to leave Formicidae behind now that the fighting was over. They consoled themselves with the thought that things could be worse, at least they didn't have to load dead bodies onto the alien transports.

"Roger that, Gunny, we'll be right down to pick you up," Bobby replied. He was even more anxious than the Marines to be headed back to the ship. Nothing had been reported regarding Mal's condition or Mizuki's since they returned to the orbiting Peggy Sue, but he and the rescue party couldn't head for home until the porcupines were headed back to what was left of their invasion fleet.

"Aye, aye, Sir," came the head Marine's reply, boredom apparent in her voice as well. "We are ready for pickup."

* * * * *

An hour later and eight hundred kilometers away from the queen's palace, the Earthlings' shuttle orbited a large opening in the forest canopy. In the clear space below sat a half dozen landing shuttles, preparing for their return to orbit. In a few minutes, the failed interplanetary invasion launched by the Fakkaa would come to an end.

"You know, those porcupines had a lot of balls," commented Steve Hitch. "Building a fleet of spaceships and flying across their star system to invade another planet."

"Sort of like the old time Vikings in their longships," Matt Jacobs agreed with his friend. "Heading out into the unknown to raid and pillage."

"They were stooges for the Dark Lords," said Kato. "Nothing admirable about that."

"They were suckered by the chillies, man," Vinny said, coming to the defense of their defeated foe. "Could happen to anyone."

Umky chuckled. "Maybe to you, Vinny. I don't know about the rest of us."

"Give it a rest, you bozos." The Gunny had seen more than enough of this world and the spiny invaders. All she wanted was to get back to the ship, grab a shower and some grub, and then get some serious rack time. "Just be thankful that the opposition was not armed with advanced weapons—we can't expect a turkey shoot every time we have to deploy."

"Or porcupine shoot," said a grinning Bosco. "Hey look! There they go!"

"Good riddance," Zeke spat. He had mixed emotions about letting any of the alien invaders go home alive. All he could think about was the sight of his brother getting hit by the RPG, flying backwards through the air, ending up with a smoking hole in his stomach. If it were up to him he'd kill them all.

The alien landing craft lifted off on tongues of flame, carrying more dead than living. Back to the ships that had brought them so far to die at the hands of creatures they had never met—dark monsters that would haunt their dreams and be used to frighten Fakkaa children for generations to come.

Peggy Sue, Four Hours Later

After a final sweep of the area, Shuttle One returned to orbit and rendezvoused with the Peggy Sue. Bobby elected to use the crew showers on 1st deck along with the rest of the human Marines, rather than go all the way forward to his quarters in a sweat soaked and fragrant pressure suit. Coming out of the shower he was accosted by Zeke, Shadi, and Dorri.

"Commander Danner, they won't let us in to see Mal up in Sick Bay!" complained Shadi. "He's been in there for hours and nobody has told us anything!"

Ah yes, the pleasures of being in command, he thought. "Please calm down. If no one is available to give you an update on Mal's condition it is probably because they are busy working on him. I'm sure Dr. White will let you know as soon as she has something to tell you."

"But we haven't even seen him or anything!" the young woman persisted. Zeke looked on silently with a worried expression on his face while Dorri showed a combination of concern and embarrassment.

"Fine, follow me. We'll go to Sick Bay and see what we can find out. I was going to go check on Mizuki anyway."

* * * * *

Ten minutes later the four of them were in Sick Bay, standing outside the isolation ward. Shortly after they arrived, Dr. White emerged. Stripping off her gloves and removing her helmet, she examined the party of visitors.

"I can guess why you are here," she said with a weary smile. Bobby, who had known Betty for years, could tell that she was tired, fatigue showing around her normally cheerful eyes. "The answer to your question is yes, Mal is going to be all right."

Zeke smiled widely and Shadi nearly swooned. Dorri poked her sister in the ribs and said, "See? I told you not to worry so much."

Recovering her composure Shadi gave her sister a sideways glance and returned her attention to the Doctor. "Thank you, Doctor, that's great! Can we see him? Can I talk to him?"

"I'm afraid that is really not possible right now," Betty answered. "He was wounded pretty badly and I have him in a medically induced coma to let him heal."

"How badly, Doc?" Zeke asked.

"I had to reconstruct his lower GI track and restore part of his abdominal musculature and skin. Even with regeneration stimulators it's going to take twenty-four hours for things to heal. Then I need to check and make sure there are no leaks or kinks, and then restore his gut microbiome. After that is done I will think about waking him up."

"But he will be all right, right?"

"Yes, yes. He's going to be fine. Here, follow Sandy and she'll take you to a viewing room outside the isolation ward where you can see him." Betty motioned to one of her nurses. "But I can tell you there isn't much to see."

"Thank you, Doctor, thank you!" the excited Shadi gushed as the trio of young people left, following behind the nurse. As they departed Bobby turned to Betty.

"How bad was it, Betty? I was there and I'm amazed that he lived at all."

"He's one lucky young man, I can tell you that. Ten centimeters lower and I doubt that I could have fixed the damage—its not like we have those magic healing chambers like on the M'tak Ka'fek. Ten centimeters higher and it would have shredded his heart and left lung, killing him almost instantly. I could grow him a new heart, but nothing his suit could do would have kept him alive to reach the ship."

271

"He's lucky his suit stopped most of it."

"Why didn't it catch all of the round? I thought those heavy suits could stop almost anything."

"The active armor repulsors did take most of the energy out of the warhead but it must have been a shaped charge with an explosively formed penetrator. Those things can burn a hole through a foot of steel plate. If the repulsors hadn't worked it probably would have blown right through him."

"That's why I found some small drops of tantalum in his abdominal cavity. He's even luckier than I thought."

"We don't need to tell his brother or the girls that."

"No. Indeed we don't. And speaking of lucky people, you can go claim Mizuki from her examination room and take her down to your quarters."

"Everything check out OK?"

"I gave her a purgative to flush out any foreign microorganisms in her digestive tract and something to help her sleep. It's time release but you shouldn't dawdle on the trip to your quarters or you'll end up carrying her."

"Did you really have to knock her out, Doc?"

"I want her out for at least eight to ten hours, and knowing her she'd be up and running around otherwise."

"You're probably right about that. Thanks, Betty." Bobby smiled at the Doctor and headed off to claim Misuki.

"And take those damned butterflies with you," Betty called after the retreating Bobby.

Polar Bear Quarters

Pulling his body from the swimming pool, Umky closed his eyes and shook himself like a dog, sending a spray of droplets into the frigid air. As much fun as hunting aliens on the planet below had been, he was glad to be back in the bear habitat with reasonable temperatures and salt water to bath in. Then he noticed Ahnah standing on the ice, flinching from the impromptu shower.

"Sorry, didn't see you there," he mumbled.

"I see you are in good spirits," the she-bear said, standing her ground. "The humans are all impressed by your tracking ability— finding Dr. Ogawa amongst all that jungle. I envy you the opportunity to breath unfiltered air for a change."

"Hey, it was not as great as you think. Breathing the air down below was like sticking your nose into an oven full of garbage. Plus I had to go through decontamination."

"Still, it was a change, and you did something the humans couldn't on their own."

"Yeah, I guess." *Why is she being so... complimentary?*

"You also made quick work of those spiny beaver creatures. Don't tell me that wasn't fun."

"It was good exercise," he said with a grin. "You should have come along."

"Maybe next time we have to rescue some crewmates." Ahnah moved closer to him. "You managed to make us bears look good all by your self, Umky."

More complements? From Ahnah? Umky was suspicious. Normally their conversations consisted of snide remarks and veiled insults.

"Everyone was watching the video feeds from your suits. You made short work of those aliens, both ants and beavers."

"It's not like I could have gotten hurt, being inside an armored suit and all." *What the hell is she up to?*

"Your being too modest. First you save me from that squid thing and now you help rescue Dr. Ogawa. You are a very heroic bear." Ahnah nuzzled the side of Umky's neck and whispered, "I had Doc White remove the IUD."

Umky's eyes went wide as the implication of Ahnah's words dawned on him. *If I didn't know better I'd think she wants to have...*

Ahnah nipped him on the side of the neck and then cuffed him so hard he almost fell over.

...SEX!

Bobby & Mizuki's Quarters

Bobby managed to get Mizuki to their quarters and dressed for bed before the sedatives fully kicked in. The *aoi chō* settled about the cabin as Mizuki perched on the edge of the bed, her sheathed katana in hand.

"This sword saved my life," Mizuki said drowsily.

"And for that I am thankful, Mizuki-chan. Please let me put it back on the mantle so you can get into bed."

"No, you don't understand," she insisted. "It saved me and I bent it."

"What?" Bobby was now thoroughly confused. Mizuki was obviously upset, but he had attributed that to the harrowing experience of surviving the shuttle crash and trekking across the primitive planet—that and the sedative.

"See?" she said, pulling the sword from its scabbard and reinserting it. "I can feel it catch when I put it in the *saya*."

"Fine, I'll take it to Arin. I'll bet his artificers can find a way to straighten it back out for you."

"No! It can only be worked on by a master swordsmith, one who knows the proper rituals. Saito-san will be so disappointed with me."

"Trust me, sweetheart. Your old sensei will be happy that you survived, bent blade and all... as am I."

In danger of nodding off, Mizuki let Bobby take the katana from her hands and place it on the mantle. He turned and looked at her, so small and delicate in appearance, yet with a spirit as strong as the folded steel of her sword.

"Bobby, hold me," she said in a quiet voice.

Bobby held her.

She fell asleep in his arms as they sat together on the bed. Once he was sure she was out, Bobby carefully slid her between the sheets and tucked her in. In repose she looked innocent, child like—not a fearsome slayer of alien daemons and rescuer of princesses.

Looking thoughtfully at the sword resting on the mantle, he turned out the lights and quietly left the cabin. The flock of alien butterflies remained, keeping watch over their goddess returned from her quest.

Chapter 33

Captain's Sea Cabin

For the first time since before the ill fated survey mission left for planet Formicidae, the four principle members of the expedition met in the Captain's cabin just off the bridge. Recovered after a full night's sleep, Mizuki was both happy to be alive and anxious to resume the search for the T'aafhal artifact still believed to be hiding on the planet.

"Yer looking no worse for wear, Mizuki. I can't tell you how relieved we all are that you survived your unplanned trip to the surface."

Mizuki averted her eyes. "You were right, Billy Ray, we should have worn armor. The shuttle crew might be alive today if we had."

At first Bobby had blamed himself for the crash. *If only I had piloted the shuttle*, he thought, *things would have been different*. After seeing the wreckage he realized that things would have been different—he would be dead instead of Lt. Lewis.

"Actually, I doubt it would have made any difference for Kate and Nigel. I examined the wreckage and nothing in the front of the shuttle could have lived through the impact."

"Thank you, Bobby, but I was still wrong—we should have worn suits."

"If its any consolation, I was in command and I let you go without it. If anyone is to blame it's me."

"Now, dear, I think some blame can be attributed to the Fakkaa," Beth chided her husband. "After all, they shot down the shuttle."

"At the behest of the Dark Lords," added Bobby.

"I guess there's blame aplenty to go around," Billy Ray admitted. "Let's try to learn from our mistakes and move forward."

"We did discover that a warp drive is possible," said Bobby, trying to steer the conversation to more positive things.

Mizuki smiled, happy to change subjects. "Yes, the Dark Lord's warp drive is quite interesting. I look forward to studying it."

"It certainly is. We definitely need to warn the fleet that other such ships may be out there."

"Yer right about that, honey bunch. Those chilly varmints bushwhacked us and almost did us in. We were lucky to escape."

"Lucky, yes, but there was more than a bit of skill involved, dear."

"I'd rather be lucky than good." Billy Ray smiled at the other three as the dark mood in the room lightened.

"Amen to that, pardner," Bobby said with a grin. "So what are we going to do about that artifact?"

"We're going back to the planet and find the darn thing, that's what."

"The four of us?" asked Beth.

"The four of us," he replied. "We can take the pinnace and start by visitin' Mizuki's pal the Queen. Maybe the ants have some knowledge about this thing, a legend or something."

"Should we all go? Something could still go wrong."

"Sweetheart, we've been in space over a year. I think the crew can find their way back home if something happens to us. Either that or we've been wasting our time trainin' them. Besides, this ain't a Navy ship, we are civilians on a trading expedition."

"You're right, Billy Ray. Between Arin and Frank and the Chief they shouldn't have a problem getting home. We've taken care of the Dark Lords and their minions—what else could go wrong?"

"Beats me, pardner, but we will all be wearin' armor this time."

Looking around the cabin the Captain saw no dissent among his officers regarding that point.

Sick Bay

Though they had been chased out of Sick Bay yesterday, Shadi and Zeke were back as soon as they were off watch the next day. Eventually, Dr. White took pity on them and let them see the still bedridden Mal.

"Now don't go wearing out my patient, you two. I just woke him up an hour ago and he's still weak and groggy."

"We won't, Doctor, promise," Shadi said earnestly. Standing behind her Zeke nodded affirmatively.

With a final stern look, Betty ushered the two young people into the room, saying, "Mal, I've got a couple of people here who want to see you."

Mal, looking pale and gaunt, lay under white sheets, his head and upper body slightly elevated. When he saw who his visitors were he smiled weakly.

"Hey, guys."

"Hey yourself, brother," replied Zeke. Suddenly the loquacious Shadi was having difficulty speaking. Eventually she managed to ask a question.

"How are you feeling, Mal?"

"I've been better," he replied. Then after a moment's thought added, "but I've been a lot worse."

"I thought they killed you. Umky and me just about brought down the ants' palace before Cmdr. Danner told us you were alive."

"I'm not that easy to get rid of, bro."

Shadi took his hand and, with tears starting to well up in her eyes, spoke again. "I thought we agreed that you wouldn't do anything heroic."

"Sorry, it seemed like a good idea at the time."

"You could have been killed!"

"I didn't do anything," he protested.

"You knucklehead," his brother chimed in, "the whole ship saw you jump in front of that RPG round."

"Oh great," Mal moaned. "Now everyone on board knows I'm an idiot."

"Are you kidding? You're a bonafide hero, brother. You even managed to impress the Gunny."

"Really?"

279

"Yeah, really. She said something about acting in the finest tradition of the Corps. Hell, I thought she was going to cry."

"Wow. I'd have paid to see that."

"Not only that, we ain't the Jumbo Twins anymore."

"No?"

"No, we are now Mal and Zeke, though some of the guys are calling you Jumper."

Mal moaned. Marines had a habit of giving squadmates nicknames, often embarrassing ones.

"It's OK," said Shadi, still gripping Mal's hand. "They are also calling Zeke 'OC'."

"OC?"

"Outta Control."

"Ouch."

"He really did almost destroy the ant Queen's palace. And Umky actually sat back and admired his handiwork, rather than help with the process."

Mal chuckled and closed his eyes.

"Alright, that's enough for one day," said Betty, reasserting control of the situation. "Let Mal rest."

"Please, Doctor, can I just sit with him? I promise not to keep him awake. Please?"

Betty looked at the young girl, desperately clutching Mal's hand, her eyes on the edge of tears. *Well, Betty, you were young and in love once,* she said to herself. "All right, honey, but you let him rest, he needs time to heal."

The look of gratitude on Shadi's face warmed Betty's heart. Turning to Zeke she said, "I suppose you want to stay as well?"

"I can't. I gotta go to the armory and finish cleaning armor and weapons. Besides, the squad will want to know how he's doing."

"OK, let's leave these two alone then." Betty ushered Zeke toward the door.

"Later, bro. You too, Shadi."

Mal waved weakly with his free hand and smiled. Shadi, seated beside the bed, held the other and gazed transfixed at his features.

Outside the room Betty shook her head and said, "if that ain't the look of love, I don't know what love looks like."

Mizuki & Bobby's Quarters

Both Mizuki and Bobby had donned the skintight pressure suits that served as inner garments for their combat armor. The suits had a tendency to highlight ever muscle and curve of a wearer's physique. Taking advantage of this, Bobby was admiring Mizuki's backside as she talked to her butterflies.

"You had better stop staring at my butt or you won't be able to get your armor on," she said without turning around. Before they put their suits on they made up for the time spent apart during Mizuki's adventure with the ants. Both had been spent by their exertions, but evidently Bobby had recovered.

"You have to admit, it's a very nice butt, and the rest isn't half bad either." Bobby smiled at his partner.

Mizuki turned and embraced him, exacerbating his armor clearance problem. "Bobby, you know I love you."

"Yes, Mizuki-chan. And you know I love you too."

"I discovered something while I was strolling through the forest and making friends among the natives, something that I always knew but was afraid to admit."

"You're talking in riddles, sweetheart." Knowing Mizuki, he realized that she would get to the point when she was ready.

"When I was alone down there, instead of giving up all I could think about was you and how disappointed you would be with me if I didn't stay alive until you came."

"I never doubted that I would find you, not for a minute. You know that you are the love of my life."

"What I discovered was that I couldn't imagine spending the rest of my life without you. What I'm trying to say is that, if you still want to, I want to get married."

Bobby was speechless. He stood mute, mouth agape, staring at her. Mizuki looked up at him from beneath raised brows. "So?"

"Yes! Yes, yes, yes, of course I still want to marry you!" He grabbed her around the waist, lifted her from the deck and spun her around. In a riot of color, the *aoi chō* took flight, surrounding the twirling couple in an ecstatic display.

After setting her back on her feet, Bobby looked lovingly at his bride to be. "You have just made me the happiest man in the galaxy."

She kissed him and pulled him close. "Some times you must almost lose everything to discover what is truly important in life."

Savoring the moment they held each other as the butterflies settled down. They might not be empathic but they certainly could sense Mizuki's, and Bobby's, emotions. Gently separating, Bobby looked at her with excitement dancing in his eyes.

"You have perfect timing, sweetheart. I have something for you, something that is now an early wedding gift."

He went to the locker next to the cabin door and produced a long bundle wrapped in cloth. Laying the bundle on the bed he began to unwrap it.

"I know that you were upset because you bent Saito-san's katana. Since you won't let the engineers try to fix it, I figured you also wouldn't want to risk any more damage to it. So I had Arin and his artificers make these."

With a flourish he threw back the last of the cloth, revealing a pair of swords. Handing one of the sheathed weapons to Mizuki, Bobby stood back and watched her reaction. Pulling the blade from its scabbard uncovered a sword like she had never seen before. It was obviously modeled after a traditional Japanese katana, with a thin, gracefully curved, single-edged blade, circular hand guard, and long grip, made to accommodate two hands.

"It's long, almost long enough to be an *ōdachi*."

Bobby nodded. "2 *shaku* 5 *sun* 5 *bu*, right at 78 centimeters. I had them made a bit longer than your katana so they would work well with gauntleted hands. The weight and balance is almost exactly the same though."

Holding the blade under the overhead light, patterns could be detected. The blade lacked the *hamon*, the distinctive tempering line found near the edge of traditionally forged Japanese blades. Instead of *horimono* engravings—depicting gods, dragons, or other mythical beings—holographic designs appeared to be part of the blade's metal itself.

"This is not steel," Mizuki observed.

"Metal ceramic like our armor or the ship's hull. Nano engineered to be flexible but hard, sharpened to an almost monomolecular edge."

"Won't the edge get chipped or nicked?"

"The scabbard holds custom nanites. When the sword is sheathed the nanites automatically repair any damage done to the blade and resharpen the cutting edge."

Mizuki made a few test swings, a smile spreading across her face. She finished her impromptu kata and again examined the blade. "It's beautiful, Bobby, thank you so much. Now I can leave Saito-san's katana on the mantle where it will not suffer further damage."

"That was my thought. That sword is more than a weapon, it is a cultural treasure—for Japanese and for all humankind. You don't have to worry about damaging your new sword."

She looked at the second sword, still laying on the bed. "You made two."

"Yes. The way I see it that sword saved your life down below."

"Many times."

"A weapon that useful should be standard equipment, at least for officers, so I had them make one for me as well—his and hers katana."

"Certainly more functional than his and hers wash towels." Mizuki grinned impishly.

"I was hoping you'd see it that way. Now come on, we need to go put on our armor and get the scabbards attached to our suits."

The two officers grabbed their new swords and headed aft, trailed by a flock of blue butterflies.

Shuttle Bay, 3rd Deck

"Captain, I just don't like it, yous four officers goin' off by yer selves, no Sir." The Chief was obviously not happy about the plan to return to the planet below.

"I've got to agree with the Chief, Captain," added the Gunny. "I don't like the idea of you going in without any backup. At least let me send a couple of Marines along."

"Or better yet, take the whole squad and the armored shuttle." The Chief put his hands on his hips and squinted at the four armored officers gathered at the boarding ramp.

"Yer objections are noted, but we are going down to pay a visit to the local monarch and then, perhaps, take a side trip up north to see if we can find any T'aafhal artifacts layin' around."

"Besides, Gunny," the First Officer added, "The Marines are needed to crew the ship, just in case some other unwelcome types show up."

"You shouldn't go down to the planet with just a couple of Jap swords," the Chief reiterated, gesturing to the katanas strapped to Mizuki and Bobby's armor. Then, realizing what he had said he added, "no offense intended, Ma'am."

"None taken, Chief," Mizuki replied. The Chief was a crusty old sailor whose language sometimes strayed from the politically correct.

"We'll take sidearms with us as well, they should prove sufficient to deal with the local fauna."

"With all due respect, Ma'am, you should be more heavily armed than that."

Billy Ray looked at his two senior noncoms and sighed. *They are probably right, better to err on the side of caution.* "OK, we'll take Hitch and Jacobs with us."

"Heavy armor?"

"Light armor, there's only so much space in the pinnace. They can bring railguns, that should handle any foreseeable local threat."

Chief Zackly looked at the Gunny, realizing that the Captain's concession was all they were likely to get. Rosey nodded her agreement. The Chief spoke into his collar pip.

"Hitch, Jacobs! Get yer sorry asses into light armor, grab some railguns and a full ammo load, and come to the shuttle bay."

"Aye, aye, Chief!" came the enthusiastic reply.

"When they arrive send 'em up," Billy Ray said. He turned and went up the airstair to the pinnace. The others followed. Bobby was the last to board, and before he did he turned to the two NCOs.

"Don't fret, you two. You know that we all can take care of ourselves if it comes to a fight, and we will have Matt and Stevie to back us up."

"Yeah, but those fair-weather sailors can be dumber than two sacks of hammers."

"Come on Chief. Sure, if they have too much spare time on their hands they can get into trouble, but they are steady in a fight and you know it. Besides, they have had experience around T'aafhal equipment, which might come in handy."

"I guess so, Sir, we just don't like you officers goin' off without an escort, that's all."

"Hell, Gunny, we blasted the Dark Lords into plasma, stopped an interplanetary invasion, and rescued Mizuki. What else could we find down there to top that?"

285

Part Four

Caverns Measureless To Man

Chapter 34

Captain's Pinnace

Bobby guided the pinnace on a slow approach to the ant Queen's palace, circling the structure before setting down on the surrounding plaza. The view from above gave him a feeling of *déjà vu*. There was activity at all three major entrances, with the northern transept being particularly crowded with workers.

"Looks like the eastern entrance is the best bet, Captain. They even seem to have repaired the doorway." Around the freshly repaired doorway a number of ant warriors stood with grounded spears, watching workers come and go.

"All right, set her down."

Bobby sat the shuttle down in front of the eastern entrance and lowered the airstair.

"Alright, let's go talk with the Queen. Hitch, Jacobs, guard the boat," Billy Ray ordered, adding, "do you think the guards will try to intercept us?"

"Don't know," Bobby replied.

"They didn't when the Chief and I were last down here," Beth added, "but things were in a state of confusion then."

The four officers deplaned and headed toward the entrance. As they approached the guards became more animated, moving to block the humans' path.

"So what do we do if they try to keep us out?" asked Bobby.

"Mizuki, can you take the lead?" Billy Ray asked. "They ought to recognize you at least, seeing how you traveled with the Queen and fought beside them."

"We can talk to them using the translation data collected by my pendant. It has been downloaded to all our suits." Mizuki halted in front of the warriors, her flock of butterflies forming an ominous cloud above the quartet of Earthlings. "I am Lord Mizuki, here to see Queen Timushi."

The ants clicked and buzzed at each other, saying nothing that the suit computers could translate. The frustration level among the humans was rising while the warriors made no move to step aside.

"So what do we do now?" Bobby said. "Somehow I doubt forcing our way past the palace guard will make a favorable impression on the Queen."

"I don't think they recognize me, I'm going to try something." With that Mizuki opened her helmet, throwing it backward and partially retracting it into her suit. The ants twitched and waggled their antennae. Picking up their spears the guards backed away, opening the path to the interior.

"Why did they do that?" Billy Ray asked. "It's not like they couldn't see you through yer helmet."

"Or the butterflies." Beth raised a single finger to point at the swirl of color overhead.

"They are not visual creatures, at least not the lower castes. They are very scent oriented."

"You mean they needed to smell you to recognize you?"

"Right, Bobby. Remember, I was not sealed inside a suit when I was helping them before."

"Probably a good thing, otherwise Umky could not have tracked you and the guards wouldn't have recognized you just now. Suddenly I feel inadequate, at least as far as my sense of smell goes."

"Let's not stand here jawin' about it, let's get inside."

At Billy Ray's prompting the four entered the palace. Workers scurried every where—in the main hall, and along the aisles and balconies—repairing and cleaning. No bodies of slain warriors or alien commandos remained. The stone floor where they laid had been scrubbed until it shined, blood stains removed and bullet holes patched.

"A lot cleaner than the last time we were here," Bobby said to Mizuki, who was walking beside him.

Mizuki looked to the right as they came to the intersection of the vaults. "The northern hall is still a mess. Zeke really did a lot of damage."

Bobby shrugged. "He thought they killed his brother. If they had harmed you I would have leveled the place."

"Hush, Bobby, we are almost to the throne platform."

Before them the raised platform on which the throne sat ascended in three wide steps. Sitting in an alabaster cradle, the Queen was surrounded by advisers, servants, and other subjects. Mizuki noted that the Queen's abdomen had already grown significantly and her vestigial wings were gone. As the humans approached, the Queen's head rose and she looked directly at Mizuki.

"My Lord Mizuki, I almost didn't recognize you in your battle armor," Timushi announced. "I thought never to see you again."

Mizuki bowed as gracefully as her armor allowed. "Your Majesty, it is good to see you again. I have brought my friends, the other leaders of our expedition, to pay their respects."

"If they are your friends then they are Our friends as well." The Queen dipped her antennae in greeting.

"This is Captain Billy Ray Vincent, our leader, Commander Beth Melaku, his mate, and you have already met Commander Bobby Danner, my mate." Taking their lead from Mizuki the other three partners bowed to the monarch.

"You are all welcome in my domain, friends of Lord Mizuki. Your aid in eliminating the spined invaders will forever be appreciated. In fact... Scribes! Take a proclamation... I Timushi, Queen of all Formicidae do hereby declare that Lord Mizuki of Earth is forever more the Queen's Daemon. All subjects will render her whatever aid or assistance she might require from this day hence."

"Yes, Your Majesty," the head scribe intoned, bowing and backing way. She conferred with her underlings and several hustled from the throne room to spread the proclamation to the far ends of the Queen's empire.

"So let it be written, so let it be done," Beth sarcastically intoned to her fellows via suit-to-suit.

291

"Your Majesty," said Mizuki, bowing again to the monarch, "you honor me greatly."

"Nonsense, it is you who has honored me with your service. Many years from now I will still recall the events of my ascension day and the part my friend from beyond the sky played in them. So tell me, my Lord Mizuki, is there something that I can do for you and your friends?"

"Well, there is something that we wished to ask you." Mizuki turned and motioned Billy Ray forward.

"Yer Majesty, the reason we came to your world is that we received a message from an entity, a very old entity that we believe has been on your world for many years."

"Really, Lord Billy Ray?"

"Yes, Ma'am. You see, our kind has inherited a problem left behind by our... predecessors. A sort of legacy that includes watching after other species and having to fight a long list of bad guys. Like the daemons who came here and meddled in your affairs."

The queen nodded encouragingly. Billy Ray continued.

"We keep looking for clues as to why the older daemons, who left us in charge of this mess, disappeared. We think the message we received came from one of their devices, left on this world a long time ago. We were wondering if you had any historical tales or legends regarding something strange, perhaps even magical, in the north?"

"Summon my scholars and sages, Majordomo, I have need of their advice," Timushi ordered. "I have no personal knowledge of such a thing, but my people have records going back to the dawn of time. Those who study and record such things will be able to tell you if there is anything untoward in the north country."

CIC, *Peggy Sue*

Arin Baldursson had come forward to the CIC, leaving the comfort of his usual haunts in Engineering. By order of rank and seniority he was technically in command of the Peggy Sue, but he had no desire to be captain. He felt much more comfortable in the engine room than on the bridge.

Joining Arin in the ship's control center were Chief Zackly and GySgt Acuna, both obviously concerned about having the ship's four senior officers together on an alien planet. Also present was Dorri, monitoring the conversation between the officers and the ant Queen, just in case some help was needed with the translation algorithm. Mizuki's prolonged exposure and interaction with the natives made that improbable, but it was a serviceable excuse to get her into the CIC where the action was.

"Everything seems ta be goin' fine so far," the Chief commented.

"It's not like the locals pose a threat to them in armor," the Gunny replied. "The Queen should surely know that from what we did to her evil sister and those spiny beavers."

"The conversation has been polite, even friendly so far," Dorri added. "Maybe the ant scholars will have some useful information."

"Where's yer sister, short stuff?" The Chief teased Dorri for being shorter than her older sister, even though she towered over the diminutive old sailor.

"Are you kidding? There is no way you can get her to leave Mal's side."

"She does seem rather smitten," the Gunny said.

"Ja." Arin shook his head. "Love seems to be breaking out all over. Evidently Umky and Ahnah have overcome their differences, either that or they are trying to kill each other."

"What?"

"The polar bear quarters are adjacent to the engineering spaces, and it has become obvious to me that the walls are not nearly thick enough."

"Death will do that to people, and to bears," Rosey said. "It makes us feel our mortality and nature's answer to mortality is procreation."

"You mean sex?" asked Dorri. She was fairly sure that was what the others were talking about, but she wanted to be sure.

"Yer too young to be hearin' this, short stuff."

"Chief, the Imam back on Paradise tried to marry me off when I was thirteen—I am well acquainted with the concept."

The Chief grimaced and squinted at the young woman. "Yer about the oldest fourteen year old I've ever met, kiddo."

"Hey look!" Dorri exclaimed, pointing at the larger wall screen. "A bunch of new ants have arrived, they must be the Queen's sages."

"You are right, Dorri," Arin replied, thankful for the interruption and change in topic. "Quiet everyone."

Queen's Palace

Having run out of small talk the Earthlings were relieved when the Queen's scholars filed into the throne room. The ant academics were all significantly smaller than the Queen, or even the bullheaded warriors, but they possessed the large compound eyes that seemed to indicate higher intelligence in the arthropods. Several of them were carrying scrolls tucked under their arms, lending them a studious air. The lead sage had a gold medallion hung around her neck on a chain, perhaps a symbol of rank. She bowed and addressed the Queen.

"You have summoned us, my Queen?" The scholar managed to sound obsequious and haughty at the same time.

"Yes, Senior Sage, these daemons wish to know if there is any lore recorded in the royal archives regarding strange or mystical events to the north."

The other scholars began chattering softly amongst themselves, while their leader bowed her head in deep cogitation. One of the subordinates leaned in and whispered something to the head scholar. She straightened up and again addressed her sovereign.

"You Majesty, it would seem that the archives of ancient times do contain stories of odd things happening to those who have traveled to the far north, close to where the mountains are white with frozen water."

"Yes?" the Queen prompted, showing signs of impatience.

"Er, yes." Another assistant handed the head scholar a scroll. With an almost theatrical flair she unrolled the scroll, nodded a few times as if reacquainting herself with the text, and then read aloud from the document.

"More than ten thousand years ago, a party of prospectors set out in search of metal deposits to mine. Their journey took them to the unexplored lands of the far north where they reported finding a cave. The cave's mouth was high on a cliff face, hidden behind a stupendously large waterfall."

The scholar paused for effect. She was definitely enjoying being the center of attention while reciting the tale. "Finding a way to reach the mouth of the cave they entered in, hoping to find treasure worthy of the trek's hardships. Sadly, few of their number left the cave alive, and even fewer lived to return to civilization. When they did, they recounted harrowing events—perils that claimed most of their companions, and even stranger things. Deep within the cavern they claim to have experienced hallucinations, strange visions that filled their heads, sending them fleeing in terror."

She looked up at the Queen. "Since that day, no one has ventured so far to the north, and none have sought the daemon haunted cavern." The head scholar lowered the scroll, bowed and stepped back from the throne.

"The old girl sure has a flair for the dramatic," Beth whispered to her companions. Billy Ray ignored his wife's commentary and directed another question to sage.

"Did they leave any description of this place? What the surrounding terrain was like, how they found it in the first place?"

"Lord Daemon, they described the waterfall as being at the northernmost end of a deep river valley, a place where mists and fog from the water never allow the rays of the sun to shine unhindered. The falls are supposedly the headwaters of the great northern river. They simply followed that river's bank, always choosing the widest tributary, until they came to the falls themselves."

"Thank you," Billy Ray said to the sage, then turned slightly and addressed the Queen. "And thank you, Your Majesty. We now have a place to start our quest."

"May the old gods smile upon your endeavors, Lord Billy Ray. I do not envy you this legacy your elder daemons bequeathed you. Is there anything more I can do for you?"

Mizuki spoke up in Billy Ray's stead. "No, Your Majesty, you have done quite enough. Thank you again, we will take our leave of you now. If we find anything of consequence we will let you know. My companions and I wish you a long and productive reign, and prosperity for all Formicidae."

"Fare thee well, my favorite daemon." The Queen nodded and dipped her antennae. Without another word, she returned to the business of running her empire.

The humans all bowed to their host and withdrew, anxious to be on their way. As they walked down the hall Bobby spoke to his fellow adventurers.

"So this is our mission, our legacy—The T'aafhal Legacy—eh?"

"Yeah, pardner. Ya gotta admit it sounds better than the giant pain in the ass it really is."

"So far, dear," added Beth.

"Trust me, things can always get worse," Mizuki finished. The *aoi chō* swirled above them in oblivious joy.

Chapter 35

Captain's Pinnace

"Looks like they're coming back," Hitch said to his friend and longtime shipmate. Both he and Jacobs were standing at the top of the airstair in the rear of the pinnace. Both petty officers had served on the Peggy Sue since the first voyage, with a few side trips along the way. They had been chosen by the Captain to accompany the officers because they were a known commodity, and they had faced strange situations without panicking in the past.

"Right, Stevie," Matt replied. "I guess we are headed north to find this big waterfall."

"Waterfalls I've seen, it's what's behind the waterfall that worries me."

"We've fought aliens on strange planets, space stations, and in outer space for years, buddy. I doubt that there's anything in this cave we're looking for that we can't handle."

"Now that makes me worry."

"What?"

"I'm the one who's always naively optimistic. You not being worried scares me half to death."

"Come on, it's a hole in the ground, and if there is anything in the hole its been here for a long, long time. You heard the officers talking—it's like some kind of lost T'aafhal weather station or something."

Hitch scoffed. "Name me one time when we have come across anything having to do with the T'aafhal that the shit hasn't hit the fan."

Jacobs waved one armored hand dismissively. "If the T'aafhal droppings do hit the fan it will be the officers in the lead."

"You wanna bet we'll be in splatter range?"

"Pipe down and belay that chatter, they are almost close enough for suit-to-suit reception."

At the bottom of the airstair they could see the tall figure of the First officer mounting the ramp into the ship. The two friends stood back from the entrance, giving each other here-we-go-again looks. They were sailors and sailors love to complain, but in truth, there was nowhere they would rather be than in the pinnace, on the threshold of adventure.

* * * * *

Minutes after boarding the shuttle the party of Earthlings was headed north, leaving behind the sprawling city of the ants. The temperate upland terrain was soon replaced by hills and then a lowland basin with a wide river meandering across it.

"According to our planetary survey this is the largest river in the north," Bobby reported from the flight deck. "If the scholar's tale is factual we should be able to follow it right to the waterfall."

"That's assuming things haven't change too much in ten thousand years," Beth observed.

"I talked with Dr. Hosseini a few minutes ago and he assures me that the headwaters of the river should not have eroded beyond recognition." Sami Hosseini was one of the scientists on Mizuki's staff, the expedition geologist. "The face of the fall may have receded several kilometers but if the strata are consistent the fall should remain. The biggest worry is that erosion of the waterfall has obstructed the cave entrance."

"We'll cross that bridge when we come to it." The pinnace's cabin was in full transparency mode, affording everyone on board a panoramic view of the lush countryside passing beneath their feet. Having spent more than a year in space, Billy Ray and the others were all enjoying the sight of so much greenery. "This is quite a pretty planet, at least from up here."

"Believe me, it is not so pretty up close."

"You only say that because things kept trying to eat you." Beth shot her friend a wry smile.

Mizuki unconsciously reached back and touched her new sword, just reassuring herself that it was there. Clinging to the cabin ceiling the butterflies rustled. Mizuki smiled back. "It was exhausting being so popular."

298

"At least there was air to breath, water to drink, and food to eat," Bobby observed.

"If you like the constant stench of rotting vegetation, getting soaked by daily showers, and eating big fleshy maggots."

"I'd say you are one lucky gal, Mizuki. After all, black crap didn't ooze out of the ground and try to dissolve you like back on Paradise."

"My paradise lies in the shadow of my sword."

"Is that an old samurai saying?" asked Beth.

"Actually, honey bunch, that was old Freddie Nietzsche from *Ecce Homo*. 'And like a wind shall I one day blow amongst them and with my spirit take away their soul's breath'."

"My favorite proto-fascist philosopher," quipped Bobby.

* * * * *

In the back of the cabin Hitch and Jacobs were quietly eavesdropping on their officers' conversation, hoping to get the real skinny on the purpose of their mission. Making sure not to be overheard, Hitch leaned over and whispered to Jacobs.

"Who's this Nietzsche character?"

"He was a 19th century German philosopher and whack job. He was a sort of predecessor to Ayn Rand, only not so warm and cuddly."

"Who?"

"Forget it. They are both long dead."

"Do officers talk about shit like this all the time?"

"It's the burden of a liberal education, Stevie, a burden you don't have to bear. Now be quiet, they may say something important."

The Cavern Beneath the Falls

Deep in the folds of the planet's crust, at the end of a cavern hollowed out by leeching water and the passage of time, an

299

intelligence of non-biological origin observed the pinnace's progress. Entangled quantum domains danced with the thoughts of a being who had been created by the T'aafhal themselves. Left on Formicidae more than a million and a half years ago, its mission was to preserve life on the small world where it resided.

Instilled with a mission it could not abandon, the AI watched over the system humans called Alpha Phoenicis. Left alone to fulfill its preprogrammed purpose it had never been contacted by the T'aafhal again—though occasional messages encoded in neutrino bursts arrived from other AIs.

Infrequent messages not withstanding, its solitary existence was seldom disturbed until recently. A web of sensors monitored stars, planets, and surrounding space while the intelligence lay dormant— even a machine intelligence would eventually be driven insane by eons of isolation if it remained fully conscious all that time.

It looks like the creatures from the T'aafhal-like ship are coming, at last. Interesting that they took the time to check on the natives before satisfying their own curiosity regarding my signal. It is possible, though not probable, that the T'aafhal sent these creatures. While they did neutralize the threat posed by the Dark Lords and their minions, that does not mean they are benign. No matter, their intentions will be known soon enough.

One thing the intelligence had in abundance was patience. But it also possessed curiosity, a hallmark of all truly sentient beings. When the visitors arrived the AI would question them, and if they threatened its mission it would deal with them.

Captain's Pinnace

The terrain beneath the shuttle was growing more rugged. Gentle hills gave way to jagged ridges and the once placid river grew wild and unkempt as it was channeled by deepening gorges.

"Well, folks, it looks like we are going to run out of daylight before we find this waterfall," Bobby announced from the pilot's seat.

"I was afraid of that, pardner, even a small planet is a pretty big place. Can you find a level area to set down for the night?"

"Why can't we just use FLIR and light amplifiers to keep looking after dark?" Beth asked.

"Since we don't really know what we're looking for I think I'd rather we bivouac for the night and get a fresh start in the morning. We've been in this system for weeks, another night won't make much difference."

"Remember that this artifact, whatever it is, may have been here for millions of years, like the T'aafhal ship that crashed on Earth," Mizuki added, always the voice of reason amongst the four. Bobby could be reckless, as she well knew, and while Beth and Billy Ray were less prone to rushing into things they too were adventurous types. Not that Mizuki was not curious, but she was a trained scientist, and tried to be methodical and patient.

"I'm surprised that you of all people would want to spend another night on this rock, sweetheart."

"Inside a shuttle, wearing armor, no problem. Better that than fly into a mountain in the dark—one shuttle crash in my lifetime is quite enough."

"All right, all right. We'll land... and no back seat flying." Bobby grinned at his soon to be wife and began a rapid descent toward a flat topped bluff bordering the river.

The Valley of Mists

After an uneventful night the explorers resumed their journey upstream. As the river snaked its way northward, the gorge through which it flowed grew narrower and its walls steeper. Low clouds wreathed the surrounding mountains and the valley below became increasingly obscured by fog.

"I hope the waterfall is tall enough to see through this soup," Bobby muttered. He was flying well above the fog obscured valley bottom.

"I hope so too," Mizuki replied. "I talked with Sami again this morning and he said that the river water showed signs of glacial silt. We must be getting near the source of the river."

Rounding a sharp bend, the river straightened out in front of them. There, rising out of the mists, was a massive water fall.

"I think we have found it," Beth said dryly.

"It looks to be about three hundred meters wide at the top and radar says it's eight hundred meters, give or take, from top to bottom," Bobby said. "That qualifies as a 'stupendously large waterfall' in my book."

"I guess it'll have to do, pardner." Billy Ray was grinning widely, as excited as the rest of the party over finding a site matching the ant scholar's description.

"So what do we do now?" asked Mizuki, viewing the falling torrent of water with some trepidation.

"I suggest we approach the fall carefully and use the sensors to scan for a cave opening," Beth replied, "and if there is, hope that a way up to it still exists."

"Yes Ma'am, let's see what secrets are hidden by the mists." Bobby eased the shuttle to within fifty meters of the falling avalanche of water and then began a slow vertical descent. The view from the cabin was quickly obscured by billowing mist, eerily illuminated by light from the red sun.

"Sort of like descending into hell," the Captain said, as swirling mist enveloped the shuttle. Fading from red to gray, things grew darker as they sank deeper into the unknown depths.

The cabin fell silent as the outside visibility dropped to zero. Bobby overlaid the forward windscreen with a holographic image, constructed from multi-spectral sensor returns. The computer generated image showed the cliff face receding away from the thundering torrent tumbling from the ledge above. About a third of the way down the cliff face a sizable hole appeared, its lower edge forming a horizontal shelf in the rock.

"Ye of little faith," Billy Ray quipped. "Just like our hard-shelled friends said, a cave entrance behind a huge waterfall."

"Yes, dear. But how do we get to the entrance?"

"I can tell you this, we are not flying through that curtain of water," Bobby said. "We'd end up on the rocks below with fifty thousand cubic meters of water a minute pounding down on our heads."

"Didn't the ant scholar say there was a way in from the side of the fall?" Mizuki said, trying to recall the words of the local historian. "It looks like the falling water causes the face of the cliff to erode more rapidly than the ledge at the top, undercutting it. Maybe there is enough gap between the water and the rock face to slip in behind the fall itself."

Hovering in front of the wall of falling water, Bobby moved the shuttle sideways while scanning for some way to access the hidden cave opening. The width of the stream did not span the entire cliff face, leaving gaps at either side.

"I don't know about you, but it doesn't look like there is any easy way to climb up that cliff," Billy Ray observed, "or to rappel down from the top."

"I don't think I would enjoy dangling on 250 meters of rope from an overhanging cliff," Beth said, adding. "We could call for more personnel from the ship."

"To do what, build us an elevator?" her husband replied. "Building anything on the cliff face would be dangerous and time consuming. Besides, most of the crew don't know the truth about the T'aafhal: how they manipulated our species's development; how the M'tak Ka'fek fiddled with those who sailed in her; how humanity was drafted to fight a galactic war we didn't start. The worst part about it is we don't even know if there's anything worthwhile in there. No, until we know what this artifact is we need to keep a tight rein on the situation."

"Are you saying that the crew might not handle the truth well?"

"I'm saying we need to know a lot more than we do now, before letting the rest of mankind in on the secret. They might not take too kindly to having been bred like some alien's prize cattle."

"Or that some of us are more than human," added Mizuki.

"Which brings us back to finding a way into the cave on our own," Bobby said, bringing the conversation full circle.

"The gap is only about ten meters, max. That's not wide enough for the pinnace to just fly in," Beth said measuring the distance with a pilot's eye.

"What are the dimensions of the cave opening?" Bobby asked.

"It is almost twenty meters wide and fifteen tall at the mouth, though it narrows farther in," Mizuki replied, giving Bobby an apprehensive look. "Why do you ask?"

"I've got an idea..."

Chapter 36

The Waterfall

"Just what do you have in mind pardner?" Billy Ray asked his friend. Having known Bobby for more than half his life, Billy Ray knew that tone of voice—it usually meant something crazy to follow.

"This shuttle is twelve meters long and eight meters or so wide, right?"

"Yes," Beth answered, cautious hesitation in her voice. "Like I said, not enough clearance between the cliff face and the cascading water."

"Not on the level."

"Why do I have the feeling that there's a 'hey y'all, watch this' moment coming."

Bobby ignored his friend and elaborated. "My point is, the pinnace is less than five meters tall. That should give sufficient clearance to fit between the rock and the water."

"Yer sayin' we can fly the pinnace, banked at an angle of ninety degrees, between the rock and the cascade."

"Right!"

"Are you joking?" asked Mizuki.

"Are you insane?" asked Beth.

"Hell no, he ain't jokin'," Billy Ray said. "And the fact that he's crazy ain't exactly a secret."

"Come on! It's not like we need aerodynamic lift to keep this puppy in the air. It can hover on its side as easily as on the level like we're doing now." Bobby's voice grew more excited as he explained his plan. "I'll just flip her on her side, snuggle up to the cliff face and slide in behind the falling water."

"And how does being sideways behind the waterfall help us?"

"The cave opening is more than big enough to level off in—if it's done carefully—and once level we can land and deplane."

The cabin was totally silent.

"Well?" he asked his companions, glancing anxiously from one to the next. "It's that or we need to find a place to land so we can try our hand at a bit of mountaineering."

Billy Ray looked to the two women. "Anybody got an alternative? Cause I got nothing."

Both shook their heads.

"This better not be as bad as the sled ride inside the metal moon," Mizuki told her partner, "I had trouble keeping food down for a week after that."

"Not a problem, sweetheart. We have deck gravity this time, you won't feel a thing."

"Like we all haven't heard that before," Beth snorted.

"OK, pardner, let me tell the ship what we are about to try and where to start looking for the pieces if it don't work."

Bobby grinned like a mad man. "What was that you said earlier... Ye of little faith?"

* * * * *

The shuttle sidled up to the rock face, spray from the raging torrent sheeting off the forward windscreen. Beth was in the co-pilot's seat, trying to look less nervous than she felt. The cabin was again in full transparency mode, giving those on board a better view than some of them might wish.

"All right people, we are about to roll ninety degrees to starboard," Bobby called from the left side pilot's seat. His hands moved imperceptively on the side stick and thruster controls.

The world outside rotated.

In the back of the cabin, Hitch reached out and steadied himself against the cabin overhead. "Woa," he exclaimed.

"Easy, Stevie," Matt encouraged his friend. "The deck gravity won't let you fall."

"Yeah, but the damned pinnace could fall!"

Outside, the water slick rocky surface that had been a vertical wall now appeared to be beneath the shuttle. The view forward showed a stream of water flying by from left to right, almost ten meters above the dark rock beneath their feet.

"Remember Bobby, it is OK to have butterflies in your stomach, as long as you make them fly in formation."

"What?"

"It was just something I read." Mizuki shrugged. "It sounded zen and seemed to fit the situation."

"You're the butterfly expert, I just fly the ship." As he was speaking, Bobby edged the shuttle closer to the seemingly horizontal airborne cascade. "OK, let's slip in between the water and the cliff."

The pinnace bounced across the rocky surface, kept from actual contact with the cliff face by its bottom repulsors. Water flew sideways across the windscreen, providing mixed signals to the crew's senses. Their vestibular systems—their inner ears—were at odds with what their eyes were telling them. A low moan came from the rear of the cabin.

"Close yer eyes if you feel like pukin'," Billy Ray suggested. "You really don't want to blow chunks inside a suit of armor."

"Thank you, dear, for bringing up the subject." Beth's dark face had turned a bit ashen but she held on. As a torpedo ship captain during the battle for Earth she had plenty of experience with similar sensory dissonance. Of course, it was easier to deal with when she was calling the shots—as most pilots will admit, they hate being passengers with somebody else doing the flying.

Soon there was nothing to be seen above the shuttle but raging water. The pinnace bobbled and bumped along, clinging to the rock, trying to avoid being sucked into the avalanche of H_2O

"My mind is a raging torrent, flooded with rivulets of thought cascading into a waterfall of creative alternatives," Bobby recited.

"What?" Mizuki asked in confusion.

"Hedley Lamarr, Blazing Saddles." Billy Ray answered.

"They are both certifiably insane! We've been hijacked by madmen!"

Smiling at Beth's sarcastic outburst, Bobby replied. "Lady, you knew I was crazy when you got on board this crate."

The shuttle wobbled and dipped as a dark hole opened up beneath it—the open mouth of the cave. Guiding the craft along the ledge formed by the floor of the cave, Bobby carefully positioned its blunt delta shape so that he could roll the shuttle into the opening. This was the trickiest part of the whole evolution.

"Hold on to your butts," he muttered as he slowly rolled the shuttle back toward a level orientation. As the left side tilted into the cave the right side tilted outward, until it was clipped by the deluge.

The shuttle flipped back to an upright position and a bit beyond. At the same time it slid down the side of the cliff, bouncing off of the cave opening.

Bobby's reflexes were amazing before being enhanced by the T'aafhal, now they were almost superhuman. He recovered the craft's attitude and stopped its downward slide.

"OK, everybody. Let's try that again."

No one else spoke.

Carefully, the shuttle climbed up the cliff face until the cave opening was once again beneath its belly. This time Bobby rolled the shuttle into the cave mouth using a combination of pitch and yaw to swing the wide rear of the craft into the opening.

Ending up a bit nose high he gingerly dropped the front while backing fully into the safety of the cave. Coming to a level hover, he deployed the landing struts and gently sat the bird down on the cave floor. Beth still had a death grip on the arms of the co-pilot's seat.

He took his hands off the controls and flexed his fingers several times. Then, looking at the others, he grinned and said, "See? Piece of cake."

* * * * *

Interesting, they have arrived at the entrance to the cavern. They are either highly confident of their skills, or they are excessively reckless. No matter, they must still traverse several kilometers of underground terrain and deal successfully with the hazards along the way.

The Cavern

"All right you two," Billy Ray said to the two petty officers. "Yer gonna stay with the shuttle and maintain a comm link to the ship. We will be dropping signal repeaters along the way, whenever the signal strength gets too low."

"But Captain," said Hitch. "The Chief told us not to let you out of our sight."

"He did, Sir," said Jacobs, backing up his friend.

"Chief Zackly isn't here to assess the situation, gentlemen. We need you two in reserve, just in case something unexpected happens. You will stay with the shuttle unless we call for you or we lose communications. Do you understand?"

The two sailors came to attention. "Aye, aye, Sir!"

Billy Ray turned and descended the open airstair. Joining the three other officers, he talked to them over suit-to-suit.

"Y'all about ready to move out?"

"Yes, dear. What was that all about?"

"NCOs, all of 'em think officers are like children to be coddled and watched over."

"They care about us, Billy Ray," Mizuki said in support of the ship's noncoms.

"They just don't want an ass chewing from the Chief when they get back to the ship," scoffed Bobby. Billy Ray snorted and Beth raised one eyebrow in bemused agreement.

"Whatever, we got a good supply of signal repeaters and a small recon drone." The size of the pinnace didn't allow for the bigger, more capable recon drones carried by the large shuttles. The grapefruit sized drone didn't have the full spectrum sensors of its larger relatives, but it could transmit high-def video and IR back to its operator's suit display.

"I've run the drone a kilometer deep into the cave and it looks like, after narrowing a bit, it opens up to a much larger space inside." Beth had assumed command of the drone, though the others could all receive telemetry from the little scout robot.

"Mizuki, do you have any way of tellin' if we are getting close to this gizmo?"

"Most of my detection equipment was destroyed in the shuttle crash and there wasn't time for engineering to fabricate replacements. I do have a nanoresonance detector that may be able to tell us if we come across something interesting."

"Sing out if you pickup anything. All right folks, let's head out."

* * * * *

Using their suit lamps for illumination, augmented by IR imaging, the quartet of friends descended into the pitch dark cavern. As promised, about a kilometer inside the cave opened up into a much larger cavern. The formerly gray-black rock became laced with color, ranging from milky white to hot pink.

Many speleothems graced the huge space—stalactites, stalagmites, and columns where the two had grown together. The ceiling was festooned with stone icicles, formed by the slow drip of mineral laced water over aeons. The sides of the cavern were so ornately decorated in places that they looked like something out of a mad king's fantasy grotto. Mizuki's butterflies flitting about only heightened the effect. The little winged aliens raced from place to place like a pack of puppies in a strange room.

"Oh wow," Beth exclaimed. "That is quite something."

"That view alone makes this trip worth while," Billy Ray agreed.

"The surrounding rock is mostly dolomite—calcium magnesium carbonate—which can occur in many colors. It is also susceptible to cave formation by ground water. Dr. Hussein says this cave must be quite old. It takes a million years or more to form large columns like those back on Earth."

"That formation to the left, where those red ribbons streak down the paler rock, it looks like the cave wall is bleeding."

"Yer just an incurable romantic, honey bunch." Billy Ray teased his wife.

"Look, there is a pool about fifty meters in," said Bobby, pointing at a crystal clear pond, "with a stone arch over it."

"It looks like a traditional Japanese bridge over a koi pond," Mizuki added, a touch of homesickness in her voice. Faced with such grandeur a hush settled over them all.

After a minute of awed reverence, Billy Ray broke the silence. "As spectacular as this is, we need to keep moving, y'all. Just watch where yer stepping."

Billy Ray strode forward, into the larger space. With tacit agreement the others moved into the cavern, following the path their captain blazed. After pausing to marvel at the tranquil stillness of the subterranean pool, staring into its turquoise depths, they crossed the stone bridge one at a time.

Among the rocks and spires, strange creatures moved cautiously. Blind scorpions with no eyes or body pigment, like miniature ghosts of their ferocious relatives on the surface. Cave newts—blind salamanders—a pale pinkish-white in color with splashes of red on their external gills. Guided by sound, one of the blind lizards tried to eat a butterfly and paid for its bad judgment with its life.

Other residents, being oblivious to the light brought by the interlopers, moved cautiously away from the vibrations made by the armored giants' footsteps, choosing self preservation over a possible meal.

* * * * *

Several kilometers deep into the cave they came upon a gentle upward slope. Trickling down the incline was a stream, and spreading outward from its banks was what appeared to be a carpet of vivid green. The improbable green blanket extended to the upward curve at the cave walls.

"Now that is strange," Mizuki commented. She was in constant communication with the science staff on board the Peggy Sue. "Dr. Krenshaw says that the ground cover looks like some form of moss or liverwort. He also says that they shouldn't be growing this deep in the cave, even such shade loving plants need sunlight."

"Everyone turn out yer lights. Let's see if there is any natural illumination down here."

One by one, the explorers shut off their suit lights, plunging the cave into darkness. Then, slowly, as their eyes adjusted, a ghostly scene faded in. The ceiling and walls of the cave glowed dimly, casting a pale light on the mossy surface. Attracted by the ceiling's glow, the butterflies flew on ahead of the ground bound humans.

Billy Ray turned his suit lights back on. "Well I guess that solved that mystery."

"Too bad," Mizuki said. "Will was very excited, thinking we had found plants that can grow in the dark."

The four walked along the meandering stream. The water soaked ground cover squished with each step.

"I'm all for making scientific discoveries, but there's bloody little profit in some of the things that excite our science boffins—no slight intended, Mizuki."

Mizuki was about to reply when a white tube, as big around as a fire hose and more than three meters in length, erupted from the ground next to her feet and coiled around her torso. She glanced back at her companions to see a forest of writhing white stalks sprouting around the Earthlings. Groping blindly for the startled explorers the giant worms seemed intent on dragging them down.

Chapter 37

The Mossy Chamber

"Oh bollocks!" Beth exclaimed as three white, segmented worms coiled around her legs and body. Drawing her side arm—a flechette pistol that fired the same 5mm projectiles as the Marines' small arms—she fired a couple of rounds into one of the worms accosting her. The pallid annelid jerked at the impacts but did not go down, the flechettes passing cleanly through its body.

Billy Ray also drew his pistol, a 10mm that fired explosive rounds. He too attempted to shoot their wriggling attackers, but one of the worms seized his forearm with its surprisingly strong mouth, throwing off his aim. The shot struck a worm near Bobby and exploded, bisecting its target by vaporizing a meter long section of the worm's body.

"Hey, easy Tex!" Bobby shouted.

"Sorry, pardner. These things are stronger than you'd think."

"I don't think side arms are going to be very effective against these things, dear."

"Ya think, honey bunch?"

"Kiai!" Mizuki yelled, reaching over her shoulder and drawing her new katana. With a single handed stroke she sliced two of the white worms in half. A back stroke claimed another, freeing her leg.

That left a single worm clinging to her waist. Inserting the sword along side her left hip, cutting edge out, she made a slicing cut that severed her last attacker. While she was dealing with her attackers, the *aoi chō* returned. Sparks flew as they swarmed the living forest that has so unexpectedly sprouted in their absence.

Looking to her left Mizuki saw Bobby had also drawn his sword and was hacking away at the swaying forest of worms with energetic abandon. As Bobby sent hunks of white worm flying in all directions, Beth and Billy Ray continued grappling with their own assailants. Billy Ray had stopped trying to shoot the worms and had drawn his survival knife. With it he was attempting to saw through the tough white flesh wrapped around his body. The worms' flexible

313

bodies were a form of muscular hydrostat and, though lacking bones or cartilage, were surprisingly strong.

Beth, becoming frustrated, fired several more flechettes at her attackers. One of them pinged off her husband's armor.

"Sweetheart, I'd greatly appreciate it if you'd stop shooting in my direction."

"Sorry, dear, any damage?"

"Naw, no blood no foul." Light combat armor was invulnerable to flechette fire except at extreme muzzle velocities, velocities that Beth's pistol was incapable of generating.

Mizuki moved toward her friend. "Hold still Beth, I will cut the worms off of you."

"Thank you, love, the buggers are proving quite recalcitrant."

Mizuki's blade was a blur as she danced around the taller First Officer. Sections of worm fell from Beth's dark armor, squirming where they lay on the mossy ground.

"Hold still, Billy Ray," Bobby shouted, hacking through several of the worms still wrapped around the Captain.

"Be careful with that thing, pardner. If I recall, you used to have trouble shaving yer self without drawing blood."

"Funny for a guy covered in worms." With a sideways swipe that missed Billy Ray's armored belly by a scant centimeters, the last worm enveloping him split in two and fell to the ground.

The worms had had enough. Those still whole retreated back into their lairs, some pulling pieces of their fallen comrades after them. All around the humans pieces of white annelid littered the mossy ground, some still twitching weakly.

"Let's get the hell outta here," Billy Ray suggested, pointing upslope. "Before something else comes looking for a free lunch."

The explorers bounded up the moss covered incline until they stood once more on bare rock. Looking back down the sloping tunnel Billy Ray shook his head.

"Well that was a new experience—attacked by giant killer earthworms."

"Now you know why I love this planet."

"Sarcasm doesn't suit you, Mizuki-chan."

"I can't wait to see what comes next," Beth added.

"I tell you what, honey bunch. Next time we decide to go walkabout on a strange planet I think we should carry swords like Mizuki and Bobby."

"No argument there, dear."

"Oh good! More students for my kendo class." Mizuki smiled brightly.

A call came over their radios.

"Captain, Pinnace, are you alright? Do you need assistance?"

"Pinnace, Captain. We're all OK. Maintain your position. We are pushing on. Captain out." The trek continued, if a bit more cautiously, with the butterflies providing air cover.

Pinnace

"You heard 'em. They are doing fine." said Jacobs. Half way through the dust-up with the cave worms, Hitch was down the airstair and ready to go after the four officers.

"It didn't sound so fine a minute ago, I thought it was gonna turn into a monkey and a football," Hitch insisted. "You saw the video feed, they were attacked by giant, mutant earthworms!"

"You don't know that they're mutants."

"You know what I mean. The furball was bad enough that the Captain was using his k-bar and the XO actually shot him trying to get those worms off."

"They're in armor, bonehead. They were never in any danger and you know it. And did you see how Dr. Ogawa and Cmdr. Danner hacked up those worm things with their swords?"

"Yeah, that was cool. We gotta get ourselves some swords, man."

"Let's talk to the armorers when we get back to the ship. In the mean time we need to be ready to go after the officers riki-tic if they get into real trouble."

"You're right about that, or the Chief will have our guts for garters."

The Cavern

Moving beyond the hall of the white worms, the explores encountered more difficult terrain. At times they were forced to crawl on their hands and knees through tight passages, to clamber up rock falls, and descend near vertical slopes. After an hour of such torture they emerged in another sizable chamber.

"To think that there are people who do this for fun," Beth commented, gratefully standing upright.

"People do a lot of stupid things, honey bunch. I've always thought that havin' to seek out danger for fun means you're playing it way too safe in yer daily life."

"What is wrong with living a safe life, Billy Ray?"

"'Far better it is to dare mighty things, to win glorious triumphs, even though checkered by failure... than to rank with those poor spirits who neither enjoy much nor suffer much, because they live in a grey twilight that knows not victory nor defeat.'" Billy Ray recited.

"Teddy Roosevelt," Bobby stated.

"I understand why he knows all these passages, but how do you know them as well, Bobby?"

"You forget that I've known him since high school, sweetheart. He's been throwing quotes at me for decades."

"I believe that the Dark Lords changed things on the challenge of life front, dear. Things have become a bit too challenging for most."

"JFK said something about that: 'Do not pray for easy lives. Pray to be stronger men.'"

While they were conversing, the four were carefully picking their way across the chamber. The rock here was dark and wet, and long root like strands hung down from the ceiling fifteen meters overhead.

"Have you always wanted to be a philosopher king?" Mizuki asked.

"Naw," he smiled, "just a philosopher captain—king's gotta stay put and rule his kingdom, a captain gets to command his ship and his ship can take him anywhere."

"These things look like plant roots," Bobby mused, reaching out to touch one of the tendrils in question. "I've heard of roots growing down into caves from surface plants. Could we be that close to the surface?"

"I don't know Bobby. We have been traveling up hill most of the time so we might be close to the surface."

There was a sound, like branches whipping through air. A number of the deceptively fragile looking roots wrapped themselves around Bobby. He vanished, yanked toward the ceiling of the chamber.

"Bobby!" Mizuki reacted instantly, drawing her sword and hacking off all of the hanging tendrils within her reach. Bobby was already half way to the ceiling.

"I can't move," he yelled, straining against the misleadingly slender threads that wrapped his arms and chest. "Somebody get me down!"

Looking up and directing their suit lights on the ceiling, the others could see that the roof of the cavern was covered with puckered mounds. The hanging tendrils sprouted from the bases of the mounds. The appendages that had kidnapped Bobby belonged to a large mound that opened to reveal a toothed, funnel-like maw.

Billy Ray drew his sidearm and fired three times in quick succession. Brilliant orange flashes erupted from where the gaping mouth awaited Bobby's arrival. Bits of creature and shards of stone flew. Bobby fell.

"Oh shiiitttttt..." he yelled. His outcry was cut short when his still bound body struck the floor of the chamber. Mizuki immediately moved to sever his bonds.

317

Beth had also drawn her pistol and was firing flechette bursts into all of the creatures she could identify, green tracers scribing lines of light from her weapon to the ceiling. Each creature she shot quickly pulled up its hanging tendrils and folded in on itself.

"Bobby, are you OK?" Mizuki asked as her butterflies formed a swirling barrier above them—they were evidently too small to trigger the ceiling creatures' snares, passing through the dangling roots without incident.

"That was just what I needed," Bobby said slowly, awaiting the verdict of his suit's medical scanners. The impact reactive layer of his armor had stiffened when he hit the ground but it didn't lessen the blow, just redistribute the force. Green lights lit on his helmet display.

"You OK, pardner? We need to get out of here ASAP."

"Yeah, yeah, no permanent damage. Doesn't mean it didn't hurt though."

"Can you stand up?" Mizuki reached down to help him. Slowly he got to his feet and they continued on. As they traversed the chamber, tendrils from other ceiling creatures retracted before them.

"Looks like they have a way of communicating," Beth observed. She still held her pistol in her hand as did her husband.

Billy Ray grimaced and holstered his weapon. "Let's hope they have a way of remembering, I don't want to go through this on the way back out."

* * * * *

A half hour later, Bobby was hardly limping and good spirits had returned. Then they came to the chasm.

"What do you make of that?" asked Billy Ray, peering over the edge.

"That is your basic issue bottomless pit," answered Beth.

Mizuki, being a scientist, measured the width of the yawning crack in the earth before them. "It is 9.3 meters across according to my laser rangefinder."

"That, if I recall, is longer than the Olympic long jump record," Bobby observed.

"Yes, but that was set under normal Earth gravity. The gravity here is only two thirds of that. That should translate into jump height 50% higher and a hang time approximately 23% longer."

"Yeah, but we ain't Olympic athletes. If we could manage seven meters on Earth we'd still come up short."

"You are forgetting that we are all enhanced. Have you tried doing a long jump since the T'aafhal nanites have been in your system?"

"No, Dr. Ogawa, I have not and I'm not real keen on testing your calculations with a leap of faith, as it were."

"Don't forget that the suits also multiply our body strength," Bobby added.

"You want to go first, Hopalong?"

Mizuki paused while listening to somebody on the ship. "The people in the CIC did a computer search and report that elite jumpers usually leave the ground at an angle of twenty degrees or less. Therefore, it is more beneficial for a jumper to concentrate on the initial speed component of the jump."

"You're saying we should trust our lives to a Google search?" Beth sounded more than a bit skeptical.

"No, you should trust basic physics." Mizuki began twitching her fingers rapidly—she was entering things using her suit's virtual keyboard mode. Finishing her calculations she looked up from the in helmet display and addressed her colleagues. "By my calculations, running at ten meters per second, with a thirty degree take off angle, you would get a hang time of 1.7 seconds and could theoretically travel 14.73 meters before striking the ground."

"That's like 22-23 miles per hour," Billy Ray converted in his head. "Yeah, I think that's doable, what do y'all think?"

"After you, Captain." Bobby smiled and made a sweeping gesture toward the chasm with one arm.

"After all, people have been jumping off cliffs since the dawn of time. How hard can it be?"

319

"Of course dear, but let me attach a safety line, just in case."

After letting Beth clip a thin safety line to the back of his suit, Billy Ray backed up twenty meters from the edge of the precipice and yelled. "Stand clear!"

Billy Ray ran toward the yawning crevasse, long legs pumping, accelerating for all he was worth. Just before the edge he landed on his right leg and leaped. Sailing well above the pit, legs pumping to keep an upright attitude, the tall Texan cleared the hurdle with several meters to spare.

Taking a few steps to slow down, Billy Ray turned to his friends and, with a wave of his arm, yelled, "Y'all come!"

One at a time the remaining explorers leaped the chasm. Last across was Bobby, who stumbled a bit on landing but handily cleared the obstacle. "I haven't had this much fun since summer camp," he muttered.

Billy Ray clapped his friend on the shoulder. "Come on, pardner, admit it—that was fun."

"I hated summer camp."

Up ahead, Beth cleared her throat.

"Uh, boys? I think you should look at the far wall up ahead..."

The Metal Wall

In response to Beth's call, the two men hurried to catch up with the women. A hundred meters ahead they spotted what she was talking about—a smooth metal wall embedded in the native rock. Nearing the wall, holographic symbols could be seen embedded in the metallic surface, shifting with the observer's point of view.

"Well, that sure looks like something the T'aafhal would make. You got any readings, Mizuki?"

"Practically nothing above background, its power supply must be either inactive or well shielded."

"There appears to be no seam at all between the metal and the surrounding rock, they abut each other perfectly," Beth observed.

Crouching down in front of the metal barrier, Bobby examined the material intently. "The metal certainly looks like the hull metal on the M'tak Ka'fek, some kind of metallic-ceramic composite. I don't see any hatch markings, but I would wager that this stuff is selectively permeable, allowing access without having to cut holes in it."

"That would be in keeping with T'aafhal design esthetics," Billy Ray agreed. "Peggy Sue, are you getting this?"

"Yes, Captain. We are recording everything from your suits and the recon drone." The drone was hovering above and behind the party of humans, providing a wide shot of the activity in front of the metal barrier.

"I'm getting no readings from behind the barrier, it must be electromagnetically shielded," Mizuki said almost absentmindedly, twiddling on a small device she had extracted from her backpack. "I don't think we can learn anymore from the outside."

"Yer sayin' we should try to go inside?"

"Yes."

"We could try to cut a hole with a utility laser," Beth suggested.

"Why don't we just do what we did when we discovered the M'tak Ka'fek?" Bobby said, standing up in front of the metal barrier.

"And that would be?"

"Just try to walk through the wall."

"That sounds like a very bold move, Bobby." Mizuki stared at him, wide eyed. Whenever she gave him that look, Bobby still couldn't tell if she was impressed with his bravery or astonished by his foolishness.

"Well, Mizuki-chan, I'm a bold kinda guy." He looked at Beth and Billy Ray. Both nodded.

Bobby turned and stepped forward—and passed through the solid metal wall.

"I've lost signal from his suit," Mizuki said.

An armor encased arm extruded itself from the metal wall and beckoned them to follow.

321

"In for a penny, in for a pound," Beth said. She too walked through the wall.

Mizuki and Billy Ray looked at each other, shrugged and followed their partners.

Chapter 38

Tanzania, Africa, circa 3.8 Million BC

A warm yellow sun shined brightly in a cloudless blue sky. Large pink birds trailing long orange legs flapped unhurriedly overhead while a dozen species of herbivore dotted the grassy plain. On the valley floor, between the wooded hills and the lake, herds of grazing animals often wandered by. Their ranks included huge shovel tusked elephants, wildebeest, rhinos, and a herd of antelope that was making its way to the lake side to drink.

Nearby in the grass, several male hominins secreted themselves in a shallow gully, waiting patiently while others from their tribal band moved into position upwind of the antelope. Most of the grazing beasts were too large for the tribe to handle, but antelope were just right. One of the herd could be brought down if lured into an ambush. That was why the males were hidden in the grass downwind.

Copses of trees littered the plain. Normally the tribe sheltered beneath the shade of those trees during the heat of the day, but today they ventured forth driven by the need for food. Though the tribe's females were skilled at gathering fruits and grain, and also digging for tubers, on occasion they all had a craving for meat. This day, the tribe was fulfilling the first part of their lifestyle as hunter/gatherers.

The primary male of the tribe was taller than most, but still quite short compared to a modern human. Not that he looked much like a modern human—jutting jaw, heavy brow, flat nose, with a head housing a brain only a third the sized of a *Homo sapiens*. His arms were long in proportion but he was not a knuckle walker like chimps and gorillas; his gate was fully bipedal, with legs inline beneath his hips and no opposable big toe. Covered with coarse brown hair, about the size of a half grown human child, anthropologists would label him *Australopithecus afarensis*.

The leader found himself crouching down in the tall grass, clutching a long stick in his hand. The tip of the stick had been shaved to a point and hardened in a wildfire. With any luck, he would be able to claim a prize with it, assuming the others did their part.

Good. We ready, catch food.

Looking to his right he spotted a smaller, stockier male. Though lacking a word for it, he thought of the smaller male as a friend. The other often backed his leadership of the tribe, happy to be number two—as long as he left the small female the other favored alone. That was a price worth paying, after all he had the dominant female to himself.

Upwind of the herd, the younger males and several of the females descended on the tribe's chosen quarry. The fleet footed antelope were far too fast for them to catch on foot so a more inventive strategy was called for. The appearance of the hominins upwind—both their physical presence and their scent—caused the herd to bolt. Fleeing in well orchestrated panic, the ungulates headed toward the nearest copse of trees, the one directly behind the hidden hunters.

The herd headed straight at the gully the hunters crouched in, their hooves making the ground tremble. The leader could feel them approaching, could smell their panic. He tightened his grip on his spear. He glanced at his friend, who grinned back.

The antelope ran through the hunters' position, bounding over the gully without slowing their headlong flight. With a guttural cry, the leader stood up and rammed his sharpened stick into the stomach of an antelope in mid-jump. It stumbled and fell to the ground, tearing the primitive spear out of the leader's hands.

The leader's friend pounced on the downed animal before it could regain its feet and runoff. The antelope was mortally wounded but that would not prevent it escaping to die later. The friend thrust his weapon into the herbivore's soft underbelly. The other males rushed up to pummel the creature with heavy sticks and rocks.

Running across the field, the rest of the hunting party rushed up to the kill site. Excited hoots and joyous arm waving spread through the hominins as the antelope expired. The tallest of the females stepped forward, pushing the celebrating males back from the carcase. A smaller female, the one favored by the leader's friend, moved forward and crouched next to the kill. In her hand she held a stone that had been knapped to expose a sharp edge.

With the sharp stone the female cut into the dead antelope and started the process of skinning and butchering the quadruped. As the females dressed the kill the males stood around, on the lookout for danger. Both the leader and his number two had recovered their primitive spears. Together they leaned on their weapons and admired the hairy backsides of the females as they bent over the kill.

CIC, Peggy Sue

"Pinnace, Peggy Sue. We have lost all communication and telemetry from the Captain's party. What is your status?" Doc White queried the sailors in the small shuttle. When the four officers entered the cave to search for the Taafhal artifact, she had come forward to monitor their progress and vital signs from the displays in the CIC.

"Peggy Sue, we lost contact as soon as they passed through that metal wall," replied PO Jacobs from the surface. "We tried following them with the recon drone but the barrier won't let it in. Not only that, those butterfly things are going crazy, dashing themselves against the wall. It won't pass them either."

"Roger, Pinnace." Betty looked at Arin, Gunny Acuna, and the Chief, who were also monitoring the surface mission from the CIC. "What the hell do we do now?"

A familiar voice interrupted the conversation—the ship's computer.

"Chief Engineer Baldursson, an outside entity has penetrated my memory system and effected a data breach."

"What! What do you mean Peggy Sue? How can an 'outside entity' access your systems?" the Chief Engineer asked the ship's computer.

"Screw how! Can it take over the ship?" the Chief demanded.

"No, Chief Zackly, the systems compromised are isolated from the ship's operation and control circuitry. Only my long-term data storage structures have been accessed."

"When did this happen?"

"The incursion began concurrently with the loss of communication from the Captain's party."

"Peggy Sue, is the entity that hacked into your system located on the planet below?" Asked the Gunny.

"That is affirmative, Gunnery Sergeant Acuna. The channel used to access my memory systems appears to be an old T'aafhal protocol. It was able to provide the requisite cyphers and passwords yielding a probability that the intruder is the suspected T'aafhal artifact greater than 99.8 percent."

"So what information did it get?" asked Arin.

"Evidently, this mechanism functions like a flight recorder on an airliner, only more extensive. It downloaded all of the historical data stored in my memory. That would include data going back to the T'aafhal ship that crashed on Earth. Portions of those data even I have been unable to access."

"So what happens now?" the Chief asked.

"I do not know, Chief Zackly."

Tanzania

In the midst of the tribe's hurried butchering a new scent drifted across the plain—cat! The leader spun around, holding his spear in a defensive position. Next to him the smaller male had done the same.

The grassland was home to many species of predator: jackals, wild dogs, hyenas, and big cats. The cats were bad and among the cats lions were the worst—they were dangerous and lazy and hunted in packs. They would much rather relieve some other hunter of its prize than hunt themselves. They were also territorial, different family groups marking off home ranges that outsiders trespassed on at their peril. For this reason the hominins staged their ambush on the boundary between two different prides.

Unfortunately, there were other big cats that prowled the plain and surrounding forest as solitary hunters. There, moving through the waste high grass was the deep golden, spotted coat of a leopard. Most of the hominins began shrieking and backing away.

326

Normally, the tribe would have hacked off as much meat as they could carry and fled into the nearby trees, knowing that other meat-eaters would soon show up to claim their kill. This time their luck was bad indeed, with the nearly lion sized spotted cat happening upon them before the butcher work was done.

The leader was incensed. *No! Antelope mine!*

He growled at the approaching cat.

Looking to the side he saw his friend, also gripping his spear, snarling at the leopard. He snorted at the shorter male, who looked back at him and grinned, displaying his canine teeth. While they lacked the large canines of more primitive hominids, the meaning of the bared dentition was unmistakable.

The leopard snarled, declaring its intention to claim the dead antelope and telling the chattering apes to move along. It slinked forward, confident of its position in the hierarchy of savanna life.

The two friends separated, one moving to either side of the approaching feline. Crouching, their sharpened sticks were held at the cat's eye level. The leopard stopped, perplexed, its tail twitching from side to side—the ape creatures should have fled.

The leopard made a lunge at the taller of the two males confronting it. The leader jumped back and jabbed at the cat with his spear. From the other side, the shorter male lunged and poked the leopard in the flank.

The big cat roared and spun on its attacker, barely missing him with a paw swipe. Before it could press its attack the tall hominin jabbed the frustrated feline in its other flank. Again it spun about to face its tormentor.

That was when the tribe's alpha female ran up behind her mate and tossed a sizable root, striking the leopard on the side of its head. It swatted ineffectually at the root and growled again. Then the smaller female, the one favored by the leader's friend, stepped up beside her mate and threw the rock she had been using to cut up the antelope carcass.

Flung with considerable force, the stone rotated in flight and struck the leopard, sharp side forward, above its right eye. The cat howled.

One by one, the rest of the tribe joined the fray, tossing sticks and stones at the big carnivore, whatever came to hand. Other males joined the leader and his friend, poking at the cat with their spears. Finally the leopard had enough.

The big cat turned and fled through the grass, back the direction it had come from. The tribe broke into a whooping, shrieking, arm waving celebration—they had driven off a dangerous predator and saved their hard won kill.

The leader and his friend stood side by side, their females beside them, and looked out across the grassland. This was something new, something unprecedented. Attacking and driving off the leopard shocked even them.

The world spun. The bright colors of the African plain mixed in a swirling pinwheel that collapsed to a single dot and winked out, leaving only blackness.

Chapter 39

The Artifact

The blackness blossomed with pinpoints of light—sprinkles of color scattered like jewels on black velvet. The components of Alpha Phoenicis appeared, with curved lines arcing through space describing the trajectories of suns and planets. The four explorers found themselves standing on a transparent balcony overlooking a gigantic planetarium. Annotations swam into focus, written in a strange yet familiar script.

"I just had the weirdest hallucination," said Billy Ray, the first to speak.

"Did it involve being all covered with hair?" asked Bobby, standing to Billy Ray's left.

"And fighting a large cat with sticks and rocks?" asked Mizuki, standing to the far side of Bobby.

"Yep, that's the one."

"Pardon me, everyone, but I don't remember being starkers when we came in here."

Billy Ray looked down, then he looked at his wife, standing to his right. His gaze lingered appreciatively on her lithe dark body. "Well, it beats being all hairy and romping around a nature park with a pointy stick."

"Oh good!" Mizuki exclaimed, looking down at her naked body. "I really didn't like having hairy breasts."

"Or hairy bottoms," added Beth.

"Not sure what the purpose of that little drama was but we have obviously found the artifact. If I'm not mistaken, that scribbling is T'aafhal."

"Indeed it is, dear."

"They seem to be astronomical coordinates, movement vectors and other information regarding objects in this star system."

"You're right, Mizuki-chan. Look, there is the remnant of the Fakkaa fleet on its way back home; and there is the Peggy Sue, in orbit around this planet."

A voice sounded in their heads.

Welcome.

"Y'all hear that?"

"I don't think 'hear' is the proper term, but yes."

"And just who, or what, are you?" Billy Ray asked.

I am the caretaker of this system.

"I'm Billy Ray Vincent, captain of the Earth starship Peggy Sue."

I know who you are, Captain Vincent. I downloaded your ship's memory.

"That's a might forward of you."

It is standard procedure for T'aafhal ships and installations.

"Well, as you might have noticed, we are not T'aafhal."

Obviously.

"Not the most forthcoming fellow, is he?" Beth said.

Ignoring his wife's rhetorical question, Billy Ray continued. "You have us at a disadvantage. You know who we are, but we don't know who you are."

I am a non-biological intelligence, created by the T'aafhal and charged with preserving life in this system.

"So what should we call you?"

I have no name.

"Really? We've met a genuine T'aafhal battle cruiser and it had a name."

Warship intelligences take the name of their vessel. I am not a warship.

"Yer on a planet, why don't you take the name of the planet?"

There was a pause.

330

Yes, that would probably make your attempts at communication less cumbersome. Call me Formicidae.

"That's what we named the place. Doesn't it have a T'aafhal name?"

No. It has a number.

"Fine. So, Formicidae, you mind telling us what that little field trip to the Serengeti was all about?"

I scanned the records from your ship, which included the records from the M'tak Ka'fek, the ship you found, and from the D'lat Me'tan.

"The what?" Bobby blurted.

The ship that crashed on your planet. The intelligence that created your species, and your companion species, Ursus maritimus. The name translates as 'Glorious Victory'.

"Holly shit," Billy Ray murmured.

That statement has no informational content.

"It is an expression of surprise," provided Mizuki. "This ship, the D'lat Me'tan, its records detail the genetic modifications made to force our evolution?"

That is correct Dr. Ogawa. I also scanned your individual genomes.

"I think we are gonna need to have a discussion about the concept of privacy," Billy Ray commented. Mizuki ignored the Captain's sarcasm.

"And what did you conclude from your examination?"

I conclude that you are the most dangerous species I have ever encountered.

The four humans looked at each other, not knowing exactly how to take that statement. Billy Ray furrowed his brow in thought.

"Let's put that point aside for now and go back to why we found ourselves hunting big game with pointy sticks. It was entertaining as all get out but I still don't understand why you did that to us."

Even your use of language is dangerous—filled with ambiguity and multiple layers of meaning. You are truly... strange, even for biological entities. But I will endeavor to explain what you experienced.

I ran a number of simulations based on the described program of genetic manipulation employed by D'lat Me'tan. That, in combination with your genomes, allowed me to reconstruct a representative history of your emergence as a fully sentient species. To test the final model's veracity I inserted your individual consciousnesses into the simulation.

"OK, and what did that tell you?"

The incident you participated in was a key moment, a tipping point. It was when your ancestors consciously became the apex predator on your world. You used intelligence and cooperation to defeat a more dangerous natural predator. From that instant on, your kind was destined to dominate the planet you lived on.

"Those hairy ape things were our ancestors?" asked Beth.

They were one of the earliest species that your anthropologists would consider a hominin, a close relative if not a direct ancestor of your modern selves. Though they would probably not grant those creatures membership in the genus Homo, they were a stepping stone.

From then onward you spread across your planet like an infection. Eventually you would inhabit almost every ecosystem, from high mountains to the deepest valleys, from frozen wastes to burning deserts, from wind swept plains to sweltering jungles. Being omnivores, there were few edible plants you would not consume and practically no animals you would not hunt.

"Yer makin' us sound like a plague of locusts."

Worse. All creatures great and small helped feed your growing ranks—not just grazing herbivores but snails, small birds, rodents, and even locust. You hunted the mammoth and mastodon to extinction. Not satisfied dominating the land, your ancestors climbed into primitive wooden ships and went to sea—an environment you are most definitely not adapted to—in order to hunt and slay whales, the largest animals on your planet.

More over, when wild beasts no longer presented a challenge you turned on each other with unprecedented savagery. It is amazing that you did not destroy yourselves. Perhaps you might have if the Dark Lords had not intervened in a failed attempt to do just that.

"Yeah, that's right, we're bad. So why did the T'aafhal, the same critters that made you, decide to whip themselves up a batch of homicidal killer monkeys?" The others could tell that Billy Ray was on the edge of losing his temper with the pedantic AI.

I am not privy to the specific instructions given D'lat Me'tan, only the steps it took to achieve its end purpose. I do know that the T'aafhal were in the process of... evolving. Advancing to the next stage of their existence as a species. For millions of years they were the Paladins, the protectors of warm life in this galaxy. When they began their withdrawal from the galaxy they evidently created you to take their place.

"We are supposed to be galactic peacekeepers? The defenders of warm life? And we don't get any say in the matter?" Billy Ray was growing angrier.

"At least you could have turned us into Jedi knights," Bobby interjected, purposefully interrupting his friend's building rage. "They got special powers and nifty light sabers, all we got was less hairy."

"What?" Billy Ray stared at his friend.

"Come on, the T'aafhal didn't create the galaxy. Right, Formicidae?"

That is correct, Commander Danner.

"So the bad guys would have come for us eventually, assuming we ever got smart enough to trip their alarms. The way I see it, this way we at least have a fighting chance. Hell, 'the most dangerous species in the galaxy'? That makes me kinda proud, brother."

"He does have a point, darling. Otherwise we might still be running around the Serengeti naked, picking lice off each other and waiting for the next major extinction event."

"When you think about it, it does make sense," Misuki chimed in. "We do seem to have a certain talent for organized violence—

we've been fighting wars against each other since the beginning of history. The T'aafhal threw us into the galactic struggle knowing that we would do what we always do."

Billy Ray nodded. "Fight. They knew we would fight."

"As we most definitely have, dear."

"But how does that make us the most dangerous species in the galaxy?"

It is a combination of characteristics: You are adaptable, as your spread across your home world and into space shows; Your fecundity is astounding, there were 7.4 billion of you on one planet before the Dark Lords attacked; You are inventive, as your recent defeat of the Dark Lord's ship illustrates; and you are curious to a fault—why else would you come searching for me? In battle you are capable of great acts of heroism and self sacrifice, though you also posses a keen sense of self preservation. You claim to crave peace yet you often harry your opponents to utter annihilation.

"Oh really?"

Your history is littered with examples. The destruction of Nineveh, the Roman sacking of Carthage, the string of ruined cities left in the wake of the Mongol hordes, the Spanish conquest of the New World. You constantly bicker among yourselves and only band together when you perceive a common threat. The Allies in the great wars of the last century demanded unconditional surrender of their foes and waged total war, firebombing cities of women and children. They invented nuclear weapons and immediately unleashed them against their all but defeated foes.

"If you bother to check, once we were done annihilatin' we rebuilt the nations that were our enemies. The rebuilding took longer than the destroying."

Yes, I see. Yet another example of your inconsistency and unpredictability. There are also other things in your nature. I can see from your history that you have great empathy for other living creatures, at least when you are not killing them. You care for the polar bears from your home world, you even keep lower animals for no reason other than you like them. Perhaps you are what the galaxy's warm life needs in a protector race, but the logic of it escapes me.

334

Billy Ray was not impressed by the AI's analysis, so he forged ahead. "So we get to fight for a couple of million years, like the T'aafhal? Then what?"

If you are successful—if you survive—when the time comes you will follow the T'aafhal, and the other Paladin races that preceded them.

"What does that mean?"

I do not know the precise details. Evidently biological sentients evolve until they reach a, for lack of a better term, a singularity. When that happens they transcend this existence. My kind do not evolve as you do, at least not to my knowledge. To find out more you would need to ask the T'aafhal.

"We'd love to do just that, if we could find any of the varmints. You wouldn't happen to know where they went to?"

I am not certain that any remain on this plane of existence. The last area where they were active in this arm of the galaxy was in a nearby open cluster of young stars, a star nursery. Observe.

The planetarium display rotated and expanded. It displayed a star cluster containing hundreds of hot, blue-white stars surrounded by intricate blue filaments of light. It was a birthplace of new stars, the nebulosity a result of starlight scattering off minute grains of interstellar dust in the vicinity.

"That looks familiar," said Mizuki. "Could you show the star cluster from the viewpoint of our home world?"

The view shifted, stars changing position and the magnification reduced. The stars dimmed until only the brightest remained. Mizuki smiled in recognition. "That is Messier 45, the Pleiades star cluster, also known as the Seven Sisters."

"And you say we can find the T'aafhal there?" asked Billy Ray.

I cannot guarantee that the T'aafhal are still there. The last communication I received from any T'aafhal installation was over two hundred thousand years ago. The Paladins were supposedly on a planet around a variable star, also partially obscured by gas and dust.

"The stars in the Pleiades are quite young. They are thought to have formed around 100 million years ago, making them much younger than our sun. They figure in the mythology of many different peoples on Earth. In Greek mythology the bright stars are the daughters of Atlas and Pleione, hence the Pleiades. In Japan they are called *Subaru*."

"Hey, I owned a Subaru once," Bobby exclaimed. "So that's why it had a constellation on its logo."

"Exactly, Bobby." Mizuki smiled and went on with her description. "Traditionally six of the stars are visible to the naked eye while the seventh is not. The missing seventh star gave rise to stories and legends of the 'lost Pleiad'."

"'Many a night I saw the Pleiads, rising through the mellow shade, Glitter like a swarm of fire-flies tangled in a silver braid.'" Billy Ray recited. "Alfred Lord Tennyson."

I see you are familiar with the cluster. There is a mystery involving the presence of several white dwarfs among the large bright stars of the cluster. Solve the mystery and you will find the knowledge you seek. Find the lost Pleiads if you wish to find the T'aafhal.

"Cryptic, much?" Beth asked archly.

"The Pleiades are a long way away. The cluster lies on the ecliptic, approximately 136 parsecs—around 440 light years—from Earth."

"We're going to have to think about that. I wish we could contact Captain Jack and the others."

Mizuki addressed another question at the alien intelligence. "You claim to be the protector of life in this system. You are aware that the primary star will turn into a red giant in less than one hundred thousand years?"

93,450 ± 6,200 years, yes.

"This will consume the planet that orbits the K type, killing the Fakkaa if they still exist."

They did not exist when I was given my mission. I am only concerned with the arthropods that inhabit this planet, as they have for more than a million years.

"A million years?" Bobby interrupted. "Why haven't they evolved, why can't they save themselves?"

The "ants" as you call them, have reached a balance with their ecosystem. They need no greater technology than they currently posses. They have remained in evolutionary stasis since soon after I arrived. The only change they experience is that every few centuries the old queen dies and a new one takes her place. Without external threats or natural catastrophes they remain as they are.

"So you keep the natives in a planetary ant farm and don't care about the other intelligent lifeform in the system because it wasn't covered by your orders? I think you criticizing us is pretty laughable given your attitude."

That may be, but I have my purpose... and I suppose you have yours. I have uploaded my historical records to your ship's computer. They may be of some help to you on your quest for our mutual creators.

"I don't give the T'aafhal credit for creatin' us, just for nudging our ancestors in the right direction. They no more created us than we created dogs."

As you will. In any case, given that you were able to find me so easily I need to relocate. Do not linger on your way out of the cavern. I bid you farewell, young Paladins.

The scene changed. The four humans found themselves back in the cave, encased in their armor, and staring at a blank rock wall.

Chapter 40

The Cavern

A flock of butterflies swirled around the four explorers, who stood dumfounded, staring at the rock wall in front of them. There was no astronomical display, no voice in their heads, no wall of T'aafhal hull metal behind them—just the cave and Mizuki's butterflies.

"What the hell was that all about?" asked Bobby.

"I think our audience with the artifact is over," said Beth.

The rock beneath their feet trembled.

"That Formicidae character told us not to dawdle on our way out. You don't think its gonna do some kind of Indiana Jones number on this cave do ya?"

"I think that is exactly what the AI's final comments implied." Mizuki looked at the others and blinked once. "We should run."

"Oh hell yeah! And don't forget about that chasm." Billy Ray turned and sprinted after Mizuki and Beth, who were already headed for the exit.

"Hey, wait for me," Bobby cried and ran after them.

The others sprinted the hundred meters to the edge of the chasm and launched themselves into the air. Mizuki hit the ground on the other side without breaking stride, closely followed by Beth and Billy Ray.

Bobby's takeoff was a bit rough and his landing even more so. He hit the far wall at about waist level and slid back into the yawing pit, desperately grabbing the surface rock with his gloved hands.

"Help!" He yelled.

Both Beth and Billy Ray pulled up short. They looked at each other for a split second and raced back to the precipice. Each grabbed an arm and yanked Bobby from the lip of the crevasse, tossing him forward. In their excitement, the enhanced strength provided by their suits made the rescue excessively energetic. Bobby hit the ground, rolled to his feet and took off running. He look back at his rescuers and shouted, "Well come on, what are you waiting for?"

Obstacles carefully negotiated on the way in were crossed at break neck speed. They came to the hall with the ensnaring roots and did not slow down. There was no sign of dangling tendrils as they passed the chamber without hindrance—perhaps the ceiling dwelling predators had sensed what was coming and fled.

Ahead, Mizuki came to the first of several vertical walls and stopped. She turned and yelled to her partner. "Bobby! Lift me up."

Bobby pulled up next to her and made a stirrup using his hands. "Step up, stand on my shoulders and lean against the rock face."

"Hai."

Mizuki complied. Standing on Bobby's shoulders the two could almost reach the top of the cliff. As Beth approached she immediately understood what to do—she climbed up the human ladder formed by her friends and pulled herself over the top of the cliff. Hot on her heals, Billy Ray repeated the maneuver and disappeared over the top.

An instant later he reappeared, reaching down to grasp Mizuki's upraised hands. Again powered armor made easy work of dead-lifting nearly two hundred kilos. With Mizuki safe, Billy Ray again dangled his arms over the edge of the cliff.

"Come on, pardner, time's a wastin'."

Bobby took two steps back and made a running jump. At the apex of his leap the two friends clasped wrists and Billy Ray pulled Bobby over the top.

"Eat yer hearts out, Flying Wallendas."

They quickly scrambled down the lose rock fall on the other side and ran after the women.

CIC, Peggy Sue

"Telemetry is back!" Shouted Betty, as her medical displays came back to life. "They are all alive, but they seem to be under significant physical stress. Elevated respiration and heart rates, I'd say they were running for their lives."

On the large wall display the video from the recon drone showed the little robot bobbing and weaving its way through twisty passages. No sign of the four explorers.

"What the Sam Hill?" The Chief swore. "Pinnace, Peggy Sue. Come in you two knuckleheads."

"Go, Peggy Sue."

"Interrogative, WTFO?"

"We just got telemetry back. The recon drone showed the metal wall disappear. One minute it was there and then, bang, it was gone. Over."

The Chief shook his head. "What about the officers? Can you see them?"

"Yeah. They were running like crazy, heading back out of the cave. I'm following them with the drone but haven't caught up with them yet."

"Well hop to it, mister! Get that drone squared away."

"Aye, aye, Chief. Uh, by the way, we've been getting some ground tremors."

"Great. Get the boat ready to cast off as soon as the Captain and them arrive."

"Affirmative. Copy that."

The Cavern

The return trip was a mad dash through an obstacle course—up hill and down, running across broken rock, belly crawling through narrow passages, scaling cliffs. They at least had the advantage of having crossed the terrain on the way in. At the top of the mossy incline where they encountered the white worms they paused to catch their breath.

"I will never complain about running laps in the cargo hold again," Billy Ray wheezed. Despite the four of them being in excellent physical condition they were all about winded.

"And I will never complain about wearing armor when on a surface expedition again," said Mizuki with feeling. "I can't imagine us making such good time without it."

"Well, dear, you were the one waxing poetic about 'caverns measureless to man'. How far have we come?"

"You really don't like that poem, do you? We just covered in twenty minutes that it took us an hour and a half to cross going in, honey bunch."

"You better watch where you're going, remember where you been. That's the way I see it, I'm a Simple Man," Beth recited. "Well, a simple woman."

"Oh fer sure, yer as simple as quantum mechanics."

"Who said that, Beth?"

"Charlie Daniels. I keep telling you, you should try listening to country music, Mizuki."

The ground trembled. Several large rocks fell from the ceiling nearby. The recon drone went flying passed them, closely followed by Mizuki's butterflies.

"I think we'd best pick up the pace, people."

"Right behind you, Captain."

The Pinnace

"Hey look! There are the officers," Hitch yelled to Jacobs. For a brief instant, four armored figures appeared on the recon drone's video feed. The drone did not stop and quickly passed by the humans. "Well, they were there. At least we know they are OK and on their way back out. Try to call 'em."

"Right, Stevie." Matt changed frequencies. "Captain, Pinnace. Interrogative your status, over."

"We're on our way back to the shuttle," the Captain panted. "Get everything powered up and ready for immediate take off."

"Roger that, Sir. Pinnace, out."

The whole shuttle shook. Resting in the cave mouth the deck gravity had been shut down. The only major system powered up was the forward repulsor shield, left on because gravel and rocks kept falling from the cave roof. Following the tremor, a large dark shape fell past the cave entrance.

"Holy shit! Did you see that?"

"See what, Stevie?"

"A humungous rock just fell past the cave opening!"

"Damn, it never rains but it pours. Let's get the shuttle powered up and ready to shove off."

"I'm with you, Matt, the sooner we get outta here the better."

The Cavern

They squished through the worm chamber without incident— evidently the tremors had sent the worms packing as well. In short order they were back in the large chamber festooned with stalactites and stalagmites. This time, instead of looking fanciful the pointed stone formations looked sinister, like the teeth of a giant monster ready to chew them up.

In the lead, Mizuki was the first across the stone bridge spanning the pool. As she stepped off the far side another tremor struck. The surface of the formerly placid pond was distorted by ripples, and then the natural bridge fell into the water.

"The Bridge is out!" Billy Ray yelled.

Ahead of him, Beth ran up the approach to the collapsed span and lept into the air. She sailed easily across the pond, landing lightly on the far side.

"Come on, we're almost out!" she shouted to the others.

The two men followed the First Officer's lead and jumped across the water. *En passant*, Billy Ray squinted at his wife and said, "show off."

As they ran for the exit another quake shook the cavern, the strongest shock yet. Bobby, who was bringing up the rear, looked at the ceiling, just in time to see a large stalactite break loose and fall. Without thinking he jumped, tackling Beth and knocking her out of the path of the falling rock.

"Oof!" Beth said as she struck the ground.

The two officers tumbled across the uneven cavern floor. The stalactite landed a couple of meters away, shattering on impact. Stone rubble landed on the armored couple, curled up together with Bobby trying to shield Beth.

Their armor's impact resistant polymers stiffened to distribute the energy from the falling rock, leaving the pair immobilized for a few seconds. As soon as full mobility returned Bobby clambered to his feet, freeing Beth.

"Thank you," she said, accepting a hand up.

"No problem."

"Come on you two!" Billy Ray shouted from the tunnel leading to the mouth of the cave. The two laggards ran for the exit.

Pinnace

Jacobs and Hitch waited nervously at the top of the airstair. The small spherical shape of the recon drone flew past them into the cabin, startling them both.

"What's with that thing?"

Hitch grinned. "I just set it on auto return and let it fend for itself."

Snatching the hovering robot from the air, Jacobs disabled the device before stowing it in a storage bin. "Next time, I program the drone."

"Whatever, bro."

Their argument was interrupted by the arrival of the *aoi chō*, who flooded up the stairs in a rush of wings and bright color. They filled the cabin with chaotic movement, flashing a warning in red and yellow.

"The bugs are back, I guess that means that Dr. Ogawa is close by." Jacobs observed.

Sure enough, Mizuki appeared at the bottom of the airstair. Glancing for a moment over her shoulder, she ascended. The two sailors stepped aside to let her pass.

"*Konichiwa,*" she said, entering the cabin proper. She then started talking to the butterflies in Japanese. Neither of the petty officers understood what she was saying but evidently the winged creatures did—they quickly settled down, alighting on seat backs and other handy surfaces.

Next up the boarding ramp was the Captain, who charged into the cabin demanding to know the status of the shuttle. "Jacobs, Hitch, are we ready to take off?"

"Aye, Captain. She's all powered up and ready to liftoff," replied Hitch.

"Good. Commanders Mekalu and Danner are right behind me."

Billy Ray took a seat in the front of the cabin just in time to avoid being run down by his wife, who charged up the stairs, down the aisle and jumped into the copilot's seat. She immediately started running preflight checks.

Another violent tremor shook the shuttle as Bobby burst into the cabin. "Secure the ramp for immediate takeoff," he shouted at the two sailors.

Without waiting for their reply, he ran to the cockpit and threw himself into the pilot's seat. "Everyone secure for take off."

The deck gravity came on, dampening the now continuous shaking of the surrounding rock. Bobby lifted the shuttle a half meter off the cave floor, retracted the landing struts, and firewalled the forward thrusters. Accelerating at 12G the blunt arrowhead shaped craft shot directly into the curtain of falling water.

The impact of the plummeting water drove the shuttle downward, but Bobby had anticipated that. Pulling the shuttle's nose up and applying power to the bottom thrusters, the pinnace burst from the fall with a tremendous spray of water, having dropped only twenty meters toward the river below. Climbing out of the river gorge, Bobby slowed the shuttle's ascent and turned to port, giving everyone a spectacular view of the waterfall.

As those on board watched, a plume of water shot out from the cliff from the location of the cave opening. Through the falling water, the torrent exploded like water escaping the spillway of an overfilled dam. The spray extended hundreds of meters from the face of the cliff, sending a rush of water down the river.

"I'm glad we didn't take any longer gettin' out of that cave," Billy Ray said with his laconic cowboy drawl.

"That, dear, is the understatement of the day," Beth said from the flight deck.

"I don't care what the rest of you do, but I am never, ever coming back to this planet again."

"I think we are all in agreement there, Mizuki-chan."

As Bobby spoke, the upper part of the fall began collapsing into the jet of water spewing from the cave. Large chunks of rock broke off the cliff face and fell into the raging torrent. The cascade only grew in size and violence as what had been the upper channel of the river receded, crumpling a section at a time. The land above the cliff sank beneath the thundering flood that carried away any trace of the once mighty waterfall.

"Mother of God," said Jacobs.

"And all her crazy cousins," added Hitch.

"That beats the rolling boulder at the start of *Raiders* all to hell, eh Captain?"

"I hope there aren't any settlements down stream," Beth said. "If there are we should warn them."

"I didn't notice anything on the trip up river," Billy Ray answered.

"From what I gathered while traveling with the Queen, the ants are not exactly fond of water, but perhaps we should fly down stream and see if there is anyone to warn."

"Sure thing, sweetheart."

Bobby, hearing no objections from the others, turned the shuttle south and retraced their journey in the opposite direction. The shuttle soon caught up with the wall of water released by the collapse of the fall, racing south at over one hundred kilometers an hour. With everyone safe and the excitement over, Billy Ray called the ship.

"Peggy Sue, Pinnace."

"Pinnace, Peggy Sue. Welcome back sir, you had us all worried for a minute there." The voice was that of GySgt Acuna.

"Yeah, I guess it just wasn't our day to die. We should rendezvous with the ship in about two hours. My compliments to the officers and crew, and please ask Mr. Baldursson to begin preparations to break orbit. We've spent enough time in this system."

"Aye, aye, Captain. Peggy Sue, standing by."

Chapter 41

The Queen's Palace

Queen Timushi noticed a clutch of scholars standing to one side in the audience hall. With her large compound eyes she quite literally saw everything that happened in her throne room. She called out to them.

"Good Sages, what brings you into my presence today?"

The most senior dipped her antennae respectfully and spoke. "Your Majesty, as you commanded, the royal astronomers have kept track of the daemon stars that recently appeared in the sky."

The Queen's antennae twitched with impatience.

"As we reported, the cluster of stars disappeared almost a week ago, but a lone star remained. We assumed that the remaining star was in some way associated with the Queen's Daemon, Lord Mizuki and her companions."

If her kind could sigh Timushi would have. *There is just no way to make a scholar come quickly to the point.*

"It appears Your Majesty, that the final wayward star has vanished as well."

"We suppose that Lord Mizuki has continued her journey to her home realm. Thank you, Senior Sage, for your report."

To the Queen's left, one of her advisers spoke up. "Majesty, this return to normalcy is most welcome news. Your ascension to the throne will be remembered as one of the most... unusual in the history of Formicidae. Never was a time that daemons fought on the sides of the royal claimants while strange gods contested the heavens."

"Indeed, my Lord Chancellor, let us all hope that the rest of my reign will be as uneventful as my ascension was notable." The Queen waved an arm dismissing the scholars and returned to the matters at hand.

I wonder, Timushi thought, *if such things might happen again. Mizuki told me that the heavens are filled with many races of daemon, all armed to the teeth as it were. It was painfully obvious that our weapons—spears, swords, and arrows—were no match for the weapons wielded by the daemons. A number of daemon weapons were collected after the battle—perhaps I should have my scholars and artisans examine them more closely. After all, Lord Mizuki might not be here to help defend the realm against the next band of interloping daemons.*

Fakkaa Fleet, Homeward Bound

Admiral Raqqee was on his flag bridge aboard the Fakkaa flagship. He was torn between two concerns: whether the Earth Captain would change his mind and decide to destroy his little armada just to be safe; and what the reaction will be when the fleet arrives home.

All the preparation, the years of building and training, trying to make the almost mystical tech provided by the 'Wise Ones' work. How could we have been so blind, to trust creatures who would not show themselves physically. Seducing us with advanced knowledge and visions of conquest. It was our own greed that made us believe the alien's tale, as questionable and full of holes as it was.

Not that his lords and masters would accept their share of the blame—the ruling class never did. He would be lucky to come away with a quick clean death sentence. *I will accept all the blame, and try to protect my officers and crew. Their only crime was to bravely accept an insanely dangerous mission, thinking that they were saving our entire race.*

Captain Tikkoo, his old friend, interrupted his depressing thoughts with a report.

"Admiral, there is no sign of the alien ship. It no longer orbits the ant planet nor can our instruments detect its presence anywhere behind us."

"The Earthlings are gone? They have quit this system?"

"So it would appear, Sir. Should we reverse course and go back and finish what we started?"

Tikkoo's statement shocked the Admiral out of his introversion. He looked his friend in the eyes and saw the mischievous twinkle that was always there when he was pulling a prank or practical joke.

"Aside from the fact that such a maneuver is impractical, I never want to see that gods-be-damned planet again, Captain. Though your fighting spirit is appreciated."

Tikkoo's quills rattled mirthfully. "You need to break out of your funk, Admiral. It looks like the aliens are not going to blast us to atoms and we will actually make it back home alive."

"That may be true, but how long some of us remain alive after our return is an open question."

"Not really, Sir. It's all in how you tell the tale."

"What do you mean? I lost half the fleet and two thirds of the expeditionary force. We didn't accomplish our primary objective and our allies, as perfidious as they were, also met with an ignominious end."

"Yes, you could definitely be in trouble if you described our mission that way. But think, what was the primary purpose of our expedition?"

Raqqee thought for a moment be for replying. "To save our race from eventual annihilation."

"Precisely! And I would contend that, under your unfaltering command, we have done just that. Think, my old friend. If all that the Earth Captain said is true then the Wise Ones would have destroyed us completely after we handed them the prize they sought, after we slaughtered the ants for them. Because of your leadership we managed to discover the truth."

"You're saying this mission was not a total debacle?"

"Some lessons are learned at great cost, Admiral. You managed to expose the alien treachery, save the Fakkaa race and escape disaster with as much of your force as possible. All in all a most impressive achievement. In fact, I say three cheers for Admiral Raqqee, savior of Fakkaa!"

With Capt. Tikkoo leading the cheer, the entire bridge crew joined in.

"Hip, Hip, Hurrah! Hip, Hip, Hurrah! Hip, Hip, Hurrah!"

"Admiral, every sailor and commando on board owes you their lives. At this point they would follow you anywhere."

"I hadn't looked at things from that... perspective."

"Something else to consider, Sir. You will be returning to Fakkaa in command of what is still the most powerful military instrument ever crafted on our planet."

Now that gave the Admiral something to think about.

Captain's Sea Cabin, Peggy Sue

The Peggy Sue had broken orbit four hours ago and was underway, still a day away from the alter-space transit point that would carry them a step closer to home. The Captain called his senior officers to a meeting in his sea cabin. In addition to the four principle partners, Dr. White and Engineer Baldursson were present, as were the Chief and the Gunny representing the crew and the Marines.

"Given the events that have taken place since our entry into this system I figured it was a good idea for us to take stock of our situation," Billy Ray said, opening the meeting. "Let's start with the condition of the ship, Arin?"

"Ja, Captain. The ship is in good shape, all major systems are fully functional: engines, reactors, shields, and sensors. Life support is actually running at 108% reflecting the planting of new food crops in the hydroponic and greenhouse spaces. The repairs to the deck gravity and shields have all passed muster and the new sensors are working as designed. In short, everything is ship shape."

"Great, my compliments to you and your engineers, Arin. They've done outstanding work under some trying conditions." The Captain looked down at his notes on the table's surface display. "Chief, how are the small boats?"

"The assault shuttle has been gone over from stem to stern following the rescue mission planet side. Same with the Pinnace. The large crew shuttle was never deployed nor were the cargo tugs. The small shuttle was lost to enemy action. All remaining boats are stowed and ready for transit, Captain."

Billy Ray nodded to the Chief. "Gunny, what about the Marines' arms and armor?"

"All suits and weapons have been cleaned, serviced and stowed for transit, Captain."

Another nod. "Dr. White, do we have any personnel in Sick Bay or unfit for duty?"

"All hands are fit for duty, Sir. Private Malachi has been discharged and returned to active duty."

"Number One, other personnel matters?"

"We lost two people during the recent hostilities. I recommend that Mr. Hoenig be promoted to sub-lieutenant and detailed as helmsman on the port watch. We have no ready replacement for Ms. Hamm, I suggest we utilize Shadi and Dorri to take up the slack where possible. Otherwise we will just have to function short handed."

"Noted. Anything else regarding readiness? Anyone?"

Heads shook all around.

"How about moral? What's the mood in the crew's mess, Chief?"

"Generally spirits are high, Captain. Everyone mourns the loss of Lt. Lawson and Kate Hamm, but recovering Dr. Ogawa alive helped soften the blow. The fact that we blew them Dark Lord bastards outta space raised morale a bunch as well. I think the crew is looking forward to be heading back to home port, Sir."

"And the Marines, Gunny?"

"They're all feeling their oats after the action on Formicidae. There's nothing like kicking some alien ass to put the squad in a good mood. Not losing anyone while doing it makes it all good, Sir."

"So both ship and crew are in good shape and high spirits. Anything else I should know before we talk about the remaining voyage?"

Betty cleared her throat. "Captain, I think you should know that Dr. Ahnah is expecting."

"Really? I guess I don't need to ask who the father is."

"No, Sir."

"When is she due?"

"That is a bit variable. Female polar bears can delay egg implantation after fertilization occurs. The process waits until the mother bear's body is fully prepared to get through winter hibernation, including pregnancy and birthing. When she has sufficient weight on her body, she'll be good to go. She won't need to den for four to five months, and actual birth won't happen for maybe nine months."

"Well that is some happy news. There are few enough polar bears that any new cubs are more than welcome." The Captain smiled like a proud prospective godparent. "And that brings us to the remainder of the voyage. Given how long we've been in space and the stressful conditions we've encountered in this system, I've instructed the Sailing Master to plot us a speedy course back to Earth."

Bobby took that as his queue. "Using the most massive stars between here and home, I've plotted a course that will consist of four alter-space transits. Including time to cross the intermediate systems we should be able to voyage back to our home system in just over one hundred days."

"So we'll be home in just over three months," said Arin, "that's fantastic."

"That's barring any complications, like bushwhacking Dark Lords or hostile natives, but I have no intention of stopping for local exploration. We have had a successful first voyage for the OATC and I know that we all share the desire to see home again as soon as possible."

There were smiles all around. Billy Ray could see the relief in the faces of some, there was no doubt that the length and hardships of the voyage far exceeded the expectations of most on board. *Well, at least we ain't being chased by a hostile enemy fleet this time.*

"Unless there is anything else, you're dismissed to your duties. As soon as we are in alter-space we will stand down for a day and issue double rum rations to all."

* * * * *

As the others filed out, the Captain signaled for the expedition partners to stay back. The door to the sea cabin slid shut and the three other officers look expectantly at Billy Ray.

"I just wanted to let y'all know that we may just break even on this trip. Of course no amount of profit can offset the lives we lost, but at least financially we will not return in debt."

"Actually, dear, I think you underestimate our booty."

"Really? Some oversized gems, broken alien recording equipment, and various native trinkets?"

"Think back when you were telling me about the ice trade."

"You mean about thinking outside the box?"

"Yes, that, but I meant when you said that the best trade good was information."

"That's right," Bobby agreed. "We now have a memory dump from another T'aafhal AI. That's gotta be about priceless."

"Bobby's correct. Plus, Formicidae unlocked records from *M'tak Ka'fek* and data from *D'lat Me'tan* we never knew was there. I think we are returning rich, sweetheart." Beth smiled broadly at her husband.

"Not only that," Mizuki added, already thinking ahead to their next voyage, "we also know where to go looking next for answers about the T'aafhal—we must find the missing Pleiad."

Epilogue

Earthside City, The Moon

As Beth had surmised, the information they had gathered about the Taafhal proved priceless. That, combined with the planetary surveys taken along the way, made the four partners very rich. Rich enough to buy new domiciles near Earthside City, the new domed settlement constructed in their absences.

Earthside, as its name implied, faced Earth, the human race's shattered home. Currently there were four completed domes, each three kilometers in diameter, with a fifth under construction. The domed areas were intended as public spaces, not places where people lived—that was in the network of tunnels carved out of the lunar rock beneath the domes. The plan was to have room for two hundred thousand people by the end of first phase construction next year.

But the truly wealthy among the solar system's new citizens didn't live in the densely packed housing attached to the domes. They lived in palatial homes excavated in the cliffs overlooking the city. Multistory transparent walls provided spectacular views of the city domes and the traffic at the spaceport beyond. Farside still handled military traffic and a significant amount of commerce—all the major shipyards were located there—but traffic to and from Earth and passenger ships bound for Mars and the outer moons now regularly departed from Earthside.

The two major lunar settlements were linked by a subterranean tube system that arced deep beneath the Moon's surface. Through it transport pods raced at thousands of kilometers per hour, whisking passengers and goods between the cities in under an hour. Wealthy merchant captains, like those who sailed for the Orion Arm Trading Company, owned their own private launches, though they would be hard put to reach Farside faster than the tube.

A month after they returned from the last voyage Mizuki and Bobby were married. Dr Yuki Saito gave the bride away, Beth was the maid of honor and Billy Ray best man. Also among the bride's maids were Shadi, Dorri, and Betty White, who cried through most of the ceremony. The attendees were a strange mix, including the crew of the Peggy Sue, faculty from the University, high ranking officers from the fleet, and all the board members of the OATC.

The bride and groom spent their honeymoon on Earth, in the Texas hill country, a trip few were allowed to take. Nearly five years after the alien bombardment ecological damage was still visible, though upland Texas retained its rugged beauty. Since their return Bobby spent most of his time watching Mizuki decorate their 9,000 square foot apartment. The only space he claimed for himself was a well appointed office-cum-man cave done up in wood and leather brought back from Texas. As with most lunar domiciles, green plants and flowing water fountains were numerous.

The Melaku-Vincents and the Ogawa-Danners lived side by side, just down from the Parkers. Their "apartments" linked by a transport tube that ran along the ancient crater rim in which they lived. Beth and Billy Ray were visiting their best friends, Mizuki and Bobby, reminiscing about old times and talking about what the future might hold for the four of them.

"It's good to see y'all are finally settling in," Billy Ray commented, standing in front of a two story transparent window with a spectacular view. In one hand he cradled a Wild Turkey, neat. Authentic, pre-bombardment liquor was quite costly, but they could afford it. Even in their wildest dreams, the profit from their voyage didn't include such luxury—palatial apartments, private launches, and a new ship under construction in the Farside shipyard.

"You know, you and Bobby should think about investing in some land in the Martian highlands," Beth told Mizuki as they sat on a wide couch overlooking the same view. "When the terraforming effort gets under way it will become obvious where the good land is and prices will skyrocket. Now is the time to buy."

"We'll think about it, but making Mars habitable will take hundreds, if not thousands of years."

"Gotta think of yer kids and grand kids, Mizuki. Land here in the solar system is gonna be at a premium in the future."

"You two sound more like TK every day," Bobby chuckled, jiggling his glass. He was drinking his Wild Turkey over ice—heresy in Billy Ray's eyes.

"Speak of the devil," Mizuki said, a notice appearing discreetly on the arm of the couch next to her. "Maria and TK have just arrived."

Mizuki rose and went to greet her guests. The others took the opportunity to freshen their cocktails in anticipation of a long conversation with TK. He and Maria were the only other investors in the new ship besides the four friends.

"Hello children!" TK bellowed as he entered the room, Maria walking behind him in conversation with Mizuki. Maria had given up years ago on housebreaking her Texas Oilman husband.

Beth went over to greet Maria and the women started a conversation among themselves. The topic of discussion was the indoor water garden and koi pond Mizuki had designed next to the entry way from the lift. Water tumbled from level to level, providing soothing sounds that the men were boisterously talking over.

"I tell ya, I never would've believed that I'd be livin' in a condo on the Moon," TK said, admiring the view while accepting a drink from the robot bartender.

"Yeah, well it still ain't Texas," Billy Ray griped.

"Texas is still there, Billy Ray, we were just down there," added Bobby.

"Yeah, and in the future we'll hopefully get much of our world back, as nature heals itself. Damn them alien scumbags anyway."

"To Earth," Billy Ray proposed a toast. "The once and future home of mankind."

"To Earth," the other two men repeated.

"So how's the work coming on the new ship?"

"Coming along just fine, TK. This time we are going to make sure we have enough room for everything we need to take along."

"Yeah," Bobby chimed in. "Like lots of laboratory space, a bigger hold, more shuttles, and room for a lot more Marines."

"Not to mention the latest in upgraded armaments." Billy Ray nodded. They had spent most of the trip back from Alpha Phoenicis discussing what they needed in a perfect exploration starship.

"I sure can't wait to see her when she goes down the ways. From the plans she should be a real beauty."

"Not just that, but TK will finally get his yacht back," said Maria, walking over to join the conversation along with the rest of the women.

"We will need to replicate the data storage from the Peggy Sue for the new ship. You never know when some obscure bit of data from the archives can be of assistance."

"Always thinkin' like a scientist, Mizuki. Hell, why don't you take the whole computer system, adapt it to the new ship."

"Really, TK? That might be easier then tryin' to figure out what to transfer."

"Sure, son," TK clapped Billy Ray on the shoulder. "We're gonna rename her anyway, Maria and me. Hell, Jack named her, she never really has been my ship."

"Well she will be soon," Beth said. "You know, that might work out well. We are all rather fond of Peggy Sue, she really does have a personality of her own."

"Yes!" Mizuki enthused. "The new ship can be Peggy Sue II. That way it will feel like home from the start."

"So yer all anxious to get back out there among the stars?" TK asked, as the six took seats in front of the picture window. "No time to settle down?"

Billy Ray smiled. "As Sir Francis Drake said, 'It's not that life ashore is distasteful to me, but life at sea is better'."

"Sooner or later I think we will start a family," Bobby said, looking at his wife. "But before we start having children I think there are some questions we'd all like to find answers to."

Beth frowned and stared down at her drink. "Yes, indeed. Like why we have been dragooned into service as galactic peacekeepers by those meddling T'aafhal."

"I do not know about everyone else, but I went from being a simple scientist, to the ant Queen's daemon, to a warm life Paladin in the span of a month. I would like to know more about what the future holds."

"I think your voyage was a bit more exciting than it was for the rest of us, Mizuki-chan. Not that I'm complaining, mind you."

"You planning on taking a bunch of yer old crew, Captain Billy?"

Billy Ray winced, he hated being called Captain Billy. "Those who are interested. A lot of the crew took their payout money and started businesses or emigrated to Mars or the outer planets."

"Not all," said Beth. "The Chief and Gunny Acuna have expressed interest and are even doing some low key recruiting."

"Will most of the Marines come back?" asked Maria.

"There are at least two of 'em who wont." Billy Ray grinned.

"Who?"

"Mal and Zeke. They are so head over heals for those Iranian sisters they won't go anywhere without them."

"Speaking of Shadi and Dorri, how is their legal suit over ownership of Paradise going?"

TK chuckled just thinking about it. "Those two little spitfires have got the Colonization Board so pissed off they can't even see straight."

"What is this, TK," Maria asked her husband, a suspicious undertone in her voice. After living together for decades and being married for years, Maria still got jealous when her husband talked about other women—at least women she did not know.

"Them and those two boys they lead around by the nose got 'em dead to rights. The planet was deeded to the colonists and they're the only survivors. Only hitch is they have to go back and occupy the planet for their claim to stand up."

"What about the contagion? How can they settle the planet if that plague is lurking in the soil?"

"Well ya see, Mizuki. We've been negotiating with them four regarding a mutually beneficial agreement."

"You aren't thinking of taking advantage of those poor young women," Beth began, protective ire rising in her voice.

"No, no, nothin' like that. The deal is that the company will cure the infestation by that black gunk in exchange for exclusive rights to any application resulting from that research. We'll ship 'em back to Paradise and provide seed organisms to build an Earth-life compatible ecosystem for the whole dang place."

"And in exchange you get a mechanism that can rapidly sterilize a planet," Bobby said, his predilection for conspiracy theories working to his advantage. "If you have a cure, that is."

"Assuming you can develop a cure you would be able to clear an alien planet of its native life and replant it with Earth-life in a few years." Mizuki was not as suspicious as Bobby, but she immediately saw the possibilities.

"You are not going to go wiping out other species with this, are you TK?" demanded Maria.

"Of course not, *querida*. We won't use it on any world with a sentient native species, or close to producing one. Only worlds that have stalled out, ecologically speaking. Or have been stripped of higher lifeforms by the Dark Lords. We need a way to establish Earth colonies on a bunch of planets as fast as possible. If we can put people on a couple dozen worlds, in a couple hundred years there will be enough humans that those cold-life bastards will never be able to exterminate us."

"And the fact that the company will own the rights to those planets, well that's all just gravy." Billy Ray shook his head sadly.

"Come on, don't be naive. Somebody has to hold the reins and I say better a bunch of free market capitalists than those military types in the Fleet or bureaucrats from the Colonization Board. Bunch of small minded authoritarian asshats from what I've seen."

"We all still have friends in the Fleet," Beth objected. "They are not all a collection of third-world colonels itching to hold a coup."

"No, there are good people there, but they won't be there forever. Checks and balances, people, checks and balances."

"What?" several of the others said at once.

"It's what America's founding fathers knew after getting' out from under the English thumb—no insult intended, Beth."

"None taken. During the time of the American Revolution my ancestors were peacefully herding cattle in the Ethiopian Highlands."

"The best government is one that is no bigger, or stronger, than it needs to be. Now granted, we need a strong fleet to fend of hostile aliens, but the military cannot be left to run things. They are the defenders of humanity but they must answer to civilian authorities. Some form of republic, with no central power figure—last thing we need is a king or an emperor. The best government invented so far was thought up by James Madison, with some help from his friends. Three co-equal branches: legislative, executive, and judicial."

"And just were does the company come in?" Bobby asked skeptically.

"Capitalism! The wealth of any nation is its people, hell the Romans understood that more than two thousand years ago. The Founding Fathers got it right—to get the most out of people you have to give 'em opportunity. Individual liberty and equality of opportunity, not equality of outcome. That's where the wheels started to come off back before the aliens attacked."

"So you are going to build a conservatarian paradise, eh TK?"

"I'm neither that bright nor that ambitious, Billy Ray. There are millions of worlds out there and I'm sure humans will eventually try every type of government and economic system you can think of. In the mean time, I am gonna try to see that my kids and grand kids have a decent place to live. Not some fascist dictatorship or a socialist paradise where everyone's lives suck equally bad. Now let's get another round of drinks and talk about where yer headin' next."

For several long seconds the room fell silent.

"It is going to be a long trip," Mizuki said, jumping into the awkward silence. "Are you familiar with the constellation called the Pleiades?"

www.ingramcontent.com/pod-product-compliance
Lightning Source LLC
Chambersburg PA
CBHW071224250626
47163CB00001B/95